# The German Boy

## PATRICIA WASTVEDT

VIKING
*an imprint of*
PENGUIN BOOKS

VIKING

Published by the Penguin Group

Penguin Books Ltd, 80 Strand, London WC2R ORL, England

Penguin Group (USA) Inc., 375 Hudson Street, New York, New York 10014, USA

Penguin Group (Canada), 90 Eglinton Avenue East, Suite 700, Toronto, Ontario, Canada M4P 2Y3
(a division of Pearson Penguin Canada Inc.)

Penguin Ireland, 25 St Stephen's Green, Dublin 2, Ireland
(a division of Penguin Books Ltd)

Penguin Group (Australia), 250 Camberwell Road, Camberwell, Victoria 3124, Australia
(a division of Pearson Australia Group Pty Ltd)

Penguin Books India Pvt Ltd, 11 Community Centre,
Panchsheel Park, New Delhi – 110 017, India

Penguin Group (NZ), 67 Apollo Drive, Rosedale, Auckland 0632, New Zealand
(a division of Pearson New Zealand Ltd)

Penguin Books (South Africa) (Pty) Ltd, 24 Sturdee Avenue,
Rosebank, Johannesburg 2196, South Africa

Penguin Books Ltd, Registered Offices: 80 Strand, London WC2R ORL, England

www.penguin.com

First published 2011

1

Copyright © Patricia Wastvedt, 2011

The moral right of the author has been

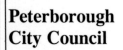

| Peterborough City Council | | |
|---|---|---|
| 60000 0000 23044 | | |
| Askews & Holts | Jun-2011 | |
| | £12.99 | |

Set in Dante 12/14.75pt
Typeset by Jouve (UK), Milton Keynes
Printed in Great Britain by Clays Ltd, St Ives plc

A CIP catalogue record for this book is available from the British Library

ISBN: 978-0-670-91942-0

www.greenpenguin.co.uk

For Gilly

*1947*

# I

At just gone five, the guest in the next room went past Elisabeth's door, his slippers flapping on the linoleum. She heard the thump of the cistern. Then the coughing horse that pulled the bread cart came and went, and soon after, the bicycle with a squeaking wheel belonging to the boy who delivered meat. Elisabeth listened to the birds singing in the rising darkness.

She had been dreaming of the garden at home in London. The sun was coming through the leaves, making patterns on the grass, and she was in her school dress collecting windfalls from underneath the pear trees. When she looked up, she saw that Karen had found a pear so big she had to hold it in her arms. It was mottled green and precious as things belonging to Karen always were. Elisabeth wanted it but Karen would only let her look. The pear wasn't perfect after all, and instead of a bee or a slug Elisabeth saw a human baby as small as a maggot inside the flesh.

'He's for you,' Karen said.

Elisabeth opened her eyes, hearing Karen's voice as if she was alive again and standing in the room. The sunlit garden hung in the darkness for a moment.

At six, the kitchen girls arrived, giggling and whispering below the window and Mrs McCrae was shushing them and chivvying them inside. The morning light slowly illuminated the dust on the bedside table, on Elisabeth's earrings and her wristwatch. It was almost seven o'clock.

She wondered how close the train would be. *So this will happen. I will inherit Karen's son, who I hate and love before I've even set eyes on him.*

• • •

'How long is it now?' Maud asked, hopscotching by the ticket gate.

'Soon, Maudie darling, soon,' said Elisabeth. 'Stay near me. Hold my hand.' The afternoon was closing over and a porter swept up litter while a sparrow dithered round a crust his broom had missed. Other people began gathering by the barrier. 'When is soon?' Maud asked.

The sparrow flew up and the train came through the mist. People winced against the flying smuts and Elisabeth held down her coat, bracing herself against the swell of noise. Doors opened all along the carriages and passengers were leaning out into the light to pass down their suitcases and bags to the porters waiting on the platform. She caught sight of George way back in the crowd, but she couldn't see anyone near him who might be Stefan.

'I've seen Daddy,' she told Maud. 'He's coming, Maudie.' Maud couldn't speak with the excitement of seeing George. Elisabeth felt it too, but even now in a crowd of faces some part of her still looked for Michael.

*Don't, for goodness sake. You won't see him here. His life is somewhere else.*

She settled her handbag on her arm, catching another glimpse of George – a middle-aged man, older than she thought her husband would ever be. He looked dazed by the long hypnotic hours of travelling and she saw him smooth his thick grey hair with the flat of his palm, adjust his hat and shoulder through a knot of people organizing their luggage. His eyes were pouched, and underneath the tan he had even in the winter his heavy handsome face was doughy as if he hadn't slept much. Perhaps he had missed her too.

He stopped at a distance and she waved, but steam was hanging over people's heads, curling down between them, and she lost sight of him again.

Two days ago he had gone to meet Karen's son from the boat at Dover. The doctor at the reception shed diagnosed malnutrition and parasites, Stefan's head was shaved, the wound to his neck was cleaned and George bought new clothes for him. The tattered *Hitlerjugend* uniform and rotting boots were thrown away.

George telephoned from Dover. 'They let him through without a fuss. No one asked him anything at all – or me.'

'Is he well, George?' Elisabeth was sitting on the bed in the bleakest hotel room she had ever seen. The floorboards were painted brown, the Lincrusta-papered walls distempered green to match the nylon eiderdown. Above the bed was *The Taj Majal at Dawn*, an embroidered picture in boiled pinks hanging on a chain. She had drawn the curtains and put on the bedside lamps but the room was still cheerless. Outside the wind moaned across the hills.

She had taken the train with Christina and Maud to this hotel near

York where George would bring the boy to join them. They would have some time to get to know each other before Stefan started his English education, boarding at George's old school nearby.

She heard a muffled voice as if the mouthpiece had been covered for a moment. 'George?'

'I'm here. There's someone waiting for the phone, I'll have to go. The doctor said he'll need time. In a few months he'll be fine.'

'Does he . . . does he seem . . .' Elisabeth wound the telephone cord round her finger so tightly it hurt.

'He's just an ordinary lad, Elisabeth. Thank God they found us. I can't believe we're letting children suffer like this after all they've been through. They had no idea what was going on.'

Elisabeth's skin prickled. *Is he a child at sixteen, George? How could he not know?*

'He's been living in a ruin somewhere,' George went on, 'scavenging from bins outside the Americans' mess tents. The bloody war wasn't the fault of boys like him any more than our children were to blame.'

She wanted to say, *Our children never wore swastikas. Our children haven't killed anyone.* Instead she said, 'We had spam fritters for supper. Banana custard for pudding, the real thing. I can't think where Mrs McCrae got bananas. Maudie was in heaven.'

The phone line crackled. 'Hello? Hello? George, are you still there? When will you be here, George? Maud keeps asking.'

'We'll be with you tomorrow. I must go. Is the hotel nice? Mrs McCrae said it's very modern. I thought you'd like some comfort.'

'It's lovely, George.'

There was a pause. 'The least we can do is give the boy a decent education. I'm going to teach him fly-fishing, and a good single malt. I'll take him shooting. He'll enjoy it, do you think?'

In spite of everything Elisabeth had smiled when she put down the receiver. Stefan wouldn't need tuition with a rifle. He'd be a better shot than George.

The first passengers were coming through the ticket barrier and a man wearing a demob suit stopped dead when he handed over his ticket as if he couldn't go on without it. He had the baffled agitated look of soldiers coming home, stranded as they were in a no-man's-land between war and peace with no way back to either. People piled up behind him, then a girl in a swirling skirt which must have used up all her coupons for the year ran across and flung herself at him. There was a tussle between them to hold each other tight enough, to find a grip that wouldn't fail again. The girl was laughing and the man lifted her up so her hair tumbled on his face and he kissed her hard, burying his face in her.

The dammed-up crowd of passengers divided around them, streaming out into the station, and Elisabeth turned her back on the girl's extravagant, optimistic skirt riding up the backs of her legs. 'Don't stare, Maudie darling.' She adjusted Maud's beret which had been knocked askew by passing elbows and when she straightened up the German boy was there, smiling as if he recognized her.

'I saw you wave,' Stefan said so softly she could hardly hear. He gulped for air, standing close so the clamour of the station wouldn't drown him out, and he tugged at his scarf. There were the stitches on his throat, as clumsy as the darning Maud might have done. 'I think you must recognize me.'

'Hello, Stefan,' Elisabeth said. She had imagined kissing him but he seemed too tall. 'I have a photo of you. It's years old but you haven't changed all that much.' She felt silly for the lie but she was flustered, not by his height or his emaciated face and caved-in chest with the raincoat hanging like a board, but by his ease and the absence of any adolescent shyness. His blue eyes made her heart twist painfully – they were scraps of Karen given back to her and she wanted to weep because Stefan was the only one who understood it was impossible for Karen to be gone. Elisabeth fixed her eyes on the stream of passengers to keep away the tears, gripping Maud's hand.

'Ow,' Maud said. 'You're hurting.'

Stefan wiped his bloodless lips, swallowing and swallowing. 'Your husband pointed out places of interest on the journey,' he said carefully. He had no accent and pronounced each word precisely like an Englishman speaking to a foreigner.

Elisabeth could feel Maud fidgeting with the worry of the introduction. 'Say hello to Stefan, Maud.'

'Hello,' said Maud and withdrew into the folds of Elisabeth's coat.

Stefan stood with his feet wide apart and swayed as if the station was rocking in a swell, leaning into the gusts of people hurrying past.

He was the tiredest person Elisabeth had ever seen. 'I'm so glad you're here,' she said, touching his arm.

He stared at her hand. 'I never met him,' he said. 'I cannot tell you anything. Everyone asks this question. Or if they don't, I see it in their mouths.'

'Who?' Elisabeth said although she knew. Stefan seemed to sag inside the raincoat as if admitting he had not seen the Führer had emptied out what was left of him. 'It's all right. I won't ask you,' she said.

At last George came through the ticket gate with a porter wheeling a battered trunk tied up with rope. Maud dashed to George and he swung her up, her mittens on their elastic and her silky hair flying. 'My baby Mouse, I've missed you such a lot,' George said and set her on the ground again. Then he leaned towards Elisabeth and she turned not quite enough so his kiss landed on her ear.

George stood swinging his arm with Maud, who had been fretting ever since he left, chirruping and dragging on his hand, and Elisabeth thought of the demobbed soldier and his girl holding each other close and not letting go. She was aware of Stefan standing quietly in the circle of her family, watching and already noticing how things were.

George smiled across at her. 'You look well,' he said in the way that meant he loved her and had forgotten all the ways she'd let him down. She felt the pieces of herself slipping back in place.

'The car's outside,' she said. 'Christina's waiting. She wouldn't come in with us.' George didn't comment and Elisabeth let her annoyance flare a little because nothing ever seemed to trouble him.

'Christina is my big sister, by the way,' Maud said to Stefan. Holding George's hand made her bold. 'And Alice is the other one but she's at home in Kent.'

'Alice,' Stefan said. 'I have three cousins. Christina. Maud. Alice.'

'You see. A house full of women. I'm glad you're here, old boy,' said George.

Elisabeth walked on ahead, searching for the car keys in her handbag, and she tried to believe in her husband's stubborn faith that anything works out if you want it to enough.

• • •

Christina rubbed a circle on the glass, breathed on it, rubbed again with her glove, hunching down in the back seat of Mr McCrae's Hillman and keeping to the spot on the leather where her back had warmed away the cold.

People were coming out of the station and she looked for a daffodil smudge that would be Maud, beside a green coat and a dark grey over-coat that would be her parents. There would be another figure too. The misted windows of the car added to the blur of Christina's short sight. She would have worn her spectacles if the German boy hadn't been arriving.

The black afternoon gusted rain and the street lamps made a span-gled chaos of reflections. She watched the shapes of passers-by, the men in raincoats, the women in threadbare make-do coats with shop-ping bags. Two nurses crossed the road, heads down and wrapped in capes like bats with folded wings. A soldier stopped to light a cigarette and a plume of smoke curled upwards in the sulphurous light, then he flicked the match into the gutter. He walked carefully as if he'd had too much to drink.

People were going home. Evenings ought to mean gramophones, Christina thought, girls smoking Craven 'A's and boys lounging on the sofa arms and being Frank Sinatra. At their hotel, evening was a time of bleakness and cutting draughts. They would all sit nearly in the hearth, scorching at the front, icicles hanging off their backs, and later Maud would creep into Christina's bed to thaw her toes and cause torment with her snuffling. It was strange to stay somewhere less comfortable than home.

The two days they had been in Yorkshire waiting for the German cousin had stretched out, wearisome and dull. The hotel provided meals and different views of rain. Christina had dust behind her eyes from too much reading, and Maud had seethed with boredom. She asked a hundred times when Stefan would arrive.

Yesterday they found a stack of jigsaw puzzles in a cupboard in the sitting room. Maud made Christina put down her book and they did *Africa, Dark Continent, A Busy Day in Toytown* and *Autumn in a Tranquil Woodland Glade* until they were stupefied with twisting little wooden pieces this way, that way. The cardboard boxes smelled of old children and the fusty innards of the cupboard.

'Will Stefan be good at jigsaws, do you think?' Maud had asked. 'Do Nazis like them?'

'You can ask him tomorrow, Maudie.'

At last the waiting was over. There was a tetchy clicking on the Hillman's windscreen as Elisabeth tapped with the keys. Maud pooched her lips against the glass. Christina unfolded herself and got out.

Elisabeth gave her a little shove. 'This is Christina,' she said cautiously as if this was a trick that didn't always work.

'Hello, Christina,' Stefan said in a rusty-iron voice. 'It is a pleasure.' His smile was so nearly a sneer it teetered on the brink of good manners and he shivered hard. 'It is a pleasure.' Saying it a second time made it sound like a disappointment he would make the best of.

Christina said, 'Golly, you look hungry.'

The German cousin was good-looking for someone with hardly any hair and as narrow as a straw but he didn't look as if he minded. The dusky yellow light was hiding him, it seemed to her, and if she could catch him from a certain angle she'd see that really he was broad and strong. It was clear he was the kind of boy who didn't care what anyone thought and she liked him in spite of his mad grim quivering and his scraping voice.

'We should go,' Elisabeth said, jingling the car keys. 'Stefan must want to rest after such a long journey. We can all get to know each other over supper.'

*Then why didn't we stay at home in Kent if the journey to Yorkshire is so long?* Christina thought. *And why leave Alice behind if he wants to get to know us?*

'Stefan is an orphan of war,' Elisabeth had said before she went into the station. 'Be nice to him, Christina. He has no one and we're his family now.'

To Christina, Stefan Landau looked like someone with no use for a family.

On the drive back to the hotel, Maud fell asleep. George tucked her against him and Christina leaned into his other side, feeling his warmth even through the overcoat.

Elisabeth drove too fast, grinding through the gears of Mr McCrae's Hillman as if she had forgotten how to drive.

The rain stopped, smoke hung above farmhouses and cottages, and faraway cut-out hills held up the granite clouds. Stefan sat in the front and Christina watched him gaze at the road ahead, with his profile against the greening evening sky, lit up sometimes by the headlamps of another car or the lamp on a pony cart going home. She had never seen a boy so shocking or so beautiful as this white-skinned, bruise-eyed German.

After a while, the hills and the sky became a single black. The car bumped along a track and the windows of the hotel flashed through the trees. Mrs McCrae was there to welcome them. The yellow light from the open door tapered away into the darkness.

'Mr Mander, here you are at last!' she said, clasping her meaty hands beneath her bosom and beaming as if George's arrival was a relief for her as well. She reared back a little when she saw Stefan. 'Good evening to you too, young man.'

They all bunched together beneath the dusty stag's head in the hall while Mrs McCrae gave directions about supper, addressing only George. Christina was used to this. Women liked her father, especially old trouts like McCrae.

•  •  •

Stefan went up to his room and fell asleep. He didn't wake up for supper, or for breakfast the next morning, or for lunch. Maud loitered by his door, kicked it softly, leaned on it, picked at the whorls in the wood. 'When's he coming out?'

'Leave him alone,' said Christina. 'He's hibernating. He's been fighting in the war and his side lost.' She took Maud's hand and they went downstairs to the guests' sitting room which looked across a lake to hills. Veils of rain washed out the colours. From time to time the clouds pulled apart to show a rag of sky miles up and solid blue, the sun shone through and everything turned opalescent. A rainbow sent Maud speeding for her boots and coat although by the time she had them on, the clouds had swollen up again, the rain had come back and the miracle had gone.

'No one's doing *anything*. What shall we *do*? He just *sleeps*.'

'What do you want to do, Maudie-mouse?' Christina said. She patted the sofa and Maud sat beside her.

'Will he live with us?' Maud asked.

'Yes, but he's going away to school.'

'Is he the enemy?'

'He was, but he isn't any more.'

'This is the nastiest holiday we've ever had,' Maud said, blowing upwards at her fringe.

'I know.' Christina pulled Maud on to her lap. 'Shall I read my book to you?'

'What is it?'

'*Valerie Learns to Love.*'

Maud put her thumb in her mouth, leaning in, and her head beneath Christina's chin smelled faintly of biscuits.

Upstairs, Elisabeth and George were talking in their room – the subject would be Stefan. It didn't matter what the details were, Christina knew it would go like this: George says it will be all right and Elisabeth says he *just isn't seeing* that it won't. George irons his hair with the flat of his palm, tests his chin for stubble and watches Elisabeth as if she is a vase about to topple off a shelf. Elisabeth twirls her earrings, fiddles with her hanky or her buttons. Her eyes have their barricaded look. Later, they will call a halt and come down for tea, but for the afternoon Christina is left with Maud.

Christina tired of skipping the paragraphs where Valerie was kissed. Maud got tired of listening, yawned and slid off the sofa to select a jigsaw puzzle from the cupboard. She tipped the pieces on the carpet, stirred them with her hands, sat back on her narrow haunches. Her pale lemon hair lit up the gloom.

After a while Mrs McCrae came in to feed a morsel of coal to the fire and as she bent, her tweed skirt creaked, so did her brogues, then she rearranged the pearls on her fawn three-ply bust and went out.

Christina pondered on what Mrs McCrae had beneath her cardigan; bosoms should be separate and pointed, as conical as possible. She hoped hers shaped up like Joan Fontaine's in *The Constant Nymph* and not like Mrs McCrae's.

Christina curled inside the brocade walls of the sofa, opened her book again and listened to the rain stop, start, stop, start, forgetting to turn the page because her eyes were closing with the soporific wheezing of the fire which was miserly with heat and generous with smoke. She leaned her head on her arms and thought of Stefan, who couldn't wake up. His sleep was trickling down between the floorboards of his room and down the staircase, piling up until she couldn't move and it didn't seem to matter any more if the rain went on forever.

# 2

There was a time when Stefan thought he wouldn't ever sleep again because his body had turned to light. He was a soldier for the Fatherland. The enemy's tanks rolled into Germany, but there was no question of defeat and glorious would be the victory in which every citizen of the Reich would have equal honour. The Führer needed everyone to fight.

When Stefan's *Hitlerjugend* troop were given a bottle of orange squash and a paper bag of bread and sausage and put on a school bus to the Front, boys were snivelling and whimpering because it was late at night and they ought to be in bed.

They woke up when the bus halted and they staggered out, huddling together and staring at blooms of red light low down in the sky. The driver threw their knapsacks in the mud and drove away. The night air was warm as if they had arrived in a resort, and after a while two soldiers came and shone a torch in their sleepy faces one by one.

'The Führer sends his greetings to you, boys.' The voice was kind and cultured, although it sounded glum. 'He commends your courage and your loyalty.'

'Jesus! Look at them. They're just kids,' said the other. 'Smarten up!' he barked. They were too tired to notice which way they were going.

After that, if they forgot to double-tie their laces or tuck in their shirts, it didn't matter because muddles in the dark with ammunition and equipment were worse. They killed each other sometimes by mistake.

At first the terror curdled in their guts. Stefan's lungs would fill in gulps because his heart was kicking his ribs like a rabbit in a sack, but after a while the fear wore itself out and Death seemed almost beautiful if he didn't turn away.

The diagrams on the blackboard at school hadn't shown the multitude of membranes, cords and liquids that make up a dying thing, nor did the drawings in a text book illustrate the intensity of colours or the possibilities of pain. Every creature was astonishing when the flesh and brains and organs were opened up, although one corpse looked much like any other; a dismantled soldier had innards like a pony, which were also like the giblets of a girl, or a dog, or a piglet, or a baby. Size and quantity were the only differences. Flesh had different textures if one paid attention. Burned black, it was all the same.

One night, he collided blindly with a piece of twisted iron and his throat was holed. He swallowed down the blood then couldn't swallow anything. So his death would be starvation, an ending to his life he hadn't thought of.

Soon after, a grinning Yank relieved him of his rifle and his ammunition, patted him on the head and told him to run home to his mother. They wouldn't even take him prisoner. Stefan was saved the humiliation of his angry tears because he fainted. He was taken to a field hospital, stitched up and fed with a bottle like a baby, then they told him to go home.

His home had turned into a mound of rubble in a rubble street. Freckled Gerda Seffert sat on an armchair in the road twitching like a rat, with scabs around her mouth and sores on both her filthy knees. 'You look a mess,' she told him, flicking her plaits. 'If you need a place to stay, there're lots of us from BDM and we've got a house in Müllerstrasse. There's a hole in the roof but you're very welcome.'

'Have soldiers been here yet?'

'Oh, yes, they found us all, even if we hid.' She flicked her plaits again. 'Some girls tried to fight but there wasn't any point and there were ladies who wiped themselves with muck or pretended to be men but that was stupid too. It didn't work. The soldiers have all gone now.'

Gerda said her mother died six months ago. Frau Seffert had been knitting with the other Party wives when the siren went. She said she would be along when she finished off her row – it was a pattern with a complicated double-cable and the shelter was only round the corner. Besides, Frau Seffert said, the siren was often a mistake. That time it wasn't.

'Your Mutti isn't here either,' Gerda told him. The muscle working in her jaw warned him not to ask. 'We have a coal hole for our shelter in Müllerstrasse,' she said. 'It's very safe.'

'The bombs are finished, Gerda.'

'I knew we'd win,' she said. '*Heil Hitler.*'

★

When there couldn't be defeat, he didn't sleep; now Germany had lost, he could do nothing else. In the enemy's bed, under a pink floral eiderdown, sleep shot him through the eyes and knocked him senseless.

He woke to see the fold of a blanket, the mountain range of his feet against the horizon of a footboard. He stretched away so many miles into the distance his brain could not locate his legs. A bluish light which could be evening or dawn came through the curtains and rain pattered on the window. He heard something else as he climbed up out of sleep – the sound of stones grinding under boots – but the noise turned into his own breath rasping up and down his windpipe.

He needed to relieve himself and with the thought he sat up. The strangeness of the movement made him dizzy. He waited for the room to right itself, drank down a glass of water from the bedside table and got out of bed.

He was a tottering old man wearing pyjamas he'd never seen before. The jacket was damp so he put on the clean one which had been left folded on a chair, and then a dressing gown as heavy as a greatcoat. This needed to be organized around him, crossed over at the front and tied with a cord at the waist. These tasks took concentration and endurance.

He remembered he'd done this before but how many times he didn't know; he had shuffled along the passageway to the freezing green-tiled lavatory, then retraced his steps, hand over hand along the wall like a mountaineer.

When he returned this time, his aunt was in the room, standing by the window with a shawl around her shoulders. 'Hello, Stefan,' she said. 'I've brought up some supper for you. You must be terribly hungry.' He got back into bed in the dressing gown, annoyed that she was treating him like a child. She had plumped his pillows and smoothed the sheet. 'You have a fever, haven't you? All this sleep should do you good but you must eat,' she said, sitting down on the bed, on his feet. She jumped up, apologizing on and on as if her weight could hurt him. She sat down again, carefully this time, and fussed with the fringe on her shawl. 'We've met before, you and I, when you were very small. Almost three, I think you were. You spoke some English even then.'

'I do not remember.'

'I met your father too. He loved your mother very much – and you too of course.'

Stefan had no memory of a time when his father and his mother loved each other. He sweated in the heavy dressing gown. This aunt, Elisabeth, was not young but she was not old either. She was wearing lipstick and scent. He didn't know what to say.

Her eyes flickered across his chest, then to a pack of cigarettes and lighter on the bedside table, and she said, 'All soldiers smoke, I expect.'

'No. Not all. An American gave me the Zippo. It is very good. Useful.'

'I expect you're practical, Stefan. I'd say you're the kind of person who doesn't keep digging over his life looking for the heart of it.'

He didn't know what she meant. Anyway, the heart of it was gone. He lit a cigarette. It seemed like weeks since he'd had a smoke.

'When your mother was a little girl she pulled up seedlings to see if they were growing. That was just like her. She was impatient for things to happen.' Elisabeth lifted her chin and discreetly blew away the smoke. 'She needed to know if something was going to work – turn out the way she wanted. It doesn't do any good to rush things, don't you think? It disturbs life's possibilities before they've taken root.'

Stefan felt the oddness of this scene, this sudden promotion to adulthood. A woman was sitting on his bed and talking to him like a lover in a cinema film.

'But then how can you know,' she went on, 'if something is right until it's in the past and then it's too late? Nothing happens the same way twice so we can't learn by our mistakes – we just go on and on making different ones.'

He had no idea if she was talking about herself, or him, or the war – or nothing in particular, just words to fill the silence.

'Do you know how you'd like your life to be, Stefan?' she asked.

'I want to serve my country,' he said and knew at once he had disappointed her. She was offering him a conversation as equals and he had lost his nerve. He sounded like a kindergarten boy who had rehearsed for a ceremony at his local *Jungvolk* group, but the words were fixed in his head and this was still the only answer.

'Of course you do,' she said. 'The Fatherland. Glorious Germany.'

'It is not any more.'

'No, it isn't. I'm sorry, that was unkind of me. You must be angry at being lied to, at being forced to fight.'

'I was not forced.' He had to stop her asking questions. 'I have a present for you,' he said. He got out of bed and went to his trunk – the effort was not so great after a cigarette – and handed her a roll of cloth.

15

In the cloth was a tattered piece of canvas. It was a painting of a girl with long copper hair, walking from sunshine into a shady village square. A man sat at a café table under trees watching the girl who was holding down her summer skirt with one hand and her sunhat with the other. A breeze had caught her hair which flickered like a flame against the bright blue sky.

Elisabeth stared at the painting. 'It's me,' she said at last.

In the corner were initials and a date, *M. R. 1929. Mazamet, Languedoc* was written in pencil on the back.

'You must know the place, Mazamet,' Stefan said.

'No. I've never been to France.'

'Then you know the artist, this M. R.?' She didn't reply and he wondered if she hadn't heard him. 'You know this painter?'

'Michael Ross. It's Michael,' she said.

So she knew the Jew. Stefan let some moments pass. 'He is a friend?'

She looked up. 'A friend?' She touched the initials with her finger. 'No.'

Stefan saw her mind circling round the puzzle of a picture of herself in a place she had never been. 'It is a good picture, is it not?' he said.

Elisabeth didn't answer. After all her talking, now she had nothing to say.

• • •

In the evening, Elisabeth took up a tray of food to Stefan. When she came down again, she sat at the table where they were waiting and poured a glass of water. George passed her a gin and tonic. Her hair was brushed back, she wore a knitted shawl to confound the draughts which marched across the dining room, corduroy trousers that had lost their shape, scarlet lipstick and too much *Evening in Paris*. She looked as if she meant to put on a dress and then forgot. Christina knew her mother's mind was on something far away. George tested his chin for stubble.

Mrs McCrae lifted a lid and released a waft of haddock soup which extinguished *Evening in Paris* in a single gust, and Elisabeth angled her spoon and dipped. No one moved.

'Where *is* he?' Maud asked eventually. 'What's he *doing*?'

'I left the tray. He's sleeping.' Elisabeth fastened off the words so neatly they all understood there would be no loose end of information to discuss. The German boy was still asleep.

★

That night, creatures blunder in the dark below Christina's bedroom window. They must be deer or cattle but they sound like elephants. They groan as if they are bereaved. They cough deeply from the chest.

All afternoon she could barely stay awake, now she can't sleep. Her pillow has a lump and the sides-to-middle seam she's lying on vexes her. She stretches out her legs which ache from being bent up to her chest for warmth but retracts them swiftly because the far end of the bed is the Arctic Ocean. The room is black and there's only the silvery ceiling for her eyes to play with. Cracks in the plaster make a map of tributaries and rivers which she examines from one side to the other, and halfway across there's a spider, not moving, biding its time. Maud is sleeping underneath it.

Christina's ears grow huge and they swivel to catch any noise that might be scuttling in the dark. The quiet throbs, then she picks up minuscule noises travelling along the water pipes. An orchestra plays faintly inside the radiator; someone in another room must be listening to a wireless and the music is being broadcast by the plumbing.

Christina's ears identify a sound she can only hear if she stays completely still. The sound isn't directional and whichever way she faces it comes from somewhere else, from under the floorboards, from behind the wardrobe, down through the ceiling. It is someone breathing, but it sounds like a saw against a piece of stone.

•  •  •

The next morning, after breakfast, they stepped outside into the unexpected brightness of a sunny day. Elisabeth put her arm through George's and they blinked at the clashing colours of the hills. Crocuses had opened up, birds were singing and damselflies bounced above the puddles on the path. There was no wind to disturb the crystal sky. 'This is a day to be born,' George said in the way he had of giving poetry to plain words.

Two sets of footprints tracked down the slope of dewy grass to the lake where Maud squatted on a rock with her hem in the water, examining something in her cupped hands. Christina stood beside her, arms folded, hips at a tilt. She dipped in the toe of her shoe and gazed out across the lake, pushing back her hair, which was the colour Elisabeth's used to be – always admired by old ladies and never fashionable. George told Christina she was a Titian angel. Christina said she was cursed and orange hair didn't go with anything except orange clothes.

There was a time when Elisabeth thought Christina might grow up to be lithe and delicate like Karen. At thirteen, Christina did have a sullen kind of grace; grey eyes, a stubborn pretty mouth and broad features inherited from George. Perhaps one day men would be attracted by her slow serenity and her uncomplicated smile.

Elisabeth and George strolled into the shade of a stand of firs and out into the sun again. A window must be open in the kitchen and sounds carried in the quiet: the clang of a saucepan, crockery being stacked and music on Mrs McCrae's tinny wireless.

Then suddenly Maud was speeding up the slope with something in her cupped hands which were leaking water down her coat. When she arrived, it had drained away and a tiny transparent fish with sequin eyes squirmed on her palms. 'What a catch!' said George. 'Quick, Maudie, take him back.' Maud about-turned and scooted back across the grass. She hunkered down again, knees up, socks half mast, the yellow coat with a stain of wet along the hem dipping into the water a second time. Christina sauntered over and leaned in to see.

There was another clatter in the kitchen and a girl began singing to the music on the wireless.

Elisabeth closed her eyes, lifted her face to the cool spring sun and walked blindly in the scarlet behind her eyelids, feeling George's solidity beside her and the rhythm of his heavy stride.

*When I open my eyes, Michael will be here.* She had imagined it so many times, the disloyalty to George had become familiar and almost benign. *It doesn't mean I don't love my husband. I enjoy my life. I have chosen to be content.*

The joy and the catastrophe of being young had dissipated to an even tempo which was peaceful and mostly happy. But Michael's painting had found its way to her. It proved this life wasn't all there'd ever been, or all there could be.

# 3

It was almost three months since Stefan had opened the trunk he brought from Germany. He had tied on ropes and carried it for miles, from lorries to trains, from camp to camp of wandering people like him who were waiting to be claimed.

George didn't ask what was in the trunk when they met at the Dover quayside. Stefan had been prepared to lie and was unnerved that he hadn't needed to.

When he opened the trunk to give the rolled-up canvas to Elisabeth, he was careful not to let her see inside. She would think he was crazy to be hoarding rubbish brought all the way from Germany. One day he would throw everything away – Hede's wooden plunger she used for mashing linen in the copper, a cooking pot, a clock without its minute hand, a tin of buttons, an old French hunting rifle found in the wreckage of his father's study. He had picked over the ruin of his home and scavenged things with barter value but in the end he never bartered anything.

There was a cup with two handles and bears around the rim which used to be his little sister's. His mother kept it on her dressing table and it would annoy him that she was sentimental and hung on to something so useless. The cup wasn't damaged when he found it in the rubble but after the journey across the Channel, it was: three pieces. He hadn't wrapped it well enough. The trunk was filled with things like this – broken filthy things he loved.

The hotel bedroom window was open and voices outside sounded silvery in the cool air. They were expecting him to go downstairs this morning and soon he would. He was almost ready.

He stood by the open trunk, which seemed to give off a gentle heat, and to calm himself he reached in amongst the jumbled things for something familiar. His hand found a piece of mildewed leather which he took out and held to his nose, shutting his eyes to find the memory in its smell.

The pictures in his mind came clear. A boy clambers over a ruined house, raising clouds of dust. He picks over the rubble and sometimes he reaches down a crevice between lumps of masonry and plaster. Suddenly, his hand touches something hairy and the boy freezes with the horror of it, then he's flinging aside the debris, terrified and wild with hope because although it's impossible that anyone is still alive, an idea flashes in his head that he has touched his mother's hair. He has found her. She'll reach up through the tangle of broken timber and masonry, scramble out and dust off her dress. She'll say he ought to change his shirt and his hands are filthy, and she'll smile and touch his cheek.

What he finds is a dog flattened by a ceiling beam. It is the gardener's wolfhound who was a puppy with milk teeth and oversized paws when the boy last saw him. Like all young things the puppy thought he was a new beginning. He was hope that wasn't blunted. He was the time before.

The dog's corpse is as rigid as cardboard as if it has no joints and never moved. The paws are still full of hard flesh but half the head is crushed. One velvet ear is tucked back as if it's sleeping. *It is only a dog,* the boy's mind tells him. His heart says nothing.

He undoes the wolfhound's collar and puts it round his own neck. A livid sun rises in the night over Dresden, while the boy buries the dog in his mother's garden of shadow petals blooming in the ash and soot and the soft deep tracks of tanks. He sniffs the earth and finds the pristine scent of worms, so he follows it, down deep into a time when this night could not happen. The perfume of the earth fills his head with lamentations that have no human words and he shakes the dust out of his fur, lifts his muzzle to the wind and hollows out the sky with the sound of blood and loneliness.

People living in the rubble across the street yell at him. 'The Landau boy's gone loopy, just like his English Mutti,' they call to one another. They throw things but he doesn't notice. He is a sound, that's all he is, a ghost-hound's song.

A racket of cawing and Stefan opened his eyes. The wolfhound's collar was in his hand. Outside the window a gang of crows tumbled in the blue and in the distance there were the snowy tops of the Yorkshire hills.

'A wireless was playing and a girl sang along in the sunshine. Stefan liked the strange soft vowels of this English he hadn't heard before. From where he stood he could see a lake and his cousin Christina standing on the shoreline with her arms folded, idly dipping in the toe of her shoe. The little one, Maud, squatted by the water like a yellow frog.

The sun through the open window warmed Stefan's face. He put on the wolfhound's collar. It might have been a minute – or more – five or ten before he reached down into the trunk and took out the hunting rifle. It was long and finely made, superior to the clumsy weapons he had used against the enemy. On the polished stock there was a pattern of flowers and trailing ribbons of inlaid mother-of-pearl and silver.

He set the butt against his shoulder and took aim. The little yellow frog was concentrating on something, peering into her cupped hands, then she stood up and ran across the grass. He tracked her in the sights, his eye following the true black line of the barrel. She was endeavouring to keep her hands steady although water was dripping down her coat, then she disappeared under the trees.

He lowered the rifle, letting it slip through his hand to rest on the floor. The branches of the fir trees bounced as if the tiny whirl of her dashing underneath had disturbed them and he watched until the trees were still. Then he saw Christina looking up towards him. She stood against the flashing water so he couldn't see her face or tell if she could see him standing in the room.

He knew he had been stupid. Sun reflecting on the barrel of a rifle is an elementary error and he was already becoming careless. Now he would have to persuade her not to tell anyone about the rifle.

Christina stared up for a moment longer, then resumed the idle dipping of her shoe in the water.

Elisabeth made a fuss when he joined them outside, overdoing the pleasure and surprise of seeing him so his heart began lurching about and he wanted to turn around and go back upstairs to his room. She said he looked marvellous this morning, very rested. George clapped him on the back and said, 'Good to see you up and about,' as if Stefan was an invalid.

'Let's all go for a walk and get some colour in our faces,' said Elisabeth. 'Maudie! Maudie!' she called to the little girl, who was still playing by the water. Christina yawned and put her arm through George's. They strolled along a grassy sheep track by the lake, with Maud skipping in front.

Elisabeth and Stefan followed behind George and Christina, and Elisabeth kept talking as they walked, running on like his mother used to when there was something on her mind.

As they climbed the hill, clouds came across, turning the water in the lake below to dark metallic green. Elisabeth was saying he would like their house in Kent because it was old and comfortable and the sea wasn't far away, but London was near enough to go up sometimes for the day. There were lots of things to do when he came home for the holidays. Did he ride? Did he enjoy the theatre?

Stefan listened well enough to smile or nod when he was meant to. He knew the question she really wanted to ask and he would never answer. She wanted to know how his mother died.

Gerda Seffert had told him one night at the house in Müllerstrasse when they were lying together on Gerda's mattress, naked under a heap of coats and scratching their flea bites. Gerda's cat smell was in his nose. She was giggling so he held her tight because he knew that soon the mirth would roll her like a wave into a sea of horror and she would punch her head and yank her hair, trying to claw the memories off her skin.

'It's all right,' he whispered and he kissed her on the mouth to stop her chortling, but she started up again if he let her take a breath. He wondered if perhaps he could knock her out to save them both another night awake. He never asked what made her laugh and fight with no one. They had all seen things they'd be better off forgetting and nothing could be done but bear it.

He tried distracting her. 'You remember kindergarten, Gerda? Remember when we made the snow house we thought was magic because it was blue inside? And the lizards sticking to the bakehouse wall in summer? And the plums hanging over and dropping in our hands?'

Gerda snorted as if he'd told a joke but she rested her head on his shoulder and he felt her breath becoming softer, and downy on his face. He searched his mind for other things to soothe her. 'What about that Christmas when we hid under the table and stuffed ourselves with truffles and *Stollen*?'

The memory of food filled his mouth with saliva. He remembered kneeling on a polished floor with firelight coming through the lace tablecloth on to Gerda's party dress, heaped around her like a dappled mushroom. Her plaits had flopping satin bows. They crammed in big insolent mouthfuls, so the gritty marzipan, cocoa, raisins and sugared cherries stuck their tongues to their teeth and they couldn't speak. Stefan smelled the oranges and cloves in the giant Dresden punchbowl and the blazing logs on the fire, and there were thumps above their heads when dishes were put down on the table. He remembered the waitresses, stiff like wood and listless as if carrying a dish was too much effort. People said Jews were sulky and considered themselves too good for honest work.

The room was full of officers and Party men and wives. Everyone was happy because it was *Weihnachten* and Germany was perfect.

But to Stefan something wasn't right. The air was trembling with the scent of the fir tree cut down from the forest and he was sorry for the tree – an innocent imprisoned thing longing for its home. It was suffering in the hot bright room and no one even noticed.

The clattering conversation above the table swelled and dipped and he heard his mother's English accent smoothing the serrated edges of the words. She made German sound questioning and hesitant, her voice lifting up above the others and then sinking like a swimmer in a choppy sea. Although she tried to hide it, he knew she wasn't sure. She wasn't as certain as a Party wife should be and it frightened him, although he did not know why.

All that was gone – the officers, the dying tree, his mother – and here he was with Gerda living in someone's burned-out house on Müllerstrasse.

Stefan pulled the coats over Gerda's shoulder. She was asleep. He was drifting too and tiredness was beginning to pull him under, then she flung out her arm and even such a skinny thing as Gerda's limb felt too heavy on his empty belly. She stirred and started muttering and he knew he had to keep talking. 'Our canoe made out of rugs, remember, Gerda? It was summer, very hot and we paddled down the Mississippi in my garden. Hede gave us honeycomb to lick.'

Gerda sat up, the covers fell off her chest, and she swivelled her waxy pointed face to him. 'Yes. Your nice fat housekeeper, Hede, gave us honeycomb. She told everyone all about it.' Her voice was conversational and perfectly normal, and even though she was awake again, he was relieved the diversion had worked. He leaned up on his elbow to pick a string of hair off Gerda's cheek. 'Did Hede tell everyone about the honeycomb? I wonder why.'

'Oh *no!*' Gerda squealed. 'Funny you! Not *that.* Hede told everyone your mother was friendly with a Jew. Didn't you know?'

'It's a bloody lie,' he said. In the dark, he could make out the shine of Gerda's eyes with the whites blinking on and off, clear white although the rest of her was badly stained. She clamped the bedclothes up under her arms, primly, as if he hadn't seen it all before. There was quiet long enough to hear the mice scrabbling in the ceiling and he lay down again, putting out his hand to touch the curve of Gerda's spine – rabbit bones under tight cold skin. 'It definitely isn't true,' he said.

'Oh, but it is.' He heard her patting the covers, fiddling with the folds in the old coats. The darkness seemed to thicken, and even the mice had quietened, waiting for whatever might come next.

'A Jewboy's whore,' said Gerda softly; 'that's what Hede called her.'

He stared up into the speckled dusk, luminescent with moonlight. There were no street lights any more. If the Zippo an American had given him wasn't out of fuel, he could light a candle. 'What Hede said, it's piss. A piece of crap.' Soldiers' words came out of his mouth as if someone else was speaking. The tattered damask curtain shifted in a draught and the armchair made a shadow on the wall like a person cowering.

Gerda tittered. 'Don't take my word for it. Ask anyone you like.'

Stefan knew she wouldn't stop unless he put his hands round her throat and pressed his thumbs down hard, but he couldn't move because his chest felt cracked apart as if he'd fallen a long way on to something hard.

'Hede told us. I swear and cross my heart,' said Gerda and bugged her eyes to emphasize her point. 'You'd gone away so you weren't there. Your Mutti couldn't be a Party wife any more and no one cared if your Pappa shot himself for Germany. They shut the door in her face and no one spoke to her. She never guessed it was Hede who told on her. Isn't that just the biggest joke!'

Gerda's shoulders started to quiver, which was a sign that laughter wasn't far away and getting nearer. 'My Mutti said a leopard doesn't change its spots even when its husband is a Party bigwig. Not a drop of German blood in Frau Landau so what can you expect, and she needed to be taken down a peg, Mutti said. She had it coming.'

Then the giggling broke out and he knew Gerda was remembering. He knew the pictures in her mind because he had seen what happened when people needed to be taken down a peg – men and women who had it coming. There was no need to make Gerda stop because the story was almost over.

'Hede said she crawled back to the house. There wasn't any point in doing much except covering her with a blanket for at least a bit of modesty. The police came later and put her in a car. They held her up because she couldn't walk.'

Gerda lay down again and she was shaking so much it wasn't surprising her mind was coming loose.

He realized he was floating way above the mattress. His mother had been beaten but it wasn't Gerda's fault. What was the difference between any of them now? No one was who they used to be, except perhaps the dead.

'Rain!' shouted Maud. She stopped on the path and her shadow stretched out on the grass. While they walked, the clouds had been gathering behind them and the hillside was glowing darkly in slanting orange light.

'We're going to get soaked,' said Elisabeth. 'Why didn't we notice?' The rain started, they turned round and jogged down the path back towards the hotel. 'Maudie, hold Stefan's hand,' said Elisabeth putting a scarf over her head.

The rain got heavier, they ran faster, bumped together, slipped on the grass. George was running with Elisabeth and Maud shrieked with the thrill of seeing grown-ups move so fast. She held tight to Stefan's hand, then Christina tripped and clutched at him so he grabbed her hand as well, and although Maud was stumbling, he pulled her hard, running faster because panic blossomed in his head like a dream he'd had of fleeing, though from what he didn't know.

Then he felt Christina yank his arm, 'Slow down, can't you, I'll fall over,' and there she was beside him with her hair plastered to her cheeks and no fear at all in her eyes. 'What's the point?' she said. 'We're soaked anyway.'

She let go of his hand and they walked. Gradually his heart stopped banging inside his ribs. The hills had disappeared inside the clouds and the rain pattered on the lake, making droplets jump. George and Elisabeth were not in sight.

Maud was exultant that the three of them were getting wet on purpose and she skipped beside him swinging on his hand. 'Will Mummy tell us off?' she asked.

Stefan licked the rain off his lips. It tasted deliciously of nothing, no sulphurous or fetid taint in it, no particles of bomb dust or ash from burned-down homes. No molecules of incinerated flesh. The rain was like it used to be in Germany – it had fallen all the way from sky to earth and nothing had spoiled it.

He wanted to tell Christina. If it hadn't been for her, he wouldn't have discovered this wonderful thing, but she was staring at the ground, rain dripping off her nose. Her skin looked warm and very smooth, and the softness where her teeth bit her lip made Stefan wish she would hold his hand again.

• • •

Later, he found her reading in the sitting room with her feet up on the sofa. Her wet hair hung over her book in dark thick ropes and when she looked up, pushing her spectacles up her nose, she asked without any preamble as if they had already been discussing it, 'Was that your rifle in the war?'

'No. It is for hunting. It is not loaded of course,' he said, sitting down on a corner of the sofa. She pulled up her knees, keeping her feet between them. The buttons of her blouse gaped and he could just make out the shadowy little cleft inside. It was still strange to see well-fed flesh.

Through the lenses of her spectacles, her eyes were huge and liquid as if she couldn't see him clearly. 'Oh,' she said. 'Actually, we're told never to point a gun at anyone even if it's empty. Daddy – George – used to take Toby hunting sometimes. Toby's gone back to America.'

Stefan had no idea who Toby was. A friend? Another cousin? Christina stretched out her legs again and there was hardly space for him. He got up. He could imagine that in a room full of people she would be the fixed point around which everyone arranged themselves.

'What music do you like?' she said. She blinked like a bulky fledgling in the light. He would have said Schumann if she'd given him the chance. She closed her book with her finger in the page. 'Do you like "Choo Choo Ch'Boogie"? It's Alice's favourite. She liked "Prisoner of Love" for ages. Actually, "I'm Always Chasing Rainbows", by Perry Como, is mine.'

He had no idea what she was talking about. It was as if she wasn't speaking English. 'The rifle was not loaded,' he said again. 'It is old.'

'Alice hates people shooting things,' Christina said. 'She thinks it's not a fair fight. My mother says killing isn't good for girls – she means killing isn't what girls should do.' She took off her spectacles and tucked her hair behind her ears. 'Actually, I should like you to teach me to shoot.' Her smile was obstinate and guileless at the same time. 'When you come home from school, would you?'

She had made it easy for him and the problem was almost solved. He waited long enough for her smile to falter, then he said, 'Yes. I will like that too. We must keep the rifle a secret. Only between us.' She looked into his face, trying to get the measure of him. He added softly, 'Perhaps you will find a place, Christina. Somewhere no one hears us.'

Her cheeks pinked and she looked down at her book. He knew she wouldn't tell anyone he had the rifle.

• • •

On their last night in the hotel, Mrs McCrae said they could use the gramophone. She announced it with the pudding, placing a little packet of needles by the custard jug.

'I dare say you'll be familiar, Mr Mander, with the rigmarole of winding and cleaning off the dust etcetera,' she said to George. 'You will kindly see to it the young people keep their arms controlled if they choose to dance.'

'I'll make sure they do,' said George. 'This is very thoughtful of you, Mrs McCrae. Say thank you, girls.'

Christina hoped, but didn't expect, Mrs McCrae's records to be something she liked, Frankie Laine for instance, or Johnny Mercer. The records turned out to be old – so old Elisabeth clapped her hands and said she remembered them.

Stefan wasn't as terrible at dancing as Christina thought he might be, although he looked like a scarecrow flapping in the wind and spent the whole time paying attention to Maud. He let her stand on his feet to do the steps and they jigged around to 'Nine Little Miles from Ten-Ten-Tennessee' and 'Sweepin' the Clouds Away'.

Christina danced with George. George danced with Elisabeth. Some other guests came in – the elderly Misses Fortey who sat on hard chairs and tapped their feet. Mr Demarne said he preferred brass, something more regimental, and only stayed ten minutes.

At nine o'clock, Mrs McCrae brought in a tray of cocoa and put the cover on the fire to keep it in. 'A very goodnight to you all,' she said, and took the gramophone records away with her.

'Well, I think it's time to say goodbye to Stefan,' Elisabeth said. He was leaving early the next morning and travelling to the school where he would board. Christina had wondered what he would tell the other boys and what they'd make of him because somehow he looked too old to be sitting in a classroom. He could probably pretend to be anyone or anything he wanted and get away with it.

'Say goodnight to Stefan, Maud.'

'Nope,' said Maud clinging like a monkey to him until Elisabeth prised her off and took her upstairs to bed.

'Goodbye, Christina,' Stefan said. He was across the room, his sleeves rolled up and his just-growing hair spiked with the exertion of hefting Maud to the music. He had his hands in his pockets and Christina wondered what she was supposed to do. They wouldn't see each other until he came home for Easter, and if he had been her brother she would have kissed him on the cheek – or perhaps she wouldn't. Would a sister say cheerio, punch his arm, hug him? What? Or should she be offhand, like Lucy Honeychurch was to Freddie in *Howards End*?

She held out her hand. He kissed it and didn't seem embarrassed.

· · ·

The darkness turned grey and hills appeared against the apricot dawn. Christina wrapped the travel blanket more tightly round herself and sat on the window seat in the sitting room, waiting for Elisabeth to come downstairs with Maud. George was seeing to the luggage. Stefan had already gone.

She watched the mist curling off the lake. A deer stood by the water with its head hanging. 'Look, look,' said Maud, running in. 'I'd love to have a deer better than a pony.'

'Shush. People are still asleep,' said Christina. 'It's waiting to die. That's what they do, just stand still when they know they can't run any more.'

'You don't know that.'

'I do,' said Christina. 'It will die today. It knows.'

'It's waking up, that's what it's doing!' shouted Maud. 'It's just sleepy. You don't know anything.'

'Quiet, girls, no, please, it's too early,' said Elisabeth, coming in. 'Where's George? Maudie, stay here, we're going any minute and I'll be cross if I have to go looking for you.' She put her coat and gloves on a chair and went out again. Christina heard her talking quietly just outside the door. 'Have you settled the bill, George? Is the luggage in the car? We should leave something for the kitchen girls, they've been so good.'

'It's all done.'

'Heavens, is that the time? We'll miss the train if we don't get a move on.' There was the click of Elisabeth's handbag closing. 'I hope Stefan will be all right travelling alone.'

'He's been through worse than sitting on a train.' There was silence and Christina thought they'd gone out to the car, then she heard George's voice again: 'We should have told them. This isn't right.'

'I know. I know.'

Christina listened, but they didn't say any more.

• • •

At first, Christina thought it was the neighbour, Mrs Saunders, waving from the shadow of the porch as they turned into the drive, but it was Alice who stepped out into the sunlight. When they had said goodbye two weeks ago, Alice was in socks with grazes on her knees. Now her hair was waved and her legs were smooth in stockings.

The dogs barked and leaped about amongst the suitcases stacked up on the gravel. 'Down! Quiet!' said Elisabeth, but she was smiling. 'Oh, I've missed you, darling.' She kissed Alice. 'But look at you! You're so grown-up.'

'Rachel took me shopping,' said Alice, smoothing her skirt with her hands. 'And I had my hair done. What do you think, Christina?'

'It's nice,' Christina said.

'Hello, Rachel darling,' said Elisabeth, leaning over an imaginary fence to kiss Mrs Saunders's cheek.

Rachel Saunders said, 'I took her to the beauty room in Selfridges. Long hair is out of fashion these days and she's not a kiddie any more.'

'Her hair was lovely,' said Elisabeth.

Christina felt it: a tug between her mother and Rachel Saunders for ownership of Alice. She picked up Elisabeth's handbag which the dogs were treading on.

Alice put her arm through Christina's. 'I've got a present for you,' she whispered. She smelled of apple blossom and Christina knew the Yorkshire souvenirs that had been beautiful would seem ugly next to Alice.

They struggled with Christina's case up to their bedroom and sat on the rug with the suitcase open between them. Christina gave Alice a wooden box with a scene of York Minster painted on the lid. 'I got you these too,' she said and looped a string of glass beads round Alice's pale neck. The colours were like Yorkshire, mauve and blue and green. 'And this as well. A swat. They have mosquitoes like the jungle.' Christina pushed up Alice's sleeve and slapped the fly swat on her arm.

Alice yelped and snatched it from Christina's hand, and they were rolling on the carpet in spite of Alice's dress and stockings.

'Watch out, my beads!'

'Get off, you lump!'

'My hair!'

'Stefan can nearly Jitterbug,' said Christina.

'What?' Alice sat up, pushing Christina off. 'But he's German.'

'He's nice,' Christina said.

'*Heil Hitler*,' said Alice. 'Ziss littel Jitterbug iss not goot. Bang.'

It was almost dark, Christina put on the electric fire and they lay on their beds in the rosy dusk. Alice said, 'You can't marry him, you know, it's a mortal sin unless you ask a bishop. You'll have mad babies.'

'He's coming home at Easter,' said Christina, 'when his school term is over.'

'Perhaps he'll fall in love with me as well.' Alice sat up. 'Open your presents.'

Christina unwrapped a book about the Princesses Elizabeth and Margaret Rose visiting the piccaninnies of Trinidad, and a bottle of shampoo crème with real beer which Rachel Saunders had recommended for coarse hair like Christina's.

'And this is the best,' Alice said. She held out a little parcel of tissue paper. 'It was in my jewellery box. You'll have forgotten all about it, I shouldn't wonder.'

Christina pulled away the paper. It was a silver heart-shaped locket.

'You found it, remember?' Alice said.

Christina did remember, but the truth was she hadn't found the locket, it had been given to her by a soldier she met once in the lane. 'I had it mended for you,' Alice went on. 'They took out the dents and polished it up. Rachel says girls should wear pearls for day and diamanté for evening. She says gold is for married women and silver is a vulgar tramp. I think it's nice even though it's silver. It's a shame the initial isn't right.'

The locket was heavier than Christina remembered, and fatter, like a heart-shaped egg. The light from the electric bar made scarlet sparks inside the silver.

When the soldier had put it in her hand six years ago, it was cold, but now it felt warm as if it was alive. The locket was engraved with a curling letter *E*.

*1927*

# 4

The front door whined on its hinges and footsteps on the bare boards in the hallway would thud through the house, so Lydia went down the area steps and let herself into the kitchen. Her son would be sleeping and she didn't want to disturb him.

In the mornings the flooding in Albert's lungs receded. He was limp and ragged like some washed-up thing, but Vera would get him up and sit him in a chair where he'd doze off again, his chest rattling like a tin of nails. Before she left for work, she pegged back the brown paper at the window so the sunlight warmed his feet – the only part of him he could bear it to touch. He would not wake again until gone twelve.

Lydia put her shopping on the kitchen table. She had been carrying too many bags to hold a brolly and her coat was heavy with the wet. She hung it in the scullery to drip. Her hat had flopped and she coaxed it back into shape and put it on the plate warmer.

The house was silent. Rachel was at school, and young Michael – heaven only knew where Michael was – drawing portraits on the street or doing odd jobs for anyone who'd pay him. He was like Albert used to be, not much to say but practical and thoughtful, quick at learning things. Albert used to understand the workings of all the modern gadgets, even engines. He could fix most things. That was finished for Albert now.

On a rainy afternoon in France in '17, Albert had tumbled into a crater for shelter to find a little breath of mustard gas sheltering there too. He couldn't climb out or shout for help – the noise of hell went on above his head. His face and hands were seared like meat against a griddle, down inside his uniform, his stomach, his lungs.

He woke to the sound of people talking in the dark, then the pain began – pliers in his guts, and scalding as if they'd boiled him. He couldn't see or move, and at first he didn't realize that the other noise that blossomed was his own voice yelling.

A nurse who sounded terrified said the blindness and the burns were secondary; the shrapnel and the fractures had been the real challenge for the surgeon. A shell had exploded almost on top of him, she said; it should have finished him. 'I don't mean *should*,' she flustered, 'what I mean is you was lucky, Mr Ross.'

Michael was ten when Albert was brought home from the hospital. Vera forbade little Rachel to see her dad at first, but Michael wanted to. He had insisted.

'Your Nanna Lydia will take you in,' Vera had said at Albert's bedroom door. 'Don't let me down. You're the man of the house now, Mikey.'

Lydia thought this was a daft thing to say to a little boy and unusual for her daughter-in-law, who normally had such sense, but Vera had gone a little crazy for a while, swinging like a pendulum between elation and horror that her husband was alive. The army doctor had assured her that Albert would heal sufficiently to lead a useful life and all he needed was time and a loyal patient wife. Mustard gas was nasty but a man could live with disfigurement and blindness – plenty did. As for the other damage, well, the courage of the man was paramount. It was important he was kept busy and not allowed to dwell.

How does one occupy a man who can't see or move and whose hearing is impaired, Lydia wondered.

'Your husband won't be quite the man he was, Mrs Ross,' the doctor had told Vera delicately. 'But with your family complete, this will not affect you.'

'Affect me?' Vera said. 'Affect me?' Lydia shushed her gently, but Vera in her anguish didn't take the hint. Lydia saw the doctor scrabble in his mind for words that would be plain enough to terminate the consultation.

'Marriage' – he pressed his palms together to illustrate the union – 'has blessed you with a son and daughter. Your family is complete, Mrs Ross. Therefore your, ah, expectations of your husband are different from those of a younger wife.'

'And what expectations would those be?' Vera said. 'I don't expect him to dig the spuds sitting in a wheelchair.'

The doctor winced. 'I simply mean that you and Mr Ross will be, as it were, loyal *friends*.' If Mrs Ross understood him now he couldn't tell but thankfully she asked nothing more.

Albert had the little room just off the stairs where the babies used to have their cots. Month by month a new skin covered him, but it fitted badly and did not follow the contours of the face and body underneath.

Albert seemed to rally for a while. In the first year, he learned to dress himself and to stand up almost straight on the good days when his skin was supple enough to stretch behind the knees. He could distinguish shapes floating in the gloom. Sometimes there were showers of lights he took for Passchendaele still raging in his head. The doctor said it was blood pumping across the damaged retinas.

'We'll have you sitting at the table in a month or two,' Vera would say. 'You have to make the effort, Albert. You have to fight.'

Lydia could see her son was already fighting on too many fronts. It was Vera's own yearnings that made her as blind as Albert.

The breakfast things were piled in the scullery sink and Lydia tutted at the mess, though not with genuine annoyance. She sat down heavily on a chair to get her breath.

She had walked the mile from her own place on the Old Kent Road, stopping at the grocer's and the butcher's to get shopping for Vera who hadn't much time now she was working for a milliner in New Cross. Lydia had called in at the fishmonger's, although it wasn't Friday, to get a pail of ice for Albert.

'How is your boy, Mrs Ross?' asked almost everyone she passed. 'Feeling better, is he? How is Albert these days?' Her boy was dying and 'these days' had turned into years.

She had passed a man – it was hard to tell if he was young or old – leaning on a crutch and playing the harmonica. He wore a filthy pin-striped suit that might have been respectable once. He'd lost an arm at the elbow, and a leg. His flapping trouser leg was knotted and his empty sleeve was tied with string. She dropped a farthing in his hat, but couldn't bring herself to acknowledge him. She hurried on, scolding herself for treating him so shabbily.

There was another beggar further up the street, whistling, with a rag laid out to catch the coins. She crossed the road to avoid him.

She should feel pity but she resented these men who could stand upright, even on the skew. They had hands to hold harmonicas, and lips and breath to whistle with. She was ashamed that she resented all the men, even her own dear husband Lemuel, who had made the leap from life to death with speed and decisiveness, when Albert was stranded halfway between.

The thoughts passed quickly. Lydia was not a woman to rake over what should or should not have been.

She tidied up and prepared the vegetables for dinner. She did the ironing and mended Rachel's gym dress.

In her day, Lydia reflected as the needle clicked against the thimble, girls didn't have tuition in doing bends. All the help they gave at home was sufficient exercise. Rachel was a clever miss and had got a scholarship to a private school in Catford and perhaps it was assumed these girls would not be scrubbing floors or fetching coal and laundering to keep themselves from getting fat.

It would be a blessing if this school which cost the earth in uniform and books would see Rachel settled with a doctor or a businessman in a nice new villa in Dulwich or Blackheath. Rachel was sensible – for a girl who'd been indulged – and had a loving generosity of heart. She made people laugh and she lightened things despite her snappish moods.

Michael was a different fish. He didn't have his sister's cheerfulness or her talent for looking like an angel while doing as she pleased. Rachel would meet trouble head on, whereas Michael had a tendency to turn away. He had his grandfather's looks, the same thick dark hair, wild if it wasn't oiled down, and those eyes that drowned you. Lydia saw her beloved husband Lemuel in their grandson's face.

Unluckily – was it disloyal to think this way? – Lemuel's need to have an artist's paintbrush in his hand, which skipped a generation in Albert, had turned up again to trouble Michael. He had the face and soul of Lemuel, but Lydia could see it: Michael had been wounded by the war no less than Albert.

On that day ten years ago when Lydia took little Michael's hand, he didn't flinch or cry out when he saw his father, but something in him changed. He stepped back from life and this caught Vera on the raw. She made him pay for it, not bullying exactly but hinting and suggesting in a hundred picky ways that he could make things right if only he were willing, as he ought to be, to take over from his dad.

Lydia did not interfere. She understood that Michael couldn't win. It would make Vera happy if he were more like Albert and filled his shoes, and it would also make her happy if Michael were less like Albert and did not remind her of what she'd lost.

But this was Vera's house. It was not Lydia's place to criticize or judge; that was the way to divide a family. It would be foolish to risk more harm to what was already in pieces.

Lydia contemplated her battered family. Their trouble had not brought them closer or made them stronger; they pretended like other families did. The war had wounded people's hearts, shrivelled them, and brought a weariness so deep the soul just longed to float away, to be free of everything, even love.

Lydia snipped a thread from Rachel's dress. There was no sense in brooding.

By lunchtime the light had gone so dim she could barely see. The rain hung in sooty veils and the stone steps outside the kitchen window were glistening. She warmed some mutton soup, put ice in a cloth and took them on a tray upstairs to Albert. He would probably not touch the soup, but he liked to melt the ice on his skin.

• • •

'Michael, thank the Lord you're here.' Francesca darted from behind the maid and tugged at his sleeve. 'Quick,' she said. 'My house is full of people who hate each other. There'll be murder. We must hide.'

The maid, Edith, moved aside, lips pursed. She could not abide racing madam to the front door when the bell sounded. Americans had no notion of position: the employee opened and the employer sat tight and waited to be told. It must be so, and Edith would not be thwarted. 'Who should I say is here, sir?' she insisted.

'Hello, Edith,' said Michael. 'It's me.' He had been here a dozen times before.

'You're wet through, you poor darling boy,' Francesca said. 'You're dripping on me.' She took off his hat and kissed him on the cheek. The tip of her tongue licked a drop of rain. 'Come upstairs and I'll find you a shirt.'

'May I take your hat, sir?' Edith tugged the hat from Francesca's hand. 'Mrs Brion will see you now.'

'Yes, I will,' said Frankie. 'I'll see him out of those wet clothes.'

A sour smell rose from the saturated wool of the old greatcoat Michael had borrowed from his father, and he was ashamed to let Edith take it. 'It's all right, Edith, I'll see to it.' He put down the parcel he was carrying.

Frankie said, 'Oh, good. The paintings for the Fairhaven. Edith, would you mind taking them to the dining room? Michael, that coat smells like a skunk.' She helped him out of the greatcoat and dropped it on the floor. 'I've been pacifying Cara for hours. I said you'd be here at seven. Where were you? Oh, Michael, you walked! I told you I'd send a car. It's too far in this damned and dratted English rain.'

Edith picked up the coat and stalked off downstairs.

Francesca took Michael's hand. 'They're in the drawing room. Run! Don't let them see us.' There was the sound of people talking and a piano being played badly. The voices were argumentative and a child was wailing.

Upstairs in Frankie's sitting room the lamps were lit and there was a fire burning. The curtains were open and the London rain pattered on the glass. 'I know, I know, the neighbours,' said Frankie. 'I'll close the drapes. I wish they knew the Yankee widow and her rabble of Bohemians had Lady Fairhaven on the premises. They respect a title, even if they don't think much of art.'

She went into her bedroom and Michael could see someone sleeping in her bed. 'It's Toby,' said Frankie smiling. 'Ingrid's youngest.' She came back with a shirt and a pair of trousers. 'They're Mac's. They'll be too small, but never mind.'

The shirt and trousers were soft expensive cloth, expertly tailored. Frankie's dead English husband had money of his own but his marriage to Francesca made him rich. 'I was too late to be a dollar princess,' Frankie had once said. 'American heiresses were out of fashion by the time I got to England. McCarthy didn't care, he married me for love. That was out of fashion too.'

She sat down on the hearthrug. 'Oh, Michael, why do my guests behave so badly? Ingrid came for lunch and has forgotten to go home, and Ollie is in her suit, provoking everyone. Douglas has brought a delicious young man – Venetia loves him too. He's a porter and Douglas found him on a train. Isn't that romantic? Poor Douglas will want to paint him nude. Venetia will see to it he doesn't.'

Frankie put a cigarette into a holder. In the firelight she could have been much younger with her short hair and clear white skin. She hugged her knees. Her stockings were green and she was wearing an outfit she might have made herself from costumes she'd found abroad. The dress was Chinese printed silk and as short as a chemise. She wore a silver belt low on her hips and a loose jacket of homespun wool with coral buttons. Ropes of turquoise and amber beads as big as pebbles looped around her neck.

There was incense burning, and a pitcher of lilies on the cabinet were dropping petals on the floor. The lilies gave off their honeysuckle sweetness and little wreaths of sandalwood smoke perfumed the air.

'I've found some new people for you to talk to – that's if we can stop everyone from arguing.' Her frown showed a crease between her eyes. 'One of them is a painter and shakes like a blancmange and the other two are nice young men who live together in a cottage – one has a wife, I think – and they do all sorts of things, designing books and carving and making prints. They knit and do needlepoint. Isn't that just so enticing? Imagine great beefy hands holding an itsy little needle.'

Frankie looked tired and her eyelids had a shadow of blue. Michael wished she could be at ease with him – then perhaps she wouldn't mind a silence sometimes.

He stood in his breeches, drying off the damp with her linen towel. The rain had gone through his shirt and it felt good standing barefoot in the warm of this peaceful room.

The voices downstairs rose and fell, muffled by the Aubusson rugs and Apache beadwork hangings, the New York Dada abstracts and the French toile curtains. The bright chaos of America and the solidity of Europe were joined by Frankie's New World dollars and her disregard for anything that England might expect of her.

So many things in Frankie's house belonged somewhere else, including him. The discordance was like an orchestra tuning up: it was unsettling and rubbed the senses raw, but made the heart fly up with hope.

This house was not soured by pain and bleached out with grief like Neate Street, where his mother simmered bitterly, Nanna Lydia had surrendered and Rachel had built a barricade of selfishness around herself. At home he was pressed back into a corner of himself and besieged by all three of them.

He finished dressing and put on the soaking boots again. They had belonged to his father. Frankie had given him a pair of her husband's hand-stitched shoes but they were too small.

'You're ready.' Frankie stubbed out her cigarette. 'Good. I'm going to get Fairhaven to open her dusty old wallet if it's the last thing I do. Her daughter is here too, so we must butter them up and get you a couple of commissions. I know you hate portraits, but this is business.' She jumped up.

'Am I respectable?' he asked.

'No, I'm glad to say,' said Frankie. 'Kiss me and let's pretend I'm young enough to be your lover.'

The drawing room was full of people. Michael glimpsed the faces as Francesca led him to Lady Fairhaven who sat sweating by the fire in raspberry crêpe de Chine. She was in conversation with a man whose feet fidgeted on the carpet and whose shoulders convulsed from time to time as if he was shaking off a spider.

'My daddy was in oil,' Lady Fairhaven was saying. The Deep South reverberated in her monumental bosom and her pearls trembled slightly. 'And my husband, dear Urban, worked tirelessly on diplomatic aspects of the friendship between our two great nations. My sons' – she patted her chest and coughed into her handkerchief – 'my sons, Huttleston and Henry, were both in military service in Jaipur. So you see, my dear Mr Maier, I am closely acquainted with the world of men, and as a woman I suffer sympathetic agonies equal to the hardships you poor soldiers endured.'

'Sympathy was just what we needed in the trenches,' the man said. His face had flushed a savage pink.

Cara Fairhaven patted his arm. 'Surely, surely. I am comforted by your gratitude.'

'May I interrupt, Cara dear?' Frankie manoeuvred Michael to face Lady Fairhaven. 'This is Michael Ross. People are just *scrambling* for his work.' Frankie waved her arm, 'He shows . . . all over the place.'

'I'm sure he does.' Lady Fairhaven lifted her hand which was as powerful as a blacksmith's. The milky fingers twinkled with gems. She waved Michael aside, grasped the arms of the Dorset chair and rose to her feet. Beneath the upsurge of crêpe de Chine there was a wheeze of silk and the creak of stays. 'I am troubled with a lung,' she said, 'I do not need to talk to him, Francesca, pleasing as he is, I only need to see what he can do.'

'Come through to the dining room, Cara,' said Frankie, standing clear as Lady Fairhaven organized her chiffon wrap. 'I've set up a little gallery and some other painters have brought work this evening too.'

Michael watched Lady Fairhaven tacking through the crowd, moving swiftly for someone so large. 'Wherever did you find him, Francesca?' he heard her say.

'Oh, I stumbled over him in Richmond Park, making exquisite

watercolours of the shrubs,' Frankie answered, following behind. The drawing room was stilled as they passed, followed by a flurry like leaves stirred up by a train. A cloud of jasmine scent hung around the Dorset chair.

The twitching man muttered, 'So help me, I could've punched her.' He looked up at Michael. 'It would've scuppered your chances of a portrait if I'd blacked her eye. You make me sick, you call yourself an artist. I know what you are.' He glared and fumbled for a cigarette. 'Mrs Brion's not bothered if you can paint – anyone can see what her interest is.'

'Let's keep it civil, sir. The gentleman's done no harm to you.' A big heavy-set man with wiry hair was standing with his back against the mantelpiece.

'It's all right,' Michael said. He didn't want an argument. He had seen this so many times in men who'd broken down; they stoked fury inside themselves to keep away the fear.

'Here you are!' A woman in a pin-striped suit kissed Michael on the cheek and put her arm through his. 'Frankie's darling Hebrew. I thought she'd hidden you.'

'Hello, Olivia,' said Michael.

'And you've met Douglas and Venetia's porter?'

'Eddie Saunders, pleased to meet you,' said the big man by the mantelpiece. His fraying collar was tight enough to choke him. In his straining clothes he looked hot and bulky, but his large face was good-tempered. 'I'm at Charing Cross, the Ashford–Dover line.'

'Charing Cross? How *thrilling*,' said Olivia, as if any other terminus would have been a disappointment. 'Francesca is just hopeless when it comes to introductions, so I suppose it falls to me.' She waved her cigarette at the glaring man on the sofa. 'This is Laurie Maier. He's been in Cornwall, Michael. He does navy skies and scarlet trees and suchlike. His pictures are a little more conventional than yours.'

'A modern are you – all ugliness and puffed-up theories,' said Laurie Maier to Michael. 'On second thoughts, I'd like to see old mother Fairhaven as a pile of cubes – or best of all inside one of Mr Jeanneret's concrete coffins.'

'But Mr Jeanneret is a visionary, is he not?' Olivia said. 'I understand he advocates large windows and a minimum of plasterwork. And underfloor heating. I'm not sure I'd want all and sundry peering in, but

I'd adore a life without people clanging about with scuttles of coal and tongs.'

'Le Corbusier, he calls himself.' Maier's nerves had set him shivering again. 'What kind of idiocy is that? Le Corbusier. Ha! He advocates ugliness, Olivia. Ugliness, and people living like chickens packed together in a coop – not the rich, of course, oh no, just the common man who's risked his life for values Mr Jeanneret wouldn't understand. He'd have us tearing down the beauty of Wren and Nash, and Mr Pugin. Even Mr Paxton constructs iron and glass with sensitivity. Jeanneret would brutalize us all.'

'Heavens! I'd no idea a builder could be so dangerous,' Olivia said. She turned her back on Maier. 'You've brought some paintings for us, Michael?'

But Maier's anger was rising. 'A painter! He licks the arses of the French; he thinks they're intellectuals. Hah! They're lunatics. Braque's spectacles must be cracked as well as his mind.' Maier slapped his thigh at his own wit. 'Picasso and his one-eyed tarts, it's a bloody insult. England, the land – that's the only thing worth painting.'

'My goodness, let's not squabble,' said Olivia. 'And isn't Mr Picasso a Spaniard? He paints bullocks and mandolins. I'm sure that isn't French.'

'I think Mr Maier's right: the land's what counts,' said Eddie Saunders peaceably. 'It's what we fought for. There's farmland lying neglected all over the country and going for a song. I've been keeping an eye out down Folkestone way and I've a mind to buy a field and a cottage for myself when I've saved some cash. I'm no artist, so working the land will have to do for me.'

'What fun,' Olivia said. 'You must talk to André and Charles – they're over there, with the plain girl in mauve. She's Charles's wife, or is it André's? They have a cottage somewhere and they find the bleakness and the hardship terribly inspiring. Well, I must leave you.' She blew a kiss in their direction. 'We're simply swamped with men this evening, all needing attention. You are so few these days, but with astonishing good fortune a little herd has gathered here. I should have worn a frock.'

Olivia moved away and Maier got up. He nodded to Michael and to Eddie Saunders. 'I meant no offence.' Head down, he shouldered his way towards a maid who held a tray of glasses.

'I had it easy compared to him,' said Eddie Saunders when Maier had gone. 'I was in France in '18 at the end and all I fought was mud. I did six months digging pits for what we couldn't identify as man or beast. The stench of it and what I saw coming home in boxes . . . I can smell it sometimes now.'

Michael felt Eddie Saunders's affable, unassuming look, waiting for him to tell his story in exchange. This was what men did for each other these days. No detail – hardly anything at all but just enough to acknowledge what was shared and could not be borne alone. Michael had nothing to say. His age was a lame excuse for standing here with no scars on his body or memories to torment him. Talk of the war always brought with it the feeling of the house on Neate Street, and something in him vanished like a wisp of smoke. So this could happen even in Frankie's house: he had disappeared and nothing was left but the clothes of a good man who was dead and the boots of one who should be.

Eddie Saunders wiped the sweat off his face and lit a cigarette. He said, 'No sense in stirring up all that.'

'I didn't fight,' said Michael. 'I was eleven when it ended.'

'Is that so? I took you for a gentleman a little older.' He put a hand on Michael's shoulder and the huge heavy palm radiated heat like a warming pan. 'My apologies. It's long past and done with and lads like you shouldn't have to hear it. So, here we are, the two of us, as sane and whole as we've ever been.' He lowered his voice: 'Not like poor Mr Maier.' He tapped his glass against Michael's. 'We should drink to our good luck, the luck of being fit and free to get on each other's nerves in whatever way we like. Here's to the future.' He took a swig. 'I don't suppose the likes of me will come to ownership of land, but I've a right to try the same as anyone, after what I've lost.'

A brother? A father? Michael didn't ask. So this was how it was: dreams could be earned with grief, and perhaps his own liberty would be earned with Albert's death. His mind always swerved away from admitting he was impatient for what would also break his heart, but this squeamishness was cowardly; it was a delusion to think that staying to witness his father's dying would absolve him of the sin of wishing for it. He felt sick with restlessness. He should leave now, get his coat and walk right out of London. 'I must get away,' he said.

'Well, it's been a pleasure,' Eddie Saunders said. 'Perhaps we'll meet again.'

'No. I mean London. I've got to leave and I don't know why I don't.'

'You should. A man is free until he marries,' said Eddie. 'And if there's love it's freedom just to be with her.'

'You have a wife?' Michael asked.

'No,' said Eddie, and fell silent.

The fire had almost died away but the air was stifling. Frankie's house had no oxygen tonight. A child bounced on a sofa with her long hair flying and her dress ballooning out above her skinny legs. Her shrieks sliced through the clatter of conversation as two older children, a boy and girl, perched on the sofa arms regarding her, bored as cats. He had often seen these children at Frankie's evenings; sometimes they were up until gone midnight. Their mother, Frankie's sister, Ingrid, must be somewhere.

Some people beckoned Eddie Saunders to join them. Michael knew he couldn't put it off any longer and he should find Frankie and Lady Fairhaven.

In the dining room the cherrywood table was covered with a cotton dust sheet on which stood the eighteen dining chairs. On each one was propped a canvas and people moved around the table to view them.

'Your work is a little slapdash for my taste, Mr Ross.' The conversations in the room were quelled by Lady Cara Fairhaven's fortissimo. She was standing at the far end of the table. 'I confess I'm rather old school in my fondness for accuracy and detail, but I much admire your portrait of the girl. You must have flattered her. It could be a whimsical notion of Salome. Who is she?'

'My sister,' Michael said. He had not flattered Rachel: she was more beautiful than he could ever paint her.

'Well, I shall sit for you, and my daughter also. Pixie's complexion is distinctive, and she is extremely good at sitting motionless. You will find her an obliging subject. Myself less so but then age has different qualities. I have discussed your fee and the appointments with Francesca.'

Frankie said, 'I've promised to let Cara know when you've finished your current work, Michael.' She rushed on, 'He's hopeless with arrangements, Cara. Thank goodness he leaves everything to me.'

'And I have purchased your charming watercolour sketch of two washerwomen in a cobbled yard hanging out a sheet,' Lady Fairhaven continued. 'It is wrapped and I shall take it now. It has an echo of the Fauves I fancy, so you see I'm not averse to modern styles. The strident colours and the coarseness of the figures are touchingly in keeping with the rustic subject.' It was a picture of his mother and Nanna Lydia. 'Well, I must say goodnight, Francesca. Urban will be fretting.'

Cara Fairhaven exited the dining room followed by a young woman with sloping shoulders and sandy hair. Pixie, Michael guessed. She turned and smiled at him, showing large teeth in a narrow hot pink face.

He looked at the other painters' work for a while, then sat with Edith downstairs in the kitchen where she made him a sandwich and a cup of tea. It was almost two o'clock. 'Mrs Brion tells me to go to bed when I like, but what's the point? How can I sleep with all that racket going on?'

He went up to Frankie's room to change back into his own shirt and trousers. The little boy was still asleep in Frankie's bed, and Michael wondered if he'd been forgotten; the other children had gone some time ago.

From the hallway he caught sight of Frankie in the drawing room. He should feel grateful to her for the money she had brought his way, but his gratitude was tempered by the prospect of the days of tedium he would endure while earning it. He did not mind so much painting the cheerful red-faced Pixie, but standing for hours studying Cara Fairhaven's flawless pearls and lantern jaw was too dreary to contemplate.

He could hear a heated argument in full swing around the canvases in the dining room. The porter, Eddie Saunders, had disappeared and so had Louis Maier. Michael tried to catch Frankie's eye to say goodnight, but couldn't.

When he closed the front door, the heat and voices were cut off. It was still raining and the pavement glittered beneath the street lamps. A sallow fog smelled of mildewed stone and soot. He thought of the soft black sky and silent fields waiting for Eddie Saunders down in Kent.

# 5

A summer morning, 1881, a silky breeze and ordinary sunshine. There was nothing to warn Lydia that by ten o'clock her life would be decided. She was seventeen.

She had been sent to collect her father's altered suit, the shop bell jingled over the door, in she went and there was young Lemuel Jacob Roth with his tailor's tape around his neck and his melted cocoa eyes. He didn't smile and he looked as flummoxed by the sight of her as she was by him. It wasn't love at first, but recognition. Her body seemed to jolt, like a dream of tripping up a kerb, her heart faltered then beat forever afterwards in time with his.

The fact that he was a Jew and she was Church was nothing to them, even when his family turned their backs and said he couldn't keep their god or their name if he went through with it. Her mother told her she was a fool if she thought two faiths and races could make a happy union and normal offspring any more than sheep could marry hens.

If the weather was fine on Sundays, Lydia and Lemuel would picnic in the park at Greenwich or at Richmond, or on Hampstead Heath. It was good to get away from Peckham for the day – they had no god to worship – and be like any other heathen family together. They gave their baby boy a solid English name, Albert, in the hope of diverting the gossip and the nastiness that came from both sides of the neighbourhood, Synagogue and Church.

Young Albert was a little Anglo-Saxon, pale and freckled. He took after Lydia in looks, and although she grieved that he had not inherited Lemy's handsomeness, a bigger part of her was glad. His path would be smoother with his Jewish blood invisible.

So the shock was all the more when at twenty-two years old, Albert announced he would not skulk as if he was a criminal, nor would he pander to other people's ignorance. He and his young wife, Vera May, would give their baby son a Jewish name: Michael Jacob.

Lemuel explained that Jewishness did not work that way. It was the mother's line that counted. If Lydia had been, then Albert would be too, but, as things were, he wasn't Jewish in the proper sense and neither was Michael.

'That's as may be,' Albert said. 'I don't know all the ins and outs, but I know the birds and bees. I'm half of you and my son's half of me. Michael's got a right to own both sides of his family.'

Then four years later came little Rachel Hannah. And the second shock was that these grandchildren were the son and daughter Lemuel should have had: dark-eyed and beautiful, with the sun of Palestine in their skin.

By the time the new king was on the throne, there were six of them for picnics. On Sundays that were wet or cold they visited the Crystal Palace or the hothouses at Kew, or Lemuel would take his little grandson Michael to look at paintings. Lydia and Vera May went off together on the tram with baby Rachel to window-shop somewhere fashionable and way beyond their purse like the Burlington Arcade.

When the orchards were in bloom, Lemuel bought tickets for the train and they'd picnic all together in real countryside in Kent.

That was another England.

In the second August of the war, the postman brought a letter from the king. Lydia did not faint or weep as some wives did. Her heart already knew. She put Lemuel's scroll and plaque amongst her stockings and her petticoats. She burned the letter. He had not fought for the king, or for any god, but for England and his fellow man.

Then came news of Albert. Her son was wounded but alive.

Since Albert had come back from France in '17, Vera refused to take Sunday trips without him. She insisted that when he was strong enough to stand and they could get him and his chair on and off the tram, the outings would resume.

Lydia knew Albert should not be seen outside when there were children to consider. Did Vera not remember the effect on little Michael all those years ago? And getting Albert down the stairs, let alone on a tram, would never be, but saying so would only anger Vera. Even Rachel's wheedling did not move her.

Then out of the blue, one Friday in early May when the weather had been warm and sweet for days, Vera said to Rachel, 'You see to it you get your homework done, my girl, we're going out on Sunday.'

Lydia and Michael looked up from their plates of herring pie. This was unexpected. Lydia said, 'I'll be here to see to Albert, and Michael will help me out, won't you, ducks? Where are you and Rachel off to, Vera?'

'Sevenoaks. You're coming too – and Michael if he likes. All of us,' said Vera. 'Ada Hobbs from Number 12 has offered to sit with Albert, so we needn't get back till tea.'

'I'll bring a friend from school,' said Rachel.

'You can take your paints, Michael. There's some nice views out at Sevenoaks,' said Lydia.

'I'll stay here, Nanna. I'll stay with Dad,' Michael said.

'I told you, Michael,' said Vera irritably, 'Ada Hobbs is coming in. What could you do for him, for goodness sake?'

On Sunday morning Lydia and Vera made the picnic and packed it in the cardboard suitcase they always used for outings. Vera had fetched it down from the attic and wiped off the dust. When they last set eyes on it, it was in a different life.

Rachel was meeting her friend off the bus at half past nine. There was a sound of giggling and voices, and then shoes clattering down the area steps to the kitchen.

'We're here,' said Rachel. 'This is Elisabeth.'

The girl was as tall as Rachel but did not look her sixteen years. It wasn't that she was younger in the face, thought Lydia, but she seemed to come from a time when children didn't grow up so fast, another age before the war when girls wore white embroidered organdie on Sundays and ribbons in their hair. The girl had such a look of sweetness that it made you worry straight away she hadn't got the hang of modern life, the way a young girl should in 1927.

She wasn't built how they liked to be these days – she was too curvy in the figure and had freckles on her nose. Like as not Elisabeth would be the ugly duckling of the class. Girls that age never know what proper beauty is; they all wanted to be like boys and have no bosom or waist to speak of, and hair chopped short as if they'd been in gaol. Beautiful carroty hair like Elisabeth's, long with natural waves, was never in the fashion pictures any more. It was worth all the worry and the scrimping to see Rachel with such a lovely friend.

And then a minute later another girl arrived, clacking down the steps outside the kitchen window and coming in without so much as a tap on the kitchen door to introduce herself. She was blonde and skinny as a spider and wore a cherry-red crêpe dress the ugly modern shape that Rachel liked but Vera wouldn't let her wear: a tube with no bodice darts or shirring, as if it was designed to fit a sausage, and a kick of cloth around the knees that called itself a skirt. This girl could have stepped out of the window of a shop in Piccadilly. She was pretty in exactly the modish way that Elisabeth would never be.

'This is Karen,' said Rachel. She gave no explanation to her mother as to why she'd invited two friends when she'd asked for only one.

As usual, Vera didn't correct Rachel for presuming but Lydia said pointedly, 'Perhaps you'd be kind enough to make an extra round of sandwiches, Rachel, and wrap up another plate for your guest.'

'I'll do it,' said Elisabeth.

The two girls were sisters who lived in Catford and were in Rachel's class at school ('Well, I couldn't just ask one of them, could I, Nanna?'). Karen was two years older than Elisabeth and Rachel but had suffered the rheumatic fever so was in a class behind her age.

Rachel propped herself against the dresser while Karen chattered and told stories about the mistresses at school. She did a little show of mimicking the Mademoiselle – *Oo la laa. Eet iz so ot een eere* – and flapped her skirt, showing a pair of slender stockinged knees and a glimpse of garter. Rachel screeched and pointed in a way that wasn't ladylike and for the first time in years Vera laughed as if she meant it.

It was plain to see that this blonde friend of Rachel was always at the hub of things but Lydia did not warm to her. Karen stirred up the air like the beginnings of a storm and made people skittery and bold. Lydia had seen her kind before.

They were almost ready to leave. Ada Hobbs arrived, the girls fussed with their hair, and Vera was rinsing off the cutlery at the sink. Then it happened.

Michael came into the kitchen and Elisabeth looked up from wrapping the extra sandwich in a paper bag. He stopped dead as if he'd hit a wall halfway between the dresser and the cellar door. It is not a myth, the arrow through the heart that stops it beating for a second.

There was a sliver of quiet so fine it slipped past unnoticed by Rachel and Vera, and by Ada Hobbs taking off her coat, but Lydia saw Karen look across, sensing what had passed between Michael and Elisabeth.

'The artist!' Karen said, raising her voice. She smiled, perhaps lifting her chin, perhaps arranging her long limbs more gracefully. 'Are you coming on our picnic, Michael?'

'No, I'm afraid I'm not.'

'Oh, how unkind of you! Our little sisters will be haring about and playing games. If you were there, I should sit quietly and you would paint me.'

Any other girl would have sounded cheap saying such a thing, but there was a touching courage in Karen. Girls who blaze so bright take too much upon themselves, Lydia thought. They overestimate what life will give them and are often hurt and disappointed.

Rachel asked, 'Elisabeth? Are you ready?'

Elisabeth had a little colour in her face – perhaps on her own account, or perhaps because of the brazenness of her sister.

Michael nodded politely to each of them and raised his hand towards Elisabeth, a strange little gesture that seemed to be his wanting to touch her, although he couldn't. 'Yes,' he said softly, as if he was speaking to himself. Then he turned and left them.

• • •

Elisabeth and Karen came to Neate Street every Sunday and the three of them spent hours in Rachel's room twittering together and preening. This was normal nowadays, but what Lydia found annoying and rather silly for girls their age was the bickering and the vying for Elisabeth, as if Karen and Rachel both wanted ownership, as if they were tussling over having her like one of them the best.

'A friendship doesn't come by fighting for it, poppet,' Lydia said gently to Rachel.

'I'm not fighting, Nanna. Who said I was? I'm stopping Karen from taking over. She thinks she knows what's best for Elisabeth and she doesn't. Elisabeth would go along with anything Karen said if someone didn't stop her.'

'You girls,' Lydia said. 'I shouldn't say it but mind you're careful and don't end up the loser. They're sisters and you can't compete with that.'

'Don't worry, Nanna darling.'

So the two of them went on scrapping like a pair of hounds over a hare.

Michael was at home less and less. He was earning money somehow, which he put in the tin on the scullery shelf. 'Portraits, Nanna,' he told Lydia when she asked. 'People pay money for them.' She could hear the bitterness but did not know its cause. He seldom talked to her these days. She could accept the rightness of a young man growing apart from his grandmother, but not the unhappiness she saw in him.

It puzzled her that Michael wasn't often in the house on Sundays when Elisabeth was there, and she began to wonder if she'd been mistaken. Perhaps he had someone – why would he not, when there were single women in their hundreds and him looking as he did?

She did not consider herself to be a sentimental woman given to imaginings or silly fancies – the weight of these last years had buried all that along with Lemuel – but what had passed between her fine young grandson and the quiet lovely girl was like a window opening and letting in a fresh new day.

It was true the world did not work the way it used to, and she wondered if she had deceived herself with wanting; she'd run ahead with dreams of love between Michael and Elisabeth when the evidence was no more than a look between them. Lydia had hoped the suffering they'd all endured had earned the family something good, but she knew she should let go of childish notions that life was fair. Reward came in subtle unexpected ways and one must have the patience and the wisdom not to question life's complexity. This was the only way to a peaceful heart.

Elisabeth might still be something to Michael, but it was not for Lydia to know what or when.

Whatever the future might be, the girls' visits made the house a more cheerful place and life seemed to begin again. There were outings and shopping trips, and Vera stopped making plans for the time when Albert's health improved.

Albert never spoke these days, and Lydia knew it was through choice and not because he couldn't. She liked to think he'd found a way to leave the ruin of his body, shut up shop and take excursions to visit Lemuel, or to watch the cricket with the lads who'd gone ahead of him. Sometimes he was out for hours.

On other days he couldn't seem to find the way and the shadow of his agony fell on every stick of furniture and every plate of food, and on every moment she breathed freely and could do nothing to share her breath with him.

# 6

In the Tottenham Court Road, omnibuses rattled up and down. The pavements were crowded with shoppers walking slowly in the heat and stopping to consider a dress or hat, or blooms in buckets, or a marble slab arranged with chops and liver. Office workers rushed between the dawdling shoppers like water around rocks, to a pub for a lunchtime drink or to a quiet square to eat their sandwiches.

Fumes of motorcars snagged the breath and horses coughed; blowing nags with loaded carts, cobs with hackney carriages, jingling the complications of their harness. The heavy oiled hoofs cupped on the cobbles and thudded on the piles of dung. Shoals of delivery boys on bicycles slipped between the motorcars and dripping flanks, pedalling hard against the thick air.

Turn down Percy Street and suddenly there was cool and quiet, not much traffic in the narrow thoroughfare and few pedestrians. The shops were the kind that people didn't wander past but went to with a purpose: picture framers, artists' colour suppliers, lithographers, with cheap rooms in the basements or painters' studios above. There were delicatessens, and foreign restaurants where the food and drink were cheap and the proprietors had no objection to their customers sitting smoking, reading, arguing about art and politics long after their plates were empty.

Frankie had booked for lunch but there was no need – the Eiffel Tower was almost empty and the only other diners were her friends. She said hello but didn't sit with them. Douglas and Venetia were deep in conversation, and Frankie wondered about the porter, Eddie Saunders, they had brought to her house six months ago. She had seen it all: Douglas smitten, Venetia patient and untroubled by another of his infatuations, and poor Saunders smitten with Venetia. It would run its course.

Frankie sat at a table by the window looking out to the street. She lit a cigarette. A waiter brought vodka and she sipped it, sucking the ice into her mouth. The day was sweltering for September. There was the murmur of conversation at her back and the hiss of frying in the kitchen. The smell of melted butter, garlic and tomatoes made her stomach growl with hunger.

Then Michael was coming along the street carrying a bundle of canvases in brown paper with his paint-spattered bag slung over his shoulder, and colours flared – the red-checked cloth, the jar of daisies on the table, the blue of Michael's shirt. The silky condensation on the vodka glass froze her fingers and Frankie's heart jumped in a way she thought it never would again. When he leaned across to kiss her, the heat of him smelled of linseed and turpentine.

She said, 'Hello, Hebrew.' He sat down opposite her, leaning his arms on the table. The sun had made them brown. 'They're still cooking. I don't know what we're having today.'

'When did you get back? You look tired, Frankie. You should have let me come to the house. Edith's lunches aren't so bad.'

'This morning. The train got in at five.'

'And how is Italy?'

'Good. Beautiful. I wish you'd been there. As you see, I'm as pale as ever. It's hotter here than it was in Naples.'

Their food arrived and Frankie ordered him a beer.

'No. Thank you.' He reached across and squeezed her hand. It was fondness, nothing more.

She said quickly, 'I have a surprise for you.'

'And I have Cara Fairhaven's pictures. We could look at them here and I'll leave them at the framer's.'

'She's pleased?'

'Yes, she's given me more work. And you have a surprise for me?' he said cautiously, as if she'd offered him another beer he didn't want.

'You'll have to wait.'

They ate and Frankie talked about Italy. She could see that he was troubled but she didn't ask. He had been painting Cara and Pixie Fairhaven at their house in Bloomsbury, that was all she knew. It was a house with neighbours who would like her more than they liked Cara, and Frankie had thought of suggesting they exchange. Regent's Park would be glad to see the last of her and have Lord and Lady Fairhaven instead, but in England one didn't do such things as swapping property.

'Now,' said Frankie, pushing back her chair when Michael put down his knife and fork. 'We don't want coffee. You can show me the paintings where we're going; it's not far.'

They crossed Goodge Street and then turned into Charlotte Street towards Fitzroy Square. The heat was heavy and the hubbub not far away was muffled as if a blanket had been thrown over the Tottenham Court Road.

In Fitzroy Street, Frankie stopped at a plain archway between two houses in a graceful dilapidated terrace. There was no porch or step, and the flagstones from the pavement continued along a dark passageway, dipping slightly with daylight at the end.

Frankie shut the door behind them and Michael followed her to an opening in the passage wall, up a wooden staircase and across a dusty windowless landing to another door. Through this was a walkway with an iron floor and a corrugated roof, lit dimly along the sides by panes of frosted glass. It was impossible to tell if they were somewhere inside the house or on a bridge across an overshadowed courtyard.

'You see? A labyrinth and you won't get out without me,' said Frankie. Their footsteps thundered on the iron floor. There was barely enough light to see and Frankie fumbled with a key.

Then suddenly they were blinking in bright white light in a dazzling whitewashed room. It was empty except for a wooden chair. The windows reached to the corniced ceiling and were pinned across with muslin so there was no view outside, only whiteness. Above a marble fireplace higher than Frankie's head was a vast misted mirror and there were others on the walls. The reflections curved away, green-tinged as if there were glass rooms filled with water on every side. They might not be inside a house in Fitzroy Street but in a nowhere place of hundreds of transparent rooms, and in each one a sunburned young man – blue shirt and paint-stained trousers – stood beside a woman in a loose yellow dress with a sunhat in her hand.

The noise of traffic was very faint, and after the clanging of the iron corridor, the quiet seemed to pulse.

Frankie held Michael's hand and dropped the key into it. In the mirrors, ranks of small neat women dropped keys into the palms of ranks of rough-haired young men.

'It's for you,' she said. She saw he was confused and she filled the silence, as she always did. 'There's a little room through there which used to be a scullery, so you have water, and the way we came in is the only entrance, so no one will bother you.' She walked to the far end of the room. 'You're painting in the street and in parks, Michael, with nowhere to work that's your own. They almost paid *me* to take it and it's yours now – the papers are in your name and it's settled so I've nothing more to do with it. Please don't say you won't. All I want is a picture now and then. You'll have to bring coal up for the fire in winter, that's the worst of it. The framer is two minutes away and . . . and you can eat just along the street,' she finished.

'I have everything I need. Thank you isn't enough, but thank you, Frankie.' Michael circled the room looking at the whiteness – there was nothing else to see and she knew he was battling inside himself. Whatever had been on his mind since they'd met an hour ago had not receded but was more pressing now.

Then he smiled at her. 'I should show you Cara Fairhaven's pictures and prove I'm worth your patronage.' That stung her and she felt her throat contract with tears. 'Oh yes!' she said, and busied herself unwrapping the canvases.

Cara Fairhaven: raspberry crêpe de Chine and pearls, exactly as she was that evening six months ago. 'You're clever, Michael. I don't mean you've been dishonest,' Frankie said. 'She'll think her scowl is majestic – damn proof at last of her aristocratic blood even though her folks were dirt poor wiener-eating immigrants like mine. And little Pixie?'

The portrait of Pixie Fairhaven: pointed chin, sharp nose, the slightly downturned lips she inherited from Mama and the heavy brow of her papa, but somehow – Frankie saw it – this girl was beautiful.

The girl's back was turned and she looked over her bare shoulder in rosy light, as if she was sitting by a fire or in candlelight. The blue-black satin of her dress disappeared in shadow, with strokes of cobalt in the folds. It was Pixie's likeness, but not the Pixie with bony shoulders and ruddy rasping cheeks that Frankie knew. This girl was as smooth as petals with the faintest flush on her skin, as if she had just bathed or had come in from the cold. Her shining copper hair curled down her back and over the midnight satin of her dress. Where was the sandy wiry chignon with a thousand pins of Pixie Fairhaven? This was Pixie but it was not.

'Do you like her?' said Michael, and Frankie knew. Her heart had been dropping and tumbling all this time since he'd touched her hand kindly and comfortably, as a friend would after two months apart in thanks for a beer offered and not wanted – and although she'd tried to save it and to hold it safely, her heart kept fluttering and struggling.

She knew when he said 'Do you like *her*?', not '*it*', that this was not another dull portrait done on sufferance for money, but a picture of a girl Michael loved.

'She's beautiful,' Frankie said. Her heart struck hard like a bird against glass, but there was no sound, only quiet in the room. There was no sensation, nothing: Michael's lover, who was eighteen, and Frankie, almost twice as old.

They stood looking at the painting and Frankie knew that in a while, if she didn't speak, he would tell her.

'Frankie, while you were away I decided to leave London.'

'Then you must go.'

'That evening before you went to Italy, I realized I can't stay here any longer. I can't paint in London.'

'Good,' said Frankie. 'You must go.'

He held out the key.

'No, the studio is yours, Michael. You might want it one day.' So he can't tell me, Frankie thought, there isn't even that much trust between us. 'I wouldn't have guessed you'd fall for Pixie,' Frankie blurted. 'Is she going away with you?' There had never been reserve between them, so why now? 'You can't hide it. I can see.' Frankie pointed to the picture. 'That's how you see her – lovely, perfect.' She was thankful to sound easy, light, and no different from the way they always spoke to one another.

Michael considered the painting for a moment. 'You're right. I should have noticed.'

Hearing him confess made Frankie's skin go cold. Once, long ago in Texas, she'd shot a cony and had this same shock when her aim was true. Some part of her had trusted she would miss.

Michael said, 'There's a girl who comes to Neate Street. My sister's friend. I haven't met her more than three or four times and she's very young, she's still at school.'

Frankie could make no sense of it: a portrait of a girl who wasn't Pixie or a lover, but who somehow was both – and neither. Then Michael said, 'I see her in my mind but it doesn't mean anything, it's what painters do. It often happens.'

Suddenly Frankie didn't want to know more or to understand. 'Let's go. I've had enough of all this dratted whiteness. I need lots of colours and some cake. Let's have tea in Regent's Park and then go dancing at the Palais. Come with me, Michael. It'll be full of women in suits like Olivia; don't make me go alone.'

He put the key in his pocket. 'I won't leave London until the New Year comes,' he said. 'Frankie, I will come back.' He touched her cheek.

The circle was complete; she had died, dust to dust, and now she was alive again.

• • •

The thin early morning sunshine was cool. The air would be sweet for a while longer before the stink of drains and horse dung was stirred up by the day. It was eight o'clock and Eddie Saunders had risen late, a free man.

Yesterday he'd given notice to the Company, bought a single ticket to Hythe and told Mrs Creak he'd pay out the month. He gave back his key to her this morning.

He had one call to make before he took his train, and he was walking from Greenwich up the Old Kent Road to find a young man, an artist, Michael Ross, who lived at an address in Peckham. Michael Ross had said he wanted to leave London and perhaps Eddie's luck would help him.

Traders were already opening and carts were unloading from the city markets. The sun had not long been up and lamps still lit the windows of the houses Eddie passed. He imagined families having breakfast together and husbands getting off to work.

He shivered. He had burned his boats and he laughed out loud with the intoxication of it. He was nuts, he was bleedin' daft, the boys at Charing Cross had told him when he emptied his locker and shook hands round the porters' room.

The station master, Mr Brisley, said Eddie shouldn't trust the man, he was probably a loony with his head not right – there were lots of them about these days. But Mr Brisley was kind enough: 'The Company will have a job for you, lad, when you come back.'

Two nights ago the man on Platform Number 4 had not seemed mad, and if he was, well, the world was so mixed up these days that anything could happen; the rich man's cream had curdled in the heat of war and now anyone could have some fat; a working man could own some land; a porter could become a Kentish farmer. The gentry weren't so high and mighty now they'd had a share of suffering, and perhaps it was grief had thawed the hearts of some of them. Rich or poor, you didn't know what was round the corner – like the man on Platform 4.

Eddie hadn't seen the land or written to the gentleman, but this chance had come and who would look a gift horse?

He walked for an hour or so and asked in a butcher's shop for directions. Neate Street turned out to be a terraced row with a park behind. The houses would have a patch of garden for vegetables and a washhouse, just what he and Lucy would have wanted if they'd stayed in London; a street where you'd be happy for your nipper, for Archie, to play outside.

It was pleasant with the plane trees and had a peaceful prettiness in spite of the overgrown hedges and scratched front doors. With husbands gone and wives struggling alone, most of London was falling into disrepair.

He asked a woman sweeping and she pointed to a house across the road. A girl opened the front door.

'Yes?'

He knew her. That evening months ago at Mrs Francesca Brion's party he had seen a painting of this girl and it wasn't a face you could forget. 'I'm looking for Mr Michael Ross,' he said.

The girl folded her arms. She was young, sixteen perhaps, not much more. 'He's out.' She looked squarely at him, not at all shy or prim, tall with slanting eyes. Her hair was black and crinkled like a pony's mane, loose on her shoulders. A Persian princess in Peckham, Eddie thought – except for the boots, the shirtsleeves and the baggy corduroy trousers. She saw him looking. 'I'm digging up some spuds. And Michael's not here.'

'I have a message for him.'

'Leave it with me if you like.' She held out a dirty hand.

'It's not written down,' said Eddie. He had retreated back down the steps. 'Could you tell him Eddie Saunders the porter has got a place in Kent? He'll remember me.'

'Oh,' said the girl.

There was a pause. His eyes were level with her breasts, her face was too beautiful, and he couldn't find a place to look. 'We met at Mrs Brion's house,' said Eddie. 'She's the one who gave me this address. Michael told me he'd like to get away from London and I have recently acquired a place in Kent.' He winced at how pompous he must sound.

'Who's Mrs Brion?' the girl said. 'I'm his sister. I'm Rachel, and he doesn't want to get away.' Suddenly she seemed annoyed as if Eddie was at fault. 'Our dad's ill, Michael can't go away.'

'Well, perhaps you'd just let him know. I don't suppose he'll come, but if he does, tell him he should take the train to Hythe and ask for me at Mr Mander's farm. That should do it.'

'And who are you?'

'I'm Eddie Saunders,' he said again. 'And Mr George Mander's farm is where I'll be.'

'A farm? You?' said Rachel. 'You said you were a porter.'

Eddie felt himself redden. His suit was tight and it always made him hot. 'I work some grazing on the Romney Marsh.' Of the two of them she looked more the farmer. 'Would you tell him, please?'

'Yes,' said Rachel. 'I'll tell him. Cows or sheep?'

It was too complicated to explain the reason why he didn't know. 'Thank you, miss,' he said. 'Good day.'

A few nights ago he was portering for late travellers as usual. He'd work every evening if he could get a chit from Mr Brisley. His room at Mrs Creak's was not a place he liked to be.

At Charing Cross the cab rank was covered by a tin canopy, but the wind gusted the drizzle underneath and Eddie had been sorry it was his turn to leave the stove and the fug of smoke inside the porters' cabin, in spite of the good tip he knew he'd get. He saw it straight away: this customer would be no trouble, and fair.

The gentleman had only one valise but he nodded when Eddie came out to offer service. The man was as big as a bear, good shoes and heavy Harris overcoat of quality but showing wear. His shoulders were wet and he must have walked for a while before he took the cab; watching his expenses perhaps, a gentleman with money but less than he would like – less than he once had, Eddie thought. People imagined they weren't giving much away but all it took was looking to pick up clues.

The gentleman paid the cab driver from change in his pocket, tucked his woollen cravat under his lapels and put on his gloves, all unhurried and deliberate.

'Goodnight to you,' he said, lifting his hat to the driver. 'Thank you,' he said to Eddie.

So: a customer with the time – or the vanity – for courtesy to the common man, and no axe to grind. He was youngish by his face, thirty-five? Not so much more than Eddie but his thick hair was going grey. A businessman or a doctor who'd been signed off active service. He didn't have the look of a man who'd fought. Had he been a con-chie? You could never tell. Whatever his life was for him, he seemed a little defeated but not bitter or grieving.

The gentleman knew the platform he wanted because he walked ahead of Eddie and directly to Number 4. The attaché case he carried was stained with rain and the valise was wet too; Italian leather with solid brass catches and buckles on the straps, and a hand-engraved lock face. The stitching had repairs, neatly done, no labels – so he didn't go abroad – and tooled initials, small and discreet, G. L. M. It was a shame to let good luggage get spoiled by wet, and Eddie hoped it was soaped properly or at least waxed once in a while as it deserved to be.

The Folkestone train should have pulled in by now but it hadn't. There was fog down in Kent. They stood on the platform, the gentle-man shifting his bulk gently from foot to foot to keep out the damp.

Usually the din inside the station was enough to wake the dead, but tonight there were only two engines dripping by the platforms and not many travellers. The rows of gas lamps had misty haloes from the steam hanging in the freezing air. It was even colder in the station than outside on the street.

Only a fortnight ago it had been a scorching autumn, more like high summer, and people were still taking trips to Margate and the Romney Sands. Then winter arrived overnight and business dropped off as it always did when the season finished.

Eddie waited to be dismissed. He did not expect to be asked to put the luggage on the train. A good five minutes passed. The man seemed to have forgotten him, then suddenly he said, 'You must want to get home to your wife. It's a filthy night.' He fumbled in his pocket.

'No hurry, sir,' said Eddie. 'I'm on duty till the ten fifty Chatham–Margate leaves. No one's waiting for me. My wife is dead, and my baby boy.' He had no idea why he said it – perhaps he was tired, per-haps he was weakened by the yearnings for another man's wife which he'd fought away because he would love no one else but Lucy.

*My wife is dead, and my baby boy*: he had told the man and they both froze with shock and embarrassment, the gentleman's gloved hand holding some coins halfway to Eddie's, and Eddie looking directly at him, which was something he'd never do, because that would be asking to be accused of insolence.

And to his horror Eddie heard himself stumbling on, stupidly, as if he was drunk or raving. 'The influenza in '19, Archie first, then my Lucy two days after.' He swallowed down the words that were a pressure in his chest even after all these years, a dam fit to break. He shut his mouth and clenched his teeth together. The man did not look away and instead of dropping the money into his palm he did an unexpected thing: he put his hand on Eddie's shoulder.

'I have no wife or children, sir, but I can't imagine how any man can bear such loss.'

That was how it happened. They began to talk as if the gentleman and he were equals, one a little older than the other but comrades like men are in war sometimes, when they know that grief and death do not recognize the differences.

The station master came down from his office to check that Eddie was not malingering and the gentleman, George Mander, as he introduced himself, confirmed that he had engaged this porter to put his luggage on the train whenever it might arrive and would pay accordingly.

Mander must be lonely, Eddie thought, but he seemed genuine and his kindness did not seem forced. To fill the time and to stop more talk of little Archie, Eddie told Mander about his plan to buy a farm, a plan he and Lucy had shared and he would carry out alone however long it took because he'd made a promise to her and that could not be broken, not even now. He went down to Kent whenever he had time off – his travel on this line was free so he could go any time he liked – and he'd talk to anyone who'd tell him about the land or livestock, anyone who'd teach him things.

After a while there was an announcement that fog at Ashford had delayed the Folkestone train but it had now passed London Bridge.

'Well, that's it, sir,' Eddie said. 'Your train. The Company's apologies for your wait.' The train pulled in and people got out. Eddie opened the carriage door. 'The driver will be in a hurry to get away, sir, what with the delay.'

Mander took out his wallet.

'No, thank you, if you don't mind, sir,' Eddie said. It hadn't been a duty after all to talk to this quiet man. For a while a weight had lightened that Eddie had not realized was so heavy.

The guard was coming along the platform, slamming doors. George Mander hesitated, holding the open wallet. He began, 'I hope I don't offend you –'

Eddie wondered if he could simply turn and walk away from this second embarrassment. The guard passed them, 'If you would, sir. All aboard.'

Mander still stood there, reluctant it seemed to board his train. 'I wouldn't wish to cause offence,' he said at last, 'but I have some land I've no use for. It's been empty since '17 and the tenant doesn't need it now.'

'Stan' away,' the guard yelled above the shrieking steam and clanging couplings.

Mander raised his voice, 'It isn't much, a cottage and a few acres grazing on the Romney Marsh. There'd be no rent of course; such land has no value these days. I'd be glad to see it worked.'

The shunted carriages lurched and the whistle blew.

'Come and look when you have the time.' He took a card out of the wallet and handed it to Eddie. 'Goodnight.' He picked up the valise and climbed into the carriage.

# 7

It was three months since Michael had seen Elisabeth. She was always in his mind and this troubled him. His friends were women like Frankie and Olivia, and his lovers were girls like the waitress at the Eiffel Tower. Elisabeth was young and gauche, and she should not preoccupy him.

He had gone out to buy paint and, walking along the Tottenham Court Road, he wondered where she was and what she might be doing at this moment – then she was there coming towards him as if he'd conjured her. She was wearing a heavy skirt, a beret and woollen gloves, and a cape with tapes that crossed over her chest. She had nearly passed him when Michael put out his hand and touched her arm.

She looked startled but he could see she knew him at once. 'I didn't think I'd see you here,' he said, racking his brains for something to say that would keep her for a moment. 'Are you visiting? Did you travel up alone?'

She patted a parcel in brown paper she was carrying. Her grey eyes were watering with the cold. 'I've come up to buy a book.'

'A special book?' he asked, then gritted his teeth at a question one would ask a child.

'*Anatomy and Physiology*. I have a place at St Paul's Hospital. It's preparatory reading. I'm going to train to be a nurse.'

'A nurse,' he repeated stupidly.

'I'm leaving school – with Rachel. Didn't you know? We're all leaving. My sister Karen too.' Her voice was confident but her eyes had not met his after that first moment. 'And are you visiting?' she asked.

'I have a studio in Fitzroy Street.'

They stood together on the pavement, pushed closer by the afternoon shoppers. It was half past three but already dusk. Christmas candles lit up the shops and sleet had made the road a mess of mud and slurry.

'Well, goodbye,' she said. 'My bus goes soon.'

'Shall I see you again at Neate Street?'

She looked puzzled and he realized how odd this question was. It was up to him; he would see her if he chose to be at home on Sundays.

'Where is your studio?' she asked.

'Just around the corner. In Fitzroy Street.'

She was not turning to go, clasping her book and shivering. Her hair was tied with ribbon that matched the collar of her school blouse.

'Would you like a cup of tea before you get your bus? I have a stove and a kettle,' he said.

She walked with him the five minutes to the studio and all the time he knew he should not have invited her.

She followed him through the archway in Fitzroy Street, down the stone passageway, up the stairs and along the clanging metal corridor. In the studio, she stood just inside the door while he lit the stove. He moved the chair next to the dying fire, which had turned the white walls to pink.

Instead of sitting down, she went along the row of pictures propped against the wall. There wasn't much. Three canvases for Cara Fairhaven: a portrait of the whiskered Urban in uniform; a stringy adolescent Fairhaven nephew; Pixie, posing coyly on a garden swing. He wished he had turned them to the wall. There was an abstract for a friend of Olivia and a few canvases he would paint over. That was all. He would leave London soon and saw no point in filling the studio with work he wouldn't finish.

On the easel was a nude he had been working on today. The model was the waitress at the Eiffel Tower and she had left half an hour ago to start her shift.

Elisabeth stopped, and, as she leaned closer to look, a curl of her hair like a lick of flame slipped forward on to the shoulder of her ugly cape. She gazed into the picture. Her cheeks were flushed with the cold, but Michael knew her skin would naturally be pale, almost blood-less if she was tired, always a little transparent and difficult to paint, blue veined on her breasts and also where the flesh was fine – the insides of her arms, the arches of her feet, the tender place between the hip and thigh.

She looked up and caught him watching. 'Your friend looks lovely without her clothes,' she said. Was it innocence or did she know what had been in his mind? She stood back from the picture, considering it. 'Her face is very peaceful, as if she's not thinking anything at all.'

'Don't we always think? Even if we take no notice.'

'Oh, I don't mean she's dreaming in an empty-headed way, she's wide awake but not fretting and worrying like the rest of us because . . . because she knows.'

'What does she know?'

'Oh, I couldn't say.' She smiled. 'Everything. Everything we forget because life muddles us.'

'It must be a better picture than I thought.'

She was still gazing at the girl. 'You are a good painter. She seems real.'

'She is real,' he said, then saw his teasing had confused her. He walked across and pointed to the model's face. 'Painters use the light – the way the light falls. You see? On the cheek and the lip. Along the jaw.'

'Yes! I see exactly what you mean.' She looked up and examined his face. 'There's light here and here.' She almost touched his cheek.

'The tea is ready,' he said, and turned away from her.

She put down her book and sat on the chair with the cup and saucer on her lap. 'If I were an artist, perhaps I should see clearly too,' she said.

'Painters see what they allow themselves to see and that's not clear at all. We're as blind as anyone. What we do is make pictures of our blindness, but we try to be truthful, I suppose.'

'Are you? Honest, I mean.'

'I'm not sure I am,' he said. 'Sometimes when I work, I imagine I'm seeing as I should if I weren't human and . . . and arrogant. And everything, even dust on a shelf or a lump of coal, is beautiful, as if the gods have shown themselves. Then later, the next day perhaps, I see my self-delusion painted on the canvas and it's hard to understand why I thought it was anything at all.' He wondered if he'd bludgeoned her into silence with this speech. Her face had changed as if she took seriously the nonsense he was talking.

'But if you see the self-delusion, then you've seen the truth about yourself and that must be good,' she said carefully.

'I wish it were true, Elisabeth.'

'I'm certain. Don't you think so?'

'No,' he said, and laughed. 'I'm not thinking any more.' He sat down on the floorboards on the other side of the fire. The corners of the room were dark with the winter afternoon closing over. The windows shuddered in the wind.

Elisabeth stared into the fire. In this light she looked beautiful, but he knew he should not say it. A model posing for him or a girl he wanted to seduce would understand that flattery was a ritual to dissolve the layers of reserve. 'I should like to make a drawing of you,' he said. 'Not now. One day.'

He got up to put on more coal. She looked down at her lap, her head bowed, and he wanted to put his hand on her dark warm hair.

The new flames came through with tiny hissing flares of blue or green. Outside, the city was quiet; snow must be falling. He heard the small sounds of her breathing and swallowing.

'I should tell you this,' she said softly. He didn't speak, knowing it would silence her. 'I've always thought I wasn't anyone at all. Like being made of air, or . . . nothing. When I met you, I knew it wasn't true. You were the beginning of knowing I am me. She chafed her hands and he wanted to hold them still. 'You see?' she said. 'I'm really rather peculiar.'

The quiet closed in again. The room seemed to have a pressure in it as if air was weighted.

'Something else, can I say?' She knotted her fingers to stop their restlessness. 'Just now, for a while – a very little while – when I looked at your painting, I wasn't in this room, I was outside too, and every-where. And I understood it all. Do you see?'

She looked up, waiting, but an answer would bind them to this moment and he said nothing. Her courage must have been greater than his because she reached across to touch his hand. 'I don't suppose you do. I shouldn't if I were you.' She wasn't tense with self-consciousness as women often were, and he was aware again of the responsibility of asking her here and her recklessness in coming with him. She hadn't known she could trust him – or perhaps she had. He did not close his hand around hers. 'It's an odd thing to be alive,' he said, not knowing what he meant.

She sat back, taking her hand away and smiling as if the doubt was gone. 'When I visit Neate Street again, would you take me to meet your father? When he's feeling better.'

'I should like you to meet him, but he won't get better.'

'Oh, he will! I'm sure he will,' she said earnestly. 'You must hope. It's wrong to give up.'

'It's wrong to pretend.'

'Well, I shall hope for you. That's what I'll do.'

She couldn't know his father was dying, but the impatience that flared up in him was a strange relief. The tenderness for her withered and he felt a kind of bitter satisfaction. He did not want to feel like this about her. He wanted nothing to keep him here in London. The need to be rid of her – her trust and hope, her naive cleverness – filled his chest like water drowning him. He got up and switched on the electric light. The glare made her wince.

'Elisabeth, I'd forgotten, I have something I should do this afternoon.'

She stared at him and he fought himself, wanting to take back what he'd said, then she jumped up, slopping tea on her skirt. 'Yes, of course.'

'I'll come with you to the bus,' he said. She was already going to the door, pulling on her gloves, and she stood with her back to him, waiting to be let out. He reached over her shoulder to turn the latch and he could smell her hair, so faint it was hardly there, like the scent of water.

They walked back to the Tottenham Court Road; snow was falling and the streets were empty. Her skirt swung heavily as she hurried beside him. He wanted to say he was sorry before they said goodbye and to repair the damage he'd done, but the bus came and she was gone.

He followed their tracks back to the studio. His boots had pressed the snow to water. Her footprints, small beside his, sparkled at the edges and each imprint of her sole was a shadow of blue. In the studio, he found her book beside the half-filled teacup.

•  •  •

As Elisabeth drops her cape on the floor, undoes the hooks on her skirt and unbuttons her blouse, she is staring at the pattern on the bedside rug, fawn and grey, and she is back in London: the slushy pavement is speeding under her, her itchy skirt is flouncing, and her feet are whisking forward, back, forward, as she walks beside Rachel's brother. She is going to his studio.

His boots are heavy hoofs beside her trotters. His arm swings and if she lets hers swing too they will bump together, his hand against her glove, but she is holding a book against her chest which is fluttering like a moth because Christmas lights are shining and she is going alone somewhere with Michael Ross.

She follows him down a flagstoned passageway, up some stairs, along a pitch-black corridor which clangs like thunder in a pantomime. In his studio, which is so far inside the house they could be lost, there is a picture of a naked girl.

69

Then it happens – she looks into the picture and the painted girl looks back. The girl begins to sing a low plain note, its pitch too perfect for a human throat. The sound expands, passing through the walls and outside to the dusk; it unfurls across the city, down into the black mud of the Thames and up into the night. Elisabeth hears the fall of time, she knows the sun's dark eye, the leaning seas, and here, inside the room, she knows the heat and bone and tide of Michael.

Then it vanishes. The girl is just a picture, the room is ordinary. Elisabeth looks up and he is watching. He sees her, far back, waiting, where no one else has ever found her.

Later, he sits on the floor and the firelight is a cave with shadows all around. He comes close and in a moment –

'Go to bed,' her mother says, palm on her forehead, looking at her face but not her eyes. She is assessing heat and colour; this daughter is unfit.

Karen comes in to look. 'Dishrag,' she says, although she isn't being unkind. 'Pastry face.' Then she shuts the bedroom door. Elisabeth takes off her stockings, her petticoat and her drawers. Her nightdress slides over, smelling of old sleep and tucked-up bedtimes gone cold. The icy cotton slithers down her back.

She has a headache, although there are no thoughts to ache, and the coldness in the bedroom makes her sweat.

Something happened – or was it nothing? – then she sipped the tea and suddenly he hated her. She must go. Now. Walking again, quicker this time, swishing her skirt and cape. The snow under her blurry feet is blank as if she isn't moving. The omnibus comes straight away so it is just as well he made her run.

She did not see his eyes again, and his voice said, *Goodbye, Elisabeth.*

•  •  •

Michael stopped to buy some flowers, carrying them awkwardly inside his greatcoat to stop the stems from snapping in the wind. He wondered if he should have chosen roses or chrysanthemums, which wouldn't be so easily damaged, but he bought delphiniums, deep blue like summer twilight. Was Elisabeth too young for flowers?

What happened yesterday still pained him, as if her hurt was hurting him. He needed to apologize.

Yesterday he couldn't think clearly but today he would explain that it was vital that he collected a picture from the framer's because it was promised to a client, and this was why he had hurried her so rudely. The lie would not excuse the discourtesy, but perhaps it would ease her hurt.

He could not tell the truth: that he had work to do; that she was too young for good conversation and asked too many questions. And there was another reason why he had sent her away – he had seen her trust and her assumption that their meeting meant something. It didn't.

It took an hour to walk to Catford. Elisabeth's address was written on the wrapping of her book and he found the house in a long street of bay-fronted villas. The garden had a laurel hedge and white-painted pebbles beside the tiled path.

He expected a maid to open but a woman in a black dress came to the door. He could see she once had beauty like Elisabeth's but it had been smothered by the years like a fall of dust. She said, 'Nothing today, and I'll thank you not to call again.' Michael saw her eyes dart wildly over his greatcoat as if it alarmed her and she stepped back to close the door.

'I have your daughter's book, Mrs Oliver,' he said. 'I'm returning it, a text book Elisabeth collected yesterday from town.' He hoped she wouldn't notice the delphiniums. He held them close to his side, the blue flowers upside down, almost touching the path. As if she heard his thoughts, she looked down and saw them.

'Perhaps you would kindly introduce yourself,' she said.

'I'm Rachel Ross's brother. Michael. Elisabeth sometimes visits our home in Peckham, on Sundays with her sister.'

He saw Elisabeth's mother take in this information, blankness first and then the thoughts chasing round as she tried to fit the pieces together – the book and him, the flowers and Elisabeth. 'I see, so you're Michael Ross.'

Suddenly he knew what she would ask next and he had no idea what Elisabeth had told her or what he should say now. The question came – 'How is it you have her book, Mr Ross? Elisabeth was unwell when she came home yesterday. I assumed she had the book. I didn't ask to see it, I had no reason to. She was upset, something had upset her.' Her voice was smooth. She waited.

He blundered through his answer. 'I saw her by chance – the snow was slippery so I walked with her. I carried her book and forgot to give it back.' He was impatient to get away; he had only planned to be there for a moment, deliver the book, his apology and the flowers, and go. He found himself cornered by his own stupidity.

'Leave the book with me,' she said at last. He held it out and she took it.

'I wonder if I could speak to her myself, if you wouldn't mind, only for a moment.'

The woman hesitated, then seemed to come to a decision. 'I told you, Elisabeth is unwell. And, as their mother, I've decided that my girls should rest on Sunday – and go to church. They won't be coming to Peckham any more. Goodbye and thank you.' Her mouth snapped shut.

He was at a loss. In spite of her hostility, her eyes were begging that he understand and go away. 'I'm sorry, Mr Ross. The flowers are most kind, I'm sure, but Elisabeth can't accept them.'

There was no doubt, but Michael could not think how to leave. Her jaw had tightened. He expected her to shut the door, instead she took a step towards him and spoke softly as if she was confiding in him. 'I don't know what happened, Mr Ross, but I should have guessed you'd have no manners. You're arrogant, your kind, as if you own the world. Don't pretend, young Michael Roth – oh, yes, I know your name, I've made enquiries.' She looked triumphant. 'Blood doesn't lie, whatever you call yourselves these days, you and your family. I'm not a fool. You tell your grandma, in Catford we know she married Lemuel Roth and we don't forget who's Jew and who's Christian. We remember things. We aren't sopped with drink and witless like the folk of Peckham.' She straightened up and went on, almost kindly, 'I expect your interest in Elisabeth came about on her Sunday visits to your sister.'

'No, that isn't –'

She cut across him. 'Elisabeth would not have encouraged it, and I'm sorry for your feelings, Mr Ross. Good day to you. I don't suppose we'll meet again.' She shut the door.

He stood on the path. The shock of what had happened made him shiver. He'd never thought much about his diluted Jewish blood. Frankie teased him but that was all.

The street was empty. He turned up his collar against the wind, and as he passed a horse trough he dropped the flowers in the icy water. He hoped someone would find them before they froze.

• • •

Elisabeth did not come to Neate Street again. Two Sundays after Michael's walk to Catford, her sister spoke to him. Karen had ignored their mother's ban on Sunday visits.

He was cleaning brushes in the scullery sink when he heard the kitchen door open. Karen came across and put her elbows on the draining board, her chin in her hands.

'My little sister says thank you for returning the book. And she says you shouldn't have paid for a delivery boy to bring it, you could've posted it, or given it to Rachel.' She dipped her finger in the oily water, leaned forward and trailed her name on the scullery window. Her hip touched against his thigh. 'I saw you at the door. I don't know why Ma didn't tell Elisabeth you'd come yourself, but never mind.' She straightened up, stretched her arms above her head and yawned. Her breath smelled faintly of oranges. 'Lovely flowers. I fished them out of the horse trough. It seemed a shame. I've got them in a vase beside my bed.' She turned to look at him. Her eyelashes were dark for someone so fair. 'You're awfully mysterious, Michael Ross.'

He scraped paint from the palette, then Rachel called from the upstairs hall; she and Karen were off to see the Christmas lights in Piccadilly. After a moment Karen turned and he heard her walk away across the kitchen flagstones.

When he looked around, she was watching him, leaning her slender body against the kitchen door. 'Don't worry. Elisabeth didn't breathe a word, not even to me, but I could tell. Sisters always know. Perhaps I should visit your studio too one day.'

He should have been amused by this girl, who was trying to be so modern. She was young and could not know the risks she took, but something warned him she was not like Elisabeth.

# 8

In December, Rachel left school and found employment in the wages office of a fashion house in Knightsbridge.

'If I get my foot in the door and get noticed, you never know, they might let me train to do designs one day. That's my dream, Nanna,' she said to Lydia. They were waiting for the kettle to steam and Lydia was knitting – she couldn't give it up even though the war was long over. 'And here's more gossip for you, Nanna. Karen is a key clerk at a posh hotel in Kensington. The customers are rich old men with money from the war. Millionaires, Karen says, with ugly wives.'

'And Elisabeth?'

'Oh, she's started training now. I don't suppose we'll see her much. Heavens, Nanna, who'd want to do it? Blood and vomit and all sorts. Rather her than me.'

'The girl's an angel,' Lydia said. 'It's such a shame she doesn't come here any more.'

'It's her mother. She says Elisabeth's got studying to do. She'd stop Karen too but Karen says she's a working woman and old enough to do what she likes.'

'Old enough to know she shouldn't disrespect her mother, is what she is,' said Lydia.

She wondered about Elisabeth, if there was another reason why the mother kept her away. There was a mismatch between their families, it was true, but Catford was surely only a whisker more genteel than Peckham.

At Christmas, Michael told them he was leaving. Lydia had known in her heart that one day soon he would. There was a time when this announcement would have made a grandmother proud, a wrench maybe but also a wistful kind of satisfaction in a job well done and finished as it should be. Now her family were like birds that kept falling out of the nest.

Michael told them there was nothing to keep him here in London.

'Nothing to keep you? Ha! There's your father,' said Vera acidly. 'You think he'll last much longer? You turn your back on all of us. You're not the only one to suffer, we're all upset.'

Lydia saw Michael flinch. 'Hush, Vera dear,' she said. 'Let him be. He hasn't turned his back on Albert, or you, and he never will, but Michael needs to go and we must let him.'

'He ought to be considering other people, not just himself.'

'He's considering cows and sheep on Eddie Saunders's farm,' said Rachel.

Michael said he had no plans, only to travel and to paint. He had saved some money. Half of it he gave to Vera.

On the morning in February when he left, Vera went to work but Rachel stayed at home with Lydia to see him off. They watched him walk down Neate Street with Granddad Lemy's old army rucksack slung over his shoulder. He turned and waved, then he was gone.

Rachel shivered. 'Come on, Nanna. It's freezing, you'll catch your death.'

Lydia looked at the empty pavement. She had thought her heart couldn't break again when it already had twice over.

• • •

*Amsterdam*

*Dear Elisabeth, an apology so long afterwards means little, but I'm sorry for that afternoon last Christmas when my rudeness to you was unforgivable. I hope that after rightly judging me ridiculous and unkind, you put the incident out of your mind.*

*I think of you often.*
*Michael Ross*

*1929*

# 9

The portrait of Pixie Fairhaven was in the drawing room of the Fair-havens' house in Bloomsbury, and Frankie was accustomed to seeing it on her visits for tea or on the rare occasions when she was invited for dinner to equalize the numbers. Cara would rise from the dining table at Urban's signal.

Forgoing a cigar is bad enough but being banished at the port! Olivia would say. *L'ancien régime*, my darling, we have to fight it.

The ladies would adjourn to the drawing room, where the painting hung above the maple chiffonier.

Cara Fairhaven had so often directed her guests' attention to the loveliness of her daughter, Pixie, as captured by a young and unknown artist whose looks were smouldering, who was modern, exclusive and abroad, that Frankie was beginning to forget the pain the first sight of it had caused her, so when she saw the girl in Fitzroy Street, she felt at first only surprise and pleasure.

She was standing on the pavement by the door to the studio, look-ing up at the façade. Her vivid hair was pinned up under a hat with an embroidered badge. Michael had not said she was a nurse. 'Hello,' Frankie said. 'Are you looking for Michael?'

'Oh, yes, I am. Is he here, do you know? He's been away, I think.' She was prettier than Pixie Fairhaven's portrait, as Frankie had known she would be, and had the kind of simple beauty that often goes unnoticed: skin that would never need powder or rouge, dark brows and clear grey eyes. She looked so young.

The old lurching and falling in her stomach caught Frankie unawares. Her mind raced but she smiled, warmly she hoped, and said, 'I'm Mrs Brion, a friend of his. I saw Michael not long ago in Amsterdam. Last June I think it was. And we were in Florence more recently. He's very well. Should I remember you to him when I see him next?'

The girl looked away. She understood. 'Thank you. You're very kind.' Frankie could see that she was trying to gather her feelings back inside herself. 'It's been so nice to meet you, Mrs Brion. I shan't delay you any longer, but when you see him, would you mind saying Elisabeth Oliver sends her regards?' She fussed with the pleats in her shapeless regulation coat. 'I'm his sister's friend. He probably won't remember me.'

'I'm sure he will,' said Frankie.

Elisabeth might not have heard the words Frankie hoped would soften the lie; she had not seen Michael in the fourteen months he'd been away. The postcards from Amsterdam and Florence were the only news she'd had. Shame for her jealousy made Frankie step back as if their conversation was finished.

Elisabeth didn't turn to go but looked down at her feet, then up at the studio again. 'Nursing must be so dreadfully exhausting,' Frankie said. She had no idea why she said it, only that it seemed impossible to say goodbye.

'I'm not a nurse, not yet. I shall enrol when I'm twenty-one but I can be an orderly and begin my study, so that's what I'm doing – in a children's fever ward. I like it very much. It's not at all tiring.' Elisabeth spoke politely and absently as if she'd said all this before, to aunts perhaps, or her mother's friends. Frankie noticed shadows of tiredness beneath her eyes.

They stood together on the pavement. There must be something that would break this impasse. 'Let's have lunch!' said Frankie, hearing the jarring brightness in her voice. 'There's a lovely little restaurant just along the street. I'll treat us.' The invitation was gushing and it was no redress for the hurt she had inflicted.

'That's very kind, Mrs Brion, but I ought to get back. It always takes my lunch hour to walk up here from the hospital.' So she often came to Fitzroy Street.

'Then you must take my card, Miss Oliver. I live not far from here, perhaps you'll visit me.'

Elisabeth must have thought the invitation as odd as the sudden offer of lunch. They had nothing in common, a young student nurse and a rich American widow, except for suffering the same complaint. 'I'll be sure to tell Michael you came to see him.'

Elisabeth took the card and put it in her purse.

•  •  •

The land George Mander gave Eddie Saunders was twenty acres of the Romney Marsh. It looked bleak to those who didn't know it. The charabancs and tandems from the holiday sands at Hythe and Dymchurch never came out here, or from the cobbled sea-less port of Rye.

Flat salt fields on the seaward side of Eddie's land were bordered by a grassy dyke with dunes beyond and a beach of gritty sand. When the tide was out, half a mile of grey-green mud wrinkled to the Channel.

Inland, willow and blackthorn grew along the marsh drains. There was an oak or elm here and there, and in the distance the spire of a church. The churches on the Marsh were often crooked on account of the sinking spongy land.

Everywhere were sheep, hundreds of them, swans and coots paddling the ditches, a heron hidden by its stillness, and larks piping high up and invisible. Seagulls came in on the storms, brawling like hooligans. At dusk, a hunting barn owl quartered Eddie's fields.

It had been eighteen months since he'd taken George Mander's offer of the land and thrown up his job of portering at Charing Cross, and every day Eddie still felt glad and grateful to be here, in spite of his exhaustion.

Since seven this morning he had been doing a repair to a gate which he thought he'd have finished by noon. When it was done, it would be two hours' work to light the stove, cook, heat water and have a wash. There were the lambs to feed and paperwork to do; the grocer in Hythe who took the eggs and milk liked to have the bills and the receipts in writing. Eddie's desk was in the parlour, which had no glass in the windows, although it did have sacks of straw stuffed into the frames. The oil lamp cast a syrupy light which smoothed over the cracks in the plaster and wormy floorboards, but made ink on paper disappear. Perhaps he needed spectacles. He had never needed to write much down before.

The sun was low and mist was rising in the chill. The slicing evening light stood each blade of grass beside its shadow, and flashes of the molten sun through the branches of the trees made Eddie squint. His collie ran in circles, rounding up gnats and gnawing at the rotten wood that had been sawn away, while the cows stood in a semicircle with their heads low, watching Eddie work, breathing hard and rocking as if their feet were cold. From time to time, they wandered off to graze, or came in close to inspect the tools.

He liked their company and mending the rotting gate was not a chore. He was still unaccustomed to the pleasure of ownership: a shabby cottage, sheds and barn, some hens, and eight dairy cows past their best. Yesterday he'd been given two early lambs a neighbour was too busy to save. Eddie put them in straw-filled cardboard boxes by the stove underneath his shirts and breeches dangling on the airer. The lambs nodded off with their new polished hoofs tucked underneath. They were overdue a feed.

Their weakness and dependence took Eddie back to all those nights when little Archie was a newborn. Lucy did the honours, then he took over with the burping and the soothing, and the changing too if need be – more fiddly than folding a lady's handkerchief and riper than a cowpat. Archie was never any trouble.

They had been gone ten years and although it seemed no time at all there was another way in which Lucy and the few short months with Archie were another life. He hadn't noticed when the change had come about, but it was a while since he'd woken in the night thinking Lucy was beside him. It used to be a feeling like a rush of sunlight in his head, then a plunging into blackness. And it had been a long time since he'd looked out for Archie in the faces of the babes he saw with their mothers at the shops, which in any case made no sense – Archie wouldn't be a baby now, he'd be at school.

It used to be a strain working with the lads at Charing Cross and a burden being attentive to his customers. There had always been an ache in his bones with the effort of being sociable. But here in Kent perhaps at last his soul was healing over with the lack of prodding and reminders. He was never caught out expecting to see Lucy at the stove stirring something in a pot when he came home, or with Archie on her hip walking out to meet him.

These last few months he had begun to like the sight of people again and to enjoy a chat from time to time – with quiet Mr Mander, who was single too, or with the grocer's boy who came out to collect the eggs.

This empty even-tempered place had organized the memories and put them in the past. The wind had flattened out the creases in his heart and blunted the razor edge of grief he thought would always cut him. He didn't feel impatient for the time when Lucy would be back to fetch him; it would come.

All this might mean that he was mended, he didn't know. Whatever it might be, he never went further in his mind than the day ahead. He worked his land, and ate and slept. He wasn't a grieving widower any more, or the father of a baby boy, or Saunders the porter late of Charing Cross. He was no one and content to be so. Occasionally he pondered the future of Eddie Saunders and felt a distant curiosity as to what the man would become.

He hefted the gate back on its hinges and leaned on it to ease his shoulders. The evening mist was a milky blanket knee deep over the fields; the moon was up with a few stars sprinkled on the curve. Sunsets on the Marsh were fragile or serene or riotous, and Eddie admired this one's carnival of colours. The sky was royal-blue lightening to turquoise with skeins of pinkish cloud low down on the horizon. The crows were clattering in their roost. A flock of starlings looped above his head in the icy shining air.

There was another sound, a distant clopping. It might be a sheep loose on the lane. A lame sheep? A two-legged sheep? The sound slowed and quickened. Eddie stared into the gloom.

It was a woman. She wobbled on heels too high for country walking and had her arms out, balancing, so her coat hung open like a cape. The day had been warm for March, but with the sun almost gone, it would be freezing soon. He could see the curve of her waist and hips, the dark blue dress against the yellow lining of her coat. Her handbag swung from her wrist. She looked at her feet, head down, legs splayed like a calf on ice. Her car must have broken down; there was no other explanation for her wandering up here.

She looked up. 'Hello, Eddie Saunders,' she called. 'I can see you don't know me in a dress. It's Rachel Ross. You haven't seen me for a while.'

She found an even patch to put her feet and stood up steadily enough to wrap the coat around her. 'You came to Neate Street looking for my brother, Michael. Remember me? Now I'm looking for him.' Her lips were red and her cheeks were powdered. 'How are you?' Underneath the make-up he could see the girl in shirt and trousers with earthy hands he remembered from all that time ago.

'I'm well, thanks,' said Eddie. 'You've come all this way from London?'

'Oh, no, we live not far. I've just come off the bus from work. You're only three stops on from us. We moved, Mum and Nanna Lydia and I. We've got a new bungalow in Hythe. Michael doesn't know. You're a friend of his and I thought you'd have an idea where he is.'

Eddie remembered her directness. It had unnerved him. When he last saw her she had long hair but it must be short now like women wore it these days; she had on a little close-fitting hat with a flower at the side, and her neck above the collar of her coat was long and smooth. Her scent made a wisp of sweetness in the air, which he caught sometimes in between the stink of sweat and chewed grass that was him and the cows.

Eddie said, 'Michael's not been here for quite a while. He stayed a month or so helping out, then went off to get the Dover boat to France. A year or more, it must be.'

'Oh.' She looked hopeful as if she thought there would be more.

'I've not heard since,' Eddie said.

'Well, thanks, Eddie. If you do, would you say . . . say we're in Hythe and we're not in Neate Street any more.'

'I will.'

'Well, bye, then.' Rachel turned herself around and he watched her tottering back along the lane.

'Have a cup of tea with me, if you've the time,' he called after her.

'In your house?' she called back.

'The only place there is.'

'I wouldn't mind. You'll have to loan me a torch, though, to see my way back.'

He tied the gate closed and packed up his tools.

In the kitchen he lit the lamp and the stove while Rachel sat on the edge of a chair. The house was cold. Some yellow flames nipped at the kindling twigs and it would take a while before the warmth came through. He left the stove door open.

The lambs woke up and looked over the sides of their boxes at the collie flat out on the lino. There would be a whiff of dog when the collie's coat began to warm. Eddie filled the kettle and used the bellows on the fire.

He could feel Rachel looking at the ruin of a room he lived in. When he'd shown her in, he suddenly saw the place as if he'd never set foot in it before. The cabbage-green distempered walls were draped with sooty cobwebs, and there was a black stain above the range and across the ceiling. In places the plaster had fallen off and wooden laths showed through like carcass ribs. The floor was bare boards with scraps of lino. He used to take off his boots when he came into the house, but he didn't any more.

'I'm not started with the decorating yet,' he said. There were rags, tools, a fence post, a box of straw in the corner where he'd hatched some chicks. His socks hung on a piece of string over the sink.

'It could do with a few jobs doing,' Rachel said. 'You're not a handyman, then?'

'The roof's seen to, and the plumbing.'

'You want to choose a colour scheme in here. Get a pot of paint at Bellamy's in Tontine Street and a nice cheerful picture. Some ornaments. You've been here a while, haven't you?'

'The sheds and the barn needed work. Things take time.'

'Looks like they do,' said Rachel. 'You're not comfy but I suppose you don't mind.'

'I get used to it. I'm out on the farm.'

'Excuse my frankness,' she said, 'but a man can't run a home and that's a fact.'

Eddie cleared away last night's plate and saucepan, wiped the table with a cloth and sat down on an upturned poultry crate while the kettle boiled. Fatigue was beginning to defeat him. He felt his blood sinking to his boots and he wished he'd not invited her. All he wanted was sleep.

Rachel tapped her fingers and jigged the toe of her shoe. She clasped her coat round her, sitting up tense with her handbag on her lap.

The kettle began to wheeze. 'Perhaps you'd like to skip the tea after all,' Eddie said.

'Oh, no, not a bit of it,' said Rachel flatly.

'I should tidy up,' he said. This thought had never occurred to him before. 'It's not a place to invite a guest. You mustn't feel obliged to stay. Perhaps another time, when I've got things straight.'

Then she smiled. 'Don't be daft. You make that tea. I'm forgetting my manners, aren't I? To tell you the truth, it's Michael I'm thinking about. I'm worried. Not worried about him exactly, just worried where he is.'

'He's all right,' said Eddie. 'He's bound to be.' He didn't know what else to say.

'Oh, I know, I know.' Rachel took off her hat and shook her hair. The hat had flattened it and her hair filled out like something taking in a breath of air. In the lamplight, her eyes looked peaty black and clear as if she saw more of him than he could see of her. 'I'm a worrier by nature. Don't mind me,' she said.

'Sugar,' he said, passing her the bag.

Rachel asked about his cows. He answered her in too much detail, he remembered later. She cooed over the lambs in their boxes and stroked the collie, which leaned against her legs. Then she told him about the shop in Folkestone where she worked and that the owner might open another one in Hythe which would be nearer and easier on the bus. 'We'll have a dressmaker for alterations on the premises – our clientele are ladies who want things exact, and the silhouette this year is glamorous and smart; Joan Crawford, Marlene Dietrich, Jean Harlow. Hythe might not be Hollywood but our ladies aren't behind.'

Eddie blinked to keep his eyelids up. It was dark outside and the yellow light cast shadows on her face and sparked lights in her hair and on her lips. The tiredness was like grit behind his eyes, but he wanted to keep on looking. He'd better walk her home.

Suddenly she said, 'I could live in a place like this.'

He laughed and the sudden force of it cracked something open in his chest like a stuck-fast door blasted off its hinges. He laughed again, but softer now; she was sitting there so clean and beautiful in the devastation of his house.

'The place we had in London was a bit like this,' Rachel said. 'You saw that old house in Neate Street. Nothing much but I loved it. We had hens, Orpingtons, the best. They're loyal, good layers and good mothers to their chicks. Pigeons too – before Dad was ill. And when we moved to the place we've got now, with no upstairs, no cracks, and all square and straight, I thought I'd go mad.' She smiled at him. 'Perfect has no heart. You don't want to do too much in here,' she said. 'It's lovely as it is.'

• • •

The death certificate of Albert Ross did not put the cause as injuries of war: he'd been too slow to go. Mr Ross had recovered satisfactorily, the doctor said, and died naturally of old age. 'At forty-eight?' Vera had said. 'Don't make me laugh.'

Were it not unseemly at a funeral, Lydia would have allowed herself a smile. She was thankful that her son was not in pain and never would be again, but she also felt the mortal injury of grief which is invisible and permanent. A soul joined with the deceased is a tree that's grown against another; it never flourishes as it should when it's half uprooted from the earth.

However, Albert's dying wasn't terrible. His passing was delicate, quiet, like the final eddy of a capsized boat going under. Just a ripple to finish what had already disappeared.

A last shudder was to come. The three of them were washing up the crockery on the January evening after Albert's wake, Lydia at the sink, Vera with a cloth and Rachel putting things away. The kitchen was peaceful with the gentle ringing in the air that comes after a houseful of guests has gone and it's just family again. People had spoken respectfully and fulsomely of Albert, and somehow the presence of the man he used to be had filled the house again.

Then Vera said it: she was selling up. She wanted somewhere fresh. She fancied a nice healthy modern house away from London.

Rachel smacked down a stack of plates on the table. 'I've had enough. I'm not choosing between you and Nanna. I can't. I'll cut myself in half, I will.' It wasn't Rachel's style to be hysterical but when Vera said her mind was set, the girl went wild with anguish, like a little one you couldn't reason with, more desperate than anyone had seen her in all the years of sadness they'd endured. What else could Lydia do but sell her cottage and go with them?

So: a bald new bungalow in Hythe a stone's throw from the Channel, pebbles for a garden and a glass lean-to at the back where they could sit and sun themselves on windy days. The windows and front door were yellow with leaded lights of rising suns, the guttering and the gate were painted sailor-blue, the walls were red brick to the windowsills, white stucco above, and the roof tiles were tinged with green. Too many colours and not Lydia's notion of a home at all.

The worst was having no upstairs. The laws of nature are disrupted without a third dimension in a house. There was back and front, left and right, but no up and down.

Leaving Peckham had affected Lydia. Since coming to the bungalow, words in conversations were sometimes like little balls in bagatelle ricocheting too fast to follow, and she was like that too: she seemed to bump about inside this bungalow; it was unknown terrain. How could a household be organized with the kitchen and the bedroom side by side, the bathroom off the hallway and the lounge adjacent to the WC, which ought to be outside? There was an attic room where Rachel slept, but the stairs were more a ladder, and Lydia could not see the point in struggling up to what should rightly store the suitcases.

Vera didn't seem to mind the oddness of their home, and in any case she was indoors much less than Lydia. It was good to see Vera full of energy again, so different from her brittle fidgets of exhaustion in the years of Albert's dying. She had found work as housekeeper to a Mr George Mander, who owned the land farmed by Rachel's young man, Eddie Saunders. Mr Mander's elderly mother was difficult and had worked her way through a string of local girls who couldn't cope or wouldn't stand for it. Eddie Saunders had brought about Vera's introduction.

It was a happy thing that Rachel had found herself a beau, although Eddie wasn't young – ten years ahead of Rachel, a farmer, a widower and not what Vera had had in mind. She said he looked uncomfortable inside his suit, inside a room, inside a house. His legs were too big underneath a table and his fingers were like sausages around a teacup. He sweated with the awkwardness of organizing that bulk of his.

'A good judge of an onion has fried more than one,' Vera told Rachel. 'Spread your wings. At your age you should be having fun.'

Eddie was the first Rachel had brought home for tea. She'd had lots of interest, as of course she would, but hadn't bothered, even for amusement.

'I wouldn't waste my time, Nanna,' Rachel had said privately to Lydia. 'I've got better things to do and they get on my nerves, these boys, fussing with their hair and trying to impress me. I want a man who knows himself.'

Eddie Saunders was a Londoner and a kind man to his bones, Lydia could tell, and Rachel had the wisdom some are born with that isn't distracted by appearances. She liked to go out dancing and was good at looking glamorous, but Rachel was also practical. She'd taken on the vegetables and hens in Neate Street when Albert couldn't and no one else had the heart. At twelve years old, she'd put on Albert's gardening things, which swamped her, struggled with the digging and taught herself to grow things without help or encouragement from anyone. Rachel would be a good wife for this farmer, Eddie Saunders, if he was her choice.

So life was unfolding for Rachel, and Vera seemed buoyant without the weight of Albert. At eight o'clock each morning, Rachel took the bus along the seafront in one direction and Vera, at half past, went in the other.

Lydia had most of the day alone, with no routine and no one needing her. She could prepare the meal any time, do a little ironing and watch the clouds that were so different by the sea.

She was baffled at the complications of having so much time and would sometimes forget her purpose between the sink and the pantry door, or puzzle over which knife was best to scale the fish, or be mesmerized like dogs and babies are by ordinary things that suddenly seem miraculous, like dust motes twinkling, a coin of sunlight on the floor, a curtain breathing in a draught.

# 10

Karen was late, as she often was, and Elisabeth ordered a pot of tea and two lunches of ham and potatoes, hoping she wouldn't have to eat them both herself.

The restaurant was full: a few gentlemen dining alone but mostly ladies together. Shafts of watery sunlight illuminated dabs of colour in the gloom: a pale green teacup, a red silk scarf, a blue corsage.

She was tired, almost too tired to eat at all. She wanted to close her eyes, lulled by the clicking cutlery and quiet voices. Tomorrow was her day off from the hospital and after having lunch with Karen she would catch her train and go home to sleep and think, and decide what must be done.

'Hello, you,' said Karen. 'I hope you're paying. I haven't got a farthing. Heaven knows how I'll live till pay day.' She leaned down and her hair smelled of cigarettes. She kissed Elisabeth on the cheek.

'You look worn out,' said Elisabeth.

'So do you. Awful. At least take off that horrid hat they make you wear. You go first. What's up? It's your doctor, isn't it?'

'He's not a doctor, he's a surgeon. And nothing's up except that you'll end up in hospital yourself one day.'

Karen took off her coat and as always people looked. She smoothed her dress and said, 'I bought it yesterday in Dickens. And gloves. See, they match. The shade is Aegean Night and the collar is the real fur of something. What do you think?'

'I think that if you don't watch out, the species of your collar won't matter much.'

Karen's eyes seemed bigger and darker, and her skin was sallow under her face powder and rouge. Sometimes Elisabeth wished she hadn't learned to recognize the damage the rheumatic fever had done to Karen nine years ago.

'What are we eating? I'm starving,' Karen said.

'Ham. You're blue under the eyes and your poor heart is struggling to keep you upright. Please, Karen, listen to me. Try to remember sometimes.'

'I will, I will, I promise. I'm so glad to see you, little nurse. I've got lots to tell you and I wish you had more time.'

'I'm here – and so are you now.'

Karen leaned closer. 'I've met someone.' She pushed the napkin and the cutlery aside. 'I think he's it. I swear he's perfect. He doesn't speak much English but he's heaven. I nearly fainted when I gave him the keys to his room. His name is Artur Landau and he's staying for two weeks to see London with his father who's doing some business thing. Artur says London is dull compared to Munich, so I said, "You should come to the Locarno in Streatham and that'll change your mind." We're going dancing there tonight.'

'How do you know he's nice if he can't talk to you?'

'You should see him, Elisabeth. There's other ways of telling.'

'What about Stanley?'

'Stan won't be bothered. He knows it wasn't serious.'

The lunches arrived and Karen ate and talked about German Artur Landau, while Elisabeth pushed her food around the plate and tried to listen to keep her mind off the nausea roiling in her stomach.

'Now you,' Karen said. 'No, wait, I'll guess; the doctor has proposed, you turned him down, then changed your mind because he's got good hands.'

Elisabeth giggled in spite of everything. Her stomach wrenched and made her eyes water. 'He's not a doctor, he's a surgeon. And he's married. He forgot to tell me.'

Karen had been giggling too but now she stared. She reached across the table and took Elisabeth's hand, knocking over a tulip in a vase which flooded both their plates. The salt cellar and a fork pirouetted off the table.

'I hate him,' Karen said. 'He's a fool.'

'I'm the fool.'

Elisabeth found she was crying and the waitress came and asked if she'd finished and was there anything wrong with the lunch as she'd barely touched it. If there was, it should be reported to Chef, so would madam like to make a complaint? Elisabeth swallowed down the tears and the sickness and couldn't speak.

'Go away,' Karen said, and the waitress scuttled off.

They sat holding hands over the wreckage of ham and potatoes and Elisabeth cried quietly although she wasn't sure why. The pain went deeper than the little cut her surgeon had inflicted; she did not love him nor had she ever really thought she would, so why did the tears keep leaking out as if he mattered?

After a while, Karen asked for the bill and fished in Elisabeth's bag for money. They walked together to the station and Elisabeth was sick into the gutter.

'Is it worse than you've told me?' Karen asked.

'No,' said Elisabeth. 'There's an infection going round, that's all. I hope you don't catch it.'

'I've got to get back to work or I'd take you home. I'll come first thing in the morning and we can talk, I promise.'

'Karen, you have to sleep. You'll be out till midnight dancing.'

Karen gave her new gloves to Elisabeth: 'To punch him if he ever bothers you again.'

They hugged and Elisabeth smelled the smoke and mustiness in Karen's hair and felt the thinness of her body. 'Tell Artur Landau he must look after you.'

• • •

Elisabeth leans her head and it bumps against the window to the rhythm of the train. She closes her eyes and more tears squeeze out and trickle down her cheeks. The carriage is empty so she lets them drip.

She wishes she wasn't going home and that the train would never stop. When she lets herself into the house in Catford, she will be careful to be quiet so it doesn't notice her. It is a stale home where no one really lives.

Her mother will be at work, but later the level chill of her will move like a cold front from room to room. Recently, a nice widower from down the road, Mr Mole, has been politely courting. When his name is mentioned, Elisabeth must look at her feet, her hands, the ceiling, but *not* at Karen, or they will both splutter and go red with laughing and that is childish silliness, their mother tells them as if they're still at school.

Mr Mole is hopeful and said as much. Their mother had almost given up the black but has taken to it again as a rebuff, a rebuke to Mr Mole.

The train shakes hard and Elisabeth feels her body collapsing. Her eyes are shut; her bones have gone and so have her muscles. Her head beats on the glass and the air bangs in her ears as the train goes into a tunnel.

Then all at once she is rushing upwards like a bubble, up out of the sickness and the thudding, up she goes, past the face of a huge smiling man who swings her and sits her on his shoulders. She holds his ears and she is safe, with her face amongst flickering sunny leaves. She reaches up and picks a giant pear. It is rough and dry and smells of pepper.

Far below, Karen circles, bobbing, fingers splayed and blue eyes goggling up. *Me, let me have it.* Elisabeth puts the heavy pear on Dadda's big creased hand and he passes it way down to Karen, who lines it up beside the others on the grass. The wooden pears will be laid out on trays, not touching, to ripen on newspaper under their beds. By Christmas, a magic spell which Dadda knows will have turned the wood to silky juicy flesh.

Then Dadda leans forward, sideways, and Elisabeth tumbles head first into nothing. This moment – the moment when she's falling and before he catches her – makes her laugh and scream together. His face, the sky and pears all whirl together.

A bang of air, and a tunnel wakes her. He is dead and Karen hardly ever comes home any more. Now it is only her mother in the house and Elisabeth dreads the days when she must leave the hospital and go home. She never would if she didn't feel guilty about her mother's solitude.

In the nurses' dormitory Elisabeth has a locker and two hangers in a wardrobe, and the air is a fug of talc and cigarettes and scent. The kettle and the ironing board are always on the go, there are uniforms hanging up and at least two dozen lisle stockings pegged across the room. There are knickers over all the iron bedsteads.

The girls laugh bawdily and raucously, half dressed in underwear and dressing gowns. They don't care, they've seen it all, they know the words, and when Elisabeth is a part of it she feels a thrill that drenches her as if she's standing in a summer downpour.

She finds it easy to be one Elisabeth on the ward and another with the girls. Matron is impressed: Nurse Oliver studies conscientiously, works hard and is respectful.

The girls are impressed too. Elisabeth Oliver is a dark horse: when she first arrived, she hardly said a word but she's different now, she's bold. She'll look a doctor in the eye and not be scared at all.

There is a surgeon who speaks to her when he need speak only to Matron. He has a seriousness darkening his handsome brow, which Elisabeth sees as sensitivity. His name is Mr Caffin. Charles. He has a flat in Pimlico.

He assumes that certain things are ordinary and although she has believed that they are special, it is almost a relief to realize she is wrong. He says that sex is for fun and secondly for reproduction, and although he loves her and this is not *just* fun, they must be careful that it isn't reproduction either. Charles is kind and also organized; he checks that Elisabeth's calculations are correct.

Elisabeth is apprehensive but mostly curious, so it's odd when at the moment she should be having fun, at the moment that interests her most, she feels as if she's slipped out through the scullery when he's come into the parlour.

Afterwards she smokes the cigarette he gives her. They lie in bed in Pimlico and Charles stares at the ceiling with his jaw silhouetted by the lamp. Elisabeth puffs her cigarette and finds that although the taste is disgusting, she can do it without coughing. This, more than what has gone before, is proof that she is now a woman.

Six weeks later, Charles Caffin tells her he was mistaken. He wrings his skilful hands and explains that he cannot marry her or take her to his house in Shropshire. He must go home to his wife and ask for her forgiveness.

Elisabeth is dazed by so much information. He has never mentioned marrying her, or Shropshire, or a wife.

'You need not tell her, need you?' says Elisabeth. 'There's nothing much to tell.'

'I must. I always do,' says the surgeon. 'The tea is ready,' he says. It is snowing in the room and Elisabeth is wearing woollen gloves. He looks up and he is Michael. He sees her, far back where no one else has ever found her, and she is running to him but not moving on the sparkling snow. I think of you often, he whispers, but it is too late because her feet are carrying her away. Goodbye, Elisabeth.

The air bangs in her ears. A tunnel wakes her.

When she lets herself into the house, she is careful to be quiet. The house smells faintly of a scent her mother hasn't worn for years, a ghost perfume.

94

Elisabeth is sick again and although she's certain it's no more than an infection, at this moment she wouldn't care if she was pregnant and had taken another turning into a life that isn't hers.

The surgeon deceived her but she sees now that she deceived him too. There's a deeper hurt she has inflicted on herself and it was done for nothing. Michael is not erased. She meant to scour him away, but she sees that her stupidity can never be undone now, because she's altered and a door is shut; the memory of the studio belongs to another Elisabeth.

She meant to punish Michael, but punish him for what? For not bringing back the book himself? For preferring, as of course he would, the lovely Mrs Brion, who is sophisticated and American?

*I think of you often.* A hundred times, she has read the chilly note from Amsterdam he sent a year ago, searching those five words for clues. What thoughts does he have? Is *often* as often as she thinks of him?

If he remembers her at all, he's thinking of a girl who's gone.

•  •  •

Downstairs, the front door opened and street sounds came into the house along with the flap and rustle of an umbrella being shaken out. The door slammed. Elisabeth heard Karen sing out, 'Hey! Where are you?' and her heels clicked on the lino in the passageway.

Elisabeth had just drawn back the bedroom curtains to a white sky laden with rain. Her eyes wanted darkness again and her skin felt bruised as if she had been fighting in a dream, but the nausea of yesterday had gone.

'It's me!' Karen shouted up the stairs. Elisabeth didn't answer. It was a habit of Karen's to call out when she came home so whatever small activities or private contemplations were in progress would be interrupted.

She needs to have us pay attention, Elisabeth thought crossly; Karen likes the audience to be ready for her entrance. The annoyance and the happiness of seeing Karen always came together.

Karen pushed open the bedroom door. 'You're not dressed yet.'

'No, I'm not. You were coming to look after me.'

'I hoped we might walk down to Cullens for a cup of coffee.' Karen's face was wet. She sniffed and shook back her damp hair.

'I've just woken up, for goodness sake, and I still have a headache.'

'In that case, I shall make us tea and toast and tell you all about the Locarno last night to take your mind off things.' Karen sat down on the bed. 'Oh, Elisabeth, he's a dream! I had just the best, most delicious time and he did too.'

'Please don't bounce. You mean the German boy, I take it, not Stanley.'

'Stan? Heavens, no! That's another story.' Karen jumped up. 'But first I'll fetch us tea. You look done to shreds. I shall make a fuss of you. I said I would and here I am. Was Ma kind to you last night?'

'She went to her Canasta evening. She didn't even come in before she went to work this morning. I could have died in the night and she wouldn't have known.' Talking made Elisabeth's head pound.

'She does her best,' said Karen softly. 'Dadda died in the night and she can't bear it. Really. I know. Death does that to people sometimes, it closes them up.'

'She's nice when you're here – more cheerful than she ever is with me.'

'I fool about to make her laugh, that's all. It's you she worries about.'

'She hardly even looks at me.'

'You were Dadda's favourite,' said Karen simply, 'and Ma loves you too much because of him.'

'Karen! That's not true – it really isn't. They love us both the same.'

'I don't mind, I honestly don't. We all love you the best. In any case, it doesn't matter now.' Karen sat down on the bed again, leaning against the footboard. She kicked off her shoes, put up her legs and pulled across the eiderdown. She yawned. 'I'm done to shreds as well.'

'Here, have a pillow. I told you you'd be tired if you went out dancing. Perhaps I should fetch the tea.'

'We didn't get back to the hotel till half past one, then I had to see to Artur's hand. I couldn't find the first-aid box and we made a dreadful noise.' She gazed up at the ceiling, smiling. 'We didn't get caught, thank goodness.'

'I should hope not.'

'Must you be so starchy? You sound like a shrivelled old aunt. Oh, Elisabeth, I just want to be with him all the time, every moment, as if something's tugging at me. You wouldn't understand.'

'I might understand perfectly well. Anyway, how did Artur hurt himself?'

'Oh, there was a fuss with Stanley.' Karen yawned again and stretched up her arms. 'It wasn't Artur's fault.' She closed her eyes and let her head rest back on the footboard. 'Rub my toes, would you? They're freezing.'

Elisabeth felt under the eiderdown for Karen's feet. 'You should wear boots when it's wet. Tell me about Stanley. Quick. I can't bear it.'

'Well, Artur and I had been dancing for a while and . . .' Karen opened her eyes and they were shining. 'He can dance, Elisabeth, really dance. Most boys push you about like a sack of spuds and they step on your feet and look scared to death of being close. When Artur had his arms around me . . . I can't describe it . . . It's as if . . . as if I don't need to worry about anything any more, or do anything, and I'm safe because I know he'll never let me go.'

'But what about *Stan?*'

'He tried to cut in. He was squiffy and I asked him nicely not to make a scene. Artur told him to go away and he did.'

'That's all?'

'It was until we were going home. Stan was outside, very drunk and silly, and he just wouldn't let up. He was dreadful, Elisabeth. Stan, I mean, cursing and putting up his fists, but he's such a weedy thing, people were laughing at him. *I know your type*, he was yelling at Artur, *you won't treat her right and I'm not standing by. Get your something hands off her, you filthy Kraut. Come on, you something coward.* And he took a swing at Artur.'

'No!'

'He did. He missed and fell over on the pavement right at our feet and then he tried to drag himself up with his arms round my legs and I would have been down on the pavement too if Artur hadn't stepped in.'

'Poor Stanley.'

'You say "poor Stanley" but he was behaving dreadfully, Elisabeth, and his language was filthy.'

'He's in love with you, Karen. Anyone can see it. You've broken his heart.'

'Well, more than that's broken now.'

'What do you mean?'

'Artur hauled him off and stood him on his feet, and Stan was swaying about, cursing and yelling and throwing punches, so Artur hit him. I don't think it was hard but there was an awful sound and another crack when Stan hit the pavement. His mouth was bleeding or it might have been his nose, but he was still saying frightful things, on and on.

So Artur put his foot on Stan's neck. *You will not speak*, he said. I think maybe it was too hard because Stan started gurgling and wheezing, and a man said, *That's enough, mate*, and someone else said, *He'll break his neck.* Then a woman was crying and other people were asking Artur to stop, but no one tried to pull him off. I think they knew they shouldn't.'

'But Artur did stop, didn't he?'

'Yes, of course. After a while, he took his foot away and people came crowding round Stan. They were sitting him up as we left. Artur said he knew Stan would be all right. He'd lost a tooth and maybe his nose was broken, that's all.'

'That's all!'

They both fell silent and Elisabeth saw Karen look away across the room, stretching up her arms again and shaking out her hair. Her face was difficult to read.

'Weren't you scared?' Elisabeth said at last. 'Poor Stanley.'

Karen turned on her at once. 'Must you keep saying that? I just wish I could forget it, get it out of my mind.'

'If I'd been there, I don't know what I should have done.'

'Afterwards, after all the noise and shouting, Artur wasn't shaken up at all, as if he didn't really mind.'

'How ghastly. How cruel and horrible.'

'Not horrible at all. Artur says this kind of thing will happen when a girl is beautiful.'

'Oh, Karen! So punching a man who's drunk and silly is forgivable?'

'Artur didn't start it. Stan had been provoking him all night. Artur was protecting me and why shouldn't he? For goodness sake, Elisabeth, you've no idea about people – about men – at all. You haven't a clue.'

'No. I don't think I have,' Elisabeth said. 'If that's how they are, I don't understand them in the least.'

They glared at each other across the eiderdown. The argument could flare or they could both decide to turn away.

The bedside clock ticked and heavy drops of morning rain splashed on the window. After a time, Elisabeth said, 'What about the tea?'

'Yes, tea!' Karen got up quickly and slipped on her shoes. 'I'm so neglectful, chatting on and on when you're not well. And toast too. You're wincing, you poor darling.' She pulled the curtains across. 'Shut your eyes for a while.' She stood by the bed and touched Elisabeth's hand. 'I can't bear it when you're ill. I just want to take it all away. Shall I fetch you an aspirin? Would that help?'

'Yes. It really would. Thank you.'

She heard Karen running down the stairs two at a time as she always did. She would swing on the newel post and slide on the drugget, which would rumple and skid on the floorboards, and when Ma came home she would tut and prod it back in place with her foot.

In a while, Karen would bring up a tray and there would be more toast than Elisabeth could eat, it would be too thickly buttered and the crusts would be burned. The tea would have too much sugar, and the cup would be overfilled so it slopped in the saucer. But Elisabeth knew the breakfast would seem lavish and miraculous like a banquet served on a ship in a stormy sea. It would restore her and seem more delicious than anything she'd ever tasted, because food Karen made for her always did.

Downstairs, the pipes groaned as the kitchen tap was turned, then Elisabeth heard the kettle crash down on the hob.

# II

Herr Gunther Landau was not displeased to see his son hand in hand with the pretty hotel key clerk although he never would have tolerated a foreign *Freundin* for his son if she were anything but English. Herr Landau admired the English. It was a pity she was in unsuitable employment, and she was a little coarser than he would have hoped, but Fräulein Karen Oliver could be polished, she could be refined – but not too much. Her raw flirtatiousness could make her an interesting and enlivening daughter-in-law, and when she smiled her quick and generous smile, Herr Landau felt an unaccustomed lightness in his chest and wistful longing for the jolly shining girl his wife once was.

His son had not shown a particular preference for this English girl, although he seemed to like her well enough; they drank cocktails together in the lounge when her shift was finished. Management disapproved and would have reprimanded her if Herr Landau Senior had not intervened.

'Come, come. My son is on holiday, and after all who would deny the young their magic times?'

Fräulein Karen Oliver smiled winningly and perhaps a touch triumphantly, and Management withdrew.

Artur was easy and politely rakish in female company. He took his pick, just as his father had in his younger days. But Herr Landau was growing weary of Artur's indecision and uneasy that he did not seem to be outgrowing a young man's natural zeal for new ideas and politics.

Herr Landau had tolerated the arguments about Jews, about capitalists – like him apparently – who cheated and oppressed the ordinary working man. He agreed with Artur that Bolsheviks and Marxists were dangerous, and that Germany was being punished with poverty, not making reparation for the war but being humiliated, ground into the dirt. Herr Landau resented Versailles as much as any patriotic German would. The Deutschmark was worth nothing and if it weren't for customers abroad their business would have failed like many others.

He had some sympathy but Artur's fervour was not diminishing and this irked Herr Landau. The National Socialists as they called themselves, to whom Artur was so loyal, would never be taken seriously, but of late they were behaving in a thuggish, embarrassingly brutish way. Artur must be diverted. At twenty-eight, it was time to choose a wife and settle down.

Fräulein Karen Oliver was near-perfect in looks and nationality, and temperament, as far as one could ever know. Her certainty in being noticed and admired came close to arrogance but Herr Landau liked a girl with character. His son would need a wife who'd match his selfishness.

She was clearly not of peasant stock: she was tall and graceful, silver-blonde. Her limbs were too long, one might say if one were critical, and her hands and feet were delicate but large as if she'd grow into them. Her face was small: a pointed chin, blue eyes – no flecks of green or brown, the irises were pure china-blue. She had the hypnotic prettiness of a child. Her expression was intelligent and hopeful.

Herr Landau was confident that his son would see all this with more appreciation in the crystal air of Bavaria, so he offered her a position as clerk at his offices in Munich. Her duties would be broad: she would learn German, typing, shorthand and cookery. She would start work in one month's time, and on the journey she would buy a wardrobe of good clothes at a particular boutique in Paris where she'd be advised on style and colour.

The arrangements were in place but it seemed Herr Landau had overestimated the effort and the money he needed to invest to bring about the igniting of the two blond hearts. During the last days of their stay in London, a change came over Artur. He was in a trance of infatuation and Fräulein Oliver was purple round the eyes.

Herr Landau knew the signs and was glad; he approved of healthy passions in the young. Artur asked to remain in London and travel with the girl to Paris, then on to Munich.

Herr Landau refused his son's request: separation from each other would be sure to strengthen the bond.

· · ·

Mrs Francesca Brion's house in Regent's Park was almost as Elisabeth imagined it would be: large, elegant, with a curved gravel drive to the pillared porch, although the Red Indian totem pole on the front lawn was puzzling, and in full view of the street there was a reclining granite figure with sturdy thighs and breasts like puddings. The sculpture was full of holes and could have been an arrangement of Swiss cheese and blancmanges.

Elisabeth's visit had no reason except that Mrs Brion's card was still in her purse and now the days were empty, this was as good a way as any to fill an afternoon.

She wore a bias skirt and tailored jacket, and the hat was Aegean Night to match the gloves that Karen had given her. She was smart enough to visit in Regent's Park. The chasm that had opened inside her was invisible.

She pulled the brass handle but didn't hear a bell. The door was opened by the housekeeper, and in the moment when the woman looked down at her, the courage that Elisabeth had guarded as she had walked from the station started to dissolve.

A voice called from somewhere inside, 'Edith? Who is it?'

As if she hadn't heard, the woman, Edith, said, 'Mrs Brion has visitors at present. May I ask if she is expecting you?'

'No. Yes. I have her card.'

'Edith!' the voice called again.

There was a long moment of appraisal. The woman's eyes saw through her. 'Perhaps you would kindly wait.'

'It's Miss Oliver! How lovely!' Mrs Brion came pattering on bare feet across the chequered marble floor, a silk kimono fluttering around her legs. She seemed completely unconcerned that Elisabeth should see her like this. 'I have some friends here who'd love to meet you. Come in, come in.' She put her arm through Elisabeth's. 'I love your hair, and that little hat, it's very pretty. Could we have more tea and sandwiches, please, Edith,' she said. 'And some toast for Toby.' Mrs Brion seemed so small without her shoes.

In the drawing room the curtains were half closed against the sunlight slanting in. The air was heavy with cigar smoke. The arms of chairs and sofas, little tables and sideboards, were scattered with empty teacups and glasses, plates of half-eaten cake and sandwiches. There were sheets of drawing paper on the floor.

Several people were in the room although Elisabeth could not take in how many, and a little boy was lying on his stomach by the fire colouring with crayons in a book that did not look as if it was meant for a child. An easel was set up and a woman in a blue cotton smock stood with charcoal in her hand.

All the faces turned to look.

'This is Miss Elisabeth Oliver, a friend of Michael,' said Mrs Brion. She waved her arm into the smoke and sunshine. 'This is my sister, Mrs Ingrid Schröeder. Mrs Venetia Gibb' – she indicated the woman at the easel – 'Miss Pixie Fairhaven and Miss Olivia Layne.'

Ingrid Schröeder was small and fragile like Mrs Brion; Pixie Fairhaven was younger than the other women, near Elisabeth in age, thin, red-faced and ginger-haired; Venetia Gibb was aristocratic.

Elisabeth was confused: there were three women and a dark young man in a suit, smoking a cigar.

'Well! The Hebrew's friend,' he said, leaping up and kissing her hand. He was wearing lipstick. 'I'm Olivia.'

'And this is Toby, my youngest nephew,' said Mrs Brion. The small boy continued his colouring.

Elisabeth perched on a Dorset chair beside the fire and the faces followed her. Suddenly the bias skirt and jacket were wrong; she was a girl in her Sunday best bought off the peg and chosen with no style or originality or taste. These women – except for Olivia in her suit – wore long soft clothes that seemed to be neither dresses nor skirts and blouses, but a mix of everything that looked comfortable and beautiful. Pixie Fairhaven was a little more conservative in dark blue, but even she had an exotic beaded cap on her wiry orange hair, and dangling amber earrings.

There was a hush and Elisabeth knew that before she arrived they had been talking and laughing and the room had been alive. She wondered when she could leave.

'Edith is bringing us more tea,' said Mrs Brion. She lay down on the sofa amongst a pile of cushions, pulling the kimono off her shoulders. 'Am I right, Venetia? Were my arms like this?' she asked the woman at the easel, who nodded and began to draw.

'This lovely girl needs refreshment. I'll get you something until the tea arrives. One never knows when Edith will turn up.' Olivia went to a tray of bottles on a cabinet and poured some spirit into a glass as big as a vase. She filled it to the rim with orange juice from a jug. 'Frankie's favourite: Russian vodka. We had ours with sandwiches so you're only catching up.'

The drink tasted of the freshest oranges but warm, as if the sun was still inside them. Elisabeth took a mouthful and the heat sunk to her stomach.

'My word! Look at the time. I should be running along,' said Pixie Fairhaven – an American like Mrs Brion. 'Shall I tell Mama you'll come in August, Francesca? And everyone, of course. We'll get a girl to help with the children, Ingrid darling. Italians are marvellous with little ones.'

'How sweet you are, Pixie,' said Mrs Schroëder. 'Toby does not take the heat but I'm sure we'll manage something.'

'Venetia? Might you persuade Douglas to abandon France this summer and join us?' asked Pixie.

'I'm not sure,' said Mrs Gibb absently. She stood back to regard her drawing. There was a smudge of charcoal on her cheek. 'He says Italians are hysterical and overwrought, not the peasants, just the middle classes. I'm not sure I shall sway him.'

'We shan't need to see Italians,' said Pixie brightly. 'Douglas need not go out. We have a pool and views from the terrace. Do try, Venetia.' She turned to Elisabeth. 'Papa has just bought a villa in Amalfi.'

'You're moving with your family to Italy?'

'Oh, heavens, no! I couldn't live there. We have a house in New York, which is home to me, and here in England we live in Bloomsbury. Mama has a little castle in Corfu – it's so sweet and tiny, nothing like the castles in your Scotland, and we have the Innsbruck chalet for when we ski. The villa in Amalfi will be a dream and I'm *longing* to take everyone to see it. It's such a thrill to spend holidays all over the place and take one's friends, don't you think so, Miss Oliver?'

'Oh, yes,' Elisabeth said.

'Americans are making money so fast they need us to help them spend it,' said Olivia.

Pixie Fairhaven did not seem offended. 'Papa has businesses on the Exchange, Miss Oliver. The Exchange is where people buy money.' She seemed to assume that Elisabeth would need an explanation. 'Isn't that just so bizarre? Why would one buy money, why not just buy things?'

'Money is just another thing,' Mrs Brion said. 'Sometimes it has value and sometimes it doesn't. The newspapers say the New York Exchange is making people too rich.'

'I love being too rich,' said Pixie simply.

'All bulls turn into bears one day,' said Olivia.

The room was quiet again, and little Toby Schroëder went on colouring by the fire. Edith brought in a tray of tea. She ignored the crockery that needed clearing. Elisabeth sipped her vodka.

'What shall you do about Lefèvre, Venetia dear?' asked Mrs Brion.

'It is depressing. I had a good deal of advice about my portrait and André said he thought it very nearly good except the head was not quite in proportion with the rest.'

'You poor, poor darling!' said Mrs Brion.

'He made me square it out,' continued Mrs Gibb. 'I can think calmly now and you'll say I'm prejudiced but I liked it better before. Lefèvre would be bad for me. They're so tiresomely narrow, they'd have us resurrecting the Academies which Douglas would adore because he can do anything he chooses, but I should die. No, I shall cancel, I think, and keep things back for the Leicester in June, where my colour will be understood.'

'How wise,' said Mrs Brion.

Pixie Fairhaven said gaily, 'Don't listen, Miss Oliver. I close my ears or I should go quite mad. Art is a mystery. Thank goodness girls like us don't have to puzzle over what it means.'

Elisabeth was annoyed at Pixie Fairhaven's assumption that they shared an ignorance of art, but it was true she hadn't a clue what or who Lefèvre was. Her mind felt slow.

'How is it you know Michael?' Olivia asked.

The room regained its sharpness. 'His sister, Rachel, is a friend of mine. In fact I'm visiting her in Kent in August and I'm hoping to see him.' Michael would not be there but it was not a lie: a part of her was always hoping. She stole a look at Mrs Brion, who had closed her eyes.

'Frankie is bereft but I expect Michael will come back to us,' said Olivia.

Mrs Brion said, 'He has work to do.'

'His letters are always vague,' said Elisabeth more loudly than she meant. She had wanted to ask where he was travelling these days but it was impossible now. 'He says he thinks of me often so I suppose that's something.'

'Indeed. It is something,' said Mrs Brion. Her voice was kind; there was no edge of falseness at all.

Olivia gave Elisabeth a slice of cake and a cup of tea. 'Your drink isn't strong, but you may like to eat something.' Elisabeth wondered if they all thought her so silly and naive that she would not know the effects of alcohol.

Pixie Fairhaven, who hadn't gone home after all, and Ingrid Schroëder were smoking coloured cigarettes in holders. Mrs Gibb and Francesca Brion said they would not smoke until the drawing was finished. No one offered a cigarette to Elisabeth.

'Miss Oliver is a nurse,' said Mrs Brion. 'Isn't that wonderful? Little children with fevers.'

'How brave,' said Venetia Gibb. 'It takes great generosity to deal with illness.'

'And selfless maturity,' added Ingrid Schroëder.

'I so admire you,' said Pixie Fairhaven. 'You girls are angels. I declare, you're positively saints.'

There was a pause in which Elisabeth realized that they expected her to speak.

She said, 'I wonder, may I have a cigarette?' The room listed gently. 'I'm not a nurse any more. I have been dismissed. My lover was a married surgeon and I told him what I thought of him for lying about his wife.'

The words unravelled smoothly and it was pleasant to have them listening.

'It was during a consultation, actually, with two doctors and a group of nurses – and Matron of course. He asked Matron to ask me to leave the room, so I told him I wasn't deaf or foreign and could follow his request without translation, and did he not remember that I understood him perfectly in his bed in Pimlico when he gave instructions on fellatio.'

She could hear her voice clear and steady, ringing slightly like a bell. 'Matron said I'd said enough. That was two weeks ago. I'm not a nurse any more.'

The quiet hissed softly in the room. There was the tiny scratching of Toby Schroëder's crayoning.

Pixie Fairhaven held a cigarette in one hand and a piece of cake in the other, both halfway to her lips. 'Italian is such a musical language, I always think,' she said. 'I'm so looking forward to Amalfi.'

# 12

After Michael left Amsterdam, he worked his way though France and Italy, earned his ticket on a steamer from Sicily to Spain, and walked inland, westwards, toiling up the baking mountain roads to Madrid. At the Prado, the work of Goya and Velázquez burned his eyes with beauty. Picasso was more sorrowful a painter than he had realized and Dalí more cunning and more arrogant.

Michael travelled north again, over the Pyrenees to Languedoc, where he stayed for several months in a loft above a bakery. The village was called Mazamet, high on a rocky hillside above the River Tarn.

He had a lover, a young widow called Delphine, and he grew fond of her. It was more than a year since he had left the house in Neate Street.

He made a painting of the square in Mazamet and what he saw in that picture – or could almost see – made him long for home. In the spring of 1929, he decided to return to England.

Delphine walked with him as far as the railway which ran east to Narbonne. They said their goodbyes without regret. 'We have been happy, I think. You will be a good husband, Michel. She will be content.' They kissed fondly and chastely, and Michael watched Delphine walk back up the dusty track to Mazamet, her dark head bowed with the effort of the steep climb. She did not look back.

At the station in Narbonne, he bought a ticket to Paris and as the train went north through France the crags and precipices became wooded hills and pastures. The southern colours were left behind.

On the luggage shelf was the hunting rifle given to him by Madame Baumanière. In his rucksack was the painting of Mazamet which had shown him he should go home.

A silver locket was in his jacket pocket and he held it in his hand, turning it over and smoothing his thumb over the engraved letter E.

He watched France moving by the carriage window, remembering a snowy afternoon in London two Christmases ago: Elisabeth walks beside him. She holds a book wrapped in brown paper against her chest, and when he looks down he sees her copper hair against the dingy cloth of her cape. Her cheek, the tip of her nose and her lips are just visible, but the memory doesn't move, she does not look up and he cannot see her face.

He calculates that he will be home in three days and even so short a time is hard to bear.

•   •   •

The mornings in Mazamet were always cold until the sun was high. The plane trees in the square were still and shreds of mist hung in the leaves and blurred the ridges of the tiled roofs. The granite cliffs rising up behind would be invisible, and from somewhere high up on a ledge muffled bleats and the clop of bells would sound as if goats were airborne in the mist.

At this hour, the old men who played boules and argued at the tables had not risen yet, only Madame Baumanière, squat as a jug and dressed in mourning would sweep her step with a twig broom. Later she would sit on a chair by her door peeling vegetables, crocheting or plucking a bird, her knees apart, her feet at ten to two, with barely room on her sloping lap for her bosom and her work.

Michael cleared away the leaves and dust with his sleeve when Delphine brought a tray to his table: coffee, bread, goat's butter and cherry jam. She shivered. '*Il fait froid ce matin, Michel, n'est ce pas?*' She leaned down to kiss his hair.

Delphine's daughters in their brown school coats and berets waited by the fountain for the bus to Carcassonne. They played hopscotch on the bald earth and puffs of dust rose from under their feet – *un, deux, trois* – and their satchels thumped on their backs. 'Look, Maman!' Eugenie cried. 'And me!' shouted Augustine. Delphine tucked the tray under her arm and watched.

Four years ago, Delphine's husband had fallen into a ravine while out hunting. He broke an arm, a rib, and cracked his skull. He seemed to recover but there was pressure on his brain, the doctor at Narbonne had told Delphine, and this accounted for her husband's agonizing headaches, the rages and the melancholia.

Gradually, he began to lose his speech and his coordination. His memory and his temper worsened. Sometimes he did not know his children, or Delphine, and her heart was numb with sorrow for the man he used to be. He tried to beat the pain out of his head and when he died his face was grey with bruises.

The darkest grief had passed. Delphine told Michael she had no wish to marry again and had become accustomed to the weightlessness of solitude. She had her daughters and the people in Mazamet were kind, but she missed the smell of a warm shirt and the level conversation of a man. She missed the leaden dreamless sleep that comes after sex.

She invited him to visit in the afternoons from time to time when her daughters were at school. 'This is our consolation, Michel,' she told him. 'We are both lost, both separated from the one we love. We are the same.'

'Am I lost, Delphine? Perhaps I am in love with you.'

'In a different life, this might be so, but I see it in your eyes. I feel it in you, Michel. There's a woman, a girl you can't forget although you run away. You fight it.'

He kissed Delphine's smooth sunburned shoulder. 'She's here. She's you, Delphine.'

'No, Michel. Not me.'

Sometimes in the evenings, Delphine sent Eugenie with a can of stew and a carafe of wine for Michael. He slept in a loft above the boulangerie, which cost him nothing in return for lighting the bread oven at four each morning and keeping out the rats.

He had not planned to stay in Languedoc and had been on his way to Switzerland – the scalding heat of Spain had made him long for ice on his breath – when the letter from Rachel reached him.

The post was delivered to the café. One morning, Delphine had brought the letter out to him along with his bread and coffee.

*Dear Michael*

*I didn't know where you were or I would have written sooner. Your letter addressed to Neate Street wasn't forwarded straight away so that's why I've been so long in replying. I tried to find you and no one knew where you had gone. Dad has died. Mum sold the house. Nanna Lydia sold her cottage too and we're all living in a new Bungalow (house with no upstairs) in Hythe. In case you don't know, Hythe is by the sea in Kent. Mum said she'd had enough of Peckham. I work in Folkestone, in a dress shop for couture.*

*Dad passed away in his sleep on December the 30th. It was a Tuesday. Nanna found him when she went up with his tea. I don't know what to say to you. There's no point in coming back now. The funeral was nice. Lots of the neighbours stayed off work and people from the shops came. Mr and Mrs Cole from the grocer's were there, Mr Faley and Eric from the fishmonger's, Mr and Mrs Almond and Dottie from the hardware shop. The church was nearly full. Ada Hobbs and her sister Glynis from Eltham did the sandwiches. There were lots of people Dad knew who I'd never even heard of.*

*You'll be wondering if we're all well and we are, although Nanna is not so sprightly as she was. Tell me where you're going next.*

*Love,*
*Rachel*

He stared at the words until they blurred. When he looked up, midges sparkled in the sunlight and a wasp struggled in the cherry jam. Delphine put a cognac in his hand.

• • •

The rattling school bus took Eugenie and Augustine away. '*Au revoir, mes enfants!*' Delphine called to them and waved. She poured a cup of coffee for herself and sat with Michael while he ate.

On the other side of the square, Madame Baumanière settled herself on her chair with a shawl around her shoulders and the first dabs of pale sunshine illuminating her silver hair. Her neat foot kicked at a cat sauntering too near, and missed.

'*Manges-tu*, Michel. You are too theen.' She cackled, sucking in the pads of her cheeks to show the hollowness of his.

*Michel Roz, the Enlishman*, was an angel, Madame Baumanière told everyone. Because of him she would live out her years content because her husband's face would never be lost, even if her mind wandered like an imbecile goat as his had done.

The night Monsieur Jean Baumanière died, Michael had been woken by the noise of banging on the wooden steps to his loft and there was Delphine with a lantern, standing in the snow and holding Eugenie's hand.

'Quick, Michel. Monsieur Baumanière, he . . .' Delphine looked helplessly at her daughter. '*Eugenie, explique à lui.*'

'Is he ill?' Michael asked. 'Should I fetch a doctor?'

'*Monsieur Baumanière est mort,*' said Eugenie. Her eyes were swimming with tears and her English had deserted her. '*Vous devez venir, Michel.*' She pulled his hand.

At the house, the body of Jean Baumanière was already dressed in a Sunday suit. The bed on which he lay was newly made with an embroidered coverlet and starched pillows. Madame Baumanière leaned over her husband, combing his thick white hair, humming softly. The lamps were lit and the room was too warm in spite of the snow outside.

'Madame says the window must be closed until you make a picture,' Eugenie whispered. 'Or he will go to heaven and his face will be empty.'

Michael fetched his paints and Jean Baumanière was propped higher on his pillows. A coin was taken from his eyelid and his wife indicated that Michael must look at the colour of her husband's eyes. She lifted the papery lid. '*Oui, oui. Brun.*' She patted Michael's hand, and then she demonstrated how the picture would be: her husband would stand behind this high-backed chair in which she would be sitting. His hands would be on her shoulders, *comme ça*. Give him again the Languedoc sun on his skin, she told Michael; Jean was not always the colour of a plucked goose.

The tableau would come later but the face must be done with haste before he departed. Here she laid her hands on Jean's chest, then up, as if she was throwing something in the air. It seemed his soul would not rise from his body gently like a waft of smoke but would fly up wildly like a bird when the window was opened. She could keep him here till dawn but after that he might not leave her at all, and he must. At this Madame Baumanière pressed her hand to her throat. Michael must be quick.

The portrait of Jean Baumanière's face was finished before sunrise.

In the days that followed, Pierre Cordot, the baker, posed for the figure on which the face of Jean Baumanière was to be superimposed. Delphine sat as the young and slender Madame Baumanière, and Michael copied the face from a faded photographic portrait of Emanuelle Baumanière at eighteen.

No, said Madame Baumanière, it didn't matter that there would be a discrepancy in the ages of the faces. For Jean, she wanted to be beautiful again. He was as handsome to her now as the day they married, so the picture was as it should be.

*

After the burial, Pierre Cordot asked Michael to paint a picture of his sister holding a tray of perfect brioches with her favourite hound at her side. Then Delphine's brother wanted a portrait of himself and his wife together with their grown-up children. A son who had died at the age of five would be included in the group.

The Mayor requested a landscape with goats to send to his daughter who had gone to live in Paris. Michael must paint the rosemary, gorse and lavender in bloom together, although they never were, and there should be snow on the rocky summits in the distance with the silhouette of a Cathar ruin. These things would bring his daughter home to Languedoc.

Michael became a maker of pictures. He was not an artist here. There were no theories on light and colour in Mazamet but only likenesses that must be accurate. He followed his customers' instructions and made the images exactly as they requested. This was his work; there was no signature or need for one, any more than a baker would sign his bread.

He knew these paintings would not be liked at Frankie Brion's soirées and would be considered sentimental. They were not provocative, nor did they say anything intelligent or witty. They did not catch the spirit of the modern age.

But these pictures were more honest, it seemed to Michael, than anything he had ever painted in London.

One day he paints a picture for himself. He leans a canvas on a café table and begins.

It shows the village square. Sunlight spots the ground beneath the planes with lemon and lavender-blue. The stone walls of the café are blocks of sour green and ochre, and the awning casts blue-black shade with some strokes of rose that are Delphine's dress as she stands in the cool.

A young man with black hair is sitting at a table but the figure is overlaid by discs of multicoloured light which filter through the leaves. He is leaning back in his chair, waiting. His arm rests on the checked tablecloth.

One side of the picture – the buildings across the square – is greenish underwater shadow; the black rectangles of doors, the aqueous glimmer of the windows. A figure, the black of grapes, is Madame Baumanière, who sits against the deeper black with reddish dabs of plucked feathers speckling her lap and the ground around her feet.

The other side, between the Mayor's house and the boulangerie, is bleached blue sky.

The figure of a woman is on the brow of the road that climbs up to the square. The sun is high and she has hardly any shadow. If she were nearer, her dress would have a flower print like the cotton dresses Delphine wears, but at this distance it is creamy white.

The woman's long bright auburn hair is tangled by the wind and her dress is blown around her legs. She holds it down, her hand flat against her thigh. With her other hand she holds her sunhat clamped down hard so it doesn't blow away. The brim is lifting with the breeze but her face is in shadow.

Michael wonders if he could paint out the hat or bring the figure nearer, but the picture is complete and the face is hidden.

'Oooh, très belle,' breathes little Augustine, her chin at his elbow. She has been skipping and is breathless. 'Eugenie!' she shrieks to her sister. 'Viens voir. C'est une peinture de la femme de Michel.'

'No, Augustine,' says Michael. 'It's just a woman.'

Eugenie runs across to look. 'She comes here, votre femme?' she asks him.

Madame Baumanière is struggling from her chair. She smirks delightedly when she sees the picture. 'C'est l'amour. La fiancée!'

'The figure is to balance the composition,' Michael tells her. They crowd in and he has no room. Augustine has oil paint on her face.

Delphine comes across and stands close beside him. She puts her hands on his shoulders and he feels her warmth through his shirt. 'Ah, oui,' she says softly.

They all understand, even Eugenie and Augustine; an artist gives himself away.

He had thought he left her behind in London but now he understands that she has been with him all along – through the weeks at Eddie Saunders's farm in Kent, on the ferry to Calais, in Amsterdam, on the journey south to Sicily, then Spain, and then north across the Pyrenees to Mazamet, where he sees her walking in the sun with the wind tangling her hair while he sits waiting.

• • •

On the morning he leaves, Augustine and Eugenie give him drawings they have made themselves. Augustine: a goat with a bell. Eugenie: the café with herself standing at the door. Delphine hands him a heavy package tied up with a cloth. It is food for the journey and looks enough to get him back to London.

His rucksack has so much tied around it he has trouble lifting it on to his shoulders, and now Madame Baumanière wants to give him something too. She beckons from her door. He puts the rucksack down again.

They are both used to miming with some words that might or might not be understood and conversation is easy with her now.

It is so dark inside her house after the sunshine in the square, for a moment he cannot see. She pats his sleeve and points into the shadows. He wonders if he will have the strength to carry whatever it is she is about to give him.

'*La carabine*,' she says, and jabs him in the chest. '*Pour toi.*' She quivers with emotion and wrings her veiny hands. He lifts the hunting rifle from its iron rest on the wall above the fireplace and she sucks her teeth as if he might drop it on the floor and break it.

For a rifle, it is beautiful. It has been oiled, the strap is supple. The polished stock is inlaid with silver and mother-of-pearl in a design of flowers and trailing ribbons. The delicate decoration suits this graceful deadly thing. He rests the butt on his foot and holds the barrel upright. The rifle is almost as tall as Madame Baumanière.

He has never held a firearm before and he lifts it and holds it across his chest. He handles it awkwardly although he feels the pleasing balance of the weight. The old lady snuffles into her handkerchief and talks quickly; he understands he must take the rifle because she will not go hunting. Jean is dead and the rifle must not die too.

Afterwards, she waddles over to the bureau, batting a cat from a chair on the way, and returns with something in her hand. It is a silver heart-shaped locket, as fat and smooth as an egg, and it hangs on a piece of tattered lace. On it is engraved a curling letter *E*.

'*E – c'est moi*,' she says. '*Emanuelle.*' Then she pulls at his sleeve and puts the locket in his hand. '*Pour Elisabeth.*'

• • •

On the train to Paris, he shared his food with a family travelling in the same compartment and found he'd learned enough French to understand most of what they said.

'You are leaving France? Are you mad?' the husband teased good-naturedly. 'I've heard the English have no wine except in church. How can they be anything but miserable.'

'Look at his face, Hervé,' the wife said. 'It isn't only wine that warms the soul.'

The parents and their three plump fair children ate the bread and pâté Delphine had made and afterwards the children and the father slept, all toppled sideways on the wooden bench against the mother, who was pressed against the window. Although the weight of the four of them was pinning her in her seat, Michael could see that her thoughts were free with her family not needing her for a while. She gazed out at the landscape wheeling by.

The afternoon wore on, and from time to time Michael got up and paced the corridor, leaned out of the window to smoke a cigarette. He tried to doze but his muscles ached with restlessness.

A sleeping child had slid over on to the mother's lap, and with her arms free now the woman took some knitting from a cloth bag at her side. Michael tried to fix his attention on the deftness of her fingers and the needles clicking a different rhythm to the thudding train. She sensed him watching and looked up. 'The journey is too slow for you, I think. You are impatient.' She regarded him, her knitting poised. 'There's someone who will be happy that you're coming home. This is so?'

'I've been away too long. She will have forgotten me.'

'We women have long memories. Too long. Like elephants.' She smiled. 'She will be there.' She resumed her knitting, frowning a little in the fading light.

Michael was reminded of Nanna Lydia and an afternoon at Neate Street not long before he left. They were sitting downstairs in the kitchen; Nanna was knitting and he was drawing – some saucepans or bowls, he had forgotten now.

Nanna had paused, looked up. Her spectacles were cloudy with scratches and he could not see her eyes. 'Do you know, Michael, once upon a time, I thought there might be feeling between you and Elisabeth.'

'Elisabeth?' He said it absently, as if he was engrossed in drawing.

When he offered nothing more, Nanna resumed her work. 'Old hearts are sentimental. They're deceived sometimes,' she said quietly.

He had felt annoyed. Her musings were an intrusion and he had baulked at giving her an answer because Elisabeth was already too much in his mind. He had to get away from London and from Neate

Street and no one would prevent it. If he felt something for Elisabeth – or any woman – it might be different, he told himself, but he didn't.

He had been dishonest, he knew now, dishonest even with himself.

• • •

The Paris air was soft and there was blossom on the café tables and on the pavements. Everything was a painting Michael recognized and he felt he knew the place already.

The Frenchman on the train had told him that the Gare du Nord would take him to the Channel coast, but couldn't say where this station was. Michael thought he would walk for a while then ask for directions.

The sky was as blue and clean as in the South. He walked in the sun beside the pale green Seine, choppy with the wash of pleasure boats and river steamers. He had thought that if he ever came to Paris, he would climb the hill to Montmartre and the Place du Tertre, as painters did, but he wanted to see these places with Elisabeth. They would come back to Paris together.

He turned off the street and into a covered market hall. Sunlight came through the rust holes in the roof and the place was warm and shadowy. He passed crates of sleeping rabbits and ducks, and underwear and tools, lace and cheese. He bought a bag of peaches. The empty stalls still gave off smells of fish or spices or leather. A butcher sawing a carcass admired the hunting rifle and was disappointed that it was not for sale.

Out on the pavement again, Michael was on a wide boulevard. It was late afternoon and the street was almost empty of carriages and motorcars. A few pedestrians walked in the shade. Ahead of him, a woman in black was carrying a basket on her arm and a small boy in a *tablier* with chalk dust on the sleeves trotted after her eating the crust of a baguette almost as tall as him. There was a milk cart under the trees with the horse resting in the shade, one hind hoof tipped on its rim and its eyes closed, and the little boy stopped to stroke the horse's nose. The woman went on past the tables of a café and across the street.

Michael hesitated, not knowing if he should call the woman back or hurry the little boy to catch up. The child was still beside the dozing horse, stroking its drooping ears, and Michael was aware of someone also watching from a nearby café table. A blonde young woman in a purple summer dress and heeled shoes sat smoking.

Suddenly the child saw that his mother had gone on without him and he dropped the bread, startling the horse awake. He ran after her. The baguette was left on the pavement.

'You'd better run after him, Michael,' the woman at the table called out. 'I'd be flat on my face if I tried to sprint in these.'

# 13

Mr Mole liked to collect the post each morning. He also liked to fetch coal, bang in nails, sharpen knives, lift weighty objects and close doors. There was very little Mrs Oliver and her daughters had not learned to manage themselves that Mr Mole could do, but Mrs Oliver, girlishly, was grateful and admiring.

Most of all, Mr Mole liked to walk with Mrs Oliver on his arm, Mrs Oliver who was now his wife.

Elisabeth wondered if the thrill of a troublesome daughter's double success – worthy employment and also removal to Bavaria – or the shock of a good daughter's dismissal and shame, or the collision of the two things in a month, had tipped her mother off balance and into Mr Mole's embrace. Whatever the reason for the change of heart, Mrs Oliver had surrendered and Mr Mole was touchingly elated.

The ceremony was simple. Elisabeth was a witness and so was Mr Mole's second cousin, Mr Baer. There was no Karen now whose eyes she must avoid, and so no risk of giggling when either of the gentlemen's names was spoken.

After the ceremony, the four of them, Mr and Mrs Oliver, Mr Baer and Elisabeth, had a lunch at the Trafalgar Hotel in Greenwich in a sunny Georgian room overlooking the mud banks of the Thames.

'Please call me Herbert, Elisabeth my dear. We're family now,' said Mr Mole.

Elisabeth was annoyed although why she didn't know.

Mr Mole, Herbert, brought a piano to the house in Catford, and also kindly warmth. He kept the fires fed and the doors closed. He played his piano cheerily and sometimes managed to coax shy Mrs Mole to sing.

Elisabeth liked him more than she thought she would. He was courteous but not colourless or dull. He was uncluttered in his mind, steady of heart and clear of purpose. He had set his cap at prickly Mrs Oliver and was certain of his judgement; beneath the spines was the woman he would love.

But happy Mrs Mole could not quite usurp grieving Mrs Oliver and Elisabeth still felt the cold front when they were alone without the warmth of Mr Mole. Elisabeth was the reminder and the residue of the desolate past and also, now, a failure in her own right.

She had thought she would never live at home again and now here she was, without work, without Karen, and in the company of two newly-weds. The days were busy with keeping out of the way, and empty except for writing letters of application which were rarely answered. Her references were not good.

Mr Mole, Herbert, tried to soften her disappointment when there was nothing in the post. 'They don't hurry themselves these days, my dear, not even when they should.'

So she was surprised to receive two items in one delivery. The first was a postcard of the Eiffel Tower, addressed in Karen's wild sprawling script: *This is where I am!!! love K xxx*.

The second was on lilac headed paper and from Mrs Ingrid Schroëder: would Miss Oliver consider the position of nanny to Tobias, aged seven? And also would she agree to live in rooms at their house in Richmond? There would be no other duties but she might be needed day or night as Toby was frequently poorly.

There would be no uniform and Miss Oliver would take her meals as family unless she had a preference for eating downstairs. The household was informal. Also she – Ingrid – and her husband, Mr Bruno Schroëder, often travelled with the older children and foreign air did not suit little Toby's health. At those times Miss Oliver would have sole charge of him.

Mrs Schroëder's handwriting was plain, and tilted downwards on the thick laid paper. Elisabeth had not left a card with Mrs Brion so how had Mrs Schroëder found her? Then she remembered that Mrs Brion had generously asked her driver to take Elisabeth all the way home to Catford on the day in April when she had visited.

The memory of that afternoon was vague. She could recall only an impression of Mrs Schroëder and all she knew of Toby was his white-blond head. How odd that Mrs Schroëder remembered her at all.

The letter continued:

*Would you perhaps be interested in this arrangement? My husband would be reassured to have Toby in the care of a proper nurse and, for myself, I admit*

*to finding most nannies fearfully dull; the afternoon in April when I met you
at my sister's house was very lively.*

*I have made up my mind so there's no need for us to meet again unless you
would like to view the house. It is ordinary, nine bedrooms and gardens on
the river. You have a pretty little sitting room for your private use on the south
side of the house, which sadly does not have a river view, but I'm sure we can
alter our arrangements if you especially enjoy waterscapes with coots.*

*Americans and various people often stay. Do you object to peacocks? We
have no religion. We celebrate Thanksgiving but do not serve poultry or pork
then or at any time of year. Neither do we eat sea creatures with shells. Toby
has a pony and a telescope. Is that sufficient information?*

*We are in Italy in August and September, and Tobias will remain in
England, so I should be extremely grateful if you would be here at your
soonest ever convenience. You might let me know when you plan to come and
I shall send a car.*

*Yours, in anticipation,*
*Ingrid Schroëder*

Elisabeth looked up from the letter to see her mother and Mr Mole watching from across the breakfast table. 'I have a job,' she said. 'In Richmond.'

'Congratulations, my dear Elisabeth, at last someone has some sense.' Mr Mole put his hand over hers. His eyes were watery with gladness, and he turned to Mrs Mole. 'We'll miss her, will we not, dearest?'

'Richmond isn't far,' her mother said.

• • •

The Schroëders were modern parents. There was no routine for the older children, who stayed up late and were completely at ease in adult company. Bruno Junior, Annabelle and Bonnie May were not under Elisabeth's supervision and barely spoke to her.

The house in Richmond-upon-Thames was always full of visitors: artists and actors who were friends of Mrs Schroëder, and manufacturers and businessmen with their wives who were friends of Mr Schroëder.

The wives ascertained within minutes that Elisabeth was the nanny, and although they might forgive Bruno's eccentric wife for this odd arrangement of staff mingling with the dinner guests, they did not forgive Elisabeth. They ignored her. The husbands flirted and seemed to find her a charming oddity of Schroëder's London home.

Elisabeth sat at the dining table each evening and listened to conversations that gusted through her head like air through an empty room. She realized she knew nothing about art or business, or politics or the world in general.

She learned to identify which guests were artists and to sit with them at table so as not to annoy the businessmen's wives. Artists included writers and musicians but were mostly painters. She also learned what was boring or bourgeois and never to admit to liking it. She must like jazz and drinking, and she should not like money or manners. She should despise pretentiousness in all its forms and this included most artists up to now and also their art, but not Art, which was the greatest thing.

Understanding business was more difficult in that it seemed bound up with politics and weather. The President of France could dictate the price of coal in Britain, and apparently the Socialists in Germany and a hurricane in the Caribbean could determine how many people bought washing machines. She wondered how Mr and Mrs Mole in Catford were affected.

The Schroëders and their friends were not taken in by gossip in the newspapers and were above the petty worries of most ordinary people who thought no further than their own front door. Elisabeth was grateful for the luck which had brought her to this sophisticated household; a thread from Rachel to Mrs Brion to Mrs Schroëder (with a brief detour to the nurses' dormitory and Mr Caffin's flat in Pimlico) had led her to this fortunate life.

The holiday in Kent might have been an unwelcome interruption but Elisabeth was glad to be leaving the Schroëders' house for a while. Something had happened and the hurt of it lingered. It concerned a young man who had come to dinner.

She knew he noticed her when he came into the room. He was thin and tall with wide-open eyes and a kind of prettiness that wasn't girlish, more like a starving angel. Elisabeth tried not to stare.

He was training as an illustrator at the Chelsea Art School and his name was River. He made woodcut prints and also little watercolours which were of no significance, he said, just pictures to go with other people's words. He sat next to her at dinner.

He sweated and quivered like a racehorse but his presence at her side was a barricade against the onslaught of conversation; there was a debate on the Society's exhibition and crossfire concerning the dollar's stability abroad.

Suddenly he said, 'You're very patient, Elisabeth.' She started and spilled wine on to her halibut. She had been wondering when he would speak to her. 'It must be annoying to see through all this.' He spoke so quietly she thought she must have misunderstood.

'All of what?' she said.

'Our insistence on dignifying our little scrawlings. And their stupidity' – here he nodded towards Mr Schroëder and his friends – 'in thinking money will keep them safe.' Close to, she saw he had a scar through his eyebrow and another on his chin. 'We should have learned, but we still believe the war was no fault of ours. There'll be another in a year, or ten, or twenty. We'll be too busy with ourselves again to see it coming.'

'I'm sure that won't happen.' She leaned away. She had wanted him to speak to her but now he was too close.

'We so-called artists talk as if we do something necessary when the world is already perfect and complete. How foolish we must seem to you.'

'How do you know I'm not an artist?' she asked a little sharply. She thought she looked very much like the other women at this end of the table.

'Oh, you're not,' he said. 'Eyes like yours could not be deceived – and they must be if you were one of us.'

He must be teasing. 'Mr Freud would say that what we see is shaped by what we are,' she countered happily. It was nice to have something to say at last. She had learned to make statements rather than ask questions, as was the custom in these exchanges.

'Ah, yes, the Viennese witch doctor. He's not the fool he's made out to be,' River said. 'And neither are you.'

Was this a compliment? 'I'm not sure I understand you,' Elisabeth said. She was pleased with the playfulness in her voice but something inside was teetering on an edge.

He paused a moment. 'There is nothing to understand other than what you are,' he said. 'People like us will make you forget even that, Elisabeth. You should not be here.' And he turned away.

Pixie Fairhaven's voice shrilled from across the table. 'I see you flirting, Mr River, with that dear sweet girl and now she's gone quite scarlet.'

His voice: 'River, Miss Fairhaven, not Mr River. If Elisabeth is too warm, it is not on my account.'

Pixie: 'She's delicate, Mr River. She is not equal to the likes of you.'

River: 'Indeed. That is her charm, and my loss, Miss Fairhaven.'

Pixie squawked delightedly and Elisabeth heard the conversations around the table sailing on. She stared down at her hands holding her knife and fork, at the tortoiseshell and ivory bracelets hanging from her wrists which Ingrid Schroëder had given her. She had been sure the young man liked her but it seemed he didn't. The humiliation was deep, but deeper still was her dismay in realizing that she did not like him. She had hoped so much she would.

There must be another man who could make the air feel heavy on her skin when he was near, and light settle in her hair after he gave her tea, and time hang on a silver thread because he almost touched her.

Elisabeth had told herself a thousand times that there was nothing special about Michael Ross and the snowy afternoon in Fitzroy Street. He did not like her then and he would not ever like her.

He had seen in her – as Mr River had seen – the tedium and ignorance of the house in Catford, the brown paintwork, the chrysanthemums and crocheted antimacassars. Michael had been kind and then was bored with her. That was all.

'Elisabeth? Elisabeth!' shrilled Pixie. 'Pay Mr River no heed! He is teasing you, don't you see? Elisabeth? Come back to us! I declare, she's in a dream!'

'No,' Elisabeth said. 'I'm here.' She was sitting in the candlelight of Mrs Schroëder's dining room, the crystal goblets, red and gold with wine, sparkled on the damask tablecloth amongst tureens and platters. People were laughing and gesticulating, or leaning together comfortably and talking. She felt the confidence, the sharpness of their minds and the ease of these people who had money.

If he could see her now, Michael would know he had been mistaken; she was not naive or silly or ignorant. And the young man at her side was mistaken too: she was not forgetting, but finding who she was.

Bruno Schroëder stood up to propose a toast: 'To the President and to His Majesty the King. To freedom and to friendship!'

The gentleman on Elisabeth's other side struck his glass with a spoon and proposed a toast – 'To the busting up of sophistication in all its forms' – at which the artists crashed their wine glasses recklessly.

But isn't sophistication good? Elisabeth thought as she raised her glass.

Francesca Brion smiled across the table.

# 14

The barrier was open for the Folkestone train and George Mander boarded and closed the door. The quiet inside the corridor was like the furthest edge of home: the din and the bitter exhalations of the engines were shut out and the next air he breathed would carry the grassy, watery scent of Kent. There would be birdsong and bleating sheep.

He slid open the door to a compartment and lifted his hat to a young woman sitting by the window with a child asleep on the seat beside her. She had bright auburn hair and the style of clothing some women liked these days – unmatched and colourful, and gracefully shapeless. Her buttoned shoes were blue, her stockings were pale yellow and her ankles were pretty. He chose the corner by the corridor.

The prospect of a peaceful journey home was some consolation for the wasted day and night in London. He had wanted to travel home yesterday because his mother was ill and he didn't like to be away, but they had kept him waiting for a decision on the loan he had asked for at the bank.

Two months ago he'd laid off the last worker who did not have a family to support. This pattern maker and son of an ironmaster had more skill than all the rich men round last night's dinner table put together. The young foundryman had refused to shake Mander's hand, and two days later he sent back in an envelope the three extra pound notes put in with his final wages. He was going to his sister in Liverpool, he said; he did not want charity.

The war was long over but the poison of it was still destroying things. These days men were being killed with shame instead of bayonets and gas.

Unless there was a miracle, it was only a matter of time before the foundry would be forced to close; for ten years it had been sinking and for four of those the books had shown a loss. Like many others, the business was being wrecked by foreign imports.

Mander felt the train move and hadn't been aware that he had closed his eyes. Last night he had been invited to a club with men he used to call his friends. The brandy had made his head sore and the odour of cigars hung on his suit and in his hair. Last night even his hair seemed proof of his failure. At almost forty he was grey but no balder than when he was a boy of twelve. Coll Grogan, a weedy weeping boy from his dormitory at school and now a cloth importer, had tugged at Mander's hair and asked him if he'd shot it or caught it in a trap. There had been honks of drunken laughter. Every man round the table, bankers, traders, property developers, every man was balding. It seemed to Mander that he should have lost his hair to make his profit.

He would lose the foundry, that was almost certain. His father and his grandfather had worked to build it and he was watching it decline. When he left university, it had seemed too brutal and ungrateful to tell his father he had no interest in making gates and railings, or fire grates or parts for machines. He knew he'd have to wait a while, then ask to learn some other line of work. He wanted to travel. A year later the war began and the small decisions a young man could make about his life were gone.

He did not enlist although he wanted to. He was needed at the foundry and this excused him active service, for which his parents were thankful. It was the beginning of a path that led nowhere. He lived at home, worked at the foundry, was introduced to his father's club in London, his father's bank, his father's friends. He lost touch with the Kentish boys he knew. Most of them were dead.

He met women from time to time: Constance at the British Library, he lunched with when he was up in town; Lilly Stephens, a divorcée who occasionally invited him to join a theatre party; Dorothy, a widow and the daughter of his mother's friend. Dorothy was not expecting love, she told him bleakly, she wanted only kindness and companionship. He – the fool he was, he thought – still believed he might find more.

The years disappeared behind him, the business slowed gently to a halt. Although he understood logically that the foundry's decline was not his fault, he had always known somehow that it would fail when it passed to him.

His mother had no idea how bad things were and he hoped he'd never need to tell her. Her interest in the present had died years ago and now she lived in tangled memories. She'd forgotten her dead daughter born two years after him, and her brother who had died at Sebastopol, and the husband who had grown tired of her.

The parcel on the luggage rack was a gift for her. It was *Touring Scotland*, a new board game he'd bought from Hamleys in Regent Street. Agnes would be eighty-two next week and the only thing she ever asked for were games with dice.

The train rocked and his mind drifted as it often did to uneasy thoughts of the freedom he would have when she died. He would sell the house and what was left of the foundry, and travel where no one would know him and there'd be nothing pressing him.

He thought of his tenant, Eddie Saunders, a man who had lost a wife and child. Saunders's life was herding cows, mending fences, shearing sheep, and Mander envied him. Despite his tragedy, Saunders seemed to have found contentment. Mander did not regret giving the land to Eddie Saunders – it was the only truly impulsive thing he'd ever done – but wondered why he'd never thought to use the land himself.

He was woken by a thud that was a half-dream of his briefcase falling from the rack. He opened his eyes and the young woman in the carriage was bending down to pick up a picture book.

'I'm sorry,' she said. 'Toby's book – I dropped it.'

It was the first time he'd looked at her face. She had grey eyes and freckles, and looked barely old enough to have a child of six or seven. She could not be more than twenty. 'I'm so sorry we disturbed you,' she said. The child was awake, leaning into her.

When they changed for the branch line, there were no porters around and he carried her travelling bag from one train to the other. She followed behind him, holding the boy's hand.

At Hythe there was someone waiting for her. He heard her call out, 'Rachel!' and a young dark-haired woman hugged her and kissed the little boy. He heard the women talking and laughing as he walked to the exit.

The few passengers for the halt at Hythe were dispersing. It was a soft, misty day and cold for August. The sands would be empty and the funfairs and the tea shops would be full. It was not quite twelve thirty but he wouldn't go to the foundry; he must go home because the housekeeper had agreed to stay the night in case, as had happened, he did not get back from London. She would want the rest of the day off in recompense. The afternoon and evening in the house with his mother stretched ahead of him.

He had left his bicycle propped against the railings. He couldn't bring himself to use the car when he was laying off his men. The saddle of the bicycle was wet: he wiped it with his handkerchief and strapped his briefcase to the back, but it slipped off before he'd got the buckles fastened and his paperwork scattered in the sopping nettles by the path. He cursed himself for being clumsy and for having scruples about the car.

The young woman and her friend were the last to come out of the station and the small boy, Toby, stared at him down on his knees gathering up sheets of paper. They walked past, the women still talking, out of the station courtyard to the lane to Hythe.

Mander was irritated by the staring child and the two young women chattering. He was tired of the Romney Marsh. If he could have stayed in London he would have spent the morning in a coffee house reading the newspapers, having lunch, looking at an exhibition and browsing some bookshops for the afternoon.

Then the feelings vanished as suddenly as they had come. He wished he had said goodbye to Toby and his mother to acknowledge the small encounter on the train so they might remember him, although she might have been alarmed and it was probably better that he hadn't.

This was how it was these days: he avoided doing anything that might risk embarrassment. He hated the careless slights that people seemed constantly to inflict on one another. He was less and less in company, but more and more he couldn't bear to be alone, as if his skin was too thin for the turbulence of people but also too thin to keep him warm alone. He would not have said that he was lonely but he supposed, perhaps, he was.

• • •

Mr and Mrs Schroëder and the other children were leaving for the Fairhavens' villa in Amalfi.

'I hope you shan't be bored when you've only got me,' Toby said to Elisabeth. She had packed crayons and a box of paints in his trunk, but she hoped she could persuade him to play outside when they were on holiday in Kent. Rachel had said in her letter: *The Dymchurch sands are full of little kiddies from London. You should see them: bandy ones, coughing ones, skinny ones, lame ones, all scampering and hopping about with buckets and spades even when it's perishing. Little Toby will soon have roses in his cheeks.*

'I must stay in the shade, Elisabeth,' Toby told her. 'I should be kept cool with calamine or rosewater. Sunlight inflames my skin and so does the wind.'

'Kent is wonderfully cloudy and you can walk behind me when there's a breeze,' Elisabeth told him.

Mr Schroëder arranged to have the pony taken down in the hope that Toby could be persuaded to ride. The pony would be stabled in Salt-wood with a blacksmith who used to be the farrier for the Schroëders' carriage horses before they were replaced by motorcars.

'Fenn will ride over with the pony and he'll find a nice gentle mount for you. Just call or send a lad,' Mr Schroëder told Elisabeth. She didn't say that 'calling' meant a letter or a bus ride. Nanna Lydia and Vera Ross's bungalow did not have a telephone nor did they have a 'lad' to take messages. And how Elisabeth would get up on to a horse's back was a mystery.

Ingrid Schroëder was thrilled that Toby would be staying with 'ordin-ary people'.

'I do so want my children to experience life in all its variations,' she said. 'Snobbishness is rather déclassé, I feel.'

The trunks had been sent on ahead and Elisabeth carried a travel-ling bag with sandwiches, a flask of tea and some picture books for Toby, who fell asleep before the train pulled out of the station.

A gentleman came into the carriage and sat in the corner by the cor-ridor; he put his briefcase on the rack, and also a parcel wrapped in Hamleys paper which must have been a present for his child. He lifted his hat to Elisabeth, then settled down and closed his eyes.

The guard was coming along the train, slamming doors. Elisabeth took off her coat and put it over Toby, tucking a sleeve underneath his face so the upholstery wouldn't irritate his cheek. Mrs Schroëder had given her the coat and other clothes too, dresses and skirts all loose cut and long so it didn't matter that Elisabeth was heavier and taller. Now here she was, almost like Francesca Brion – an elegant gypsy with expensive luggage and a taste for Russian cigarettes and vodka.

The train would soon be out of London and she could forget River-not-Mr-River from the Chelsea Art School, who didn't know her at all.

Toby would sleep for a while and the other passenger was already sleeping too. His jowly pleasant face was blank and peaceful. She searched in her bag for the letter from Karen which she'd had no time to read.

*Dear Little Sister*

*I've just had your lovely letter full of news. The new job sounds wonderful and I'm so happy for you, darling. Toby is such a little character, from what you say, and all those fascinating people coming and going, I almost envy you.*

*I meant to write sooner but it's so hard to settle. Here is my Big News: I'm getting married! No, don't faint – I know I said I never would, at least not for years, but I knew I was in love with Artur the first moment I saw him. I've never felt like this about anyone before, and I know in my heart, with all my heart, that he is the man I will love for the rest of my life. The wedding will be in November and Mutti Landau is helping me to choose a dress. It's being made for me.*

*You asked me if I've been well and mostly I have. Dear Doktor Hartog, who is a family friend and has known Artur all his life, was called the other week when I was poorly with swollen ankles and tiredness, but I'm better now although he said I must rest more. You'll be cross because you've been telling me this same thing for years. Yes, I know. I'm very silly, but I've promised Doktor Hartog so you can be at least a little pleased with me.*

*I'm in a rush to go out so that's all for now. I'm so happy, I can't tell you. Elisabeth darling, now I know I'd never been in love, although I thought I had. When you meet the right man, you will feel this way too.*

*Your*
*Karen*

Elisabeth looked out of the carriage window at the trees and fields. She felt nothing much about the letter. What should she feel about a husband who is Karen's? The news was like a story in a book.

There must have been a time – a day perhaps, and a moment in that day – when they cast off from the life they shared without knowing that they had. The distance between them now was more than miles and what made them sisters was disappearing. There was no Dadda and Ma any more, or pears ripening under the beds in the house in Catford.

Elisabeth tried to conjure Karen's face, which she used to know better than her own, but could catch only a glimpse, a lightning flash of blonde hair and a smile before Karen switched off the light. They have never said they love each other in all their lives, and what they are to each other is so embedded that Elisabeth can't feel it, any more than she can feel her own bones and blood.

The edginess between them tips one way into closeness and the other into fury. Elisabeth is towed along as if Karen is a blustery kite and Karen is maddened at being tethered. Elisabeth seethes because she is 'the good one', but she could be more selfish, have more fun if Karen didn't hog it all. She would fight anyone to save Karen from being hurt and in the same moment could want to punch her.

There is everything and nothing to guard against with Karen, who won't let her get away with being false even for a second, and sometimes she longs to be with Karen so much it makes her ache.

Elisabeth caught sight of her reflection in the carriage window. She was smiling. Excitement had flooded into her, anticipation with no shape and no direction, like a river that had burst its banks. So this thing can't be severed after all, and this was the comfort of it; the husband meant nothing to her but Elisabeth was happy because Karen was.

Toby woke up at Paddock Wood. Elisabeth gave him a sandwich and they looked at a picture book together. There was an awkward moment when Toby dropped his book and disturbed the man in their compartment. Elisabeth apologized and he was kind; he apologized to her for being so rude as to fall asleep.

At the change for Hythe he carried her case and they stood on the platform waiting for the branch-line train. He made courteous conversation for fifteen minutes without asking her a single question or making any reference to himself. For once she felt delicate and small. He smelled of good cigars. For the remainder of the journey he read his newspaper.

The train slowed down and Elisabeth stood up and struggled with the leather strap on the window. She pressed her face against the glass to see along the platform.

Rachel looked older – they would both be nineteen this year. They hugged each other. 'Guess what. Karen's got a husband,' said Elisabeth. 'Almost.'

'No!' said Rachel, linking arms. 'Spill the beans.'

As they left the station, they passed the gentleman gathering up sheets of paper which had fallen from his briefcase into the nettles.

The Hamleys parcel was on the saddle of an old bicycle leaning against the railings. Elisabeth thought a man like him ought to have a car.

· · ·

Vera Ross met Mander at his front door. 'You're back.'

'Hello, Vera.' He was used to her abruptness.

'We've had right old fun and games, your mother and I. Not to worry you but she had another turn at teatime yesterday. Anyway, she's upstairs barricaded in her room. You look fit to drop.'

'I'd better go up.' He put down his briefcase.

'I've heard her tiptoeing about so I know she's all right.' Vera stood squarely in his path. 'I've made you a sandwich, Mr Mander, but I shall have to go, I've got visitors coming to the bungalow.'

'I'm sorry you've had all this trouble.'

'Just look at you. London saps you dry and don't I know it. I'll make a pot of tea, then I'll be off.'

Mander tapped on his mother's bedroom door and a moment later the key turned and Agnes peered out. 'Where's Ross?' she said. Agnes was wearing a silk evening gown that matched the fawn of her skin, and an array of brooches. Her hair was swept back in its usual misty chignon, today with a Spanish comb and veil. 'Would you have a word with her, George? I sent her to her room.'

'Of course.' He'd given up explaining that Vera was not a Kentish servant girl with no Christian name or home of her own. 'Vera's made me a sandwich,' he said. 'Would you like one?'

Agnes disappeared for a moment, then came out with a marabou cape around her shoulders. 'Who's Vera?'

In the afternoon, after Vera Ross had gone, he gave his mother the *Touring Scotland* game and lost count of the number of games they played. He was tired but the pattering of the dice on the board and Agnes's impatience kept him awake. She would rap on the table with the shaker if he didn't pay attention. Her eyes were shining, and she drove the little model car along the cardboard roads fuelled by numbers on the dice.

# 15

It was nearly two years since Lydia had seen Elisabeth. She was coming for a holiday and would bring her little charge, Tobias Schroëder, a seven-year-old American.

The arrangements: Vera said she didn't mind the ladder and would sleep up in Rachel's attic. Lydia would move into Vera's room and Elisabeth would share with Rachel in Lydia's room, which was large enough for the camp bed and also next to the box room where the little boy would sleep, so Elisabeth would hear him if he woke up in the night.

Lydia was invigorated by the pressure of the jobs that must be done, the extra shopping and baking and all the beds that needed to be changed. She had always enjoyed the contemplation that chores inspire, the drift of the mind being so much sweeter when one is busy. She unfurled a sheet, smoothed and snapped the corners under. She was thinking of Elisabeth, of the first time she came to Neate Street all those years ago.

It seems, Lydia thought, that the woman inside the girl is glimpsed sometimes like the colours in a starling or the fire inside an opal. It might be a tilt of her head, a gesture of her hands, a look of understanding or annoyance much older than her years, but there she is, her grown-up self waiting for her time.

Then the girl is gone. The young woman is calamity; sullenness and hope all mixed up in a pot of vanity. She's lost the ease inside herself when she didn't know her own perfection and didn't know the harshness of the world.

But there's a time between, Lydia believed, when there could be girl and woman equally together. It's short, this time, a heartbeat in a life. It might be just a month or even days, but you breathe the moments, you watch her and you know: she is everything that she should be, she is the moon, a songbird, a quiet sea.

Lydia remembered Elisabeth when she first came to Neate Street. Rachel was past the time, and Karen even further, but Elisabeth was like water washing through the house, rinsing off the dust, illuminating colours and making the air fit to breathe again.

Vera didn't notice, blinded as she was by the dazzle of the sister, but Michael did, and Lydia still didn't understand why Elisabeth had made him fearful.

Suddenly, straightening the eiderdown, Lydia felt the odd crumpling-up of time, which happened often lately. Her memory seemed to order things according to their weight and not their placement in the past. How long was it since Michael walked away with Albert's kitbag on his shoulder? Last week was already blank – perhaps then? She could see Michael waving from the corner of Neate Street, not outside the bungalow, so that couldn't be.

Their old life in Peckham was as clear as being there again, but this morning Vera had asked Lydia to call on someone to collect something, but who and what Lydia could not for the life of her remember.

It was grief that caused this perturbation in the brain, and Lydia had seen it enough times in Peckham widows to recognize the signs. She should knit again, like they did in times of war. The pacifying clacking of the needles and orderly ravelling of yarn seemed to ravel up the mind.

The clock on the mantelpiece in the sitting room chimed twelve. The bungalow was ready, the pie and Bakewell tart were warming in the oven. Rachel had taken the day off work to meet Elisabeth, and Vera would be back from old Mrs Mander's at one.

Michael was coming too, although Lydia had forgotten how she knew or when he said he would arrive. She was certain that his fear had left him and he was on his way home to Elisabeth.

• • •

The first night, everyone was late to bed. Elisabeth undressed and got into the camp bed. The sea wind bumped the walls and across the road the tide was scrabbling at the pebbles. Vera snored softly overhead.

Rachel turned out the light. 'Right,' she said. 'I want the lot. I'm ready and don't spare the horses.'

They had pushed their beds together and Elisabeth could feel how close they were, even in the dark. London was a long way away and as she talked everything she told Rachel seemed interesting and funny, as if it had happened to someone else: the unpleasant River-not-Mr-River, and Pixie Fairhaven, the Schroëders, the beautiful Mrs Brion, who were all so rich they didn't even know it. She confessed about the treacherous Mr Caffin and what she'd said in front of Matron.

'No!' shouted Rachel. They giggled and shushed each other, biting the sheets and trying to be quiet. 'You wouldn't have the nerve to say that – did you?' Rachel squealed. 'You *did*!'

Rachel told Elisabeth about the farmer she was walking out with. 'Eddie's right for me,' said Rachel. 'Mum doesn't think much of him but she'll come round. Nanna's on my side.'

'Do you love him?'

'I will.'

Elisabeth pondered Rachel's certainty, which was so like Karen's. They didn't flounder or agonize when it came to deciding what they wanted; they seemed to cut through all the doubt and complications.

'Rachel? I wonder where Michael is.'

There was no answer. Vera snored. The silence stretched out. Perhaps Rachel had fallen asleep. Then suddenly she said, 'He's in Germany.'

'Oh, how funny that he's there too. I wonder if he's anywhere near Munich, where Karen lives. He doesn't ever write to me – not that I thought he would.'

She heard Rachel turn over and the creak of bedsprings. There was a different pause, reluctance or turning thoughts.

'What is it, Rachel?'

'It's nothing.'

'There is something. What is it?'

'I thought Karen would have told you. They met in Paris four months ago and he went with her to Munich. I had a letter from him, not saying much. You know how Michael is.'

• • •

Karen Oliver's hair was blonder than he remembered. The Paris sun lit the silk sheen of the purple dress.

'If you're not going after him, you should sit down and stop gawping at me,' she said.

He put the little boy's forgotten baguette and the bag of peaches on the table, unloaded the rucksack from his back and the rifle from his shoulder.

'I thought artists were supposed to be pale and feeble. You look as if you've been hunting bears and living in a cave.' She pushed the other chair with the toe of her shoe. 'We must celebrate. I shall buy you a drink. Oh, here's Mama, back for her bread.'

The woman had returned with the little boy, who had the rawness of a fright on his face. The woman said in French, 'Thank you, mademoiselle, monsieur. My son loves that old horse and I should have known to keep an eye on him. Say thank you, Pierre.'

'*Merci, madame*,' said Pierre. The effort made him wince and tears trickled down his face.

'Oh, darling, don't cry. Here, I have a hanky in my bag.' Karen smoothed the child's face and gave him the handkerchief. 'You keep it, just in case.' The boy held it to his nose and Michael knew it would smell of Karen's perfume. The French woman nodded her thanks again and Michael saw her notice the mismatch – his unshaven face, a rifle and a filthy rucksack, and the sophisticated English girl sitting with him.

The woman and the little boy left them, the boy skipping with the broken baguette flopping over his shoulder.

Karen signalled to the waiter to bring another glass. 'I've discovered these.' She waved her cigarette. 'Much nicer than the Woodbines Stanley used to smoke. And this too – it's like drinking aniseed balls. And, since you're about to ask, I'm on my way to Munich. I have a job and I'm being paid to stop off to do some shopping. Isn't that glorious? My train goes this evening.'

She told him about the guest who stayed at the London hotel where she was working. Old Herr Landau from Bavaria had employed her. It was luck, she said, he must have liked her face. She reached across and filled Michael's glass, spilling anis on the table. 'Now you.'

'I'm on my way home.'

'I heard about your father. I'm sorry, Michael.' She lit another cigarette. 'Death makes things clear, don't you think? It shows who you really are. When my father died, Ma blamed everyone, everything, even him. Then I realized she'd always been like that, simmering, gritting her teeth, waiting for proof the world was bad. She blamed us too, for needing her, for reminding her of Dadda – everything. Elisabeth wailed if I went out of the room. She was eight and I was ten. What a joke.' Karen filled her glass again. 'At least I know now not to waste time.' She counted on her fingers. 'I've learned that being good won't make you happy; that life isn't fair; that love should be given for nothing and not as some kind of trade; that it's better to risk it than never to know. There! You have my list.'

He had never heard her talk like this and he felt caught up with her in a way he never had before. She leaned her arms on the table. 'What a speech. Hark at me, just like one of your gloomy intellectuals. And you need cheering up. Let's talk about this later, in about twenty years – then you can tell me if I'm wrong.'

The high clouds over Paris moved across the sky, obscuring the afternoon sun, and the dazzle of colours dulled over, the air cooled and a breeze stirred around the dusty blossom on the pavement. Then sunshine bloomed again, the warmth returned, and shadows spread like blots of ink under the trees and tables.

She filled their glasses. 'Here's to us. And Paris! You can't want to go home. Surely you don't.'

'I've never wanted anything so much.'

'I tell you, Michael, I prayed to God to get away. People in London are knotted up inside. They think being miserable proves they're virtuous. Drink up. I'm paying.' She pushed the water jug towards him. 'I'm getting serious again. I swear I'll be cheerful from now on. So, tell me why you mean to die of dreariness in England?'

He could see she'd had too much to drink. They would look like a couple flirting, arguing, getting drunk together.

'I must see your sister. I may be in love with her,' he said.

Karen laughed softly, reaching across the table to tap her glass against his. 'Oh, bravo! You *may* be in love? How strange you are! But you haven't seen Elisabeth for years. You can't mean it, Michael.'

'I do.'

'How *can* you tease me? Elisabeth? The little goody-goody, the shrinking violet who's as tough as steel?' Karen laughed. Her teeth were small and perfect. 'I'll never work you out and I adore it because you never bore me. We're the same, Michael, we hate bores – and martyrs and pretenders.'

His mind was thick like honey and he felt suddenly besotted with the beautiful Paris street, the downy hairs on Karen's bare arms and the sunlight in her hair. He wanted to touch her because she was made of the same flesh as Elisabeth. 'I love her.'

Karen pushed her glass away, sat back. Something had altered in the light. 'You *are* serious.'

'Yes.'

She lit another cigarette. The sun was full on her face and she put back her head and closed her eyes. She said, 'I think you should know, Michael, Elisabeth is married.'

The shock was so swift, for a moment he didn't feel it.

'Don't spoil things for her, Michael. And I'll tell you this, it wouldn't ever have worked between you. My little sister wouldn't want a life like yours.'

'I hadn't thought that far.'

'I don't suppose you have, but I have and –'

'If she's happy, then I'm glad.' He cut across to stop more words he didn't want to hear.

Karen didn't say any more and Michael was grateful to her. Café tables along the street emptied. The waiter brought coffee. A cat had curled up on the rucksack.

The gauzy clouds were still luminous but the air had the dusk in it. They sat in silence for a time. Karen put a cardigan around her shoulders and tidied her hair. 'Walk with me to the station, will you, Michael?'

The porters were loading the luggage and Karen tried to explain that a dressing case and a travelling bag were to be taken to her compartment but the trunks should be stowed in the luggage wagon. She was annoyed at being unable to make herself understood and two liveried attendants tried to help, anxious to placate this first-class passenger.

Michael spoke to them in French, raising his voice above the din of the station. Karen was ushered by an attendant to the steps, and she turned, perhaps to say goodbye, but the noise was too much and she beckoned Michael to follow her.

They stood in the quiet of her compartment, close together in the small space beside the single bunk made up with white sheets and dark blue blankets.

'Michael, where will you go now?'

'I shall go home anyway. I should see my family.'

'Sit down for a moment. You look awful. Wait there. I'll be back in a moment.'

He sat on the bunk and the blankets gave off a quiet scent of lilac that made him think of Nanna Lydia. He was tired and his clothes were filthy. The carriage shifted and doors were slamming along the train.

He heard Karen talking in the corridor, some altercation with the attendant which she must have won because a boy struggled into the compartment with the rucksack and the rifle.

Karen was standing in the doorway. 'Come to Munich, Michael. There's no reason to go back. I have money. I'll give you plenty, and when we get there you can go anywhere you like.'

There were shadows moving although the carriage seemed still, and he looked round to see Paris sliding past the window.

'There,' she said. 'It's easy.'

·   ·   ·

It was after midnight. Munich Station was deserted except for a man in a dark coat waiting beneath a lamp and smoking a cigarette. In the light his hair was the same white-gold as Karen's.

She introduced them and although Artur Landau's English was halting, he welcomed Michael to Germany and apologized for the train from Paris arriving so late at night. Karen smiled, standing close to Landau, but he would not look at her and Michael knew the feelings that would move a man to act this way. He had seen Landau's expression when they disembarked, understanding that Karen had not travelled alone. Whatever he was feeling, Artur Landau would hide it. He asked how long Michael planned to stay.

'A couple of days. No more.'

'I'm *so* disappointed,' Karen said. 'It was such luck to meet up on the train. Artur, you'll persuade him to stay longer, won't you? Please do. Michael takes no notice of me.'

'He has plans, I am sure,' said Landau.

'Michael is a painter. There must be galleries he should visit. If you won't persuade him, then I shall tie him up and make him stay!' She laughed, one hand lightly resting on Landau's arm and the other on Michael's. 'At least a month, Michael, and you shan't argue.'

Now Landau was watching her. He was searching for more than friendship in her smile for Michael; intimacy perhaps, or guilt. She is reckless, Michael thought, or perhaps she simply doesn't think that either of us might care.

An hour ago, the wagon-lit attendant had knocked on the door of their compartment to bring coffee and to announce that the train would shortly arrive in Munich. They had got up and dressed. Karen steadied herself in the rocking carriage, leaning her hip or her foot on the panelling to put on underwear and stockings, and Michael sat on the narrow bunk and watched her, knowing she should look beautiful to him. He saw how graceful she was, the fineness of her bones under the pale even flesh. She twisted to fasten the suspenders and she smiled at him through a tangle of creamy silver hair.

When the train swayed, she fell on him and the weight of her, her breasts in silk against his chest and her thigh under his hand, made him want her again. She pushed herself away, laughing softly and scrambling up, then kneeling on the floor by her dressing-case mirror to put on earrings and lipstick. She unpacked a skirt and blouse. The purple dress she had worn in Paris was on the floor and she left it there.

When she was ready, they sat side by side, not knowing what to do for the last minutes of the journey. Michael turned off the light, pulling back the curtains, and they watched the blackness streaking past.

'I'm sorry, Michael. You shouldn't be here but I'm glad you are,' Karen said. He wanted to tell her he was sorry too, because throughout the journey the longing for Elisabeth hadn't lessened. They were silent for a while, then she said, 'I should tell you, someone will meet me at the station.'

'Then we must say goodbye now.'

'No, it doesn't matter. I shall tell him you're my friend from England, and you are.'

'He'll know, Karen.'

'I wish you loved me and I loved you,' she said. She put her hands on his face, turning him to look at her, and he kissed away her lipstick.

Now they were in Munich with another man who was her lover and Michael couldn't understand why he felt as if he was deserting her. She might be oblivious of the hurt she could inflict, but there was more tenderness and honesty in Karen than he had understood before and something made him reluctant to leave her with Artur Landau.

They came out of the station on to the empty street and Landau said, 'The journey has been long, I think.' Karen looked away and yawned. The Paris sun had disappeared from her skin and the street lamps hollowed out her cheeks. Her eyes were dark with fatigue. She hadn't slept, or eaten anything but peaches since leaving France.

Two young men were lounging against Landau's car. They were good-looking, almost beautiful, heavy and tall like Landau. They nodded to

Michael, looked at the rifle with interest, glanced briefly at Karen. Landau opened the door for her and she got in. She didn't say goodbye and perhaps she sensed she should let things be.

He lifted the rucksack on to his shoulders. Landau's handshake was fierce. 'Goodbye, Michael Ross. Good luck,' and he opened the driver's door, taking off his coat and throwing it over Karen's lap. He bent inside the car, tucking it round her, and Michael heard him say, 'It is cold in Germany, *Liebling*.' His voice was tender for the first time.

Then there was a shout, '*Monsieur! Pardon, monsieur!*' A boy in uniform came hurrying out of the station. It was the wagon-lit attendant who had served them coffee. '*Attendez-vous, monsieur!*' he called.

Landau stood up.

'I found this, monsieur,' the boy said in French to Michael. 'Your wife left it on the floor of your compartment.' He held out Karen's purple dress. 'Apologies, monsieur, it is not damaged, I hope.'

Michael took the dress, in that instant knowing he should not. He should look perplexed, say there was some mistake, but it was too late and the boy had gone.

After the briefest hesitation Landau said, 'You have friends in Munich? You have a room to stay?' He might not have noticed the dress, or perhaps he didn't understand French.

'I'll find somewhere. Thank you.' The cloth gathered easily into Michael's palm.

'Do you speak German, Michael?'

'No. None.'

'Then my friends will take you to a place for tonight. It is suitable, I think. A fair price.' Landau went around the car to the young men and flung his arms around their shoulders. There was some discussion in which Landau seemed emphatic. The two men moved away and stood waiting. 'It is arranged,' Landau said. 'You will see you are wrong in England, Michael Ross. We Germans are hospitable.' He slapped Michael softly on the back. 'Goodbye, old chap, old sport,' he said, smiling at his own joke.

He got in behind the wheel. The car drove off, turning down a side street. The sound of the engine faded.

The two young men began to argue: one seemed angry and the other tried to pacify him, and Michael wondered if they wouldn't bother to take him to a boarding house now Landau had gone. But after a few minutes they nodded to him, turned together and started walking. He pushed the crumpled dress into the rucksack and followed them. The two were shoulder to shoulder, a few yards ahead. They turned up their collars against the cold and dug their hands into their pockets.

From time to time they glanced back. Michael had no idea how far this place might be and the weariness of travel, the lack of sleep and the weight of his belongings made keeping up with them more and more of an effort.

The streets were straight and the square provincial buildings had painted plasterwork and shutters, wrought-iron grilles bolted on the windows and heavy carvings on the doors. Yellow street lamps shone thickly through the trees, and the coldness had a northern chill that smelled of earth and sap. There were no lights in the houses and no sign of people, such as open windows, or the scent of wood smoke, or a bicycle leaning on the railings. Munich could have been deserted. There was only the sound of their boots on the pavement.

The two men walked for half an hour or more, turning from street to street, until Michael was lost and had no idea in which direction they were going, then they slowed and walked on each side of him.

Nothing was said; the men looked ahead, hunched down into their shoulders, and the three of them went on walking. Michael knew they weren't taking him to a boarding house. They all understood that he wouldn't run. He couldn't pull the rucksack off his shoulders unless he dropped the rifle first. There wasn't a chance he would get away.

He wondered where they were taking him, why they had walked so far to rob him and if they would ask for money before they took the rifle – this was what they must want because he had nothing else worth stealing.

They stopped in a silent street of gabled houses set back in leafy gardens. The two men faced him and Michael saw that in spite of their size they were not much more than boys. One squared his shoulders but they both looked anxious as if they didn't know how to start.

Michael unslung the rifle and then the rucksack from his shoulders. He could run now but his back was against an iron gate. He would have offered them the rifle if he spoke German but they would take it anyway, and he felt them stoking up their anger so they weren't weakened by any doubt that he deserved what they would do. They must hate him for witnessing their fear.

Across the street, there was the sound of a door opening; a pause; then it was shut quietly and locked. The boys looked at each other as if this could still turn into a joke and they would laugh, take him to the boarding house and say goodnight.

Then one boy lunged, punching him so hard his head smashed back against the iron gate; the other kicked his legs away. As he was falling, white thoughts told him that his head was split, his knee was broken and these boy-men were flying on the joy of cruelty and wouldn't want to stop.

· · ·

On the first occasion, the body was left on the pavement; more recently, another one inside the gates. Last night they had dragged the Jew right to the front door, leaving blood along the path and on the step.

The neighbour and his son came immediately when Ruben Hartog called them. He had no strength in his arms these days, and between them they carried the man along the passage to the surgery. Hartog told his wife to keep the grandchildren and the dog inside and that Esther should throw water on the step. To beat a man outside a doctor's house might seem perverse but he knew it was another warning.

There was nothing to see of this man's face, which was swollen tight, black with bruises and split open like a gourd. They had broken his hands. What other injuries there might be would be known soon enough and might not matter.

Hartog could see he was young, this Jew, by his black hair and lean body. He had no money or papers, and nothing in his pockets except a silver locket engraved with the letter E.

## 16

It was a crush with all of them in the bungalow. Elisabeth and Toby seemed to swell their numbers by more than two, and Lydia felt the rush and busyness of guests clearing her head and carrying her on as if she was a bit of driftwood being rolled by a wave.

It was good to have a little one to look after again, and original as he was, Master Tobias Schroëder made life normal and familiar. Lydia needed to remind herself to turn in the kettle spout and the handles of the saucepans, put across the fire guard and not to leave a cup too near an edge. Anything sharp or dangerous was put away although Toby was not the kind of child to dash about or meddle with a matchbox or a knife.

He had a face that haunted you – too pretty for a boy, angelic, as if he already had a toe beyond this life. He needed sun and puddings, Lydia decided, to give him colour and some ballast, or the Dymchurch breeze would knock him flat. She had never heard a boy so confident in conversation, even paying compliments and offering opinions, which Lydia didn't think was healthy for a child. For all the indulgences he was accustomed to, it was as if he'd never been treated like a little one before. It was clear he loved Elisabeth.

And Elisabeth, still with the thoughtfulness and hesitation she used to have, but fuller now and colourful in graceful exotic clothes that Lydia had seen only in *Woman's Sphere*. Her hair was short. She smoked cigarettes like Vera and Rachel and most women did these days as something stylish and feminine, although Lydia couldn't see the appeal of breathing smoke when there was enough of that with fat dripping in the oven and fires that wouldn't draw.

The evening they arrived in Kent, Elisabeth seemed almost as she used to be. Vera made a pot of tea after dinner and Nanna and Rachel sang songs for Toby, who sat on Elisabeth's lap.

If you can't afford a carriage, forget about the marriage;
I won't be jammed, I won't be crammed
On a bicycle built for two.

'What queer words,' Toby said. 'What does "afford" mean, Elisabeth?'
Elisabeth sang too.

There's a long, long night of waiting, until my dreams all come true,
Till the day when I'll be going down that long, long trail with you.

She put Toby to bed, and not long after they all turned in too.

Lydia heard Rachel and Elisabeth giggling like they used to do as girls. Their voices kept at bay the monsters which shouldered through Lydia's mind when the bedside lamp was out. She often couldn't keep them away even if she talked to Lemuel, what with the groaning sea and cackling pebbles and the thick tar of nothingness against the window glass. But that night, the gossamer thread of Elisabeth and Rachel's whispering held Lydia floating, and she bobbed away on sleep as she'd not done in months.

She woke up to shouting seagulls and thoughts she'd not had for an age: the preparation of breakfast. Snip bacon rind, stab sausages, wipe mushrooms with the Irish linen cloth that was coarse enough to slough off the earth but would not break the skin. Elisabeth had offered to help and Lydia looked forward to the talk they would have while they worked together. Lydia would pass on some tips on coaxing little Toby into line.

But in the morning, Elisabeth's happiness had vanished and some trouble had overtaken her.

• • •

The Kentish wind bangs her hair against her ears and sounds are wavering and tinny as if they are coming through a wireless set; squealing children, a yapping dog and the skirl of gulls. Seaweed and rotting fish are sometimes at the edges of the wind but mostly the air smells of nothing and seems to fizz inside her head like liver salts.

The sand is full of colours. Elisabeth digs her fingers down and scoops a cool damp handful. She pokes through the grains and they're spangled black and purple, white and pink. The mystery is there's no yellow although the beach that stretches in both directions is the colour of straw.

The sky is white, the tide is out so far on greenish mud it's only visible by the wrinkle of a wave that barely heaves itself over the popping suds of the one that went before.

The sea is doing nothing. It's khaki to the pencil line of France. There's no passion in it. She needs foamy horses flinging up their manes to match the tempest in her mind. Karen met Michael in Paris and they went to Munich, and why shouldn't they? But why didn't Karen say? There was nothing in the postcard from Paris, and nothing in the letters since.

Toby wants to fill up the tin bucket Nanna Lydia has given him so Elisabeth claps the sand off her hands and walks with him to the sea. They labour across the soft dry sand, then the hard ridges that press into the arches of their feet. He patters in the wet beside her, worrying that he'll step on worm coils or rags of seaweed or bits of crab claw. She holds a fistful of her skirt to hoist it higher but the soaking hem slaps her legs. They walk into the wind. Ahead, the sea seems to get no nearer, while the bungalows behind them shrink to cubes of white and people are coloured dots along the promenade. Toby shivers at the emptiness.

At last they are standing in a few inches of water. The Channel is so listless they don't know where it begins. Toby trawls the bucket and suspended in the water are tiny transparent creatures with tentacles and bobble eyes. He shrieks, flings the bucket in the sea.

'That's kind of you, Toby. We should always put creatures back,' Elisabeth says, hitching up her hem again and wading for the bucket.

Now she is sitting on the sand once more and Toby digs with a spade. He has no coordination, Elisabeth observes. He can't keep the spade level and the sand keeps sliding off. He can't visualize a moat and castle so the trench he's dug and the pile of sand make no sense.

A moat, a castle and a spade. It began here. Or perhaps before.

Karen is six. She wears white bloomers, sailor pinafore and sunhat. It is hot; bleached-out sky, tawny sand, and their mother is knitting in a deckchair in a flowered dress and sunglasses. Their father lets the sun polish up his face. He has a book open on his chest, but he doesn't read or doze because Karen keeps on and on telling him he must watch.

She squats like a grasshopper, knees up, head down, and her thin legs are brown. She says Elisabeth is a piglet because she's pink and fat. Elisabeth is four. Her skin is scorched by the sun and her bare feet are tormented by prickling things in the sand.

They have dug a moat and when the sea comes in they'll stand on top of the mound that is their castle. The moat will fill up and overflow, then join the tide, and they'll be way out in the ocean. The ramparts will slide away under their feet, the towers with paper flags will topple and dissolve, and they'll screech with terror although the water is only inches deep and if they wanted they could splash to the shore any time.

Rescue will come when their father rolls up his trousers and paddles across. He says Karen doesn't need to be carried any more with those long legs but he'll swing Elisabeth on to his shoulders because she is small. He'll save her.

But not yet. They dig the moat, piling up sand for the castle, and they needn't talk because they have a system: Elisabeth works from one corner, and Karen from another.

The sea is coming. The deckchairs are moved back, resettled, their mother is knitting again, their father stands with his hands in his pockets and his summer trousers snapping in the breeze.

The sea is coming and it pushes a creamy scum ahead of it. They climb on to the castle and Karen has her arms around Elisabeth, hugging her. They shiver, wrapped together, waiting for the siege. The water sidles up, backs off. Nudges, sinks away. This time is it. The froth spews into the moat, stirs around the corners and maroons them.

The sea comes quickly now it's made a start. It's confident. They cling and squeal, trample the collapsing castle, and their bloomers are splashed, their sunhats drip. Their castle is doomed and they will drown together.

Then Karen is squealing differently, louder. She hops, pushes Elisabeth away and topples her knee-deep in the water. Karen lifts her foot, mewing. Perhaps she stepped on a shell, perhaps a stone, a piece of glass, perhaps, perhaps . . .

She stands on one leg, keening, and Dadda is coming, four strides, and here he is. 'Carry me,' Karen says, holding up her arms, and then, 'My toe hurt on her spade.' She looks coldly at Elisabeth. He lifts Karen up and carries her.

Elisabeth is alone in the circling sea which sucks at her feet, shoves her knees craftily when no one sees. Their castle has nearly gone, and real fear, not pretend, is muddling up her limbs. She will drown this time, properly, because she can't keep up with Dadda's legs scything through the water. Karen looks over his shoulder. She smirks down at Elisabeth.

It is nothing. They splash out of the sea, Karen's toe is better, the things are packed up, and they go home.

Nothing happened but something did, and this is how it has always been: moments Elisabeth can't foresee or guard against when Karen proves that things can always be adjusted to her liking. The balance between them is corrected although Elisabeth hadn't known anything was wrong.

And now, again, it's nothing. Karen saw Michael in Paris and they went together on the train to Munich. Why shouldn't they?

Elisabeth mashes sand between her palms. The day seems endless.

Karen is marrying Artur Landau and must have forgotten meeting Michael – that's why her letters never said. If she was here, she would laugh and say it doesn't matter because Michael is just someone they used to know in London and Elisabeth is tying herself in knots. She's inventing drama where there is none.

Elisabeth can't keep this thought from being pushed aside by another: Karen didn't tell her and there's a lie in the omission, a deceit that is impossible to grasp and as slippery as sand.

• • •

It had been five months since Karen arrived in Munich. She had learned some German words. '*Karte*, Hede, please. Map of Munich, *bitte*,' she said to Hede's rear and the pinned-tight coils of her yellow plaits. Hede was bending over, putting clothes away, and there wasn't a flicker of a pause in her folding. There would be no hurrying someone so substantial with so methodical a hairstyle.

At last Hede straightened up, rubbed away the bend in her back and sighed. The embroidery of alpine flowers on the bosom of her blouse lifted up and settled again. 'Ah mep?' she said. Her face was as flawless as an egg, with a puff of pink on each cheek from the exertion. Close to, there would be lupin-blue reflections in Hede's eyes of Karen's face staring up out of a mound of pillows.

'*Fund*, Hede. *Karte*. Chop, chop,' said Karen.

Hede was learning to make sense of the skinny Fräulein's flailing German. She filled the bath and laid out Karen's clothes, then went off downstairs, returning with a breakfast tray and an atlas.

'But there are no *streets* in this, Hede. A map of *München*. Oh, bother.

Oh, never mind.' Karen waved away the atlas. Not knowing how to ask for things was like being small again. There must have been a time like this long ago when the world was made of wild things that didn't answer to a name. It was lonely when the sounds you made were gibberish to everyone. No wonder babies cried so much.

Artur was the only one who understood. He was teaching her to summon all the skulking, untamed things: like hairbrush, *Haarbürste*; brassière, *Büstenhalter*; lipstick, *Lippenstift*.

In the mornings Karen saw no one except for Hede. Pappa Landau left for work at six and Mutti Landau didn't come downstairs until lunch.

Soon, Karen and Artur would move into the house Pappa Landau was giving them as a wedding gift. The house was already furnished: heavy lace, dark wood and crystal lamps – a small version of this one. Karen had nothing to do.

There had been a fuss a month ago when she had a bout of the tiredness. Her ankles and stomach swelled, which had never happened before, and she explained to the kindly Doktor Hartog who spoke English that it must be because of the rheumatic fever she had when she was ten.

Then there were some different symptoms, and yesterday the Doktor had confirmed the news, telling Pappa and Mutti Landau that Karen should not work from now on and that she must rest in the afternoons.

Artur did not know yet. He had not come home again last night.

This morning she would find the restaurant where Artur met his friends and she would surprise him. He would be sitting at a crowded table and he'd look up and not recognize her at first with her hair put up and wearing a new pale pink velvet coat. He would get up to kiss her, put his arm around her waist and introduce her to his friends as his fiancée, his *Verlobte*. Then she would tell him she was pregnant.

At the mirror, she smiled, didn't smile, licked her lips and pulled the pins out of her hair, which looked too severe. She noticed that her hands were shaking. She hadn't expected to feel like this about Artur Landau and never in her life had she missed a boy before. It made her edgy. Artur was out so much, her nerves were taut, and even when she was distracted for a while, part of her was always listening for his car.

When he was home and close to her, the bunching of her nerves didn't stop because the missing went too deep. There was never time enough for her heart to settle, to drink her fill, to let him soak her through before he left again.

He was out most days and often at night too, busy with Party work. 'There are sacrifices when a cause is great,' he often told her. She wondered what the cause might be, but she must trust him; he was working for their future and for Germany's.

Karen understood this, although Pappa Landau clearly did not. He and Artur had arguments over dinner which Karen could not follow. Artur would shout and bang his fist on the table.

If she didn't know he cared for her so much, she'd think he was furious with her as well. He made love as if he was taking out his anger on her body. Afterwards he fell asleep in the wreckage of the sheets that were soaked with his sweat and hers, and she would ache from the wrenching of her arms and legs. Her skin was stinging with the roughness of his hands, and his making love so hard she had to stop herself from crying.

In the morning, Artur would touch the marks he'd made and tell her he was sorry. He stroked her face and kissed her. He would spread out her arms and legs, kiss her bruises, her breasts and her aching belly, and she knew the pain wasn't only hers but shared between them.

When he stayed away for a night, or two or three, she would remind herself how much he needed her.

He seemed different since she had come to Munich, and perhaps this was the proper change from the first infatuation. In London he had been doped and drunk with love for her; now his eyes had other thoughts in them as if he looked at her through glass. But the wedding plans were being made so everything must be right.

The car drove through the suburbs, large square houses with wooden shutters, iron gates and stands of blackish firs that looked like remnants of an ancient forest, then into the city.

As they passed the station, Karen thought of Michael Ross. It seemed odd he hadn't been in touch. Artur told her he had called at the boarding house but Michael had already gone. He had left behind a rolled-up canvas. 'You should have it,' Artur said to her. 'He is your friend. A picture of a pretty girl. Not thin. Not you.'

In the painting, the girl held on to her sunhat and her hair was wild in the breeze. Her face was in shadow but Karen knew it was Elisabeth. The picture proved how right it was that Michael had not returned to England; he might think he was in love but he would never be a man like Artur. Elisabeth should have a husband who could look after her. What good was love when you were scraping out a dreary little existence with nothing to look forward to? There had been enough of that in Catford.

But the colours in the picture, Elisabeth's bright hair like a flame against the sky, made Karen's heart drag as if a part of her was breaking. Was it because she missed Elisabeth, or was it longing for the feelings that had painted her this way?

Whatever it might be, the picture was too much to bear. Karen put it away in a cupboard.

The car stopped near the Hofgarten. The place where Artur met his friends was just along the street and she didn't need a map after all. When she opened the door, the heat fell on her, the tables were full with lunchtime diners and people were standing drinking. Karen pushed her way between them, asking if they would please move, although mostly they ignored her or couldn't hear. Empty plates had smears of fat, full ones were loaded up with meat. She could taste cigarette smoke in her mouth.

There was the embarrassment of not knowing her destination, of having to turn around and ask people to move a second time. Everyone could see she was alone. Two women with vermilion lipstick looked her up and down, and smirked. A group of men wouldn't move aside and Karen was forced between them. They unfolded their arms, lifting them so she was pressed between their paunches. She sweated in the velvet coat.

Then she saw Artur. The heat was spiking up his hair and his shirt was open to the chest. He was sitting with his back against a wall amongst a crowd of men who were leaning on tables pushed together and loaded with beer flagons, steins and empty coffee cups. He chopped the air with his hand, emphasizing something, then he laughed. She watched, waiting for the moment when he would look across and see her.

He leaned forward to light a cigarette from someone sitting across the table. With both hands, Artur steadied the hand held out to him – a smooth muscular arm with the sleeve rolled up. His blue eyes looked up at the man she could not see; two seconds, three, four. This look was not through glass. She wanted to turn now and go.

Then Artur noticed her, stood up and smiled. He clambered out from his seat, climbing across his friends who were shouting and jeering. They hardly glanced at her. The tables rocked and glasses tipped and spiralled in the puddles. She waited, buffeted at her back, until he reached her, then he took her hand and led her through the crowd towards the door.

She can see he expects an explanation so she says it in a rush, clumsily, almost like an accusation. In the street with people walking past, she tells him she is pregnant.

So many thoughts are in his eyes she can't follow what they are. His skin is waxy as if he hasn't slept, he smells of stale cigarettes and beer, but his face is beautiful and she has to stare because he is new again, astonishing.

Then he drops his jacket on the pavement and he kisses her. Exhaustion sinks through her as it always does when she's close to him again. It has only been two days but it feels so long. Her legs are heavy and she wants to lie against him in his arms, not making love, just sleeping. This weariness always comes after the hours and days and nights alone. She is so tired she would fall down right here on the pavement if he wasn't holding her.

The noise of passers-by and traffic is far away. He kisses her again with his warm hands caressing her face.

But it was nothing. He is hers and there is nothing else. He loves her. 'My baby,' he whispers.

Everything should stop, now, here, always in this moment, because she will never be happier than this.

• • •

They moved into a new house twelve miles outside Munich. Pappa Landau said to her, 'This is good. Artur will stay at home now there is more distance from his friends. For you, it will be better.'

Artur had a car. He drove to Munich as often as before.

The house was surrounded by fir trees and Hede said an ogre lived in the forest, which was why the birds didn't sing. When the baby was born, he must not be put outside in his pram, she said, especially if he was blond and fat. The ogre was often hungry and he didn't like intruders on his patch.

One evening they were eating dinner at the big oak table. Artur was at home and Hede had cooked soft meat and yellow cabbage which she served on the Dresden china Mutti Landau had given them.

'Hede says we must be careful of the ogre in the forest, Artur.' Karen reached across and touched his hand. The happiness of this meal with him took away her appetite.

'Hede is full of silly stories.' He sawed the meat from the bone and the flesh fell away, rosy red inside.

A smile skidded across Hede's face. 'I only tell her take care of fresh baby in old worn-out place,' she said, hands on hips and her neck flushed from cooking. 'It is English story too, *ja*? Ogre he is licking his lips about his face. Ho Hum, Ho Hum. He is not up a stalk in Deutschland, he comes gently sneaking out of trees.'

'Hede, you'll frighten her,' Artur said. Then he spoke in German and Hede laughed with her mouth wide open.

'What is it?' Karen asked. 'Artur? What did you say?'

Artur chewed, smiling, and he swallowed. 'It doesn't matter.'

• • •

Karen thought she would forget the ogre but he hunkered down inside her mind. Mutti Landau had told her that pregnancy was a blissful shut-in world where nothing troubled you; it was the Virgin's legacy, a treat to soften what came next, which was the opposite of bliss. If any woman told you otherwise she was crazy or pretending.

Karen already felt the opposite of bliss. Her mind felt thick like glue, with sudden terrors swelling up like boils and puffing out their poison: Artur would be killed, shot through the head; Elisabeth had forgotten her; the baby would grow up to be a murderer; the forest would imprison her and she would never get away from Germany.

At night, beneath the silence, she heard the ogre breathing. His shadow leaned against the wall while she lay in bed alone, and he took to moaning in the dusk as he settled down to sleep with a wolf curled behind his knees and another for a pillow. The shutters must stay closed and not the smallest chip of light should bother him, but if she turned off all the lamps, she could sit looking out at the bristling firs with the moon wheeling along their spikes and through the stacks of clouds. She could watch for the lights of Artur's car coming up the hill.

• • •

One morning, she asked the question which had been troubling her: 'Artur, who was the man who lit your cigarette?'

'Kurt,' he answered, and turned away. Something in the way he said the name told her. Nothing could be worse than this thing which must be false but she knew was true. She grasped his hand. 'Stay at home today, Artur, please.'

He sat down on the bed, pulling her on to his lap, but she knew his mind was far away and he was impatient to be gone. He talked about the progress of the Party – their leader was the finest man, a man with vision who was giving his life to Germany. 'We will succeed in the election this time, but there is work to do.'

The restaurant didn't look like work, Karen thought but didn't say.

'Germany will be great again.' Artur stroked her hair. 'I work for you and for our baby. I have to go.'

Then, because it didn't matter, because something between them was already breaking, she said, 'It's not for me you're going, it's Kurt.'

Artur stood up, tipping her off his lap.

'I'm sorry, Artur. I don't know why I said that.' Karen lifted her hand to touch him but he caught her wrist and his grip was painful. He didn't let her go, but squeezed tighter and twisted so she sat down on the floor at his feet, then he dropped her wrist as if it was something filthy in his hand. He picked up his jacket and suddenly her heart was bursting with fear of the door closing after him and being left alone again. She shouted, 'You won't go! I forbid it! I'm having your baby, you'll be my husband soon.'

'And you'll be my wife,' he said quietly. 'You won't tell me what to do.'

She was still sitting on the floor, clutching her wrist. 'But you love me. You said so in London.' He was at the door. 'Artur! I only came here because of you.'

He turned, came back and sat beside her on the floor. He closed his eyes, let his head fall back. 'You came for your own reasons, *Liebling*,' he said. 'Not for me.'

She wanted to tell him she was different now, she hadn't loved him then but now she did – more than anyone in her life.

'I thought I would never find a woman I would want,' he said.

She kissed his cold cheek. 'You have. You have and I love you.'

He took her hand and held it. 'You don't listen to me, Karen. Listen. I had never loved a woman and thought I could not. But you changed me and I was happy. I thought, she is my heart, my blood, this English girl. Now I am as I should be.'

'You see?' She laughed. 'I'm right. We're meant to be together. You know it too.'

He didn't seem to hear her. 'But then the Englishman. The mongrel Jew. Explain him to me. You were coming here to be my wife.'

Karen sat back, surprised. He had never mentioned Michael before. 'There's nothing to explain,' she said. 'We travelled on the train together, that's all.' The lie was necessary. The past was gone so why hurt him now?

The thoughts were rushing in his eyes like the moment on the street when she told him she was pregnant, and now she understood that all this time he had been thinking of the night when she arrived with Michael.

'You should tell the truth to me,' he said.

'I have. It is the truth.'

He still held her hand, uncurling her fingers, stroking them. 'I know, you see. I know.' He kissed her palm and for a moment she thought something was healed, or beginning to be healed. 'It doesn't matter now.'

'My darling, I shall make you happy.'

He kissed her hand once more and let it go. 'I think not. But we will not be unkind. It is good for us both that we marry, *Liebling*. You will have money, anything you want. I will have a wife and my father will be satisfied.' He stood up. 'Now I must go.'

'No!' She leaped up too, quick with the panic in her blood, and pushed him hard against the wall. 'You shan't go!' she shouted in his face. 'You love me and you're staying here!' Now she couldn't stop the words. Her fury would burn through the ice in him and she would make him care again as he had in London. 'You won't go. I won't stand for it! I'll take our baby back to England. I'll tell your father about Kurt –'

He hit her hard, the room wheeled over and she was lying on the floor with the iron taste of blood trickling down her throat.

Artur stood above her looking down into her face for a long time – or perhaps it was no time at all; then he put his feet astride her body, pinning her hands to the floor. His weight crushed her fingers on the wooden boards and the pain was so fierce and sudden, she was squealing like a skewered rabbit, on and on. Then he stepped away.

She curled up, pressing her burning hands into herself and crying with the pain. She didn't hear him walk away and when she opened her eyes his shoes were still near her face and she knew she must be quiet. She must be still.

She heard him breathing; he bent down and cuffed her head almost tenderly, so her hair fell across her face and into the blood dripping from her mouth. She heard him going to the door, his footsteps on the stairs and sometime later the car driving away.

• • •

In the morning, her cheek was purple, there was a crust of blood in her hair and her lip was split. Although the pillowcase was stained and she had forgotten to undress, she had slept soundly through the night. She filled the basin in the bathroom and lapped, and threads of blood floated in the water. Later, Hede tapped on the door. 'I come in, madam?'

'I'm tired. I shall sleep this morning, Hede.'

'It is good to rest, madam,' Hede said. There was something in Hede's voice which made Karen wonder if she knew.

When she woke the second time, she had been dreaming of the house in Catford. Elisabeth had fallen on the path and cut her hands, blood was running down her dress and over her socks and shoes, but when Karen opened her eyes, the pain was in her own hands and she remembered that she, and not Elisabeth, had cut herself that day at home. *My brave Kay*, Dadda had said. *My little soldier.*

After Dadda died, Elisabeth would sleep in Karen's bed and eat from Karen's spoon, following her everywhere as if Karen might disappear as well. Elisabeth would stare at Dadda's empty shoes, at his hat hanging on the hook, at his dusty chair, but she would almost smile if Karen played the fool. And Ma couldn't look away from grief even for a second unless Karen was distracting her with wildness and bad behaviour.

It was so long ago. They didn't need her now.

Outside, the sun was shining. The ogre and his wolves would be relaxing in a hollow, blinking at the light, but they would have smelled the blood and Karen kept the curtains closed.

• • •

*Munich*

*Darling,*

*Here is the most exciting news and I know it will make you happy. You are going to be an aunty!*

*The doctor has confirmed it and Artur and I will be married sooner than we thought. I mustn't get too fat for the dress Mutti Landau helped me choose but if the baby shows before the wedding, there's no worry of a scandal here. It seems Germans are not so starchy and ready to disapprove as people in England.*

*Pappa Landau is giving us a house! I haven't seen it yet but it will be beautiful, I know. Doktor Hartog says I should have no excitement so the wedding must be small. You need not worry, he is looking after me very carefully.*

*Isn't it strange that so many wonderful things are happening to me? I thought my life would always be tedious and I should probably go slowly mad, but now it all looks different.*

*You must marry someone and have a baby too, Elisabeth. It is the most wonderful happiness. All the things Ma fretted over after Dadda died, money and the roof, getting up the coal and tradesmen, etc., all that is taken care of. For the first time in my life, when I wake up in the morning, there is nothing to worry about or feel down about, only missing you. Please come and see me if you can. I shall ask Artur to buy your ticket if you will allow it. Please come.*

*Karen*

• • •

Toby's mother wrote to say that Mr Schroëder had been called suddenly to New York but she would stay in Italy with the other children for a further month. Therefore, Ingrid Schroëder's letter said, if Elisabeth wanted to remain in Kent she should find a little vacant cottage for herself and Toby.

'You'll stay with us,' said Vera.

'We're vacant and beyond,' said Rachel.

Elisabeth did not miss the Schroëders' house in Richmond. She was happy to stay in Kent although thoughts of Karen still preoccupied her. At first, the letters had seemed fond and full of joy, but now, rereading them, the tone was strange and smug. *You have nothing, little sister,* Karen seemed to say, *I have everything, and I have Michael too.* Why should she go to Munich to have Karen gloat? She took even what she didn't want just because she could. At one time it would have been impossible to stay away if Karen wanted her to come, but everything was different now.

# 17

Toby's pony was stabled six miles away in Saltwood. By the time the blacksmith had brought the pony to the bungalow for Toby to ride, it was almost time to take it back again.

'Poor little scrap, he's waiting in his riding breeches and always disappointed. We'll keep it here,' said Nanna Lydia, arms akimbo. 'We'll move the mangle out and the horse can have the lean-to.'

'He's not a horse,' Toby said. 'He's an Appaloosa Dartmoor cross.'

'Its feet will ruin the floor,' said Vera. 'I don't want hoof prints on brand-new linoleum.'

'He shan't be standing on the floor, he must have bedding,' Toby explained.

'I know he must, my chicky,' said Lydia. 'We'll see to that.'

'There's no bedding spare,' said Vera. She turned to Lydia. 'The animal won't walk around on tiptoes. And it won't be house-trained. And I'm not about to do the mangling outside in the rain.'

Elisabeth could feel the temperature rising. 'The sea is just across the road, and the donkeys. Toby has plenty to occupy him.'

'The donkeys aren't schooled sufficiently to go forward,' Toby said.

'My life!' said Vera. 'So all you poor little kiddies are going backwards for good money. It didn't used to happen.'

Lydia said, 'I rest my case.'

'For goodness sake,' Rachel said, 'let Eddie look after Toby's pony. His place is nearer than Saltwood, and Elisabeth and Toby can walk along the beach to Eddie's farm when Toby wants a ride.'

'There you are, poppet,' said Nanna Lydia to Toby. 'Your horse will be just a step away and Vera can mangle in the dry, so everyone is happy.'

The Saltwood blacksmith brought the pony and also two saddle mares. 'You've got to ride along beside the little lad,' he said to Elisabeth, 'and someone's got to ride along with you. They all belong to Mr Schroëder, so it's all the same to me if you take the three.'

The animals stood on the concrete path, nosing softly in the alyssum and marigolds. The two mares were black with clean white socks and polished hoofs. The spotted pony looked out from under its chocolate fringe. All three wore red saddle cloths with gold braid. They stood against the backdrop of a rinsed-out sea and powdery sky like cut-outs pasted on a faded postcard.

'Aren't they just as smart as paint in those nice coats?' said Nanna Lydia. 'Almost military.'

'Military is what they are,' the blacksmith said. 'The camp at Shorncliffe cleared out their harness room. No one's got a use for equines like they did. They'll be sorry if there's another war.' He tugged his cap and the horses swung up their heads to watch him go, their manes blowing back like dark-haired girls. The blacksmith seemed to wade as he went on his way, knees apart as if his trouser legs were damp. The horses sniggered in their throats, but it was kindly and affectionate.

• • •

The evening was quiet; a low white sky, a flat rug of sea and not a breath of wind as if the world was suddenly indoors. Toby rode his pony and Elisabeth and Rachel walked the horses along the sands to Eddie's farm.

Rachel wore her gardening clothes. 'It's what Eddie likes. He says he can't bear to see me go home in another dress with paw prints down the front. The collie loves me but Eddie says I'll make the dog too soft to do its work.'

Elisabeth was wearing a skirt and jumper she'd had since school. It was nice to be herself again and not dressed like Mrs Schroëder or Mrs Brion.

The beach was empty. The holidaymakers had gone home, seagulls were picking over lumps of seaweed, and a man in waders dug for lugworms far out on the mud.

They turned inland over grassy shingle with bits of driftwood and fishing net thrown up by the tide, and across the fields were some iron sheds, a barn and a white cottage with two chimneys. 'That's Eddie's place,' Rachel said. 'It's in a state but Eddie's practical and all it needs is time. When we're married I can help him more.'

'Married?' said Elisabeth, stopping dead. 'Rachel! When?'

'He hasn't proposed exactly, but I know he will. We shan't bother with an engagement ring. I wouldn't have him shelling out just for me to show off to the girls in the shop.'

Eddie Saunders came to meet them and the wagging collie was nudging up to Rachel. 'Good evening, sir,' Toby said to him. 'Tobias Schroëder. And this is my pony, Little Bear.'

Eddie was a big kind-faced man in clothes the colour of earth. He nodded to Elisabeth, and while they were walking back towards his farm she saw him often take a little sideways glance at Rachel, a sip of her as if a proper look might be too much.

'It's three horses after all, Eddie – do you mind?' Rachel said. 'I know I only told you one but Toby's dad is paying.'

'The pony I can cater for, but those mares are nervous. I'm not sure.' The two horses stood peacefully in Eddie's dusty yard and at last he said, 'We'll put them with the flock. There won't be much to trouble them in the company of sheep.'

It took a while to unsaddle the mares and the pony. 'I don't normally do this myself,' Toby said.

When they had finished and the gate was shut, Eddie said quietly, 'Rachel, I have something for you. We talked about it and you said it was what you'd like sometime, when we could afford it.'

'Eddie!' Rachel said. 'Oh, Eddie! I said I wasn't in a hurry and I meant it.' She smiled quickly at Elisabeth, who took Toby's hand and moved away. Eddie would reach into his pocket for the little velvet box or perhaps already have it hidden in his hand.

But Eddie sidestepped to the shed, leaving Rachel poised in anticipation. He unhooked the latch, propping the shed door open with his foot.

'Oooh,' said Rachel carefully, doubling back from the excitement she'd assumed without first ascertaining Eddie's direction. Eddie had his boot heel planted out to hold the door and he leaned away to give Rachel a better view of the gloom inside, then he banged the shed hard, once, with his hand.

Nothing happened for a blink, then a bundle of hens came out as if someone had thrown them. The clattering and upset calmed and the hens settled, rearranging their feathers and muttering.

'Orpingtons,' Eddie said. 'Good layers, good mothers to their chicks, and loyal.'

The hens beadily considered this. 'The same as your dad kept at your old home in Neate Street. You said it was a dream of yours to have Orpingtons again.'

Rachel was staring at the hens and Eddie said, 'When you came to visit me that first time, Orpingtons, you said, that's what I'd like. You remember?' Eddie waited, his big hands hanging and doubt beginning to cloud him over.

'I do,' Rachel said at last. 'I do.' She went across to Eddie, hooking her arm through his and they watched the hens tacking back towards the shed, their feathers shimmering in the dusk.

· · ·

Agnes Mander's reclusive life seemed at odds with the stack of condolence letters George Mander received after the notice appeared in *The Times*. He asked Vera Ross if she could recommend a caterer for the wake and she told him there was no need, she'd be glad to do her bit. She had grown fond of Agnes in spite of their quarrels.

'There might be more than forty, Vera. Are you sure?'

The dining room and drawing room were opened up, but the guests gathered in the little sitting room, then spilled out into the garden. The late September sun brightened up the dark old leaves of summer and the bruised red roses with their petals falling. Along the borders, fading foliage and tattered flowers were wound around with bindweed.

George Mander saw his home in a way he never had before. The furniture was a sociable mix of good Georgian and overstuffed Victorian, there were smoke stains on the wallpaper, some fine porcelain and hideous paintings. The mahogany curtain poles had warped. Now his mother was gone, everything looked more vulnerable in his ownership.

On the morning of the funeral, Vera brought some extra help: her daughter, Rachel, and a friend from London, Elisabeth Oliver. To Mander's surprise, he knew them both. Miss Oliver was the young woman he had seen on the train the last time he came down from London, but when Vera introduced her, Miss Oliver didn't seem to remember him. Vera had already told him that her daughter Rachel was Eddie Saunders's girl and Rachel turned out to be the friend who'd met Elisabeth Oliver at Hythe Station.

The dining table was laid out with platters of cold meats and savouries, ham, tongue, lobster-paste sandwiches. The two young women serving tea to his guests added to the feeling that the house was not his own. Miss Oliver and Rachel Ross were lithe and glossy, like young cats amongst staggering ancient dogs.

Mander moved from group to group and by late afternoon he had drunk more than he intended. No one seemed to want to leave and he wandered outside to the terrace where he stood for while enjoying the air and the gentle view across the mossy lawns and the paths with their ragged box and rosemary. On one side, by the orchard wall, there was a stone seat beneath an iron arch where his mother used to sit on days when she could walk outside. The arch was overgrown now with rose and jasmine. A puff of smoke was rising through the leaves.

He found Elisabeth Oliver sitting staring at her feet. She looked up and he saw her panic for a second as if she'd been caught out. She dropped her cigarette beneath the seat and covered it with her heel. 'I'm sorry about your mother,' she said almost belligerently as if to fend him off.

'Thank you. That's kind of you. I don't suppose you remember but we met on the train in August. It must have been six or seven weeks ago.'

'Yes, I do. Thank you for carrying my case.'

He could feel she'd rather be alone and he would leave her as soon as was polite. Her fingers were tapping her knee. She didn't wear a ring.

'I hope your little boy is enjoying his holiday. Is he at the sands today?'

'He's with Nanna Lydia – Rachel's grandmother. He's not mine, by the way.'

'There are dunes out at Camber. They're great fun for a child. You should take him.'

'I'm not sure I will. It's rather too far.' She stood up.

He didn't know why, perhaps it was the oddness of the day, perhaps it was the sherry, but he said, 'Why don't I drive you out tomorrow? The wireless forecast said it should be warm. The boy would enjoy it. I used to love the dunes when I was his age.'

'You have a car?' she asked.

'The bicycle is only for special occasions.'

She nearly smiled, looking at him directly for the first time, and he was suddenly embarrassed at having asked her. 'I have an appointment in Rye at twelve,' he said, feeling ridiculous for the lie. 'I'll leave you at Camber for an hour or two and then I'll bring you back. It would be no trouble.'

'Thank you. It's very kind but we have plans tomorrow.' She gazed past him as if she didn't know how to get away, then Vera's voice was calling. 'I must go,' she said. She walked quickly along the path and up the steps, two at a time, her arms stiff and her head down as if she knew he was watching her.

After a while he went back inside. People were leaving and it took an hour or more to get them all into the cars.

When everyone had gone, Mander shut himself in his study to keep out of the way while they cleared the crockery into the kitchen. He could hear Vera chivvying the girls, who were singing a popular song he had heard lately on the wireless.

He must have dozed off because when he opened his eyes it was dusk and Elisabeth was standing in the lighted doorway. 'Please come in,' he said, getting up hurriedly. She must have seen him sleeping in his chair like an old man.

'We're just going,' she said flatly. 'I wanted to tell you I'd like to go to Camber after all.'

He switched on the lamp on his desk. 'You've changed your plans?'
She looked tired. 'Yes.'
'Then I'll collect you and Toby at ten.'
'You know his name.'
'You told me on the train from London.'
Her smile was almost warm, almost a smile of gratitude.

• • •

When he pulled up in the car, Elisabeth was waiting on the seafront with the little boy. 'Good morning,' Toby said. 'My father has a Daimler too. Ours is black. I like your yellow one better.'

Mander said, 'Thank you, Toby. I find it rather bright, I'm afraid. It was my mother's choice.'

'I thought I'd save you coming in,' Elisabeth said, as Mander opened the car door for her. He wondered if she'd not told Vera she was meeting him.

She was wearing a cheap summer suit, slightly too tight and too short as if she had suddenly grown. On the train all those weeks ago she had looked older, stylish, although he didn't much care for expensive Bohemian clothes, which seemed rather fake to him.

Elisabeth sat with her hands in her lap and Mander tried to make conversation. She looked across at him politely from time to time. He felt old and a fool. Last night he hadn't slept. The whole day yesterday seemed unreal: his house crowded with strangers and black-plumed horses fidgeting on the balding gravel by the porch. And now the young woman who had kept him awake seemed unconnected with this awkward girl beside him. She was behaving as if he was a tedious uncle who had insisted on her company. Or perhaps she was just wishing he was someone else. The child was quiet in the back.

Mander parked the car by the dunes at Camber, and now that they had arrived it seemed odd to leave the two of them alone, but she didn't invite him to stay. She had a basket with towels and beach things. He wondered if she would swim.

'I've brought sandwiches,' she said. She had already kicked off her shoes and dropped her jacket on the sand. Her blouse suited her, white without sleeves or any fussiness. She tied a scarf round her hair. 'We'll wait here for you. It doesn't matter what time you come for us.'

He walked back to the car feeling overdressed in his summer suit and hat. Sand had already filled his shoes. There was nowhere to wait nearby except a wind-blown café with metal chairs, so he drove on to Rye, where he strolled through the cobbled streets, had lunch in a hotel and visited an exhibition of local antiquities.

When he went back for her at three, the boy was digging with a spade and Elisabeth was lying on a towel in her bathing costume. Mander realized that young women probably did this kind of thing nowadays, unaccompanied. She was on her stomach reading and she didn't hear him. She had taken off the scarf and her hair was falling forward over her book. The skirt of her swimsuit fluttered on the backs of her thighs. She did not look up but it came to him that she knew he was there.

'Why are you wearing shoes?' the boy said to him. 'Why are you wearing a tie?'

Elisabeth stood up, brushed sand off her legs and put on the skirt over her swimsuit, stepping into it and reaching round for the button. Mander fixed his eyes on the horizon. 'Shall I wait for you in the car?'

165

'No, it's all right. I won't be long. There's a hook on my blouse. Would you mind?' She came across to him and scooped up her coppery hair. He wanted to bend down and kiss her neck.

'Thanks,' she said, not turning round. She packed up the basket.

'Would you like a game of cricket, Mr Mander?' Toby said.

Mander was glad Elisabeth didn't cut across the boy as women often do and say, 'I'm sure Mr Mander wouldn't want to play' or 'It's much too late for cricket.' She was shaking out the towels and folding them.

'Yes. Why not. A couple of overs,' Mander said.

They set up the stumps, Mander took off his shoes and socks and stooped over the little bat. Elisabeth sat down on the sand again.

They played for a while. Toby bowled and Mander remembered when his joints were loose like Toby's and his arms and legs were learning. They changed places and he showed Toby a better grip and how to block the ball. A cold evening breeze came in off the sea. They finished their game and shook hands.

'I'd like to buy you a cup of tea,' Elisabeth said. 'You've been very kind to bring us all this way. We've had a lovely time. Thank you.' This was more than she'd said to him all day.

They sat at a table outside the beach café and she poured the tea. 'Sugar? One or two?' She lived with Toby's family, she told him. 'Sit up, Toby darling, or you'll fall off your chair.' Her sister was getting married soon and lived in Germany, Rachel worked in a ladies' fashion shop in Folkestone, and the three of them were at school together. 'Would you like more tea, Mr Mander? More tea?' She was born in Catford. 'Mind out, Toby, your milk is on the edge.' She was not engaged nor did she have a particular young man, although of course she met lots of interesting people, friends of her employers. Mr Mander shouldn't assume she was the kind of girl who –

'I'm not sure I'd assume you were any kind of girl.' He smiled to soften the discourtesy of interrupting her.

'Well, what you must think isn't how I am,' she said bluntly.

He was caught off guard and didn't know how to answer her. The boy looked from one to the other. Mander looked into the teapot. 'We need more hot water. Shall I order cake? And what must I think?'

She didn't speak and he waited, at the edge of irritation because she was making this awkward for them both. 'I don't know,' she said at last. 'I'm sorry I was very rude yesterday – and this morning too.'

'Elisabeth, I'm afraid I've forgotten most of yesterday, and as for this morning I still have a thick head, I'm ashamed to say, so the quiet was welcome.'

She seemed relieved, as if a weight had lifted or something was resolved. For the first time she seemed happy to be with him.

Toby asked, 'Why do you ride a bicycle when you have a Daimler Double Six?'

'It's good for me,' said Mander. 'I save the car for special days like today.'

'That isn't what you told me yesterday.' Elisabeth smiled and he saw how pretty her grey eyes were. 'Vera says you own a factory.'

'A foundry.'

'I thought you'd have a farm, or a few farms that people like Eddie run for you.'

'I don't know anything about animals or growing crops. All I know is iron.'

'And your business is doing well?' she asked politely. Suddenly, he cared what she thought of him and he was searching in his mind for a reply. A woman's expression could switch from interest to disappointment in a blink, like the shutters in a cat's eyes. Elisabeth would assume his feelings were blunt with age; she didn't know yet that getting older – and thirty-eight would seem old to her – isn't any protection from embarrassment and hurt. The silence between them had stretched too long. He said, 'I'd have preferred a different line of work but things happen and one finds oneself in a life one never intended.' He cringed to hear himself sounding like a disappointed man.

'I expect that happens to lots of people,' she said softly. She gave the boy a handkerchief to wipe his hands and face, and when they left, she asked to pay the bill.

The sun was low behind them on the drive home. Toby fell asleep and Elisabeth leaned over to cover him with her jacket. 'Didn't you want children?' she said.

He felt hurt that she put it in the past for him.

He drove carefully so as not to wake the boy, and slowly to prolong the journey home with her.

She sent a thank-you note a few days later, saying it would be nice to see him when he next came up to London and the afternoon at Camber had been one of the nicest of their holiday. She gave him her address in Richmond. Her handwriting was neat and rounded, set out on lines.

He was glad of the invitation to meet in London and he appreciated her politeness about the outing to Camber Sands, but he thought he would probably not see her again.

• • •

Over these last two months, with Elisabeth's company for most of the day and with little Toby's too, Lydia felt efficient in her mind again, as if she was plugged in to the Electric and moving smoothly and usefully about the bungalow.

In the mornings, after Rachel and Vera had gone off to work, Lydia and Elisabeth would sit together at the kitchen table with their second cups of tea and discuss tactics for the housework as a mother and a married daughter would – except they were probably more in tune than most and neither had a husband.

Elisabeth wasn't bothering with her London outfits any more and had borrowed a cotton dress from Rachel. Toby was almost chubby, rosy in his cheeks with a pretty shade of sunshine in his skin. He was not so quick with his opinions, more able to leave it to Elisabeth to decide what was best for him.

The arrangement with the pony had worked out nicely. Most afternoons, Elisabeth took Toby along the beach to Eddie's farm. She would walk beside the pony, Little Bear, for miles across the Marsh.

The two black mares were having themselves a holiday. Eddie had offered to teach Elisabeth to ride but she said she was more likely to take off from Dymchurch beach on a pair of wings than stay astride a horse and she was better with both feet on the ground.

Only once in their morning conversations did they refer to Michael and not much was said. Elisabeth asked if there had been any news since the letter saying he was in Munich. 'We're due to hear from him any day,' said Lydia. 'He promised Rachel he'd keep in touch.'

But something troubled Lydia. When she reached out in her mind to him, Michael wasn't there – not like Lemy, who was dead but still contactable. She often talked to Lemy, and in all their years of marriage, she always had a sense of where he was. It was the same with Michael right from when he was a baby, but in the last few months he seemed to have disappeared. It was as if his wireless was switched off – or hers. She wondered why his most recent letter had been written by someone else with no explanation – it looked like the handwriting of a child. And Rachel said he'd gone to Munich with Elisabeth's sister, who was marrying a German fellow, so what was anyone to make of that?

Lydia had always known the shine on Karen Oliver would cast a shadow. No sisters could turn out so differently as these two.

Elisabeth said, 'What's Munich like, I wonder, Nanna. And Paris.' She sounded as if that wasn't what she was thinking of at all.

'Big and noisy, I shouldn't wonder.' Lydia was rolling out the pastry for a pie and Elisabeth was stringing beans. Some moments passed, each pretending to be busy. Lydia decided she would say it: 'Once upon a time, I was so sure you and Michael would be a pair.'

'Were you, Nanna? Why?' Elisabeth looked up. Her eyes were wide and clear as they used to be.

'It's not easy to explain. Something went between the two of you that first time you came to Neate Street.'

'What was it? What went between us?'

'It isn't something you can see and it isn't love – not yet. The heart is slow to know itself, but you can't stop a soul from flying to its nest. I saw it once before and I'd put my life on it.'

Elisabeth picked up another runner bean from the pile on the table and resumed her work. 'Perhaps it's just as well you didn't.'

• • •

The Schroëders were due back in London, although Elisabeth had heard nothing for a month. The trunks were packed and waiting for Railway Collection. Elisabeth and Toby would leave tomorrow on the train.

There was a knock at the front door and Elisabeth called out, 'It's all right, Nanna. It'll be the luggage men.' Lydia heard voices in the hall, then quiet. Toby appeared at the kitchen door.

'What is it, cherub?' said Lydia. 'Has there been a hitch?'

'I don't know, Nanna. Our Daimler is here and not the luggage men. Elisabeth is reading a letter and you'd better come.'

'Well, there's a thing,' said Lydia, wiping her hands on her apron.

Elisabeth was staring at a letter in her hand and through the front-room window Lydia could see a long black car with a driver in a cap silhouetted against the misty autumn sea. She felt her blood sinking. Elisabeth said, 'It's from Toby's mother.'

*My dear Elisabeth,*

*I am sorry to write abruptly. The house in Richmond is sold. Your belongings have been delivered to your mama's home in Catford and I have asked the driver to take you there today.*

*Toby will be brought to my sister's house in Regent's Park, which is where I am at present with Bruno Junior, Annabelle and Bonnie May.*

*There has been an emergency in America. What has happened I am at a loss to understand, but it seems that everyone who had money suddenly does not. My husband's business is a mystery made up of guesses, hope and arithmetic, none of which is reliable in my opinion.*

*Suffice to say there has been a catastrophe: people have been buying with dollars they do not have and then selling to pay for what they have already bought. Is this lunatic or am I? Now they are selling investments frantically but doing so makes them worthless. It is all absurd.*

*My husband tells me the Wall Street Exchange has been unsteady for some time, which was why he returned to New York last month to safeguard his businesses. Alas, the lunacy took hold and he could not.*

*I have no interest in the world of money, as you know. Bruno always says that commerce is the scaffolding upon which my artists dangle – no, 'the edifice your artists cling to' are his words. I have never understood quite what he meant but it seems the edifice has fallen flat and so have we.*

*This is not the end, it will get worse, my husband says. The Fairhavens have suffered also and will be forced to sell the villa in Amalfi. The trompe-l'œil jungle in the loggia is barely dry. Poor Cara and darling Pixie, they cannot take it in.*

*I will stay with the children at my sister's house – Francesca Brion, you will remember – until we get a passage to New York. Thank God Francesca has not been affected by this calamity, her money is in gold and suchlike. Our mother always said my sister has the Midas touch.*

*I cannot think clearly at present and I will write again when I do not have a headache. I will send your salary.*

*Please give my apologies to your dear friends for the unexpected arrival of the car. As you can understand, I had to intercept you before you went to Richmond.*

*Wishing you a pleasant drive. Toby loves the Daimler. It will be the last he sees of it.*

*That's all, I think. I cannot trouble my husband with the question of the pony.*

*Yours in disarray,*
*Ingrid Schroëder*

On the journey up from Kent, Elisabeth had Toby sitting on her lap and he squirmed with incomprehension. He was hot with the struggle to understand and it was too difficult to explain so she only told him some things, and that was hard enough. She said she would not be looking after him any more.

'We'll see each other, darling. I'll come to visit you as often as I can.'

'No, I'll stay with you.'

'My darling, you're going to your mamma and Aunt Francesca at her lovely house in Regent's Park. You'll have Bruno Junior and Bonnie May and Annabelle to play with.'

'They never do. I'll stay with you and Nanna, and Little Bear.'

She struggled to keep her voice from giving way. 'Toby, this isn't goodbye, I promise you.'

He stared at her, suddenly younger than his seven years. His face squeezed shut, his mouth opened and he wailed a long note of anguish. 'I stay with you.' And so their conversation circled.

The Channel and the misty Romney Marsh, the yellow hop fields, the apple orchards heaped with fallen leaves, slipped behind them. Miles of hawthorn hedges, rosehips and blackberries, with autumn licking flames along the green, and the car came to the little towns of Orpington and Bromley, then on through the village of Beckenham where the cottages were mixed with terraces of new brick houses. At Catford, the hedgerows changed to privet.

Ringstead Road, Catford, was agog when the black Daimler smoothed to the kerb outside the house of Mr and Mrs Mole. Elisabeth's mother stood at the front door with Mr Mole behind her, his hand resting on her shoulder as if they were posing for a photograph. Other doors along the street had opened too.

Elisabeth sat with Toby in the car and his silence in these last minutes was more painful than the tears. The chauffeur turned around and spoke to them. Perhaps this was his last drive in the Daimler too and it didn't matter any more. 'I'll take care of Master Toby,' he said. 'There'd be no harm if he sits up front with me. A young gentleman should learn to drive a motorcar.'

Toby climbed in beside the chauffeur and his resignation made Elisabeth want to scramble in with him, ask to be taken back to Kent, refuse to be a piece of nothing thrown up by the tide. But the Daimler was gliding away and Toby was just a smudge of brightness inside.

As the car turned the corner, his face appeared in the rear window. He must have climbed over the seat to see her. Then he was gone.

'Elisabeth, my dear,' said Mr Mole. 'The Kentish air has suited you.'

'Back again,' her mother said. 'There's a lodger in your room and another in the spare so you'll have to think again.'

# 18

On Tuesdays, Gunter Landau had coffee and schnapps with Doktor Ruben Hartog after morning surgery had finished. Gunter walked to Ruben's house, enjoying the exercise and the prospect of Hannah's coffee, which she made by simmering a vanilla pod in the cream, and adding a dash of brandy.

Hannah made coffee like this almost forty years ago in her little attic room above a bookshop in Vienna. Ruben was studying medicine. Gunter and Hannah were classics students and also lovers then. Their parting had not been painful thanks to Anna-Marie Fischer.

She was in the university library reaching for a book, her long brown hair curling to her waist. Gunter had never seen a girl so lovely from the back. When she turned, he saw that her face was unremarkable and less beautiful than Hannah's, but Gunter was already smitten.

Hannah didn't weep. She kissed him fondly on the cheek and confessed that she and Ruben had long been anguishing over how to tell him they were in love, fearful this would end the friendship of the three of them. Anna-Marie had solved it.

And now, here they were, all four in Munich, content and getting old. The war was behind them, they had been spared tragedy and grief, and also the hardships so many families were suffering in Germany, Ruben and Hannah Hartog with three grandchildren, and Gunter and Anna-Marie Landau, their first on the way.

As Gunter turned into the leafy street where the Hartogs lived, a shadow in his thoughts was spoiling his anticipation. It would be hard to give Ruben the message and Gunter must impress upon Ruben how ridiculous he considered his son's decision. It was only a matter of time before these latest idiotic ideas of Artur's were forgotten, but for now they must comply. After all, sweet English Karen was Artur's wife, this was their first child and his wishes must be respected.

Hannah opened the door. 'Dear Gunter.'

He noticed, always with a little shock, her thickened waist and the flesh around her jaw. Somehow he could never quite remember she was middle aged. The memory of her at twenty was still so clear.

The youngest grandchild was swinging on her skirt and Gunter lifted the baby into his arms. The house smelled of coffee, as he knew it would – the scent of friendship, student days when they were hungry and so poor that Hannah's extravagance with the cream and brandy sustained them. It was the smell of mornings, before Anna-Marie, when he'd wake with Hannah. Now Hannah's black hair was silver-grey. Coffee was the smell of conversation through the night, talk of politics and books, and God, and then mornings when the four of them were speechless with exhaustion from the feeds and the tantrums of their babies.

Now here they were, not so much changed apart from creaking in the joints a little.

'Ruben is in the garden,' Hannah said. 'Go through and I'll bring the coffee out to you.' Gunter put down the baby, who tottered behind her grandmother into the kitchen. Hannah still liked to cook, although they could all afford to pay servants these days.

Ruben was attending to the roses wearing an old sunhat and with a pair of secateurs in his hand.

'No scalpel, this morning, Ruben, old fellow?' Gunter said.

'My operating days should be long over,' Ruben said. 'Sadly they are not. Another emergency last night for our poor guest. His wounds have putrefied again and I had to cut away more flesh and amputate a digit at the second joint.'

'Have pity on me, Ruben. I don't have your stomach for these things.' They sat down on the willow chairs under a parasol. 'And you're too generous, you and Hannah. You can't take in every stray you find upon your doorstep.'

'He is no stray, my friend. And it was not by chance he was beaten outside my house and left at my door.'

'You take too much upon yourself. You still think it was your speaking against those thugs that is the reason?' Gunter said.

'Three times it has happened. It cannot be coincidence. Here's Hannah with our coffee,' said Ruben quickly.

They sat talking for a while. Hannah asked after Anna-Marie and Karen. 'Is Karen resting as Ruben said? Ruben, you haven't seen Karen for a week and you should visit. You hear me?'

'I will call when I am asked,' said Ruben quietly.

He knows, Gunter thought, perhaps nothing need be said. 'How is the patient upstairs?' he asked, wanting to steer the conversation away from this awkwardness.

'He was conscious for a while when they moved him from the hospital. He asked that we write to his sister in England,' Ruben said.

Hannah went on, 'It's fortunate that little Judith has learned some English. She took his dictation but speaking exhausted him – an hour or more to write a dozen lines. She was so calm and brave. Esther sat with her all the time. His injuries are terrible.'

'He is unconscious again,' Ruben said. 'We have a nurse with him. Last night's amputation and scouring of the wound was probably quite pointless. His blood is poisoned and it's unlikely he will live but we pray, do we not, Hannah?'

'We do.' Hannah refilled their cups and left them. She knew they would talk about the beatings and Ruben would say he was responsible somehow – which was ridiculous. Someone must speak out. After the horrors of the war and the hardships of these recent years, it was madness that Germans were inflicting suffering on each other now. The hatred had contaminated the Landaus' son. She and Ruben had loved Artur as if he was their own, and he used to be such a sweet quiet boy, a little spoiled perhaps, but always thoughtful and polite. Now he looked at them with contempt – if he acknowledged them at all.

But there was a new generation of babies to take care of, Hannah thought. Life must go forward. She prepared Leah's food and lifted the baby on to her lap.

Gunter and Ruben were silent until they heard Hannah talking to the baby in the kitchen.

'You know how young men are, Ruben. It was just a brawl.'

'Out here? In these quiet streets where families live? No, Gunter, they mean to punish me – punish any Jew who crosses them. It has worked. I'll say nothing against them now, not with the children here.'

'This will pass. It will, believe me. They're just a few young men, a very few, full of restlessness and itching for a cause. This whole thing will die away. The silly little ranting Austrian failed miserably at the election. He'll be forgotten soon, you'll see.'

'Perhaps.' Ruben filled their cups. They sat quietly for a while and

Gunter wrestled with the words in his head, trying to find the best, the most diplomatic. 'Ruben . . . it is with the deepest shame . . . and sadness that I must ask you –'

'Do not distress yourself. I understand. Artur would prefer me not to attend Karen again.'

'It pains me to have such a son. He is a fool.'

'My concern is for Karen. Her heart is weak, you know this, Gunter. Make sure he finds the best of care for her.'

'He will, though I fear the marriage is in trouble. Artur does not love Karen as he should. He neglects her. They are unhappy, I think.'

'New marriages are often difficult, Gunter. Do you not remember how Hannah and I would bicker over nothing in the early days?'

'I know, I know. But this is different. I know my son. In London he was in love. Waiting for Karen to come to Munich tortured him, but something changed when she arrived. Poor Karen. He need not marry her, I told him this, but he wants to. I cannot understand it.'

'He has a good heart, Gunter. He pretends to be tough but he is easily hurt, anyone can see. Artur is a little lost, perhaps, and troubled, but he will find himself again. You'll see, he and Karen will be happy, as we have been.'

'His mind is too much on politics.'

'Hannah and I, we pray he doesn't get mixed up with the violence. The bullies may be few but they know how to inflict damage. The young man upstairs might not use his hands again and will have pain in his legs when he walks, if he ever walks or needs his hands in this life.'

'With your care he has a hope, a chance – the best.'

'Why they hate us, I cannot understand. But Artur should take care, Gunter. There are Jews in Germany who are not as cowardly as me.'

'I'm sure he doesn't hate you. Not really. And you're no coward, Ruben. You put your wife and family first. I ask you humbly to forgive us for our son. You and Hannah are so dear to us, and Anna-Marie is beside herself with worry that we'll lose you.'

Ruben laughed, slapped him on the back. 'We're good Germans together, are we not? It will take more than a young man's foolishness to rid you of us.'

★

*Darling,*

*I shan't write much because my new doctor said I must rest almost all the time. Doktor Grundmann is very strict and I liked dear Doktor Hartog better but Artur said he was unsuitable, whatever that might mean. I didn't ask.*

*Artur has employed more people and they start work today. He has engaged a cook, a gardener and a girl to help Hede with the housework. I'm not sure how to give them instructions. It's hard enough with Hede.*

*Artur is away a lot and I miss him although I don't make a fuss. His work is important and he travels all over Germany speaking in town halls on behalf of his Party. He says there are too many old-fashioned, narrow-thinking Germans who are frightened of new ideas, and even men like darling Pappa Landau are rather backward, Artur says.*

*The meetings get quite noisy and Artur's Party friends, young men called Sturmabteilung, are firm in discouraging anyone who heckles. How can people learn if others interrupt?*

*He tells me most good honest Germans don't understand the reasons why their country is rotten to the core because they're too busy complaining and struggling to get by. Corruption has ruined everything, he says, and the countries that won the war made Germany the whipping boy.*

*The war was twelve years ago, how can it matter any more? I wouldn't say it to anyone but you, but sometimes I think Artur cares too much about these things – that's my selfishness, which I must curb. Of course, he's patient when people are slow to understand, but I've heard some members of his Party bully anyone who disagrees. There's no excuse for nastiness over something as silly as politics, but it's wrong to stand in the way of progress. It's all so complicated. I don't understand the ins and outs, and I don't suppose I ever shall.*

*Oh, darling, Mutti Landau gave us a cradle! It was Artur's when he was a baby and Pappa Landau's before that, and back and back in the family. Birds and animals are carved on the sides and a scene of fairies by the pillows. Mutti Landau cried when she gave it to us. Artur isn't really interested, although he says he is.*

*I'm doing my best to see that there are more important things at stake than the two of us and our baby. Artur says it will take hard work and clear thinking for Germany to be great again and then everyone, not just us, will be better off. I'm sure he's right. He is a fine man and I am the luckiest of girls.*

*With my love,*
*Karen*

• • •

Elisabeth decided she would not go to see George Mander again. That day in Camber she had tried him out, as Karen would have done, as Mr Caffin the surgeon had tried her out, and George Mander, Elisabeth had discovered, could be charmed.

But something wouldn't fit, wouldn't settle her decision, even though it would solve everything to marry him and live in his big old house a mile from the sea, to be Rachel's neighbour, to live close to Vera, and close to Nanna Lydia, who was more a mother to her now than Mrs Mole.

However many reasons piled up in favour of George Mander, Elisabeth knew he was too good a man to have a wife who didn't love him. After she sent the note giving him her address in Richmond, she wished she hadn't.

That was before Ingrid Schroëder's letter came. Elisabeth stood in the Post Office in the Tottenham Court Road while the woman behind the counter looked up the number on a list. 'We have a Mander & Son Foundry at Bourne and we have a Mr G. L. Mander, near Hythe. Which is the connection you require?'

'Mr G. L. Mander,' Elisabeth said.

'Very good, miss.' The woman wrote the number on a card and Elisabeth went to the booth, closed the door and sat down on the bench inside to wait for her call to be put through. She had not rehearsed anything, she was tired from a sleepless night and all the walking of the last three hours. She gazed out through the glass at the people in the Post Office coming and going silently like a moving picture.

Last night, she had slept in the dining room on Mr Mole's camp bed. 'From the Transvaal campaign, my dear,' he told her. The October cold came up through the canvas meant for Africa and she couldn't sleep. She was up at six to put away her bed and lay the breakfast table for the lodgers, Miss Lewin and Miss Brownsort. At eight she caught the train from Catford to Charing Cross.

By eleven thirty, she was dazed with the traffic and the rush of peo-ple. She looked for the agency where she would register for work but lost her way amongst the thousands of little journeys whose trajecto-ries she crossed. Her brain was numb with the suddenness of being here, the spiteful London wind whisking up her skirt and ironing down her hair. The air was laden with soot and too thick to breathe.

She walked aimlessly towards Mrs Brion's house in Regent's Park, Toby filling her mind, but then found she had turned into Fitzroy Street.

There was the archway between the houses in the shabby graceful terrace, no porch or step, the shadowy passageway sloping down. An opening would lead to wooden stairs, a landing and a clanging iron corridor, then another door would open on a bare white room col-oured pink by the embers of a fire.

For a while, in that room, Michael had seemed to love her. She remembered the sensation, so light it didn't take away her breath or make her heart beat faster, but the air was luminous and the smells of turpentine and linseed, the wooden boards and the fire, were each separate and complex. She had felt the weight and texture of her clothes against her skin and her mind had fallen quiet for the first time in her life.

Elisabeth looked up at the façade. She never knew which windows were the studio's. If she went through the archway now, up the stairs and along the corridor, the door would be locked. Michael had been away for so long, he must have forgotten this place, as he had forgot-ten her.

How could it take so long to understand? What she had felt was an illusion and it would go on and on eating up her life until she smoth-ered it, disowned it, cut it away, as Mr Caffin the surgeon failed to do.

She turned around, walked to the Post Office in the Tottenham Court Road and telephoned George Mander.

The telephone in her booth rings and she jumps. She has never made a long-distance call before and suddenly she has stage fright. It goes on ringing and people in the Post Office hear it even through the glass door of the booth. They're staring so she unhooks the ear piece and listens for his voice. There are clicks as the operator makes the connection, then silence. 'You're through-hooo,' sings a tinny telephone girl. Any moment now George Mander will speak and she must say something.

'This is the residence of Mr Mander,' says Vera's voice.

Elisabeth's mind scrabbles to grasp the surprise. Of course, he will be at work and she should have asked to be connected to the foundry.

'Hello, hello, hello,' trills Vera, and the sound of her is like coming home. Elisabeth still can't speak but for a different reason – because tears are strangling her.

At last she says, 'Vera, it's me.'

'Elisabeth? Elisabeth, is that you? Nanna told me all about it, what a shame. And little Toby, he's going to miss you, poor mite, pushed from pillar to post, it isn't right. A child shouldn't be uprooted, it distracts them, takes their mind off growing, that's my opinion. You're lucky you caught me, I was just off to the shop, but here I am.' There is a pause. 'What can I do, my poppet? This call will be costing you.' Another pause. 'Is your mum all right? Are you settling back?'

The strangulation gets fiercer and Elisabeth can hardly breathe. The longing for Nanna Lydia and Toby, and for Rachel and Vera too, squeezes her rib cage and she can only open and shut her mouth.

'Oh, ducky,' says Vera softly, and that's enough. Elisabeth heaves in a breath and the sobbing starts. It's bursting out of her, she's braying like a calf and people in the Post Office can hear this as well. They stare some more. Elisabeth hangs up and leaves, forgets to pay, has to go back. She has only been out of the door for a moment but already people have resumed their business of buying stamps and sending telegrams. They have forgotten the small event of a girl crying into a telephone.

• • •

Elisabeth knew George Mander was there when she walked up Ringstead Road and saw the yellow Daimler parked outside the house. The Ablett boys from Number 12 were lurking round the car and just the look of them could blister paint.

'Paws off,' Elisabeth shouted over her shoulder, hurrying up the path.

'Some awfully nice friends you've got, dear,' called Mrs Riddick sourly from across the road. 'Two Daimlers in a week.'

Elisabeth fussed in the hall, fumbling with the buttons on her coat. George Mander taking tea with Mr and Mrs Mole would be two universes colliding. She could hear her mother's voice. '. . . my other girl took a similar arrangement with a German gentleman and it worked out very nicely. She's married to his son. I wonder, Mr Mander –'

Elisabeth sprinted down the passage, 'Hello, everyone. Hello, George.' She hadn't called him George before.

'Here she is,' said Mr Mole.

'Mr Mander has a proposal for you, dear,' her mother said. 'He has explained to Herbert and myself and we have consented to his asking you.'

George Mander smiled at Elisabeth. 'No, not that, you'll be relieved to know. Employment, if you're interested. We need a clerk at the foundry and I've been looking for a while for someone who'll do first-aid too. Just minor things – they happen from time to time. Vera tells me you were a nurse.'

'You spoke to Vera?'

'Yes, the other day. She mentioned you. She said your job looking after Toby had ended, unfortunately.'

He gave nothing away. If he knew about the telephone call, he would not embarrass her. He would probably never tell her this was why he came.

His suntanned face and black Harris overcoat were one world, as she had thought, and the pallid Moles in their sepia sitting room were another.

'You've only just come back and now you're off again,' said Ernest Mole bleakly.

'I'm sure Elisabeth will have other offers of employment, Mr Mole,' said George Mander. 'Perhaps you'd rather your daughter stayed at home.'

'Elisabeth is too pretty and too clever to be mine,' said Mr Mole, now chivalrous. 'She's her mother's daughter and I want whatever makes her happy.'

'Happy *and* independent,' added her mother, whose cardigan and skirt blended with the furniture as if she was wearing camouflage. Mr Mole's bald spot glinted with a bright reflection of the electric bulb.

'Yes,' said Elisabeth. 'I'll take it.'

'You'd like to think about it, I expect,' George Mander said.

'No, I wouldn't. Thank you. I accept.'

Her mother clapped as if Elisabeth had won something.

George Mander must have seen the trapdoor springing open and he stood up. 'I could take you with me now, if that's convenient. It would save another journey on the train and I'll send for your trunk tomorrow.'

Her mother bristled. In a blink she was on guard for her daughter's reputation. *Years too late*, Elisabeth thought.

With perfect timing George Mander added, 'Mrs Ross, my housekeeper, has a room for Elisabeth until she finds accommodation.'

So he and Vera had arranged it all between them.

When they went outside, a pack of children were circling the Daimler and the Ablett boys were sitting in the gutter, poking at the tyres. Across the road and all down the street, people were suddenly busy putting out the milk bottles, the cat, getting the children in, chatting over the gate in spite of the perishing cold, sweeping the path regardless of there being no leaves left in Ringstead Road.

'Goodbye, goodbye, my darling,' her mother said loudly, kissing her. Anyone who wasn't already looking would be now.

George Mander seemed untroubled by the audience. He shook Mr Mole's hand, then her mother's, and opened the car door for Elisabeth. When they drove away, people waved and Elisabeth waved back at the neighbours flapping handkerchiefs as if she'd turned into royalty. Children ran beside the pale yellow car squealing and yelling nothing, just making noise.

The car turned out of Ringstead Road towards the coast, back along the lanes she'd travelled a week ago with Toby.

A week ago she couldn't breathe with the longing to be in Kent. There was nothing in the future except a feeble pointless hope. A week ago she hadn't been to the studio in Fitzroy Street and understood at last that Michael had forgotten her.

She was balling up her handkerchief and pushing it against her eyes. George Mander must have noticed but he didn't ask her why or try to comfort her, and she was grateful to him for yet another kindness.

When she woke up, a rug was over her knees. She must have been sleeping for an hour because a golden moon was hanging in the blue above the Downs and the headlamps of the car were pushing furrows through the dusk.

Elisabeth said, 'Thank you, Mr Mander. George.'

The miles went past and the evening turned into night. They didn't speak again, and the quiet in the car with him, the icy air, the warmth under the rug, were like a dream of travelling. The road was rushing water, flashes in the dark of bare twigs and hanging leaves, each one separate and furred with rime, trees looming up, white bones against the stars, a gate of chalk, a hare loping over frosty stubble. The moon was hardening and shrinking, high up now and silvering the hills.

At Lympne, the road came to the rim of the Romney Marsh and there it was, spread out below, flat as a plate from Hythe across to Rye, a thousand pearly squares of pasture marked out with ditches. Sheep sheds and lambing pens, cottages and barns, were charcoal lines and smudges in the moonlight. And beyond was the English Channel glittering like a bank of coal dust up to the horizon.

• • •

*Dear Elisabeth,*

*I wish you would settle although I'm glad you have a job. A foundry in Kent sounds dreadfully dull but it's better than nothing, I suppose.*

*I'm well but very tired. The birth is soon and Artur does everything he can for me but it's my responsibility to bear a healthy child. We want a son.*

*My doctor tells me I'm a cask of precious wine maturing. I say I'm a barrel. My Paris dresses will never fit again but Artur says I was too thin and I see now that I wasn't womanly. I also didn't understand the duties of a wife or the importance of seeing my weaknesses and faults and working at improvement.*

*Happiness is found in dedication to your husband and your country. I had silly notions of what I had a right to but now I appreciate that happiness must be earned. You'll discover this too when marriage comes for you.*

*I forgot your birthday and I know you'll forgive me, darling. Pregnancy has made me stupid as well as fat and Artur is so patient with all my muddles.*

*We now have a kitchen girl as well as Cook, two gardeners, a boy to see to the dogs, and Hede too, of course. People are grateful to work for next to nothing and we do our best to employ as many as we can.*

*Please don't think badly of me but I had to dismiss a gardener last week. I told him to cut down some firs which overhang the garden and he said it is unlucky to harm the trees. He said, poor man, the baby would be affected. How stupid can that be?*

*He's elderly so I explained kindly and very simply that I'm only suggesting felling half a dozen, not the whole forest, and the trees can't know I'm pregnant. I think these people can be dense on purpose. He dug his heels in and wouldn't do it.*

*Artur is too busy to get involved and says the staff are my domain. I see now exactly what he means: that some people are determined to stagnate in ignorance and laziness.*

*And something else. I was upset and didn't understand at first, but Artur has told Pappa and Mutti Landau they are no longer welcome in our house. I returned the cradle. Artur says they are exactly the kind of people who have brought Germany so low and we will soon have our child to consider.*

*We hear about the dreadful situation in America. It is greediness and Jews that have caused this disaster and we must learn from it. There is little sympathy here but the financial collapse affects us too and people are losing jobs and going out of business.*

*Thank goodness there is a guiding light. Our Leader, Herr Adolf Hitler is his name, shines brightly and we in the Party follow him with hope in our hearts. Herr Hitler personally signed a letter congratulating Artur on his talent for speaking passionately in public. He mentioned me! He thanked me for supporting Artur's work. Our Leader seems to understand the lives of women as well as men. (He's rather attractive, actually, and if I weren't a married woman . . .!!!)*

*When the baby is born I shan't have much time to write but I'll think of you all the time, my darling, and keep my fingers crossed that you'll find happiness too.*

*Marriage is making me a better person, and I'm beginning to understand how to lead a useful life. I feel as if I'm home. I belong to Artur and to Germany.*

*Karen*

*1930*

# 19

George Mander's house was built of Kentish brick and knapped flint. It had the ease and presence of an important residence but was smaller than it seemed from a distance and on a scale that made it welcoming and homely. The façade was evenly proportioned, the walls had settled and the tiled roof had sunk in undulations. The back was a jumble of gables and pitches and fancy brick chimneys.

The twisted trunk of a wisteria leaned over a black oak porch; the blooms had finished and now the house was bearded with greenery which curled around the windows and gave the rooms a peaceful dusky light.

Every Friday, Elisabeth made up the wage packets in George's study. She would drive from the foundry in the morning, then back again to give the men their cash. This had come about because she couldn't concentrate at work with all the noise.

When she finished counting the money, entering the figures in the ledger and sticking down the envelopes, she would sit in the drawing room with a cup of tea, looking out at the garden.

She and George had played a board game on Sunday afternoon and the pieces were as they'd left them. Elisabeth tipped them in the box and folded up the wooden board. His mother must have loved games with dice because there was a cupboard full of them. He used to hate these games, he told Elisabeth, but it was different now.

It was almost a year since Elisabeth had come here to help with Mrs Mander's funeral. The old lady's things had been everywhere: a board like this one halfway through a game, hatpins and gloves on the table in the hall, a romance with the page marked by an envelope on a footstool by the sofa.

Vera said that Mrs Agnes Mander had been ailing but it looked as if death had caught her by surprise. So that must be another way: not inch by inch like Albert Ross but suddenly. Full stop. Life bangs shut like a book whether it's finished properly or not, and all the things half done, all the plans and the practical belongings of a life, are adrift without a purpose or a destination.

Elisabeth thought of Nanna Lydia and wondered if there was any news. The doctor came almost every day now.

George was paying for the visits; Elisabeth had seen the bills. He took them from the pile of opened post on her desk in the office and put them in his pocket. He said nothing and she didn't ask. He might be doing it for her because she loved Nanna, or for Vera, or just because he was the man he was. In this past year there were so many times when she had seen his generosity. She knew from the foundry ledgers he could not afford it.

The sun was streaming into the sitting room and showing up the worn upholstery and the stain along the ceiling. The wallpaper of exotic birds and flowers on pale blue silk had curled at the edges and come unstuck. Dusty needlepoint cushions were lined up along the sofas, and the piano stool was tapestry too. Perhaps Agnes Mander was a wife who passed her days playing sonatas and sewing.

On the piano there were photographs in little silver frames of family and friends. One was of Michael with Eddie Saunders and George, and the three of them had lambs around their necks like scarves, holding bunches of little hoofs in their fists and grinning at the camera.

'Rachel's brother,' George had told her. 'He stayed with Eddie one spring. It was years ago and he went off travelling, to paint in Europe. How I envied him. You're old friends with Rachel so you know him, I expect.'

'No,' Elisabeth said. 'Not really.'

These days, she was used to seeing the photograph and it was her habit to pick it up, look, put it down.

Today, she hardly glanced at all, easily ignored him and put the picture back amongst the others. She didn't fool herself any more.

She trailed her finger along the mantelpiece and over a bronze figurine of a slender naked girl whose black face was expressionless. The girl held a swathe of bronze cloth that clung around her narrow hips. She seemed to be the only thing that never needed dusting. Perhaps George ran his hand over this naked girl.

The house was silent. Elisabeth opened the French doors and the sound of the sea was carried on the wind with the constant peevish bleating of the Romney sheep. A whistle trailed up through the air with the shushing of the engine pulsing underneath. A train must be on its way to Dungeness. She stood listening with the salty air on her face.

Then a voice shouted her name and someone was banging on the front door. It was Eddie Saunders with his hair on end, his shirt clinging and, behind him, a black mare sweating and blowing in the sun. 'You'd better come,' he said. 'Nanna is asking for you.'

Vera is waiting on the doorstep when Elisabeth runs up the path and stumbles on the welcome mat. She's already past, already opening Nanna's bedroom door when Vera calls, 'Michael has come home.'

Her hand is pushing on the door, her feet are carrying her into Nanna's room, and her mind has stopped, wiped blank because this cannot be.

He is there, sitting by the bed holding Nanna's hand. He turns and sees her, stands up, and everything is tipping as if the room is sliding them together like the pieces on a board sliding to the fold.

But they are still, Elisabeth just inside the door and Michael by Nanna's side, because the moment they touch it will be the same and there will be no end. It was never an illusion.

She can't move until Nanna pats the counterpane and says, 'Sit over here, my chicky, on my other side, then I can see you both.'

Elisabeth sits down and her head is empty air. Two days have arrived together – the one she prayed would never happen but knew must come, and the one she couldn't even think of because she wanted it too much. She is cancelled out to nothing because Nanna is leaving her and Michael has come back.

But in this moment, she has them both.

She holds Nanna's hand. It's cold and clammy like a piece of uncooked chicken, but it is precious and Elisabeth examines the texture of skin, the shape and details of the fingers that have done a lifetime's work. She holds firmly to memorize the feeling and to imprint Nanna's hand inside her own. The room smells powerfully of disinfectant. Nanna's Yardley Lilac flutters like a moth.

Michael takes Nanna's other hand.

'Here we go,' says Nanna, closing her eyes. 'Mind the dog.'

Elisabeth looks into Nanna's face, trying to concentrate until her senses calm. Michael is so changed.

'Would you like a slice?' Nanna says. 'Go on. It's cold out there.' She is a wisp. Her breathing whistles and her lips are tinged with blue, but they have been for weeks, it might mean nothing. Then she's snoring.

Vera comes in and stands watching for a while. 'The doctor's on his way. Rachel's coming home from work.' Then she leaves.

'Elisabeth,' says Michael softly, and Elisabeth looks up. She has seen scars before but this one is bewildering. It carves into him, cuts across his temple and down his cheek. It is brutal, she thinks. 'I know,' he whispers.

Then Nanna is awake again. 'Look out! The oranges are on the loose,' she shouts. 'Here they come, chook, chook, they're being friendly, but oh no, little Bertie, he's not fooled.' She chuckles, but her eyes are troubled.

Then the cloudiness clears and she looks squarely at Elisabeth. 'You see, my sweet. I always told you.' She lifts their hands, puts them together on the coverlet, Michael's on Elisabeth's. 'I always knew,' says Nanna sleepily, 'didn't I, my poppet? I said you and Michael would find each other one day.'

His hand burns. It's heavy. His fingers touch her ring. Nanna has forgotten about the wedding.

Michael doesn't flinch. He will say it for Nanna and Elisabeth will too.

'You were right all along, Nanna,' he says.

'You were, Nanna darling,' says Elisabeth. 'We're together now.'

*1931*

# 20

The great shingle bank of Dungeness sprawls seven miles into the English Channel. This promontory of the Romney Marshes is pushed northwards by the sea; every tide scours six cartloads of pebbles from the southern side and carries them around the point. The summer long-shore raking is slow, but winter gales and spring tides gush through the rabbit warrens and badger setts in the Broomhill Wall and Green Wall bank, filling up the land's capillaries and seeping northwards underground towards the old town of Lydd. These are the hidden tides of Dungeness, moving through the peat and shingle, under the black tarred fishermen's huts and old railway carriages with stove pipes and washing lines, under the upturned boats and the hoofs of goats and ponies browsing the acres of sea kale.

The shingle bank of Dungeness seems like land, but salt water moves under it and mists roll over it as if it is the sea.

Elisabeth pedals hard, head down, into the wind. Her coat flaps and her face and knees are wet from the salt rain hanging in the air. Sometimes she takes the little train if she has too much to carry in the basket of the bicycle; a pie or potatoes in a bag to peel when she gets there, or mutton cut into cubes for a stew. Today she has a ripe cheese which is too unsociable for the train, and a loaf of bread which she'll slice before she leaves. She knows Rachel took some eggs to Michael a few days ago and also a rabbit Eddie shot, so that will need cooking too if Rachel didn't have time.

When Michael came home, he couldn't hold a cup, or shave, or fasten buttons. He couldn't lift a saucepan unless it wasn't hot, and then he would hold it in his arms. Now he has learned to do most things. He can't use an axe or a knife. He still can't hold a paintbrush.

There is kiddle fishing on the shingle beach near his hut and he knows how to string a net along the poles. If he catches anything, he shares it with his neighbours, who share their catches with him. The neighbours are better fishermen. They sell their surplus at the market in Rye and bring back tea and tobacco which they exchange with him for whisky. Elisabeth brings the whisky for him because it dulls the pain.

She turns on to the track to Michael's hut. The compacted shingle glitters under her bicycle wheels, which judder in and out of potholes and splash in puddles. Huts are dotted here and there across the flats as if the gales have scattered them. The people who live out here are generous and solitary. They nod to her when they see her passing on her bicycle or walking across the pebbles from the train, but even after all this time they rarely speak.

Today the sky is blue, the clouds are blowing inland and the April sun climbs higher. Sometimes this place is almost colourless but today the brilliance makes her eyes ache. In the sunshine the black huts are like holes in the tumps of flickering pink and yellow flowers. A goat looks up, chewing, and its creamy coat could be a splash of bleach on patterned cloth. She can see Michael's blue shirt hanging on the washing line and, out on the point, the lighthouse cut out red and white as if it's made of cardboard.

There are no contours in the land to cast shadows, no subtle tones and no indecisive curves. Everything is flat and bright like Toby's paint-by-numbers pictures. The horizon looks higher than the land and the sea seems to encircle Dungeness as if it is an island.

Long before she gets there, Elisabeth sees Michael stacking drift-wood by the hut and from here he looks the same: his hair is too long, he's wearing working clothes, an ochre shirt with the sleeves rolled up, and his arms are brown. She smiles although he hasn't seen her yet and she pedals harder and skids sideways, jumping off the bike. The shingle scatters and he looks up.

'Here I am,' she says.

He raises his hand as if she's a long way off even though she's standing right in front of him. Since Nanna held their hands together on the day she died, they do not touch unless it is by accident. A month after he came back to Kent, this almost changed.

It had been a day of thick sea mist and the waves were pressed flat by the weight of water in the air. When Elisabeth arrived, the fire in the stove had gone out and the hut was cold. The windows were blank as if the hut was floating in a cloud.

Michael was sleeping. She put a blanket over him and sat down at the table. There was food to cook, but if she moved around in so small a space she would disturb him. The silence seemed to thicken like the whiteness at the windows and it was dark enough to light the lamp, but Elisabeth remained still, watching Michael sleeping in the dusk.

He had been lying with his face to the wooden wall, now he turned on to his back. There was no scar on this side. His skin was smooth, with a sheen of sweat from the pain he felt even in his sleep.

She got up from the table and knelt on the floor beside the narrow bed, leaning over him, and she shut her eyes to breathe in the smell of soap and brine, and linseed, very faint, as if he was still a painter. She could taste the warmth of him.

There wasn't the yearning or the sadness she thought she'd feel so close to him, but only wonder. It was as simple as another breath; she would lie down beside him.

She slipped off her shoes, unbuttoned her coat and put it on the table. The sounds she made dropped into the silence and disappeared. There was no ticking clock to separate the minutes. Time had folded like a wave. The dark hut with blank white windows was a white room coloured pink by firelight with a painting on an easel of a naked girl. There was no difference between then and now. She took off her ring.

Her body had never felt like this before and the longing for him dragged inside her. His face had been imprinted on her heart for so many years, but it was unfamiliar, barely known. Elisabeth unbuttoned her dress and let it fall on to the floor. The cold poured over her like icy water.

Then the thought came: what would happen after this? Hurt and guilt. George could not know she cherished him, that she tried so hard to be a loving wife. And Michael – did he want her now? He had seen her wedding ring the day they said goodbye to Nanna Lydia and he had never tried to persuade her. He told her he would not go away again and being near her was enough. He had not asked for more.

If he opened his eyes, he would see her stranded stupidly in her slip, shivering with cold and caught out halfway to betrayal. After so many years, this was not how it should be.

When he woke, the stove was alight and Elisabeth was peeling potatoes on a newspaper at the table.

Today, Michael picks up her bicycle, leans it against the hut and takes the loaf of bread and the package of cheese out of the basket. He walks easily now and is upright again, not hunched with pain as he was for so long. He doesn't look so different from the person she remembers. The change in him is subtle and sometimes she thinks she imagines it, because she never knew him well. His battle with his damaged hands absorbs him and there's something else – is it indifference? Or disappointment. He never looks at her as he did in the studio in Fitzroy Street. He does not seem to see her.

She follows him into the hut, talking about nothing much and not expecting him to answer. In spite of everything, the happiness of being with him never lessens. Dungeness is like an island and Michael is too. He is another life.

She loves her husband, his company, the fairness in him that puts her heart in balance whenever he is there. George does not understand deceit. His strength is in the clarity with which he sees the world; his weakness is in trusting her.

*1932*

# 21

'People tell you lots of ways to stop a baby but not a scrap of good advice when it comes to making one,' said Rachel. The Orpingtons were scuffling round her feet and she fed them corn from the pocket of her overall. 'I wish we still had Nanna to give us tips.' Then she giggled, 'Eddie's worn to shreds with trying.'

'Don't think about babies when you're doing it,' said Elisabeth, sitting on the edge of the cattle trough in Eddie's yard and banging her heels. 'Fretting gets the spermatozoa going round in circles.'

Rachel shrieked. 'My life, Elisabeth! The things you say!' She flung some corn and the hens sprinted after it with their bloomers fluttering. 'At his age, George must want a kiddie. What should we be up to that we aren't? You're a nurse, you should know.'

'It's luck, Rachel. That's all.'

Elisabeth didn't mind her failure to have a child with George and it didn't surprise her: her heart and body were separate. Rachel was impatient and beginning to feel anxious. Eddie had already been a father to poor baby Archie so it couldn't be because of him that Rachel wasn't pregnant yet.

Little Toby Schroëder had to be shared between the four of them. He was nine years old, and the remnants of the Schroëders' fortune paid the boarding fees at a school in Kent. His father was building a new career in armaments and had taken the family home to New York, but Toby suffered so badly with the separation from Elisabeth that Ingrid Schroëder agreed to send him back to England.

Every Friday, George would drive the Daimler to collect him from the school in Tunbridge Wells and Toby spent weekends with them. His spotted pony, Little Bear, still grazed in Eddie and Rachel's pasture. Sometimes Toby helped Eddie with the milking or Rachel with the hens, or he rode along the beach to Vera's bungalow, where she fed him and scolded him for looking like a gypsy boy. No one worried where he was because all the land was home. He lived wild like a fox cub. The boy who used to worry about sun and wind didn't care now if it rained when he was swimming with Little Bear in the sea, if he lost his shoes or slept in straw.

His aunt, Francesca Brion, drove down from London occasionally to visit and she seemed to approve of the change in him. She was as lovely as Elisabeth remembered her, still neat and gracious. The silver in her hair made her dark eyes more beautiful.

Once, on a visit, when they were having tea in the little sitting room and waiting for Toby to come home, Francesca Brion said lightly to Elisabeth, 'I haven't heard from Michael Ross for some time. He always lets me know his whereabouts. I'm wondering if you've heard anything at all?'

For a moment Elisabeth didn't know what to say. 'Yes,' she said. 'I see Michael often. He's living not far from here.' She saw a minute flicker in Francesca's eyes and it was acknowledged: the equalizing of that moment when they first met all those years ago outside Michael's studio and Francesca had subtly claimed him. She had not been honest, Elisabeth knew that now.

Francesca Brion looked down at her teacup. 'I'm so glad he's well.'

'He came home when his grandmother was dying. I was close to Nanna and she asked for me. Michael and I –'

'I wonder, do you have his address?'

'There's no address. I could take a letter to him, if you like.'

'How can there be no address? How strange.' Her sweet American voice didn't falter in its gentleness and good manners.

Anger that should have died long ago rose up inside Elisabeth. She did not feel guilty for inflicting this humiliation; it was deserved. 'Dungeness doesn't have streets. If you send a letter it might be delivered or it might not.'

Francesca smoothed the pair of blue kid gloves lying on her lap. 'Then perhaps you would tell him,' she said evenly, 'that the studio in Fitzroy Street is still in his name. I should like Michael to know the lease will be renewed for him.'

'He doesn't paint any more.' Elisabeth was swept along by spite and it came easily now. 'He won't want your studio.'

Francesca sipped her tea. 'He may not want it now, but things change, Elisabeth. When we last met you were not married, as I remember.'

They never mentioned Michael again and somehow they found a way around this boulder on the path of a friendship which must be maintained because of Toby.

Elisabeth knew when Francesca had found Michael on Dungeness because the blue gloves were on his table. He didn't hide them and Elisabeth didn't ask. What was between them could not be altered by Francesca Brion, but Elisabeth took the gloves and flung them in the sea.

• • •

The house in Munich had been oppressive for so long, but now, almost empty and being left behind, it seemed to Karen to be full of wistful benevolence. The fir trees weren't sinister any more and she couldn't imagine why she'd ever thought their branches moving in the wind were an ogre in the forest.

She was eating lunch in the dining room. The dust disturbed by all the movement in the house streamed in the icy sunshine, and if she blew softly up into light, the motes wheeled and twinkled.

It was easy to be alone now. Solitude was simple and she could not recall how it felt when she was never by herself. Far away, in a different life, snoring Betty had shared her room at the hotel – or Stan sneaked in when Betty was bribed to spend the night elsewhere. And all the years at home in Catford, Elisabeth was always trailing after her.

The house was full of people today but Karen had no part in the work that needed to be done, so she was eating slowly, keeping out of the way and waiting to be told when to move so the dining table could be loaded on to the lorry. The legs of the table and the chairs were already wrapped in cardboard, the curtains had been taken down and the carpets rolled up. The furniture to be left behind was covered with sheets and looked like icebergs sailing across the bare floor.

Outside on the gravel were trunks of linen and crates of crystal and china packed in straw. The mirrors were laid flat on the lawn, and various armchairs, armoires and tables huddled together in the cold breeze like people waiting, aimless and homeless, for whatever might happen to them next.

The largest pieces of furniture were being carried out of the front door, up the ramp into the lorry with Hede shouting directions to the men.

Hede had seen the house in Salzburg, although Karen hadn't. Their new home was large and well decorated, Hede said, and the previous inhabitants had left behind a library of books and dozens of oil paintings on the walls. The Jewish family who used to live there had decided to emigrate, as many were these days, and hadn't wanted the inconvenience and expense of taking all their things. Although it was odd, Hede said, that the cupboards were still full of clothes and the beds were made.

The bodies of two shepherd hounds had been thrown into a flower-bed and a starving kitten was mewing in the cellar. Hede brought back the kitten in a box, but when she opened the lid to show little Stefan, it shot away into the forest and disappeared.

Artur had gone ahead to Salzburg a month ago. Karen did not know much about his work these days. She understood the new administration was reforming the economy in Germany and, necessarily, it was Jews who were most affected. Only those who opposed the general good were forced in any way – and that was the same for anyone who did not support the Führer's plans.

Some people were more fervent in their views than others and at first it had been shocking to see the insults daubed across the shops and businesses of Jewish people, but now it just seemed part of the change in Germany.

Elisabeth had written that newspapers in England were full of stories of bullying and violence. People outside Germany didn't understand, Karen wrote back. Progress is always painful for a few, but the difficulties weren't significant and no one was being hurt. It was a matter of putting proper Germans first. No one shopped at Rosenbaum's any more and that was the only way she was personally affected. Rosenbaum's used to have the nicest dresses anywhere in Munich.

Karen was careful. As Artur's wife, she should write nothing that might be misunderstood so she didn't tell Elisabeth how unkind it was of Artur to dismiss the sweet, hard-working Küchen girl because she had a Jewish grandmother, or that Mr Rosenbaum's little dog was tied up by the paws and hung outside his shop, almost strangled and painted yellow.

There was another thing she couldn't tell Elisabeth, and if it could be written down, if Karen could explain why she had done nothing to help, perhaps the memory would begin to fade.

It had been an ordinary day and Karen was shopping for winter boots with Hede. Ahead in the busy street there was a snag in the flow of pedestrians, and people stepped off the kerb to go round an obstruction on the pavement. When they drew closer, Karen saw six or seven *Hitlerjugend* boys swaggering and guffawing, blocking the way. The boys were big, almost men.

There was a gentleman and a little girl pressed back into a doorway, and the boys were jabbing at the man, who had his arm around the child. She was twelve or thirteen, dark and pretty, and he held her tight against him with his hand shielding her cheek, pressing her face against his coat so she couldn't see the boys. Perhaps he covered her ears so she couldn't hear them either. The girl sagged into him. Her mittens and her satchel had fallen on the pavement and the boys were jeering, leaning in at her.

Karen stopped and people barged against her back, but Hede grabbed her sleeve and pulled her on. 'Juden,' Hede said.

'How do you know? You can't tell. How can you?'

Hede looked at her with disbelief. 'Open up your eyes. *Jude*, he is sly like a skinny dog. It is boo-hoo tears pretending fear. It is obvious.' She spat delicately into the gutter.

The child had her arms wrapped around the man as if she was trying to protect him, and she keened softly with spit and tears dribbling down her chin. The man's eyes were darting past the boys to the passers-by and he caught sight of Karen. A tall blonde girl with a Nazi brooch on her lapel would not help him.

Then Karen was pushed forward by the people behind, and she was walking past with all the other good Germans who would not interfere. What could she have done? It would have been foolish to intervene. The man wasn't hurt, she told herself, neither was the child, and the boys were strong and drunk on the power of their uniforms and swastikas.

But the memory wouldn't fade. She still saw the little girl's face against the coat, the spot of livid pink on her cheek. How could such a thing have happened and she did nothing to stop it?

The thudding of the furniture-removal men's boots up and down the stairs put Karen's nerves on edge. This morning something else had disturbed the blankness which made the days pass smoothly.

On top of the wardrobe in her bedroom, the men had found the picture of Elisabeth painted by Michael Ross and the sight of it stirred a feeling of disquiet. It reminded her of a letter from Elisabeth saying that Michael had been beaten by some men in Munich, and a Jewish doctor and his wife had cared for him until he was well enough to travel home to England.

He must have been hurt soon after they parted at the station and

Karen had puzzled over why, in all the months of his recuperation, he had not been in touch.

She could hear the men in Artur's study along the hall. The files and papers had already all been moved and today the furniture would be cleared. The thudding and grinding of heavy objects being shifted was enough to make the wine shudder in the glass beside her plate, and through the open double doors of the dining room she saw a man go past carrying a leather chair. A bookcase followed and a brass floor lamp, a filing cabinet and a boy leaning backwards carrying some wooden drawers.

Then Hede was standing at the doorway. 'This is not good, I think.' She held up a filthy rucksack. 'I will put it for the mice to eat. But this is very good.' It was a hunting rifle. 'I find it in Herr Landau's cupboard under old flea-bite coat and other rubbish. Is luck we find it or your husband is not happy.' She dropped the rucksack on the floor and held the rifle across her bosom. There was a decoration of flowers and trailing ribbons on the stock. 'The weight is good. *Ja*, I have never held so good in all my life. We ask Herr Landau, why do you not oil this gun and put it with the others?'

Karen felt the cool smooth table beneath her palms and let her mind empty. There was no answer she could give. The rifle belonged to Michael. There was no explanation as to why it might be here, only a question that could not be asked.

Her heart was still. The dust streamed in the sunlight and the men passed back and forth carrying things to the lorry. Hede fidgeted, waiting for instructions. 'I ask Herr Landau, *ja*?'

Karen stood up, picked up her plate and glass. She was a wife who did not meddle or ask questions. 'It's just a gun, Hede. I don't care.'

Hede shrugged. 'It is the same to me. So what if fine gun has dust? I shall put it in the lorry, and that is that.'

• • •

ARRIVE FOUR STOP

WILL STAY AT HOTEL STOP KAREN

The words were typed on paper tape and stuck down like a ransom note. Nine words. Karen had changed the plan. Elisabeth stared at the telegram and felt the old humiliation burning. Even after all this time, Karen could lure her into feeling safe, into *assuming*.

Everything was done, a cake baked and flowers put in the room. Elisabeth had gone up to the attic and brought down, piece by piece, the bed which her father had painted for her when she was five and in Stepney Hospital with the whooping cough. Dadda had painted a picture on the headboard of a farmyard with ducks and hens, and it had been a homecoming surprise.

The bed was for little Stefan and Elisabeth put it in a corner of the guest room where she had thought Karen and her husband would sleep.

She stood at the door where the telegram boy had left her and caught herself turning the telegram over to look at the back, like an animal who looks behind a mirror because it makes no sense.

She sat down on the doorstep in the shelter of the porch. The summer wind rocked the branches of the cedar in the garden, slowly, like a great ship in a swell. Out across the Marsh, blond reeds along the ditches were bending.

She wondered what she would do with all the extra eggs and butter. Her housekeeping money was already stretched and she hadn't a clue how women managed this for years and years.

Now supper would be just her and George. There was nothing else to do today but wait. She had time to go out to Dungeness to see Michael, but she couldn't; she hadn't told him Karen was coming. The reason why he mustn't know slipped away from her and she didn't try to catch it. So many feelings flitted in the shadows now, not all cunning and evasive – some were quick and beautiful, like half-seen birds. She let them fly up and disappear.

She sat on the doorstep for a long time, watching the cedar dipping and rising, and listening to the sheep complaining. The happiness and excitement seeped back. Karen was coming. Nothing mattered as much as seeing her again. It had been more than three years.

At half past three, Elisabeth went upstairs to change, brush her hair and put on lipstick. Bending over the dressing-table mirror, she heard a car, doors opening and footsteps on the gravel. She ran too fast down the stairs, swinging on the banister and almost slipping on the flagstones in the hall.

Karen was there standing at the open front door. 'Oh! Oh!' they both cried. 'It's you! It's you!' Karen's arms around Elisabeth felt bony and her eyes looked feverish, and Elisabeth almost recoiled as if Karen was a gushing stranger, then the feeling disappeared and they were holding hands and smiling. Elisabeth had thought there might be an instant of assessment which Karen could not hide – at the wedding, Ma's face had given away her disappointment that the marriage to George Mander had not provided Elisabeth with a house or wardrobe to boast about – but Karen showed no sign of noticing anything.

Her husband stood beside the car, waiting for his wife to introduce him.

'I'm so pleased to meet you at last, Artur,' said Elisabeth. It was impossible not to stare. It was clear why Karen had chosen Artur Landau. He was a match for her – a man who would always be noticed and admired. He was indifferent to his handsomeness but certain of it.

'Karen has told me so much of you,' he said. His accent was slight and only the preciseness of the consonants and an odd inflection gave him away. He held Elisabeth's hand a moment longer than he needed and she saw him take in her clothes, her face and body. The little boy was standing close to him and Artur stroked the child's blond head. Stefan was dressed in a tweed jacket and leather shorts with woollen socks turned over at the knees. The stiff clothes seemed strange on such a tiny child.

'Stefan darling, say hello,' said Karen. Stefan gave a little bow. 'Oh, Stefan.' Karen laughed. She seemed flustered. 'There's no need for that. Give Tante Elisabeth a kiss.'

'He behaves correctly,' said Artur. There was a breath of ice Elisabeth might have imagined, then Karen took Artur's arm and he gazed down at her as if they were still so much in love.

'Let's go in and have some tea,' Elisabeth said. To her surprise, Stefan took her hand.

Artur stretched his long legs towards the hearth and Elisabeth worried about the feathers leaking from the sofa on to his spotless clothes. From time to time, he spoke softly in German to his son, who sat cross-legged on the rug and ate his cake.

Karen sat on a fireside chair, a tea plate on her lap, holding her cup and saucer in her hands. The flames in the fire lit up her skin and her pale hair. Her dress was the black red of roses. 'How is George?' she asked. 'Will we see him today?'

'He won't be home until six. He's so looking forward to meeting you and Artur.'

Karen turned to Artur. 'Elisabeth's husband has a factory which makes iron gates and railings and things. Is that right, Elisabeth?' Karen seemed shy – or cautious. Was she still overwhelmed with love for Artur Landau? There was a time when Elisabeth knew what Karen felt, but the thread between them was fragile now. It used to be too strong, too tiring, but now suddenly it was weak and slack as if they barely knew each other.

'I am not a businessman. I have no aptitude,' Artur said to Elisabeth. 'I am an administrator, I think you would say in England.'

'Artur is dedicated to his work,' said Karen. 'The Party is his life. And mine. How is Toby?'

Stefan looked up from his plate. 'Cake is good,' he said.

'You speak very good English, Stefan,' said Elisabeth.

'Karen did not tell me you have a son,' Artur said. 'His name is Toby? I am happy for you.'

'Oh, Toby isn't ours. He comes to us at weekends. His parents are in New York and I worked for them in London before I married, but they went back after the Crash in '29. Toby is at school not far from here.' Elisabeth wondered if she'd said too much.

'Of course.' Artur's voice was neutral. 'Your home should have a child and a boy should have a proper education whatever the circumstances of his parents. He is fortunate.'

Elisabeth didn't know if this was approval or not. She offered Artur another cup of tea and he complimented her on the china which had belonged to George's mother. He questioned her on English attitudes. Did they not envy the transformation of Germany?

She didn't know. He laughed and said he could forgive her for having no interest in these things, it was as it should be in a wife.

After an hour or so, he said, 'I'm afraid it is time for us to go to our hotel. It has been very pleasant, Elisabeth. We will meet again before I leave.'

Karen was buttoning Stefan into his jacket. 'Artur is going home when his business in London is finished,' she said. 'He'll take Stefan with him, so you and I can have some time together.' She fussed over Stefan's clothes. 'I should so love to see Rachel.' Her hands were shaking and Elisabeth realized that something was wrong and had been all the time. 'Will we see her?'

'Yes, of course. If you'd like to.'

At the porch, Artur kissed Elisabeth's cheek and took Stefan to the car.

Karen pulled her close. 'Is he here?' she whispered. For a moment Elisabeth didn't understand. 'Is Michael here?'

'Karen, you mustn't.'

'Tell me. Quickly.' Her hand gripped Elisabeth's too tightly.

'Yes.'

Karen turned away, smiling to her husband. She walked across to him and waved to Elisabeth before she got into the car.

• • •

'They didn't stay?' George asked her.

'They've gone to a hotel. It was all arranged. It doesn't matter.' Elisabeth took his coat and hung it on the hall stand.

'You look lovely today,' George said, as he always did.

'I'm not lovely at all,' she said, kissing him. 'You need your eyes tested.'

Suddenly, she was relieved he hadn't been here to meet Karen and Artur and their angelic child. George was too good a man to notice but she would have felt for him; grey-haired and ageing with an untidy wife and home – and a boy who wasn't even his. The truth was she had been ashamed. The flowers from the garden, the sunken cake and all the extra groceries that would go to waste seemed silly now, like the efforts of a schoolgirl.

She hadn't paid attention to Karen's letters, she knew that now. Karen had been careful not to say where they would stay and it was Elisabeth's mistake to assume it would be with her and George. Karen had come to see Michael and that had probably always been her plan.

George picked up the post on the hall table, whistling softly while Elisabeth brushed his hat. She would make herself forget Michael, as she always did when George was home. She would forget Karen too.

George stood watching her with the letters in his hand and Elisabeth turned away. The disappointment of the day was still inside her and he would know something had gone wrong. It was hard to have her every mood and smallest upset noticed. 'Supper will be a while. Shall I make some tea?' she said.

'I'll get more coal. It will be cold this evening.'

She watched him change his shoes. She was sorry she was grieving over Karen and sorry that the longing for Michael still took hold of her sometimes. George was part of her in a way that Karen had ceased to be and he loved her in a way that Michael never would.

The evening would be peaceful. George would read the newspaper, write letters for his secretary to type the next day, and Elisabeth would knit or do some mending, listening to the wireless.

And later, in the high old bed, he would kiss her softly and say it didn't matter. When he was asleep, she would lean into him in the warm hollow in the mattress – the dip he made was too deep to roll out of even if she'd wanted to – and she could believe that, after all, this was where she should be and in time, at last, it could be right.

● ● ●

It was a sunny morning and a sea wind blew in over the fields. Karen arrived alone at ten o'clock. 'Where's Stefan?' asked Elisabeth.

'Hede's taking him to the beach.'

'Hede?'

'Our *Kindermädchen*. I've forgotten the word. Oh, yes, our nanny. Stefan loves her.'

'I know who Hede is, but he could have come with us,' said Elisabeth. 'I want to see him while he's here.'

'We can just be ourselves,' said Karen. 'Do anything.'

'We could have been ourselves with Stefan.'

'Where is Rachel working?' Karen asked. 'Let's surprise her.'

'Folkestone, and we'll have to get the bus,' said Elisabeth. 'Do you mind?' At one time it would not have occurred to her to ask.

On the bus, Karen talked happily about her new house, which was bigger than the one in Munich and had a view of mountains.

The Kentish lanes were narrow and the hedgerows scratched along the windows of the bus, from time to time showing glimpses of the chalk downs rising up on one side and the Channel on the other. Elisabeth wondered when a question about Michael would come but if Karen was thinking of anything other than her life in Germany she didn't show it.

They found the dress shop where Rachel worked. '*Guten Morgen, meine Damen*,' said Karen. The women in the shop looked flustered.

'Look at you!' said Rachel, hugging her. 'You've scrubbed up nice.'

'I'm going to take us out for lunch,' said Karen. 'And while we're here I want to buy Elisabeth a dress. No, two.'

'Karen, thank you. I couldn't let you.'

But that was how the morning went. Karen chose a dozen dresses from the rails for Elisabeth to try; plain creams and pale blues and yellows, and all impractical. At first Elisabeth felt shy standing in her underwear in the fitting room with Karen and Rachel going in and out, tweaking at the cloth, arranging her and standing back, hands on hips. If she looked good enough, they'd send her out to show the other assistants and after a while it was a game of dressing up and Elisabeth began to enjoy parading in the shop and having everyone give their verdict.

'The place looks like a jumble sale,' said Rachel. 'You'd better buy something, Karen, or I'm throwing you out, lunch or no lunch.'

Karen draped some dresses over her arm. 'We'll have this and this. And I want Elisabeth to have this one too.'

'No, Karen,' Elisabeth said. 'They're lovely but I wouldn't wear any of them except maybe the cotton one.'

Karen ignored her. 'You don't know when you might go up to London or out for dinner with George. Wear this one now, today, for me.' Elisabeth put on a sky-blue crêpe suit. The material fitted softly, close to her body. 'George will love you in it,' Karen told her.

He loves me anyway, Elisabeth wanted to say.

They walked along the Leas and a promenade photographer took their picture. 'Cuddle up, you lovely ladies,' he bellowed from under the black cloth. They giggled and put their arms around each other. Karen wrote the name of her hotel on a card and gave it to him. 'Bring a set for each of us – if they're any good. And you'll have to be quick, I'm not staying in England long.' The man nodded, waiting. 'My husband will pay you,' Karen said.

'My life!' said Rachel, when he'd gone. 'Since when were you the Queen of Sheba.'

Lunch was in a tea room looking out over the Channel, and Karen and Rachel chatted while Elisabeth watched the boats go by, listening to the gulls and the sea wind rattling the windows. Then she heard Karen ask, 'Where's Michael living these days?'

'Let's go to the fair in Rye tomorrow,' said Elisabeth quickly, but no one heard because at the same moment Rachel said, 'He lives out on Dungeness Point.'

'Then I shall visit him,' Karen said.

Elisabeth was watching an old man over on a grassy promenade with a paper bag of bread. 'You can't,' she said. 'You're married.'

Seagulls were hanging in the air and screeching like harpies, dipping and fighting over the crusts he was throwing up to them.

'I'm only going to say hello,' said Karen, patting Elisabeth's hand.

'How will you get there? I can't ask George to drive you.' Elisabeth heard her voice sounding quarrelsome.

'The hotel car will take me.'

'And you'll tell Artur?'

'For goodness sake. Artur won't mind, so why should you?'

'There's no point worrying, Elisabeth,' said Rachel. 'She'll do what she wants. She always has.'

Rachel went back to work and Karen called the waitress for the bill. They walked along the promenade in silence and Elisabeth knew there was nothing more to say.

'I know what you think,' said Karen after a while. 'But you don't understand.'

'No, I don't. And you think I don't know when you're not telling me the truth.'

Karen's blue eyes looked away, out to the blue horizon. She said evenly, 'The truth is, I did something which turned out badly for Michael. I should like to talk to him, that's all. I must tell him I'm sorry.'

So Karen had a past with Michael, as of course she would. They had seen Paris together and travelled on a train to Germany; there was a story between them and something which must be resolved.

'Artur won't know, I promise you,' Karen said. 'He's gone to London. I told him I would stay with you because that was what you wanted.'

# 22

Karen didn't come to the house the day after they took the bus to Folkestone, or the next. On the third morning, Elisabeth walked to Vera's bungalow.

It was hot and she tied up her hair in a scarf. She took the path across Eddie Saunders's fields, past the two black mares standing knee deep in buttercups. They turned their heads to watch her. In the lanes, she kept to the shade.

Vera made a pot of tea and the conversation was laundry and baking and the price of coal. Elisabeth wanted to ask if Michael had been home or if Karen had visited, when Vera sat back squarely in her chair and said, 'Your big sister! Well! She's always been a pretty thing but she's grown into a real beauty. She came here the other afternoon, so lovely and expensive-looking, but no airs. No, not a bit – you'd think she still lived round the corner. She had tea with me, a chop and veg, just like she did in Peckham when you girls were in and out the house like fleas.'

'Did she tell you where she would be today?' asked Elisabeth.

'She was going off to London, you didn't know? It's her husband's business so she probably didn't have time to tell you. She showed me a picture of him and I nearly swooned.'

'Did she say when they'd be back?'

'What's her husband's name? What is she now? She'll always be Karen Oliver to me.'

'His name is Artur. She's Karen Landau now,' said Elisabeth. 'Vera, do you know when they'll be back from London?'

'She didn't say. Do you mind the ironing board? You sit there, don't move yourself, I only need a corner.'

Elisabeth wanted to go home but her teacup had been filled again.

'She'll tell you all about it, I shouldn't wonder,' Vera said, 'but it was such a chance – Michael turned up when she was here and he said he'd see her home, back to her hotel. She told him her stockings didn't matter, she wasn't bothered, and she'd ride on the saddle of his bicycle.' Vera unrolled a pillowcase and spat on the iron. 'She looked so pretty sitting there, her skirt hitched up and laughing, holding on to him. I said, you were slow, my lad, she's the one that got away. Well, he said, she's here now. And off they went together.'

The midday heat was hard like metal. Elisabeth followed the path from Vera Ross's bungalow, back through the meadows where the black mares lifted their heads from the buttercups as they had earlier.

She had always known this would happen. How could it not be so? Michael would want Karen and she wouldn't care who was hurt.

Selfishness meant freedom and Elisabeth envied her.

And it seemed natural that Artur Landau was waiting when Elisabeth arrived home. He was sitting on the garden wall in his shirtsleeves, looking out at the fields. He watched her walk towards him but he didn't speak, and she wondered if perhaps he didn't recognize her with her hair tied up. She could feel the sun had burned her face and she was wearing an old blouse and a summer skirt she'd had for years.

'How nice to see you again, Artur, I thought you were in London. I'm sorry you've had to sit outside. I was visiting a friend.' What else could be said? An apology for her sister meant nothing.

His eyes flickered over her and he looked away. He was sweating. His hair was ruffled and he looked younger than the man she had met three days ago. 'I am returning to Germany with my son. Perhaps you would let Karen know this when you see her.'

'Please come in, Artur. It's very hot out here.'

He followed her into the kitchen and she put a glass of water in his hand. He drank it down and water trickled down his neck and inside his shirt. She gave him another.

He stood beside her at the sink, out of breath from drinking, and wiped his mouth with the back of his hand, watching her. 'My wife told me she would stay with you. She has not been here.' It was not a question. 'A man, Michael Ross, perhaps he lives near but I do not ask you where. Even if you know, you will not tell me.' He put his hand lightly on her shoulder and the anger in his eyes kept her still. He lifted a strand of hair away from her face and his fingers touched her cheek. 'Perhaps you are a good wife,' he said. Then he left.

★

Another car came later. Elisabeth was planting seedlings. She wanted to be occupied because it had been impossible to wash away the touch of Artur Landau on her face. She heard the car pull up and expected to hear footsteps on the gravel, but a moment later Karen's bare feet were standing on the earth next to the trowel.

'You told him,' she said.

Elisabeth put down the trowel. 'Artur came here looking for you,' she said. 'What happened to your shoes?'

'How could you? All you had to do was keep quiet.'

'Artur knew. I didn't tell him.' Elisabeth got to her feet, brushing the earth from her hands, dusting off her skirt. She felt ashamed, as if she was the one who had caused this chaos. 'He knew you were with Michael.'

'You could have helped me,' Karen shouted. Her face would have looked spiteful if Elisabeth hadn't known it was fear. 'You could have made up something.'

'I told you, he already knew. He knew Michael's name.'

Karen wasn't listening. 'I should have known I couldn't trust you. Why do you always do this? You watch me, you watch everyone, and decide what's right and never have any feelings of your own.' She paced to and fro, stamping down the earth where the seedlings were to go. 'I had to see Michael. I told you why. I explained it all to you.'

'You didn't explain anything. And I don't trust you any more,' said Elisabeth.

Karen stopped pacing. 'What?'

'You never told me about meeting him in Paris. Michael went to Germany with you and you didn't say. You never told me in your letters and you could have, but you didn't.'

Karen's face was blank. 'Why should I? And what does it matter?' She started pacing again, impatient to get past this distraction. 'You're happy with George. He looks after you and Michael never could. Michael said he loved you and I stopped him coming back. I didn't tell you because I dealt with it. That's all. I did it for you.'

Elisabeth wondered if it would feel like this to be shot – a moment of agony, then nothing; Michael had been coming back, and Karen had taken him away. She watched Karen's feet walking back and forth again on the soft turned earth.

'I always think of you,' said Karen peevishly. 'You don't know how much it cost me to help you, and when I need just one small thing from you, it's too much to ask.' She sat down suddenly on the empty flowerbed. 'Artur's gone. I don't know what to do.' She picked up the trowel and began to scrape hollows in the earth. 'He left money for me at the hotel, not even a message, just money.'

Elisabeth sat down beside her. The seedlings had already wilted and she began poking them into the earth one by one with her finger. She wished George would come home. It was late and the sun was low on the horizon.

Karen said, 'I didn't think Artur would come back here. He went to London to meet someone then he was taking Stefan home.' Her arms were sunburned like a farm girl's and there were tiny cuts on her legs.

Elisabeth touched her skin. 'What happened?'

'We went swimming in the sea last night. There were mussels on the rocks. I lost my shoes somewhere.'

They said nothing for a while and Karen kept on scraping at the earth.

'I couldn't bear it, Elisabeth. Michael's hands and his poor face. I didn't mean to stay.' For once, there was no triumph in her voice. 'When I saw him, I didn't care what happened or what I did, because I hated Artur.'

Suddenly the deadness vanished. 'You make excuses. You always forgive yourself whatever you do and you never really care if people are hurt. And why hate Artur? Michael's beating wasn't his fault.'

Karen put down the trowel beside the seedlings. 'It was mine.'

'But that's crazy. You think things happen because of you, but there are people you don't matter to at all. You make a game of everything – Michael loving me, and even Dadda dying.' This time Karen flinched and Elisabeth felt a rush of fear. Too much had been said.

Karen stood up, shading her eyes against the setting sun. 'I should go.' She seemed preoccupied, as if she had already forgotten what Elisabeth had said. 'This is how it always is. Whatever Artur does, I can't hate him. Will he forgive me, do you think?'

'Tell him nothing happened. He'll believe you; people always do. You'd better go.' Elisabeth turned away. She watched the starlings flocking to the trees and didn't hear Karen leave, only a car starting up and wheels turning on the gravel.

*

Elisabeth dragged her bicycle from the coach house and rode out to Dungeness. The evening sun was slanting and disintegrating now, and the sea was a tender evening blue. Michael didn't look surprised to see her even though she'd never come so late before, and she stood in front of him, gasping like a fish, the bicycle flung down and its wheels still clicking round. She wanted to slap his face and punch him, and sink down on the ground and weep.

She couldn't speak because the thoughts were stampeding in her head. She had no right to be hurt so there was nothing she could say.

The day's sun still scorched on her skin but the air seemed cold and she shivered. In the hut, Michael sat her down on the wooden bed and put a coat around her shoulders then he gave her a glass of water as she had Artur Landau a few hours before. Her eyes darted everywhere before the thought even came into her mind that she was searching for signs of Karen.

'I didn't bring her here,' Michael said. He sat on a chair at the table. A slab of sunlight came through the open door and Elisabeth leaned back against the wooden wall. The soft percussion of the waves and the rolling pebbles made her tired suddenly in spite of the storm inside her.

'I suppose you've loved her all this time since Paris,' she said, and her voice sounded quite ordinary.

Michael gave a dry laugh. 'Not love, Elisabeth.' He got up and took a bottle from the shelf, poured whisky in a cup and gave it to her, then one for himself, spilling some on the table. He was clumsy when his hands were tired.

'You don't care she's married? You've spoiled everything for her.' There was a feeble spark of anger but Elisabeth had no heart for it. 'And what about me?' She knew she sounded childish. The jealousy got dusty but it never went away.

He swirled the spirit in the cup and drank it down. 'This has nothing to do with you.'

The pain of what he said brought a rush of fury. 'How can you say that? Knowing how I feel, how can you say it?'

He regarded her. 'And how do you feel? You've never told me.' His coldness hurt but soothed her too; there was no love for Karen in his voice. 'Why shouldn't I have Karen – or any woman. God knows, there's no point in wanting you.'

Her mind was leaping from one thing to another. 'She says it's her fault you were beaten. I think she's going mad.'

'We all are. The world is, Elisabeth.'

'And she said you were coming home to me when you met in Paris, so why did you go with her to Munich?'

He looked up quickly, as if this wasn't a question he'd expected. 'It makes no difference now.'

She waited. She knew there would be more.

'You were married. Karen told me. I was too late.'

She looked down at her hands, the gold ring and the redness from the housework, and wondered at this life she thought was hers. The cogs and levers of events she thought she understood had synchronized without her knowing. The stars had taken up their places, the machinery had set and locked a course in Paris long ago. 'It wasn't true,' she said. 'I wasn't married then.'

Outside the light had almost gone. George would be home by now and he was bringing Toby back from school. Over supper in the kitchen, Toby would tell her about his week – the rugby games, the fights and food, and which items of his uniform needed to be mended. They would wonder where she was.

'I must go.' She stood up and Michael stood up too. A chair fell over and the sound when it hit the floor cracked apart the quiet.

'There's a place in France, Elisabeth. I've seen you there.' His voice rasped.

'Yes,' she said, although she didn't understand.

'You're walking up the hill to me and your hair is long like it used to be. We'll take the boat tonight. We'll go to Paris, to the market to buy peaches, and we'll take the train south to Mazamet.'

It was too painful to hear him say it as if it was a possibility. She must go home, but he was standing in her way. Then he put out his hand and took away the touch of Artur Landau on her face. 'It's not too late.'

He took her hands in his and when she looked up, she was in his eyes again after so many weeks and months and years when he hadn't seemed to see her.

'I must say goodbye to George and Toby,' she said.

'Then you'll come with me.'

'Yes.'

This was all it took to realign the stars. The machinery could be stopped and reconfigured. Karen's lie could be erased.

• • •

It is raining hard, and the air is so warm it clings like wet cloth. The English summer has suddenly turned feverish and the garden is a jungle of sagging greenery and saturated earth. Fat worms sprawl about looking more naked in the wet, the slugs are feasting and so are the snails. It's a time of plenty for the birds too. Thrushes and blackbirds are on the rampage in the herbaceous borders, skewering their victims and smashing snails on the path.

Across the Marsh, heat rises from the ground and the clouds do not seem to move or empty out. The sheep are drenched and stoical.

Elisabeth opens all the doors to let a draught through the house but the early morning air is viscous, almost fleshy, like something that has risen from the sea. She sits in the kitchen in her nightdress with her bare feet cooling on the flagstones. It is only eight o'clock but already the heat is oppressive. The gutters are overflowing and rain streams down the windows as if someone has turned a hose on them.

George and Toby have gone shooting today with Eddie Saunders. They have just left. Toby was looking forward to it so much they decided to ignore the rain. She waved to them elaborately like someone acting, and it's as if she has already forgotten how to be. She'll see them off only one more time because her plan is to leave tomorrow when Toby has gone back to school and George is at work.

This is the day when she must say goodbye to her husband and her almost-son, but she knows she can't tell George and Toby she is leaving them. She can't bear to see their hurt and incomprehension, or their anger either, hating her, not understanding that she loves them.

Her heart will die if she doesn't go with Michael. Guilt mutters in her head and when she listens she hears a trickle of excuses. *It's best you leave, you haven't given George a child. He can find a better wife. You can nullify the damage. Toby will come to understand that you love him just the same.*

All last night she was awake, staring up into the darkness, conjuring Michael's body close to hers. He leans over her, kisses her, softly pulls back the sheet. Her mind swerves around thoughts of making love because her stomach flies up as if she is falling and the current sparking through her seems to twist her nerves. The longing for him was denied for so long that now it has been named it overwhelms her.

She imagines that they live in France. Their house is cool although it's hot outside, and she loves being there alone because she knows Michael will come home. He paints, the pain has gone, the scar has faded, they have breakfast together, swim in a river in the mountains, sleep, feel the presence of each other in the house. They meet people who assume they've always been together. They have friends. They have a child.

She has guarded against these thoughts but now that they've taken flight she's weightless and can do nothing to tether herself again, although it's hard to silence the voice that keeps intruding. Is this love or jealousy? Why did she not leave George when Michael first came back? She has not thought of it in all the time he's lived at Dungeness, and she has organized her feelings so nothing is disrupted. George is her life and Michael is her soul and so, she tells herself, there is no need to make a choice. She is loyal to them both.

She has fooled herself that Michael will stay with nothing to sustain him. She brings him food, that's all, morsels of the life she has with George. The taste must always turn bitter when she leaves.

Then Karen comes and proves how easily Michael can be taken. Elisabeth should be grateful because now there is no doubt.

This morning she is sick with sleeplessness and the truth of what it means to go is crushing her. She loves Toby as if he is her own. George, she respects more than anyone she's ever known and she loves him, although she thought she never would – but the truth is she could be apart from him and bear it. It would not be a death inside her.

She sits listening to the rain, puts up her hair with her hands on her head, leans back and looks at the ceiling. A tap drips in the sink. The heat is increasing. Her nightdress sticks to her stomach and she finds a cool place on the flagstones for her feet.

Then something makes her sit up and turn around, scrabbling for her dressing gown, which has fallen on the floor. Two men stand at the open door in the shadow of the porch, their silhouettes against the opaque curtain of rain.

They do not come in yet, they wait in the porch and watch her bend down to pick up her dressing gown, put it on, tie the cord, before they walk through the hall and into the kitchen. One is Artur Landau. The other man is younger, his hair is plastered down and he is soaking as if he's been standing in the rain. Artur is almost dry and Elisabeth notices how odd it looks, one man dripping and the other immaculate. Her mind is flickering and she can't fix on anything for long enough to speak, but part of her is simply astonished that this is happening. Artur smiles over her head. 'What is your opinion of my sister-in-law, eh, Kurt? Is she to your taste?'

The man, Kurt, doesn't answer. He moves behind her and she feels his nearness at her back.

Artur's expression is cheerful. This chills her more than what he's said. Then she knows the reason he isn't soaked is because he has been waiting in a car somewhere along the lane, out of sight, while the other man stood in the rain and watched George and Toby leaving. She knows this in a flash and she sees that Artur knows she's worked it out and understood that he has come for her.

'I would like to know where I can find Michael Ross,' he says. 'I asked Karen, of course, and I believe she doesn't know.'

There is a long moment when Elisabeth feels the emptiness around her and she's flying through the silent house, across the garden and the miles of deserted fields to find the only people who can help her, but they are walking away and will hear only the rain.

Artur looks her up and down. 'Not skinny like her sister, a healthy figure, firm. A pleasing mouth would you say, Kurt? Unfortunately, another little English whore.'

He can't have said it. She hasn't heard correctly. Her face is fixed and so are her limbs. Kurt says something in German and Artur laughs. She can almost believe that this is nothing, she has misunderstood it all. But her instinct tells her there is no doubt and soon he will touch her.

Artur regards her, frowns a little. 'She receives us in her nightdress, Kurt. Perhaps she knows where we might find her friend but would rather we do not leave just yet. She teases us, keeps it to herself.'

There is nothing in his eyes, as if he doesn't see her any more. He reaches out and strokes along her jaw, under her chin and down to the opening of her dressing gown.

Then something changes so swiftly that the movement is invisible, like sleight of hand. Now Artur is not close and the man, Kurt, leans casually against the dresser. They're both looking towards the door to the garden, but when she tries to turn around, her legs give way and she sits down in a chair.

George and Toby and Eddie Saunders are dripping in their oilskins and gumboots, hunting satchels, guns, game sacks tied around their chests. George's deep sociable voice is filling up the kitchen and they are all shaking hands, introducing themselves. There's so much noise and movement she can't follow what they're saying. Toby comes to stand beside her chair and absently puts his wet hand on her arm.

Artur lies smoothly. He is showing Kurt the English coast, they were passing when they noticed the front door was open and, knowing that country people everywhere rise early, he decided to call on his English family.

'It's fortunate we came back. I should have been sorry to miss you a second time,' George says, and the tension that was pulsing in the air is rolled away by his voice. He does nothing to indicate he's noticed anything is wrong, but Elisabeth knows he has because he doesn't look at her, and he didn't kiss her as he always does when he comes home; all the time he stands facing Artur Landau, talking amiably. 'The rain is too heavy to take a shot,' George says. 'So here we are. We won't be going out again.'

The minutes move on and Elisabeth can't formulate the words to interrupt and tell George what happened, because nothing did. She understands that Artur will leave soon, but before he does he'll try again to get the information he came for. She takes Toby's hand and whispers to him, 'Let's find some dry clothes for you,' and for once he doesn't question her. She must get away and take Toby with her because there's nothing else she can do. They walk towards the door and George continues talking. She notices that Eddie has not put down his gun and stands against the wall.

'We should trouble you no longer,' Artur says. 'Kurt and I, we hope to find an English friend. He lives near here but we're not sure of the address. Do you know him by any chance? His name is Michael Ross.'

'I can't help you, I'm afraid.' George does not miss a beat. He looks across at Eddie. Eddie shakes his head.

She has to walk near Artur and if she did not have hold of Toby's hand she wouldn't have the courage, even now.

'It is a pity if we do not find him. Perhaps a postal office? Is there one nearby?'

'Hythe,' George says, 'but it's Sunday. They'll be closed.'

'So this name means nothing?' Artur looks at Eddie now. 'Michael Ross?'

Then Elisabeth feels Toby's hand in hers tighten and in that second she knows he will speak and she can do nothing to stop him. They are at the door, almost through, but Toby turns and says, 'Michael lives at Dungeness.'

Elisabeth closes the door behind them and, standing in the hall with Toby, she hears George say, 'You'll have breakfast before you go, Artur? Kurt? The English never let their visitors go away hungry.'

Now the fear begins to flood her and she feels so weak her legs are nearly giving way again, but she pulls Toby into George's study and shuts the door.

'What is it?' Toby asks. He looks frightened so she makes herself smile and says she wants to ask him something, that's all.

'Why didn't you tell him where Michael lives?' Toby isn't listening because her fear has entered into him. 'You wanted them to go away, didn't you?' She should reassure him but desperation is almost overwhelming her and she struggles to be patient.

'It doesn't matter, Toby.' They both know she hasn't given him an answer. 'Will you do something important for me?' There's a flicker of interest in his eyes. She finds paper and a pen, scribbles a note, puts it in an envelope and seals it. 'I'd like you to take this to Michael.'

'Why?' asks Toby.

She must make up something quickly and she must make him hurry. 'Michael was expecting me to visit this morning, but we have visitors. It would be best if you ride Little Bear and go the quickest way you know.'

Toby looks at her and she sees him sifting through to find the lies, to understand the truth of what she's asking him to do. 'Why?' he says.

'Because they . . . because Michael . . .' She has pushed the envelope into Toby's hand and fights away the panic at the wasted time.

'But my coat is in the kitchen,' he says reasonably. She dashes to the boot room, hears the men still talking in the kitchen and finds a coat of her own for him. They go out through the front door and into the downpour, her dressing gown is soaked in seconds and she watches Toby put a bridle on the pony and ride off across the fields.

Then she sits down in the mud. After a while, there are footsteps on the gravel on the other side of the house and a car in the lane starts up and drives away. She can't think – not even clearly enough to get out of the rain.

Sometime later, George finds her and he carries her into the house, undresses her and wraps her in a blanket, puts her to bed. He gives her brandy, holding the glass to her lips because she's shivering. 'Eddie has gone to Dungeness,' he tells her. 'I told Landau to take the New Romney road through Lydd. They won't get there for an hour or so. Eddie has time.'

She is crying and can't stop, and she has no idea how George has understood but somehow he has. He sits with her, holding her and stroking her hair, and he asks where Toby is. When she tells him, it's the first time he has ever looked at her with anger.

'He is a child, Elisabeth. How could you send him?'

He stands up and leaves her. She never knew before how much she needs him and how safe he makes her feel. She hears him go downstairs and soon after there is the sound of the Daimler's engine starting up.

He will take the big old car along flooded farm tracks direct to Dungeness, Eddie is striding as he does, knowing the land so well he will not waste a second, Artur Landau is driving on fast metalled roads but goes the long way through Lydd, Toby and Little Bear are trotting across the fields in the rain.

• • •

The envelope inside Toby's shirt was sticking to his chest. Perhaps the rain had already soaked the paper and the ink on Elisabeth's letter would be running. The message would be washed away. He told Little Bear to canter but the ground was too soft and they could only trot.

What had happened this morning was puzzling, and now that he was away from the two men from Germany, Toby couldn't remember why they had frightened him so much. This letter he was carrying was a puzzle too because Elisabeth hadn't told the truth.

She had been different since she came home late on Friday, so late they had started making supper. He was buttering bread at the table, George was frying sausages in a pan and it was almost dark outside when she walked in and smiled without really seeing them. She was looking at something else behind them, or through them, as if they were ghosts.

She said she had been washing the eggs with Rachel but that wasn't right. Rachel never did the eggs on Friday, always Sunday afternoon – Toby knew this because he helped her. Rachel scrubbed the muck off them with a little stiff brush and he dried them with a rag, wrote the date in pencil on the shell, wrapped each egg in straw and put it in the box. The boy from the grocer's collected the box on Monday.

And why would no one tell the men from Germany where Michael lived? And why did this letter have to be delivered now?

Toby reined in Little Bear in the shelter of a beech tree. The rain beating on the leaves and splashing on the ground was like standing under a huge umbrella with the grey Marsh all around. He took out the envelope and opened it.

> *Michael, go now. Now.*
>
> *Artur Landau and another man are on their way to Dungeness.*
>
> *Find some way of telling Toby where I should meet you tomorrow and please wait for me. You know I will come.*
>
> *E*

So the men were bad but this was no surprise. Toby had known as soon as he came into the kitchen that Elisabeth was frightened. The air around the men was spiteful.

The rest of the message he couldn't fathom, but it felt thick, knotted up, and perhaps this had stuck the envelope to his chest.

He hated the clammy letter with the private words. He hated Elisabeth, who was suddenly different and strange. He screwed up the paper, threw it out from under the shelter of the tree and watched the shining rain close around it.

He tore up the envelope too and let the pieces fall in the mud, then turned Little Bear's head towards Dungeness again. He would ride as slowly as he liked. He would tell Michael Ross about the men but that was all.

By the time he was walking Little Bear across the shingle, the rain had stopped and a sideways sun was barging through the clouds. Everything was glistening except the waves, which were the colour of old metal, and dingy with the rain moving out to sea and beating off the sparkle.

Toby did not dismount when he reached the hut because it wouldn't take long to deliver the message about the men. He had decided he hated Michael too.

'Hello, Toby,' said Michael, putting out his hand to Little Bear, who touched his nose to Michael's palm.

'Did you know Elisabeth was coming to see you this morning?' Toby asked, to check if anything she had said was true.

'No, I didn't.'

'Well, two men are coming, Elisabeth says to tell you. They're from Germany. I told them where you live because they asked. You'd probably better not be here when they come and they will any minute, I should think.'

Michael seemed to believe him straight away, but he said he would not go until Little Bear was out of sight so Toby must leave at once.

As Toby rode away, there was the sound of a car a long way off across the shingle, but then the rain began again and that was all he heard.

# 23

The old flowered curtains were pulled across, and in the half-light the floorboards were dark and glittering like water. Elisabeth was too drowsy to think why she should be in bed with daylight outside and her mind was empty. The wardrobe and the chests made heaped-up shadows and a little silver lozenge in the corner was the dressing-table mirror. Her body was so heavy she couldn't move.

Then she remembered: Toby's hand on her arm, the spotted rump of Little Bear disappearing in the rain, mud soaking through her dressing gown.

She sat up. The bedside clock said half past four and she had been sleeping almost all day. She started dressing, fumbling as if she had been ill. A headache from the brandy George had given her was swelling behind her eyes.

Downstairs, the front door was still wide open. She slammed it shut and bolted it although she knew Artur Landau would not come back. The house was empty. George and Eddie and Toby must still be out on the Marsh. She pulled on her boots. Toby had her coat but George's oilskin was still on the hook on the kitchen door and she reached up and put it on. Then she saw a note on the table:

*Elisabeth,*

*Michael Ross has gone. Eddie and I arrived together as he was leaving. We are looking for Toby. Do not go out. You must be here if he comes home.*

Michael was safe, but Toby had been gone since half past eight that morning – eight hours.

Now she knew what she had done. She sent Toby alone to Dungeness, into the path of Artur Landau who was as callous because of jealousy as she was because of love.

It seemed impossible to wait, to do nothing, though after a minute or two a dead weight of exhaustion descended on her. She sat down and put her head on her arms on the kitchen table. Perhaps she slept again.

'Are you all right?' Toby was standing beside her, filthy with spatters of mud and sand sticking to his coat – her coat – and she hugged him so tightly he squeaked. She kissed his soaking sand-spiked hair. 'You've been gone for hours and hours,' she said and she couldn't let him go.

'I went to Camber.' He shuffled her off and moved back. 'Little Bear likes the sand.'

'It's all right, darling, although you should have told me. George and Eddie are looking for you and I was worried too.' Toby's eyes slid away and he sniffed the water trickling from his hair and down his face. She kept her voice light. 'It doesn't matter, you're home now, and look at you. What a sight! I'll run a bath and make you something to eat.' Toby stared at the floor. 'Did Michael give you a message for me, darling? What did he say?'

'I want to go to Rachel's for tea today,' Toby said.

'No, Toby. It's school tomorrow. Did you hear me? What did Michael say?' Elisabeth shook Toby's shoulder gently but his eyes were blank. She knew she must look crazy, her face was hot and her hair was wild. She smiled as normally as she could and stroked the wet from his cheek but he stiffened and then he burst out, 'You weren't going to Michael's like you said. You lied and there's other things you lied about and that's all I'm saying.' Then he turned on his heel. 'I ripped up your stupid letter.'

In a second she grabbed him and slapped his face. They were both astonished. Toby's eyes filled up with tears – so did Elisabeth's. He ran out through the kitchen door and she called after him, but she let him go.

•   •   •

The certainty had disappeared. There had been too much time to scrutinize herself, to pick herself apart, and now she did not know if it would be a just punishment if Michael had gone without her.

Since Artur Landau came to the house four days ago, Toby had not returned to school and George stayed home from the foundry, saying they had missed their day's shooting and had earned some time together.

It seemed 'together' meant himself and Toby. They cleaned the guns, the Daimler and the bicycles, laying out bits of oily metal on newspaper in the courtyard. They came into the kitchen and found food when they were hungry. It was as if she wasn't there.

Elisabeth fell asleep on the sofa, at the kitchen table, sitting on the stairs, dreaming and forgetting, and half hearing George and Toby in the house. Sometimes she believed they wouldn't care and wouldn't even notice if she left, and sometimes she wanted more than anything for them to prevent her.

When she stood watching them, they glanced up sometimes, briefly, as if she was something bumping softly on the window.

Rachel came to help Elisabeth wash her hair and to change the sheets which were still stained with mud. 'It's your sister's caused all this trouble, what with her permanent wave and Paris coats and German la-di-da, and woe betide anyone who gets mixed up with her.' Rachel yanked the blankets straight and thumped the pillows. 'She's always been the same. Eddie didn't tell me much, but he said her husband was after Michael. What were they thinking of, the fools, going off like that?'

Elisabeth looked out of the window. Sunshine was flickering across the Marsh. Over Dungeness, the clouds were like mountains in the sky.

Rachel's voice was punctuated with slaps of her hand flattening the eiderdown. 'Don't bother telling me what went on, I can't keep up. I just hope Michael comes back soon.' The headboard rattled as she pushed the bed back against the wall. 'Mum needs him, what with Nanna and Grandpa Lemy passing on, and all those years looking after Dad.' There was a pause. 'Elisabeth?' Rachel's arms were folded across her aproned chest. 'Michael didn't even say goodbye.'

There was nothing Elisabeth could tell her. She closed her eyes. Her head was too heavy, her wet hair dripped down her neck, smelling sweet now after days when it was as rank as a pond.

'Perhaps I shouldn't care,' Rachel said. 'No one knows what's in my brother's mind so there's no use in speculating.' She rubbed Elisabeth's hair with a towel as if she was putting out a fire, then set about the tangles with a comb, but gradually the disquiet worked out of her hands and she said gently, 'I'm sorry. I shouldn't take it out on you. None of this is your fault.'

In the evenings, George came into the bedroom to say goodnight. He was solicitous, remote, and Elisabeth held his hands tightly. 'Please stay with me, George. Please talk to me. I'm sorry.'

228

'There's no need to be sorry, Elisabeth. It was my mistake for assuming I knew you better than I did. I thought Toby was like a son to you. He is to me. Now I understand what Michael Ross must mean to you.'

Whatever Michael meant eluded her because it had sunk too deep to bring up to the light. The days of Karen's visit were in shadow too, and the story was too long and complicated to explain: the house in Neate Street, the studio, Francesca Brion, the New York Crash, and somewhere in that time was Paris. Chinese whispers. Each little change evolves from what went before, but bit by bit the meaning disappears, the direction meanders, loops, turns inside out.

George stood at the foot of the bed, his hands in his trouser pockets, his big handsome face half in lamplight and half in shadow, and his voice had an edge she'd never heard before. 'I wonder if our marriage makes you happy, Elisabeth.'

'Of course I'm happy, George. I *am* happy,' she said. It was true but also a lie. How could it be both?

'There's something wrong between us and I think you know. Perhaps there always will be. You can be honest. There's no dishonour if we've done our best. I won't be unreasonable should you decide to leave.'

She could not be honest because the truth was shameful and it was not what George deserved. There was nowhere she would rather be than here with him, if Michael had gone without her.

• • •

George and Toby were sitting at the kitchen table, looking through a catalogue of bicycles. Perhaps it was their impenetrable attention to each other which made it possible to pick up her cardigan and purse and go out through the open door. She kept her head down, knowing George would notice, and she waited for him to read her guilt in the set of her shoulders and call out to her, but he didn't. She walked across the fields to the station and took the little train to Dungeness.

A heap of burned timbers was on the shingle where Michael's hut had been. The tar paint had been boiled by the flames and was still stinking, but the fire had been dead for days and sand was blowing across the charred remains.

A piece of the floor was intact, with the stove standing on its slab, and after a while her eyes could separate black from black and she saw a saucepan in the wreckage, a spoon, a window latch, a cup.

The pile of wood for the stove was untouched by the fire and a shirt was still pegged on the washing line. It had come half free, hanging on by a cuff, and Elisabeth reached up and pulled off the peg, but the wind grabbed the shirt and it looped up over her head, over the shingle bank, and flopped like a bird in the sea.

She had the peg in her hand. This was all he had left her.

A gull landed on the stove, planting its wide fleshy feet on the hot-plate where the kettle used to warm. The seagull's hooked beak was tipped with red: black-backed gull. *Larus marinus.* Toby had taught her the names.

A long time after, a car came. She heard the shingle crack under the tyres and the sonorous murmur of the engine on the wind. She had listened for this car so many times. There was no need to look. It was the yellow Daimler and George had come to take her home.

· · ·

*Mrs Francesca Blanche McCarthy Brion*
*Woburn Square, Bloomsbury*

*My dear Elisabeth*

*I trust all is well in Kent. I write because my nephew has asked to stay with me at weekends. Children often have these whims, and I'm sure before too long Toby will be asking to come to Kent again.*

*My sister is agreeable to whatever makes Toby happy and she thanks you and your husband for all you've done for him. I have told her how content and healthy he has been with you. I will send a car to his school in Tunbridge Wells on Fridays and bring him to London from now on.*

*As you see from this letter, I no longer live in Regent's Park but in Bloomsbury in the house that belonged to Pixie Fairhaven's family. You will remember Pixie? Michael Ross made a rather lovely portrait of her some years ago when he was working in his studio in Fitzroy Street.*

*Do come up and visit us – you and your husband will be most welcome.*

*Kindest regards,*
*Francesca Brion*

# 24

In the weeks after they returned to Germany, Karen expected some retribution, but Artur seemed equable, absorbed. They never spoke about what happened in Kent.

When Hede found the rifle in his study, Karen had tried hard to explain it to herself. Perhaps Michael had given it to Artur. Perhaps it was a different rifle.

In her heart, she knew that Artur had guessed what happened on the train from Paris and punished Michael. The rifle was a trophy. She should despise her husband for what he'd done, but she felt a furtive heady joy in knowing she could inspire such jealousy. Artur would fight any man who tried to take her.

The past could not be changed, and saying she was sorry for her husband's cruelty was all that she could do, but when Karen saw the scar on Michael's face and his broken tortured hands, Artur had seemed to deserve a second infidelity, even if he hadn't earned the first.

Michael's forgiveness was a sweet relief. He said he wanted to relive the memory of the Paris train and, in that moment, so did she.

Now all she wanted was to show contrition and convince Artur that what she did in Kent was not her fault. He would not divorce her because the failure of a marriage would damage his career. He would do something else to make her pay.

Since Stefan's birth, he had come into her room only when he wanted her, and since they returned from England, only once. She had woken early, it was barely light and Artur was standing by her bed. His boots were covered in earth and his uniform was filthy. An iron smell was in his hair.

Afterwards she knew it was hatred of Michael Ross that made him want her, not forgiveness or love. That was the last time. His indifference was her punishment.

But this would end one day, she told herself. He would desire her again and the thrill of it would breathe life into her like nothing else she'd ever known. The question of blame or guilt would cease to matter because he would belong to her again as she belonged to him.

There was no letter from Elisabeth, and Karen didn't write. Elisabeth was too far away to help and anyway she would never understand how all this had happened because of her.

*1933*

# 25

*Elisabeth, my darling,*

*You must have heard the news. Artur and I, we feel like crying and laughing at the same time. We wonder if it's a dream and we might wake up. Our Leader is Chancellor!*

*We went to Berlin last week. Herr Hitler was sworn in and there were thousands of people celebrating outside the Kaiserhof. Just the sight of it – a strong handsome man standing beside the old worn-out President – was enough to make everyone feel hopeful again.*

*Artur and I have been closer to our Leader than anyone around us in the crowd would have guessed, but we were happy to be with ordinary people, cheering and carrying our torches past the Chancellery. The noise was deafening, people couldn't shout loud enough, women and children too, not just the men. There were Hitlerjugend boys climbing the trees in Wilhelmplatz.*

*It was a freezing night and little Stefan was wrapped up in his sheepskin jerkin and his hat. He rode on Artur's shoulders and I swear he knew who the excitement was about. His sweet face was turned towards Herr Hitler all the time – people say he has this effect on children, and on animals too. They can sense his goodness and his kindness. It's an instinct of all innocent things to recognize those who have integrity.*

*I wore my dark green Paris coat. You've always said real fur looks good next to my skin.*

*We are waiting to hear what post Artur will be appointed to. We've been assured of his place in the Party and we may have to move, but now our Leader will be more in Berlin, it doesn't matter where we go.*

*Gunter and Anna-Marie are not as happy as us. We don't see them much these days and when we do, they don't acknowledge Artur's success, which I feel shows their ignorance. They didn't celebrate. Anna-Marie is proud of Artur secretly, I think, but she and Gunter don't understand why Germany must change. They are stuck in the past, and liberal in the worst ways. They have Jewish friends, Artur tells me – need I say more!*

*But they do see I'm a good wife to Artur, perhaps better than they thought I would be. A good marriage depends on duty even more than love, and on husband and wife excelling in their different roles, which are equally important. Each person's contribution can be measured – and perhaps their failures too – without the excuse of shared responsibility. I'm not sure how it works with you and George, and I can't imagine how I would have learned without our Leader's wisdom. Ma never told us anything useful.*

*I'm baking a cake for Artur's birthday – or rather I shall watch the kitchen girl. I'm still hopeless at cooking. Stefan wanted to help, but Artur doesn't like him doing girlish things. Stefan is so sweet and serious, I wish you could see him, darling. He knows numbers already and he speaks some English too. Artur is very proud of him.*

*I've had my hair permanently waved and it's such a boon with all there is to do at home and entertaining too. You should ask George if you can have yours done. It means sleeping in a hair net, but it's worth it.*

*As ever,*
*Karen*

• • •

With her face over the sink, Karen could taste the odour of the flannel, the stinking drain and the metallic bitterness of the brass taps. Her mouth flooded with saliva and she sweated, leaning her arms on the rim of the basin and seeing nothing because her mind was turned inwards to her stomach.

The reflection in the mirror showed a yellow tinge beneath her skin. Her eyelids were thick with too much sleep and her cheeks were hollow. Two creases cut between her eyebrows.

She should see a doctor; she had been warned that her heart was weak. Artur must have guessed what was wrong and decided that a dead wife was preferable to the embarrassment if this one lived.

The heaving in her stomach subsided. She washed her face and sat down on the bathroom chair, leaning her cheek on the tiled wall. The thought of food was repulsive but her stomach cramped with emptiness. She waited for the sourness to rise up her throat again as she knew it would.

On the train from Salzburg, she imagined taking another when she got to Munich. She could go on to Paris, then to the coast and take a boat to England. The loneliness would be left behind, along with Hede's smirk and Artur's silence, and the ranting Führer.

The German train was sleek supercilious chrome, with pork and cabbage in the air and little scarlet swastikas like drops of blood on the crockery, the corners of the napkins, the studs on the stewards' cuffs.

The French train would be polished wood and old blue velvet. The Channel ferry would be painted brown with olive-green upholstery in the cabins and swinging ten-watt lightbulbs. This would be home.

Nothing more than miles separated her from England. She could live with Elisabeth in her peaceful house on Romney Marsh with sheep outside the windows and starlings in the Kentish sky. One step followed by another would take her there.

But if she left now she would never see her son again so she must stay, and Doktor Hartog would help her. He had put a card in her hand the last time they spoke. 'I am here, Karen my dear,' Ruben Hartog had said, 'should you ever need me.'

It was strange to be in Munich again, alone. She took a taxi from the station to the suburb named on Doktor Hartog's card. The house was in a leafy street of large shuttered villas with iron gates. The young woman who opened the door was tall and blonde like Karen. Perhaps in another place, some other time, they would have been friends.

'I wonder, is the Doktor here?' Karen asked. The sickness gathering in her throat was so slight she could almost be imagining it, but she knew it would build and she must be quick. She held out the card.

The woman did not look. Her smile soured. 'He is not here.'

Karen's jaw had begun to ache as if she was eating salt. She swallowed down the thought of vomiting on Doktor Hartog's doorstep. 'I'd very much like to wait.' She clenched her teeth together and concentrated on the woman's face. 'If you wouldn't mind.'

'You are a friend?' the young woman asked.

'Oh, no, not a friend. I'm not acquainted with Doktor Hartog personally. Not at all.' An instinct for deception was learned just breathing the air of this new Germany. 'He is a friend of a cousin of mine in London – also a doctor. I'm English, you see, although I live here in Munich and it's not important but I've been asked to deliver a letter – just a card.'

Too long a speech, too many embellishments. Lies must be quick and lean. Karen gave the woman her nicest smile. 'Between you and me, it's rather a nuisance and I shan't worry if I can't.'

There was a pause. 'He has gone. His wife and daughter travelled east, apparently, with the grandchildren.' The woman sniffed. 'I understand the Doktor did not go with them. Where he is, I've no idea.' Her pupils seemed to narrow like a cat's, then the question came, lightly, as if it was a kindness. 'You need to see the Doktor for some other reason, perhaps?'

'No. No. Just the letter.' Karen could feel the blood draining from her face with the curdling sickness. The woman missed nothing. 'It doesn't matter in the least. I'm sorry to have troubled you.'

'You would like to leave your letter? I cannot promise it will be delivered.'

'Oh . . . thank you, no. I couldn't. I promised to see to it myself – which is silly, but there it is.'

'Of course.' The woman's face showed satisfaction and distaste as though she'd lanced a boil. 'It is a pity, but it seems I cannot help. Good day.' She stepped back to close the door. '*Heil Hitler.*'

'*Heil Hitler,*' Karen answered.

*1937*

# 26

Every hour there was daylight, Eddie had been digging out his animals. Ewes could tolerate the snow, but lambs wet from birth would freeze to death before they'd even suckled.

The lanes had disappeared and the marsh drains were smoothed over, so a person had to use a stick to poke along like a blind man feeling his way or he'd end up buried to the armpits. Everything that marked the land was gone, hidden inside great banks of snow sculpted by the wind and which could contain a tree, a shepherd's hut or a flock of sheep.

Then a thaw and the snow was water. After all the whiteness, the colours of grass and mud, the bark and berries seemed exotic, and slick like new paint on a picture. The Romney Marsh looked level to the eye until a flood showed up the subtle rises and hollows; now Eddie was spending his days wading to the islands of saturated ground to fetch his sheep and bring them home, or haul them to places that would take a corrugated shelter and a heap of straw. He used a half-barrel as a ferry for the lambs, loading them into their little boat to tempt the waterlogged ewes to swim with the collie bullying them behind.

He had been up since dawn, and he leaned his aching back against a tree and looked across the shimmer of floodwater to the swans fixed to their reflections. Beyond the swans was Fairfield Church on its temporary island. He lit a cigarette and held the smoke in his lungs to savour the warmth of it.

The day was closing over and he must cross the two hundred yards to the church to rescue any of his flock marooned there. There was no track across the pasture and even in the summer it was a tiresome walk for the women in their skirts and heels, and for the old folk. This coming Sunday, the parson and his congregation would take rowing boats to worship as they always did in times of inundation. The path to salvation in this parish required resourcefulness and stamina.

He had married Rachel in this church. He had never seen a girl so lovely, with her honey skin showing through the white lace sleeves, and smiling, head up, not shy at all. A bee was bumping round the posy she carried and a butterfly had settled on the flower in her hair. Inside the church was twilight, greenish, and cold as water in a well, but Eddie remembered the warmth that hope was pouring on his skin, and Rachel, bright and beautiful, just like the hymn.

Elisabeth in a blue costume was standing next to George. Nanna Lydia and Vera beaming fit to burst, and afterwards they all flung petals and bits of coloured paper that went up on the breeze.

Rachel put her arm through his to have the photographic portrait taken which George Mander had arranged. Eddie stood motionless but Rachel suddenly turned to kiss him, and in the printed picture her face and the posy ribbons were like a puff of mist, the dress and her hair streaming out like smoke.

There he was, smart in every detail, fixed to the earth, and Rachel like a wraith around him. She said it didn't matter because this was how they were, him clear and still, and her all restlessness and muddle.

Rachel had suffered sadness in her life just like him but she wasn't cowed or beaten, and gradually he believed her when she said they'd both had their share of mourning.

Now he knew they'd been distracted, looking in the wrong direction when all the time a different grief was stalking them.

There was a shallow rise where Eddie stood against the tree and smoked. The apathy that wore him out these days made the effort of wading seem impossible. He could feel the tender sponginess of his feet after two long days of being submerged in old canvas ditcher's boots and he thought of London streets with cobbles, a pavement and lamps along the kerb. It seemed miraculous that he had lived in a place where he could walk without the ground sucking at his feet.

London brick never altered with the weather, the horizon of roofs and chimneys was rigid and dependable. Even in the freeze of winter, London smells were smeared across whole neighbourhoods and stirred around with drains and soot; the brewery at Greenwich, the abattoir and the stinking tannery at Deptford, were proof of activity and toil, proof he was alive because his lungs would heave and his nose was assaulted with every breath he took.

Here in Kent the air was nothing. No shape to it and no knowing if anything his eyes could see was more than a watery illusion. Perhaps he should be grateful that at least one soft rank smell – damp dog – was available to convince him he was still alive on this dreary afternoon. The collie leaned against his leg, gazing out across the water.

Eddie flicked away his cigarette and the movement let in the chill under his coat, distracting him for a second from the melancholy that had settled over him. The wind was getting up, roughing the surface of the water and scribbling over the perfect reflection of the church. There would be a skin of ice so fine it would feel almost soft when he started wading through it, and under the surface each blade of grass and twig and leaf would be magnified like something fixed in glass.

He was thinking of Lucy and his baby boy again. The seven years with Rachel were not taking him away from Lucy but home to her. More and more, his mind flew back to London, back through the years.

Lucy cradles new-born Archie at her breast. She looks up and smiles.

The door to the street is open and Lucy stands on the pavement with Archie on her hip. She's giggling with Florrie Tanner, and Archie swivels his head to gaze at Eddie, then seems to come to a decision. He will speak. DAAAAA, he shrieks, flinging out his arms as if the word has knocked him backwards.

Then Eddie is sitting on a hard chair beside Lucy's bed as he has been for three days and nights. Sometimes when he opens his eyes he doesn't know if he's been asleep or if this waking is another dream. There are noises in the ward, coughs and rasping breath, squeaking shoes on the waxed linoleum, and the sounds are part of him as if he's lived here all his life.

The curtain around the bed has a pattern of roses and pink ribbons. He knows he will never forget how the petals fold so tenderly and the ribbons are the colour of watery blood. When a nurse draws across the curtain and no one can see, he leans close to Lucy. She breathes slowly as if she is inhaling perfume, exhales, and he pulls down his mask and sucks in her poisoned breath.

Lucy opens her eyes. Has Archie taken food today, she asks. She strains against the rawness in her throat and her voice barks, then disappears. Eddie strokes her hair, which has been cut because the Matron said the heat of it was worsening the fever. It will make no difference, Eddie knows it and the Matron must know it too. Lucy's plait of hair was thrown away. Eddie wanted it but couldn't bring himself to ask.

Lucy says again, has Archie taken nourishment? Is he all right? Eddie tells her, yes. It is the only lie there has ever been between them, but it's nearly the truth because Archie isn't hungry. He is waiting.

Lucy seems satisfied. Good. Our baby boy.

Eddie kisses her and his tongue touches her lips but they're dry as chalk and there's nothing for him. He is trying to steal from her, to take his share, although she doesn't know and she smiles sleepily as if what he's done is ordinary and nice.

A creature with a blank white muzzle flaps aside the curtain and the runners screech along the rail. Her eyes flick across the bed, then fix on him. You should go home, Mr Saunders, and get yourself some sleep.

A swan was landing and its great webbed feet skidded out in front, rumpling the silky flatness of the water. It settled, the wings folding away like a magic trick.

He must get on with his work and he should keep his mind on Rachel, who deserved better than him fleeing to be secretly with Lucy.

He must remember how Rachel used to be and must still be underneath the longing that tormented her. She used to sing to the hens and swing the bucket on her arm. She could bring back a lamb almost from the dead with whispering her will into the creature's soul. And in their bedroom, in the lamplight, she didn't used to care about the little cries she made like the night sounds outside in the blackness. Eddie remembered her smooth heavy limbs, and her smile through the tangle of her hair.

Three years ago, Elisabeth had a baby girl, Christina, and that was the beginning of the change. Rachel was happy for Elisabeth but it had started – the closing up against him.

'I can't explain,' Rachel told him angrily. 'It's all of me, all the time, every second, even when I'm busy, or talking, or thinking other things. It's like being thirsty – the deepest thirst you ever could imagine and I'm not allowed to drink. I'm not a proper wife like Lucy was.'

'I'm happy, Rachel,' he used to tell her. 'I don't want anything but you.'

This morning, in the dark, he could feel her mind clenched away and smouldering. She'd had a dream, she said, that she had a baby but she had forgotten where she'd left it. The baby was a sparrow in a knitted coat, then it was a foal with silver eyes, and then it was a human baby so tiny that she looked in all her pockets, in the kitchen drawers and behind the cushions on the sofa. The baby would die if she didn't find it.

The dream was terrible, she said, but still better than waking up and finding she had nothing. Her face was spiteful and triumphant as if this was a challenge he could not meet, a provocation to an argument he could never win.

At one time, Eddie would have said, 'You've got me, we've got each other,' but he didn't any more. She wanted to hurt him and to make him feel her pain. As if he didn't.

When he got up and dressed, Rachel didn't come down with him to make his bottle of tea. She didn't say goodbye and that was proof enough they had reached the end. Love always knows that any parting could be the last. A man and woman who don't say goodbye have stopped caring if they're tempting fate.

The collie fidgeted and Eddie felt the chill where the dog's heat had been. All this thinking would not save his sheep. Eddie flexed his hands and stamped his feet. The dog was wagging, looking back, and there was Rachel, wading out towards him. Her coat trailed in the water and a hunting satchel was slung across her chest. She looked mournful as a shadow with her long hair loose and her dark eyes so grave.

'Hello, dog. Hello, Eddie,' she said. 'I brought some tea for you.'

He told her he couldn't stop because the evening was coming on, but the truth was he didn't want her peace offering. He didn't want to soften like he always did and be punished all over again.

'I'll come with you,' she said, as if it was so simple.

He said he'd have to carry her across or she'd be useless with the cold and he hoped she would decline, hearing the discouragement in his voice.

'All right,' she said.

He didn't want her company but he longed to be with her. He was glad she asked to be with him and angry with himself for giving in. He didn't want more harm to his love for her, but then perhaps he'd never loved anyone but Lucy. The contradiction of it all took away his voice. The dog looked from one to the other, waiting for a resolution.

At last, Eddie nodded and turned his back, and Rachel put her hands up on his shoulders and gave a little jump, like children do, expecting him to catch her. She put her arms around his neck and her cheek side by side with his.

He had almost forgotten the feel of her, her faint musky smell like fresh planed wood and roses. She was a good even weight that would not trouble him. His arms were under her knees, her legs were around his waist and there was a time when this would have made him hot and tight with need for her and she would want him too, but their bodies were silent now, as if all the spark and hope between them had run down, useless.

He started wading and Rachel's feet made furrows in the water. The collie swam beside the half-barrel for the rescued lambs floating on its rope. The evening yawned across the water. The cold was bitter.

Up ahead, there was an arrowhead of phosphorescence and they saw a vixen swimming, then they came upon her cubs far behind her and almost drowned, with their heads straining up and their skinny bodies sinking. Their eyes were staring into death. Eddie scooped them up, the three of them, and put them in the barrel.

His legs below him were scissoring in slow motion and so numb they might not be his. The pasture under his feet looked more luscious through the lens of water and the collie swam beside him, seeming to be running in mid-air with streamers of bubbles from its paws.

A swimming hare, her nose a little prow, was pointing away from the church and out towards empty water. The collie circled twice using the tiller of its tail, then left the hare alone. Eddie was beside her, within reach of the flattened sodden ears, the bony skull and long dark body with its wake of turbulence. He had rescued the fox cubs – and him a farmer who should know better than to interfere – so why not a hare? Her eyes showed fear, not of drowning but of him, of the dog and cubs she knew were close. He would be pulling her from one terror to another, compounding her helplessness for his own sake, not for hers, and he fought inside himself to save the creature's life. Then he saw it: the will to live was in the graceful motion of her legs and he knew the wisdom of a hare could be trusted more than his own. He let her swim.

Rachel seemed heavier and heavier, silent, resting her chin on his shoulder and her arms around him. They passed a drowned lamb floating, spread-eagled like a woolly starfish, revolving slowly.

The ground was rising and the weight of the water lessened against Eddie's legs. Rachel slipped off his back.

They found a single ewe on the island at Fairfield Church. Two lambs were dead on the grass and three were packed tight in the shelter of a buttress, their heads resting on their hooflets. The church doors were open and more sheep huddled by the pulpit. A steaming mud-caked plough horse was standing in the nave.

They sat in the pews drinking tea from the flask, and the quiet between them was peaceful, as if the fury had gone for a while from Rachel's grief. Outside, across the Marsh, the wind was picking up. The vixen and her cubs slipped underneath the shadows.

Later, when the light had almost gone, they gathered up the sleeping lambs and put them into the half-barrel boat. The collie chivvied the ewes to follow.

They rode the plough horse back through the flood, Eddie sitting behind Rachel, who leaned back on him with her hands on his hands holding the horse's mane.

Something had altered in her, surrendered. It might be that she was coming back to him or she might have set off swimming into nothing like the hare.

· · ·

Karen remembered how eager she used to be, and sure of herself, leaping from one hope to another. Now she didn't have the energy or the taste for taking chances and wasn't fool enough to think the effort would be worth it.

Her greatest wish was that she should remain exactly as she was, going through the days like a cow along a path. She would keep her eyes on small things on the ground and ignore the little diamond glints of happiness that vanished if she looked at them. Elisabeth used to tell her she was reckless and contrary. She was the opposite now – she was the absence of anything at all. The mystery was how still a life could be, so still its passing and its dying couldn't be detected.

*I make myself busy doing this and that, but I'm inert. I'm nailed to the black.*

There was nothing she liked about herself except her patience and her marvellous ability to pretend. Hypocrisy hung round her neck as such deceits do hang, and it tired her. Every morning there was the job of raking around inside herself for sufficient docile cunning to get through the day and she would lie in bed and close her eyes – for trenches are best dug in the dark – until she felt invisible.

*I even fool my children. They don't know I've given in. I pretend our life is wonderful but the world is mean, it cuts you down to nothing. Everything in*

*Germany is squeezed too tight and stewing. Perhaps this is how a mother has to be because there's nothing she can do.*

She knew there must be other women in Germany who were as false as her, but they would be hiding too, so how could they ever know each other?

She needed Elisabeth. A sister is an anchor to the truth about one-self and Karen had drifted into nowhere. Even Elisabeth might not recognize her now, seeing the healthy flesh on Karen's body but not understanding that the fat was not contentment but part of the dis-guise. It filled the bodice of an evening dress and distracted from the thinness of her conversation. She made as good a show as anyone at loyalty and hatred in accordance with Party lines.

Artur seemed satisfied. He never minded if his statuesque English wife was surrounded all evening by leering Party friends, and this was how dinner this coming Saturday would go. Karen's ravishing décolle-tage and perfect manners would mesmerize her guests, and her mind would be as blank as a plate.

• • •

Karen asked Knitted Dog and One-eared Bear, 'Where's Antje? Where can she be?' Antje squealed behind the curtain, screwing up the tassels in her fists – more marks on the silk for Hede to suck her teeth at, Karen thought. It didn't matter; they would have new curtains. Karen crawled across the floor looking under the chairs and her hair came out of its pins. She looked inside a puzzle box, in Antje's shoes and behind the cushions on the sofa. 'No, she's not here. Or here. Or here.'

Antje lost her balance and fell out from behind the curtain, dashed away across the polished floor, slithered in her socks and Karen chased her, scooped her up. *'Ich habe dich.* I've got you!' Antje squirmed in her arms. 'Quick, off you go. I'm counting again. *One. Two. Three* . . .' Antje fled.

'Is Stefan home yet, Hede?' Karen called. On these summer eve-nings, Stefan would be with his troop learning to pitch a tent and march straight, practising his *Heil Hitlers* to get them exactly right.

'Mutti, I'm here,' Stefan said. He had Artur's skill of slipping in unnoticed and Artur's habit of swallowing down a smile. Karen kissed his hair. Antje hugged his waist and Stefan pretended to gnaw at her. 'I'm the ogre. Yum Yum.'

Antje's shrieks brought Hede to the door, hands on hips. 'Our baby child is breaking glass in Timbuktu. The food is ready. Now, madam.'

Karen had given up asking Hede not to call her madam; it was Hede's notion of Englishness and class, Karen supposed. The dishes were on the table and Hede was cutting up Antje's food.

'I'll do it, Hede.'

'You see how I cut it, madam? Our baby girl likes her food just so,' said Hede fondly. 'Heddy knows a game and Antje will finish everything.'

'Antje will sit by me, Hede. I'll see to her.'

Hede settled her bulk and loaded up her plate. Since Antje was born and Artur was away so much, Hede ate with them. They had Cook and girls to serve, so Hede had become a companion of sorts to Karen, although they had little to talk about other than the children and the running of the household.

The meal was quiet. Stefan made faces across the table and hummed his *Hitlerjugend* songs for Antje, who giggled and forgot to eat unless Karen reminded her. Hede chopped and ate methodically. The maid brought in the pudding.

'I've decided on the menu for Saturday, Hede,' Karen said. 'There'll be eighteen of us so the caterers will come. Tell Cook to take the evening off. Herr Bölling and Doktor Grundmann will sit near Artur.'

'*Ja*, madam, okay.'

'Stefan will stay up for dinner and I should like you to bring Antje in to say goodnight.'

Hede looked up, chewing slowly. 'To see Herr Bölling and Doktor Grundmann? These men, madam?'

'Antje is old enough to meet people, don't you think? It will be good for her.'

Hede put down her spoon.

'What is it, Hede?'

'It is nothing.'

'If you've finished, Stefan darling, would you take Antje in the garden,' Karen said. Stefan took Antje's hand and a moment later, through the window, Karen saw them on the lawn, Antje on Stefan's shoulders, holding his ears and swiping at the blossom on the cherry tree.

'What is it, Hede?'

Hede dabbed her lips, tipped her plate for the last drop of cream. 'You are her Mutti and must know best.'

'You think it's too late in the evening for her? I'm sure just this once won't hurt.'

Hede put down her spoon, delicately positioning it to line up with the pattern on the plate. She frowned as if she needed to gather up her thoughts. 'It is not that, madam. Ah, my mind is such a muddle. You will tell me I am crazy. Mad, you say in English, as a hat.' Hede folded her hands in her lap and looked up to the ceiling. 'It is this. We visit England . . . it is, I think, five years ago. Herr Landau, little Stefan and me, we were in London and you were staying with your friend.'

'That was years ago, Hede. I can't see –'

'I finish, madam, very quickly. For two days, maybe three, you were with this friend, Herr . . . Mr . . . What was his name? My memory is not good.' Hede tapped her fingers on the tablecloth. 'I have it! Mr Ross. Michael Ross, an artist Herr Landau tells me. It is a big surprise, I almost fainted. *Jude!* Herr Landau tells me your friend is a Jew!' Hede flapped her hands, patted her chest. 'I say to myself, Frau Landau is young and English. She knows no better in her friends.'

'He's the brother of an old schoolfriend of mine, Hede. And this really isn't any concern of yours. I'm –'

Hede held up her hand to silence Karen. 'Soon baby Antje comes along and she is *so* beautiful a baby as I have ever seen. I say to myself, Antje cannot be the only little girl whose Mutti and Pappi and big *Bruder* all have blue blue eyes but she is not the same. She has brown. Brown as a nigger.' Hede looked out at Antje gathering blossom on the grass. 'Brown as a Jew.'

Karen waited. Her skin was cold. 'What are you saying, Hede?'

'It is not *saying* that will hurt, madam. It is plain to see for anyone who looks at Antje.'

'I've no idea what you're talking about.' Karen stood up and began to stack the plates. 'I'll put the children to bed. You may go now. Thank you, Hede.'

Then Hede reached across and grasped her arm. 'I am not so simple as you think.' she said softly. 'Trouble will come and it is no good saying it will not.'

Karen pulled her arm away. She sat down again.

'Good,' Hede said. 'So. Antje's Pappi is the Jew. Hush, don't tell me he is not. It is too late for stories. You see, madam, I love our baby girl but I am cut in half. What would you have me do? I am German and have one duty. No, do not frown, this fault is not mine. Herr Landau loves his little Antje as any pappi would and he pretends he does not see, or perhaps he cannot bear to. But soon he must because others will – men like Herr Bölling and Doktor Grundmann. The story will come out, and if they ask, I cannot lie. You understand this must be so, madam, although it breaks my heart.'

Karen's mind was frozen still.

'Herr Landau is dismissed, young Stefan is no longer in his boys' corps, and you, madam, what happens to you? But Antje is the one who suffers most.' Sweat had appeared above Hede's lip. 'I ask myself, what can we do to keep her safe? I have thought and thought and I cannot see a better plan.'

The quiet thickened in the room and Karen knew some horror would come to life when Hede spoke. Outside Antje ran to and fro throwing up handfuls of blossom and dashing through the petals.

'I will say it now,' Hede whispered. 'It is this. They say put washing bleach into the eyes and this will make them blue. The sight is lost and there is pain, but in time the pain will go.'

Karen could not move. She should slap Hede's face, dismiss her, call someone, but who? 'I'll tell my husband,' she said at last – the most stupid thing of all.

'Ja, you tell him, madam.' Hede stood up. She leaned across the table and Karen felt a breath of hatred burning her. 'You think I cannot see? You break Herr Landau's heart not once but twice. You torture him – a good fine man who loves you. I try to help, to find a way to help us all. You think Antje is invisible?' A blade of evening sunshine cast silver in Hede's eyes, and Karen saw that they were depthless, like metal. 'You think the Führer will turn away his head because you are a pretty Party wife? No, madam. He will not.'

'Mutti?' Stefan was standing at the door. How long he had been there Karen had no idea and she got up, flustered. 'Oh, darling, don't creep about so! Is Antje still outside?' Stefan gazed at her. 'We were gossiping as usual.' Karen smiled, holding out her hand. 'I shall come outside. What should we play, do you think?'

She knew that Stefan was not easily fooled. His eyes were as unfathomable as Hede's. He stood at the door for a moment, then he turned and she heard him walking back along the passageway, out into the garden.

# 27

Salzburg

*Michael,*

*I shall hope your mother sends this letter on to you. You might tear it up and if you do, it would be no more than I deserve, but will you meet me one last time?*

*In June I shall come to Kent for a few days. If you contact the bookings clerk, Mr Stubbard, at the Metropole Hotel in Folkestone, he will tell you the dates I shall stay. If you would telephone me at the hotel, I will meet you anywhere you suggest. I must talk to you, Michael. Please say you will.*

*Karen*

• • •

Ronald Stubbard smoothed the pages of his bookings ledger in preparation for the guest coming up the steps. In a blink, he had folded up his newspaper and tucked it behind the cash tin where Mr Tart wouldn't poke about. The position of Head Clerk for twenty-seven years should give a person privileges and a bit of slack, Stubbard thought, but old Lemon Tart still prowled around, checking up. It was an insult if a man couldn't read the paper when business was quiet.

The news was grim with things coming to the boil in Europe and Spain tearing out her own heart. The pompous little German Führer had pledged support to Señor Franco, and young men from countries who shouldn't get involved were swarming south to help the Spanish rebels who sounded like a pack of savages. The Orientals were at each other's throats, and if Mr Chamberlain didn't take a stand in Europe, they'd all be back fighting in the trenches though they vowed they never would again in all eternity. The promises that there would never be another war weren't adding up to much.

But perhaps it was all best forgotten on such a sunny optimistic day. Stubbard tweaked back his sleeves to show the buttons on his cuffs – nice nigger-brown enamel his mother had given him last Christmas.

He composed his professional smile but the young woman still did not come through the door. She had stopped in the shadow of the entrance and a pleasing picture she made, with her pretty silhouette against the grassy Leas and yellow gorse, the splintery sea and, far away, a streak of nothing that was France.

Stubbard couldn't see the woman's face but her figure was shapely and her coat was nicely tailored, square shouldered, flared to just below the knee. She wore her hair up with her hat at a hopeful angle and it had an embellishment of some sort on the brim with a little veil over her eyes. She carried a vanity case on her arm.

He noted that her neck was fine and her waist was trim; this was his personal method of assessing the quality of lady he was receiving. Neck and girth were signs of class.

Years ago, when the hotel was residential chambers, he used to pride himself on his skill at guessing which gentleman a visitor would ask for. The atmosphere in the place was more congenial then and one could even have a brandy occasionally after hours in the little staff room adjoining the Snug. In his time he'd smoked in the presence of an Indian prince and a minister of His Majesty's government.

These days, the place was modish but rather dull, although it was still the second-best hotel in Folkestone.

Through the glass door, Stubbard could see the doorman, old Mr Pearce, fixed in a half-bow with his gloved hand holding the brass handle, his epaulettes frisking in the breeze and his buttons winking. The young porter, Awkward Sidney, stood to one side waiting for instructions although it seemed the woman had no luggage.

She patted her hat edgily and tucked back a wisp of hair. The three figures were sharp and black against the sunshine and the glittering sea: the woman, old Pearce and Sidney. Then Pearce pulled open the door, a little too flamboyantly perhaps, and in she came.

An oval face, bright auburn hair and a nice enough complexion, clear grey eyes, but no lipstick or powder. Stubbard was a touch disappointed. She was pretty but not as sophisticated as her figure promised.

She was perhaps twenty-five, twenty-six, it was hard to tell. Her chin and nose had pinked as if she'd caught the sun and her lips were full; not to his taste. But her faults gave maturity to her childish face and made her rather fetching. He had assumed she was reluctant to enter because of shyness, but she had a look of wary excitement he'd seen so many times in the past. She must be visiting a gentleman.

She leaned forward as if they might be overheard. 'Good morning. Is Mrs Landau here?' she said. So he was wrong about the gentleman.

The tall and plainly dressed Frau Landau was not to his taste either. She was a beauty, that could not be denied, but she had an arrogance that spoiled her in spite of the exquisite eyes and golden hair.

She had been here two days and a small mystery had gathered itself around her; she had reserved adjoining rooms and given permission to disclose her booking dates to a gentleman, a Mr Michael Ross, who would telephone to enquire. Stubbard had enjoyed the prospect of overseeing the smooth running of a discreet liaison, as he had often in the past. The gentleman's call was put through to her room on the first evening of her stay, but she didn't go out and no one came. It was anyone's guess what that was all about.

The Frau was demanding, as if she considered herself more than just a visiting foreigner – and mean with tips. The room staff squabbled over who should answer her bell and he'd had to intervene. He told them there was a policy of appeasement to the Hun. They looked blank. He shouldn't have expected them to read the newspapers.

'Perhaps madam would like to wait comfortably,' Stubbard said to the Frau's visitor, gesturing to the winged leather chairs arm to arm along the wall.

'Oh, thank you, no, I really don't need to sit down.' She seemed to think he was being kind. 'I expect Mrs Landau will come as soon as she knows I'm here.' On the desk was a bouquet in a glass vase and she sniffed a lily. 'The flowers are lovely. They always make me cheerful, don't they you?' Her smile was so innocent Stubbard forgave her for her embarrassing friendliness. The blooms gave off a feeble joyous scent of the outdoors which Stubbard found uplifting too, and he warmed to this novice guest who now had pollen on her nose. She looked too gentle and too nice to be a friend of the Frau.

'Who would madam wish me to inform Mrs Landau is here to see her?'

The woman stared. Stubbard tried again. 'Madam, may I ask your name?'

'Elisabeth. Thank you. Mrs Elisabeth Mander.'

Sidney was sent to alert the Frau. She came down directly and Stubbard took on the colours of his background so he could observe.

'I'm fatter and you're thinner,' he heard Frau Landau say bluntly as soon as she set eyes on Mrs Mander. 'You've got pollen on your nose.'

Poor Mrs Mander looked overcome and cautious all at once. She scrubbed at her pretty nose while tangling with the Frau's embrace.

'Your room is next to mine,' announced Frau Landau when they'd got over all the kissing and dishevelment of meeting. 'We can see the sea and we've got a door in between so we can leave it open and talk. Let's take up your bag.' And off they went together.

• • •

Elisabeth wondered why Karen had never mentioned the chaos of the last time they were together. Has Artur forgiven you? Elisabeth asked in her letters more than once, but Karen seemed absorbed in married life, and in the Führer whom she spoke of as often as she spoke of Artur. They had another child, a little girl, Antje Eva, so Karen's marriage had survived.

To George's delight, Elisabeth had fallen pregnant at last. She gave birth to a daughter in the same month as little Antje was born. Karen sent an embroidered shawl for baby Christina, Elisabeth sent a teddy bear for Antje and a matinee coat she knitted herself.

Karen's letters became infrequent, so it was a surprise when she wrote to say she would be coming to England again, on her own this time. She would book a hotel in Folkestone for two nights. It'll just be us, she wrote, like it used to be before we had husbands and children.

Elisabeth had packed her case, aware that her excitement was tinged with dread that something she could not foresee would send everything into chaos again. She resolved to keep her distance this time, wondering if Karen knew where Michael was and if this visit was another excuse to see him.

The hotel was expensive. There were flowers on the reception desk and oil paintings on the walls.

When Karen came down the stairs, Elisabeth saw that these last five years had altered her. She seemed more guarded somehow. She put her arms around Elisabeth, hugging her as if nothing had happened. 'I'm fatter and you're thinner. You've got pollen on your nose,' she said.

Elisabeth thought the man at the desk could have warned her about the lilies. She had felt nice in her new hat – although the veil was like looking through a cloud of smuts – but with a yellow nose she must look ridiculous.

Their rooms were at the front and the long bay windows looked out along a crescent of white seafront villas. The furnishings were modern: maple wood and pale green watered silk. There were chrome lamps and glass tables. Elisabeth took off her hat and coat and put her vanity case in the mirrored bathroom where a dozen reflections spat on their hankies and scrubbed at their noses with their hair lopsided from the hurricane on the Folkestone bus. She powdered her face and applied some lipstick.

'What are you doing in there?' Karen called out. 'It doesn't matter if you look a sight. The place is full of geriatrics and they're all as blind as bats.'

Downstairs in the sun room, some elderly ladies were drinking sherry. Ironed newspapers on poles were hanging on a rack. The cotton blinds were drawn down against the morning sunshine, and a young man with oiled hair played popular ballads at the grand piano. He stared into space as if he had no interest in the fingers on the keys.

'This is nice,' said Elisabeth.

'I hate hotels,' Karen said. 'How's George? I liked your hat. He must be giving you more money for clothes these days.'

'Thanks,' said Elisabeth. 'He always gave me plenty, Karen.'

There was a time when Elisabeth made almost all her clothes, but the foundry was doing well and money wasn't tight at home any more. George had taken her to London shopping more than once this year already. He had engaged a man to do the bookkeeping, and also a wages clerk, so Elisabeth no longer helped out in the office. It was strange that this comfortable life was thanks to Karen's Führer, whose belligerence had provoked rearmament. The foundry had orders for months ahead, although it troubled George. 'We should be grateful, shouldn't we?' Elisabeth had said to him. 'We're only making rivets and bolts and things, not guns. Mr Chamberlain says having weapons will stop another war, not make one. You're keeping us safe, George. You're helping peace.' She always wanted him to say, yes, that was it, but he never did.

The young man at the piano finished the piece with a sardonic rippling chord.

Karen said, 'I always knew George would be a good husband for you.'

'What an odd thing to say. Yes, he is. I'm very lucky.'

After they finished drinking coffee in the sun room, they walked along the Leas promenade and sat in deckchairs looking out over the Channel. A brass band in the bandstand honked 'Hello, Mr Sunshine' and when the conductor closed his music and the boys put down their instruments and started on their sandwiches, Karen took Elisabeth's arm and they followed a little zigzag path down the cliff through mock grottos of shell-encrusted rock where lizards basked, down steep steps with a wooden handrail, beneath pines and tamarisk, down to a path by the sea.

They walked with their faces to the afternoon sun as far as the cottages at Sandgate, where they teetered along the sea wall, holding their arms out for balance, or their skirts down for modesty. Elisabeth knew they were too old to behave like this but she was slipping up through the silt of wifeliness and motherhood that had settled over her, and popping like a bubble in the air where she and Karen would always be the same.

The upset of Karen's last visit was disappearing. Those days were only four in the thousands of their lives together. So few should not matter.

They had forgotten lunch. Elisabeth had a headache and her face was sore from the sun and the salt air. A little weatherboard shop sold ices and when they'd finished they left the saucers and spoons on a tray outside, then sat on the pebbles with their backs against a wooden groyne to watch the fishing boats waiting for mackerel to come in on the evening tide.

After a while, Karen said, 'I've always known you would be happy because you're good.'

'I'm not good at all.'

Then Karen grasped her hand. 'I'm sorry for what happened last time I was here. Can you forgive me?'

Elisabeth was astonished. She had never known Karen to be ashamed of anything she'd done and it came to her in an instant of bleak certainty that there was something false in this whole day together. Karen wanted something and she was waiting for her moment, biding her time.

But Ma had taught them that forgiveness must follow an apology, however unresolved the battle, so Elisabeth put her arms around Karen and held her close. It wasn't affection that made it hard to let go but the blankness when they touched. The feel of Karen was baffling, like hugging a bolt of cloth. Elisabeth looked over Karen's hair, not knowing when the reconciliation was complete, and she watched the old ladies knitting and gossiping in the sun outside their painted cottages and the children turning somersaults on the promenade railings.

After a while, Karen said meekly, 'Thank you.' They walked in silence back to the hotel.

When she dressed for dinner, Elisabeth put on the opal earrings George had given her. She had bought a new cashmere jacket and an expensive lipstick. For the first time, at least in one way, she and Karen would be equal.

In the dining room, Karen looked scornfully at the other guests. 'I've wasted so much time and money on clothes and silly unnecessary things. Women who spend hours adorning themselves are pitiful. Thank goodness I know now that health and motherhood are all a woman needs to make her beautiful.'

This didn't seem to be directed at Elisabeth but the opals and the Coral Secret lipstick felt coarse and silly.

Karen drank too much and argued with the couple at the next table. 'Juden,' she said, not bothering to lower her voice. She accused the old gentleman of staring. She was insulted, she said, and it was also an insult to his wife. The woman looked alarmed and the white-haired gentleman said he was sorry if he had offended her but Karen had misunderstood: he had an interest in Germany and he'd merely been wondering if they'd like to join them at their table. The other diners gawped.

Elisabeth would not have blamed the gentleman, or anyone, for wanting to look. Nothing, not even her frumpish blouse, could make Karen less beautiful.

It was late when they went upstairs. Elisabeth found their keys and Karen leaned against the door frame. In the room the lamps had been lit and the covers turned down. Karen stumbled in, kicking off her shoes. She pulled out her hair pins and yanked at her blouse. It was half undone and she dragged it off her shoulders, fumbling with the buttons. She stood swaying by the bed, then sat down suddenly and flopped back against the pillows. Tears trickled into her hair and she was asleep.

Elisabeth looked at her and felt nothing except longing to be at home with George. She switched off the bedside lamp. Whatever the reason for Karen's tears, they would be for herself.

Once upon a time, long ago, she always wanted to sleep beside Karen. Elisabeth remembered scooting across the freezing lino in the bedroom in Catford, so quickly the shadows couldn't grab her ankles, jumping in, wriggling close but careful not to cling or Karen would be cross. There was often no room for Elisabeth's legs, not enough blanket, a flat corner of the pillow, but it was still the best place to be.

Back in her room, Elisabeth undressed in the dark and opened the curtains. There was no moon. Yellow lights that must be the lamps of fishing boats were low down in the black like stars that had fallen in the sea. She could hear Karen whimpering and she closed the door between them.

In the morning the sea was white capped and brown. The grassy promenade was empty, and rain and sea spray spattered on the window. Elisabeth stood in her dressing gown looking out and she wondered what George and Christina were doing.

It was past nine when she knocked on Karen's door, expecting the room to be in darkness but the curtains and the balcony doors were open. Rain blew in on the clammy wind, wetting the polished floor and the rug. Karen was standing in her nightdress.

'For heaven's sake, Karen, you'll catch your death and they won't like their carpet getting soaked.'

'I'm paying, aren't I?' Karen said.

Elisabeth closed the doors, pulled the breakfast trolley to the table, and put out the cups and plates, lifting lids and dish covers. 'Here's our toast. Hot water. Jam. Do you want grapefruit? We have marmalade too.'

'I must tell you something.'

'Milk, and cream –'

Karen banged the table and the china rattled. 'Your fussing goes on and on! You never hear anything because you never listen.'

Elisabeth felt a closing-up inside herself she hadn't known for years, and it occurred to her that she could get up and leave and didn't have to bear this any more.

'Are you listening, Elisabeth?'

Elisabeth said nothing.

'I shall give Antje to you,' Karen said.

Elisabeth heard the words but what should be the reply? She picked up the teapot, put it down, lifted the lid from a silver dish. Her mind felt scrambled.

'You will love her because of me, Elisabeth. That's why I've chosen you.' Karen spoke quickly as if she had rehearsed the speech. 'I thought Artur wouldn't ever know, but now it's obvious. It's impossible to have a mistake in his family. He can't have a wife who has done . . . who has been disloyal. He – we are bringing up a child who is . . . who is . . . who isn't German, so this is what I must do. You shall have her.'

The quiet beat softly on the walls. Elisabeth poured tea into their cups, because it seemed wrong somehow to let it stew.

'You have Stefan, so how can Antje be wrong? Your children are the same,' she said, setting down the pot on the silver stand. She had forgotten to put milk in their cups and a thought flitted in her mind that Karen would be cross.

'Not the same,' Karen said. 'She's Michael's daughter.'

Elisabeth watched her own hand reach across to take a piece of toast. What she had heard was impossible, and inevitable. Michael was never hers. She stirred her tea and felt as weightless as the ringing of the spoon against the cup.

'Say something.' Karen sounded exasperated. 'Do you hear me? Antje is a Jew and she can't stay in Germany.'

There were muffled voices outside in the passageway, footsteps receded and a door slammed shut.

'I must set an example,' Karen continued as if Elisabeth had spoken. 'I must be beyond reproach because of Artur. We're trying to achieve something wonderful in Germany and everyone must search themselves, the Führer says, everyone must make sacrifices –'

'Stop it, Karen. I'm not listening to any more. You used to say everyone should do as they please. You should have told me. How could you say nothing in all this time.'

Karen got up and wandered to the window. She stood in the puddle of sea rain and put her hands on the glass. 'They read our letters.'

'Who? Who reads your letters?'

The panes were running with water and the curtains were soaked as if it was raining inside the room. 'Please don't ask me any more.'

The second night in the hotel that Karen had booked was pointless now. They sat in the empty sun room waiting for Elisabeth's taxi while the summer rain washed the windows and beat on the glass roof. Karen talked about the future all true German people shared, like a close and loyal family. She barely paused for breath as if the wall of words would stop any doubt or argument. Elisabeth felt numbed by the logic of it.

Karen lit a cigarette and arranged the pleats of her skirt. 'If you don't want Antje, a family in Holland will take her. It's all arranged. It'll be no trouble.'

Elisabeth had thought nothing Karen might say could shock her now. She leaned across and grasped Karen's hand. 'What's happened, Karen? I want to understand. Please.'

Karen gazed out at the rain. Her voice was calm, as if she had been waiting for this moment all along. 'You're like a child. You expect people to take care of you and you've no idea how the world is. You couldn't understand because you think life is fair and everyone is nice.'

The old humiliation. Karen knew her better than she knew herself. Arguing was useless, but Elisabeth was on her feet, stamping her foot – like a child, just as Karen had said. 'You don't know me at all! You take what you want and you don't care what it costs. You hurt people, Karen, everywhere you go.'

Karen stubbed out her cigarette. 'Well? Will you have her?'

'I'm not sure what I shall tell George.'

'Thank you,' Karen said, as if everything was settled.

•  •  •

Mr Pearce, the doorman, was on his break, so Awkward Sidney was at the ready, blushing with the challenge of showing Mrs Mander to her car. Her mood had changed since her arrival yesterday, Stubbard thought. She looked tired as if she'd had a sleepless night, and blank as if she'd had a shock – or perhaps she was counting down the minutes till she could say goodbye to the Frau, just like they all were.

Now the two were leaving and Stubbard busied himself behind the desk. He was interested in the women's farewell. Ladies usually made a show of pecking at the air on account of not wanting to disrupt the powder and the lipstick, or they gave an icy little gloves-on squeeze, but these two embraced hard and tight, though only for a moment, as if they loved and loathed each other.

Frau Landau looked the worse for wear this morning – not surprising after last's night débâcle in the dining room. Elsie told him the story at the start of morning shift. Apparently a waiter – Walter, most likely, seeing as he and Chef were 'friendly' – had told Chef, who'd told Mrs Cubsy, who told the girls in the laundry room, who told Elsie.

Frau Landau had fired a broadside at old Mr Aaronheim, Elsie said, suggesting he was leering, and Mrs A, who was teetotal on account of her tablets, downed a scotch and didn't touch her Cabinet Pudding. This morning, the two ladies hadn't eaten their breakfast, there was rainwater all over the floor and the carpet was wringing wet. The girls downstairs were already run ragged in the summer season without grown women larking about and making extra work. The curtains in the Frau's room were damp and would have to be taken down and pressed, and silk moiré was never the same after water had been on it.

Stubbard watched Frau Landau gazing after her friend's departing car and she stood there long after it had disappeared, looking queenly in spite of the hangover she must be suffering. Her hair was loose and she was informal in a way that ladies these days seemed to think acceptable. He wondered how long she'd stand there looking out at nothing.

Then it happened. She collapsed as if someone had cut her strings. Her lovely body folded over and there she was on the carpet, with her bleached silk hair spread out and her cheeks all milk and roses. The bad temper was smoothed away and she could have been a sleeping angel. It unsettled him – somewhat unprofessionally – to see her lying there.

They called a doctor and she came to in no time, then she was taken to her room. Stubbard sent up a message saying the hotel would organize a telegram, free of charge, to her husband or some member of the family she might like to escort her home, but the Frau did not contact anyone at all.

Later that day, whey-faced and civil for once, she asked for her luggage to be brought down, settled her account and left.

# 28

In 1928, when Michael left England, British artists knew their place – above the coarse Americans and well below the French. Modernism belonged in Europe although weak rays of its glassy intellect reached across the Channel and Michael had believed he was one of the few in London who were illuminated. He felt at home in the icy Gallic light. A glow worm thinks he has something in common with the moon.

In Mazamet he learned his mistake. His art is plain; a subject is observed and remade in paint. But his efforts are deficient because a likeness, however true, can't catch the birth and death of every moment. Time cannot be preserved. It is a grief to Michael to see a shadow sliding on a curve of ground, a yawning cat, a drop of water on a tap, and know it can't be saved.

Then Artur Landau taught him another lesson. Michael is a coward who only paints to save himself. It is his own life he strives to preserve, and so the years on Dungeness when he could not paint had been a kind of dying. If Elisabeth had not been near, he would have walked into the sea.

She saved him but she also made him suffer. A thousand moments of Elisabeth are lost; she walks across the shingle with a basket on her arm. She reaches up to the washing line, her bare heels are dusty and her sunburned hands peg his shirt against the sky. There's a breeze and the shirt billows green and yellow shadows on the blue. The sun is in her eyes as she sits at his table peeling an orange on the grey wood.

Life fades like a comet's tail and there is no trace of her. No proof of him.

He returns to London and lives in the studio on Fitzroy Street. He learns to paint again and finds solace in leafy streets with people walking, markets, parks, children playing on the pavements. He can't control a brush as he once did, but there are buyers for his work, ordinary people who want a picture for a drawing room or study. 'We don't understand the modern art,' they tell him. 'It's everywhere these days – all cleverness and temper. You are a good painter,' they say, as if he is a good man.

• • •

On a hot summer morning, Michael walked from the studio to the Post Office on the corner of Warren Street. There was rarely anything for him to collect, although his mother wrote occasionally and sent a card with some small gift for his birthday. Her writing was becoming spidery as Nanna Lydia's had been and the messages were brief. Vera had never asked him why he left Dungeness five years ago, abandoning her for a second time.

In the Post Office, Michael signed at the counter for his correspondence, mostly envelopes containing money orders from the galleries which sold his work. He made a living and had loyal customers but his paintings were an oddity in London now, and so was he. He did not align himself with any of the warring factions – Modernists, Realists, Abstractionists, Surrealists – and at their gatherings, he would be received with warmth and tolerance like an eccentric cousin who cannot grasp the intricacies of the family feud.

A new style of soirée had superseded the good-natured evenings of the kind that Frankie used to hold. The drink these days was beer, the food was nil, the mood was cynical and grim. The demons were Fascism and poverty, the grail was Eternal Truth.

Some believed that Art in the modern age should be a vision of perfect order, others said it must be spontaneous. Art should poke fun at bourgeois vanities, but it must strive for social unity. Art is timeless. Art is now. It is a madman's scribbles, a raw pork chop, a tiger in spectacles, a diver's suit with a mask of roses.

One publication said, *Left, right, black, red (and white too, for the fools who won't take part and so constitute a battle line all of their own), Hampstead, Bloomsbury, surrealist, abstract, social realist, Spain, Germany, Heaven, Hell . . . All colours turn to mud when stirred together.*

Michael sorted through the bundle of correspondence he had collected from the Post Office, standing in the shade of the Warren Street Underground to open the envelopes. One had German stamps and had been forwarded from the bungalow in Hythe where his mother lived.

He sat for a while in a café with the envelope in front of him on the table. It was a note from Karen Landau.

. . . *You might tear it up and if you do, it would be no more than I deserve* . . . It made him sad that Karen assumed he was angry when the anger should rightfully be hers. His hatred of Artur Landau had dissipated and the residue was shame for the hurt he had done her the last time she was in England.

*In June I shall come to Kent for a few days. If you contact the bookings clerk, Mr Stubbard, at the Metropole in Folkestone . . . I must talk to you, Michael. Please say you will.*

The letter was dated six weeks ago and he might have missed it but for the chance collection of his post. He left the café and returned to the Post Office to telephone the Metropole Hotel. The desk clerk told him that Mrs Landau would arrive in Folkestone the following week.

When Michael called again to speak to Karen, it took several attempts for the switchboard to make the connection. Karen's voice sounded weary and she seemed exasperated by the hissing and clicking on the line. She made the arrangement quickly and without warmth; she would come up to London and meet him in the tea lounge at the Charing Cross Hotel. What she had to tell him would not take long.

He was early and he met her walking along the Embankment, filling time as he was. He almost passed her when she said, 'It's me, Michael. Hello.' If she hadn't spoken, he might not have known her, but he would still have noticed her. She wore a drab green coat of some stiff hairy cloth which would be ugly on any other woman but Karen looked modest and rather touching, like a peasant girl who doesn't know how beautiful she is. She had lost the raw, electric quickness he remembered, she was heavier and her hair was held tight in an elaborate plaited coil at her neck. Her thickened features seemed immobile. She looked oddly still standing beneath the wind-blown trees by the choppy water of the Thames.

'You look well, Karen,' he said lamely.

'I look like a school matron,' she said, and for an instant he recognized the smile as if the intervening years had disappeared. He took a step towards her to kiss her but her stillness made him stop. He had never seen indifference and the flatness of neutrality in her.

'It's cold. Shall we walk?' she suggested. They came to some steps down to a concrete landing just above the waterline. 'I'd like to be out of the wind,' she said. On the steps, she slipped, clutching at him, and he caught her and held her until she steadied. The feel of her in his arms brought back memories of the Paris train. She pulled away, her eyes not meeting his, and she flicked at her coat fussily as if she was brushing off his touch. There was nothing to show that she remembered.

They stood on the landing looking out across the river. A swan came, expecting to be fed.

Then she opened her handbag and took out a photograph. 'This is Antje Eva.' The little girl had dark eyes, an elfin face and fair curling hair. Karen put the photograph away again.

Afterwards, when she had gone, Michael could not recollect the words she had used to tell him this child was his daughter. He remembered watching the oily water with the swan glowing bluish-white as if the moon was in its feathers, and the world had seemed to shift while she was speaking, the understanding dawning in his senses rather than in his mind, like an alteration in temperature or light. He remembered his wonder at the miracle of a child who was part of him.

'Antje can't stay in Germany,' Karen had said. 'You know why, Michael. She is . . .' She faltered. 'Antje isn't safe.'

'I should like to see her, Karen, if she's mine.'

Karen laughed, a shrill kind of yelp. 'Oh, yes, she's yours! If there were any doubt, do you think I would be here? You mustn't ever contact her, Michael, that's why I needed to see you. You must promise me you won't.'

'I'd like to know her.'

'Don't you see it isn't fair? She must belong to her new family. She mustn't know you and she must forget me. If she ever looked for me, if the authorities in Germany should ever know . . . I can't tell you . . . if someone were to hear of it . . .' He saw in Karen's eyes that she was desperate and would have begged if it had been in her nature.

'What should I do?' he asked.

'Nothing. There's nothing you need do.'

'Then why tell me? I'd never have found out.'

'I think you might have. Elisabeth is taking her.'

So, another piece of him would be beyond his reach. He could not see Elisabeth and now he could not see his daughter.

The swan rose out of the water and beat its wings, stirring up a little tempest, then settled back. When Karen spoke again, the desperation had gone from her voice. She sounded unconcerned, as if she was returning to ordinary things before they parted. 'I once thought Artur had you beaten because he loved me. Isn't that so silly? It was because you are a Jew.'

Michael had come to realize that his Jewish blood was visible to everyone but him. Israel was in the bones of his face; he was Francesca Brion's Hebrew, and the Jewish boy from Peckham bringing flowers to Elisabeth, and the English Jew who deserved a beating in Artur Landau's Germany.

What Karen said was true but he could see how much it hurt her to acknowledge it. There was hurt whichever way she turned: either she had caused his beating, or, if she hadn't, it was because Artur Landau had not loved her.

Cold was coming off the river. They watched the filthy tide rippling against the swan's white breast. Karen's face was tinged with blue as if bruises were just beneath the skin. She didn't shiver any more. The life in her seemed almost to have disappeared.

After a while, they climbed the steps again and walked in silence. The swan came too, gliding on the wind-scuffed water beside them as if the three were going somewhere together. Karen took his arm, leaning into him, and another memory came: five years ago, a warm summer night, lying with her on a Kentish beach and listening to the drag of shingle under the sea. She had smiled up at the stars, elated because he'd said he'd forgiven her. The beating in Munich didn't matter any more, he told her. The lie seemed easy.

They had gone swimming in the moonlight, she cut her legs on a mussel bed and afterwards couldn't find her shoes. He knew she should go back to her hotel but she seemed drunk with gratitude and said she must be with him.

Now he was ashamed because Karen had been hurt more terribly than she deserved. The past was a knot of sins and punishments with no way of knowing where justice lay. She had lied in Paris for reasons he could not understand; jealousy of Elisabeth, perhaps, or protectiveness, or simply Karen's need to shape life to her will. Whatever the reason, her lie had hurt them all.

They walked for a while along the Embankment, then back again towards Charing Cross. In the shelter of the bridge, Karen stopped and took her arm from his. Her voice was desolate. 'I must do this. You see, don't you? I must let Antje go. If I don't, they'll take her. They'll punish me, send me away to die and be forgotten. It's what happens in Germany to women like me.'

She smoothed her tight hair. 'I shan't want tea now. I must catch my train.' She looked impatient to be gone. 'I don't think we'll meet again. Goodbye, Michael.' She turned quickly and he watched her walk away.

# 29

When the Fairhavens returned to Texas after the Crash of '29, Francesca Brion bought their house in Woburn Square. She had always thought Bloomsbury would suit her better than the stupefying gentility of Regent's Park, and that the artists, writers and poets who came to her soirées would prefer it too.

Along with the house, she purchased the Fairhavens' furniture as a kindness to Lady Cara, who said she couldn't face auctioneers and dealers 'flicking their rattle-snakey tongues' in her darling English home. 'But I will not be parted from my Art. It is one's soul, one's consolation,' she told Frankie, 'and Urban says oil paint is the only safe investment left on God's green earth.' Cara's paintings were shipped out to America.

Frankie was glad she would not see Pixie Fairhaven's portrait again, haunted as it was by the luminous ghost beneath Pixie's skin, the ghost of the girl Michael loved.

A rectangular shadow was visible on the wallpaper in Cara's drawing room where the portrait had been, so Frankie had the men put up a mirror. She needed to look at herself, not at a reminder of Elisabeth.

The last time she saw Michael was so long ago. She had found him living in a fisherman's hut out on the godforsaken pebble banks of Dungeness, and she understood why he had not come back to London. It was not because his face was scarred and he couldn't paint, but because of Elisabeth. He didn't say it – he didn't need to; he stayed in Kent for her.

He had put on a show of being glad when Frankie arrived unannounced. He was taller than she remembered, and heavier, a man now, not a boy. He seemed to be existing on what people gave him but he looked untroubled by his poverty and at ease living in a wooden hut, as he would be in a London villa or in a castle or in a cave. Michael could live anywhere, or he didn't care.

They were so different, Frankie could see it now. He wore washed-out colours like the shingle, Frankie needed to be vivid or she would be lost. She sat at his driftwood table in her crimson coat and yellow scarf and cobalt velvet shoes, and wanted to apologize.

She took off her gloves but he didn't take her hand or touch her. She had forgotten if they had ever kissed. Gulls were mewing and their cries were almost musical, like lamentations. Frankie wondered how people lived with so sorrowful a sound. The weight of each wave breaking on the pebbles came up through her feet as if the sea was underneath the wooden floor, and she could not stop the thought that Michael must make love to Elisabeth here. When they were lying in each other's arms the birds would sound wild and magical and not lonely, as they did to Frankie.

She didn't drink the tea that Michael made for her. His fondness had never been enough and now even that had gone cold. He seemed unmoved by her anguish at the injuries he'd suffered. She asked him to come back to London with her to see a surgeon, whom she would pay for. The studio in Fitzroy Street was still leased in his name, she told him, and she had two houses now, one in Regent's Park and one in Bloomsbury. He could live in either, or anywhere he liked.

He was only half listening, half seeing her. The truth was he didn't want her concern any more, or her money.

When she left, she forgot her blue kid gloves but could not go back. It would be humiliating to have him think she'd left them on purpose.

A long time afterwards, without her even noticing the change, she thought of Michael less. His absence closed over like the wound when a branch is broken off a tree. She was sealed up again. And although a part of her was lost, the freedom from missing him and wanting to see him one more time almost felt like happiness.

It would have been impossible, she told herself. She was forty-two, a widow, and asking for disaster if she tried to make a life with a man of twenty-nine. She was wealthy and he was poor. It was for the best that they had never been lovers and she had nothing to regret. She would forget him. It was good to visualize a future and only see herself.

So it was like crashing through a mirror when she came across the painting in a little gallery on the Embankment. The picture was bitter, restless colours: a hillside of acid-yellow grass and a green bruised sky. There was no card in the window saying who the artist was, but Frankie knew. It seemed he'd learned to paint again although the work was crude. She felt her own hands ache remembering the injuries to his.

She drove to Fitzroy Street. For years she had avoided the place and she didn't know what she hoped for. Her body sparked like a girl's but her mind was weighed down with defeat. After all this time she was still weak. She was opening a trapdoor and would fall into the past.

Night was coming down and the windows of his studio still had sheets pinned across the glass and she imagined the great mirrors on every side reflecting candle flames like constellations stretching off into infinity.

She walked down the passageway, up the stairs and along the echoing metal corridor to Michael's door.

• • •

Toby Schroëder's inky letters never said much, but Elisabeth was touched that he wrote at all. He was fifteen, still at school in Tunbridge Wells, had holidays in New York with his parents – Ingrid and Bruno, he called them – and weekends with his aunt, 'Frankie', in London.

Elisabeth went to London from time to time to see him, although he never asked her to. They would meet at a café, a museum, or take the ferry up to Kew or down to Greenwich. Toby looked pleased to see her and at least he didn't seem bored in her company. He said he liked to hear about George and about little Christina. He asked after Rachel and Eddie and the spotted pony, Little Bear, who would be too small for him to ride now.

There was no residue of hurt in Toby's eyes behind his flopping hair. Whatever Elisabeth had done in Kent to wound him all those years ago was probably too far in the past to matter. She was a not-quite aunt from an episode of his childhood that had shrunk into the distance behind him like something viewed through the wrong end of a telescope.

He had written that he wanted to see the ruin of the Crystal Palace at Sydenham before the site was cleared, so they arranged that he would take the train from Victoria out to Penge. Elisabeth would drive from Kent and meet him at the station.

When he walked towards her on the platform, she stopped herself from saying how much he'd grown. He was taller than her now. She told herself not to stare at his face, which looked new, not quite finished or properly proportioned, but so big, so almost like a man's. He was wearing long tweed trousers, a blue silk scarf and an olive leather coat. The coat and the trousers flapped around his stringy frame. Elisabeth thought the clothes unsuitable – too flamboyant for a schoolboy, but typical of his mother and his aunt to encourage him to dress that way.

Elisabeth remembered she once dressed like this too, a long time ago in a life that had come and gone, left her married and wearing mealy tailored coats and provincial hats that nobody would notice.

She walked with Toby through the park to see the great cage of buckled iron which used to be the Crystal Palace on the crest of Sydenham Hill, and from the distance of the safety fence the wrecked structure looked almost delicate, like a giant heap of blackened lace. The stone head of Sir Joseph Paxton on its plinth stared at empty air and a pair of sphinxes guarded a flight of steps up to nothing. There were already weeds pushing up through the grand terraces and walks, and everywhere was green broken glass, acres of it. Someone had climbed up and put a tin hat on a marble nymph.

Toby was impressed by the devastation. 'Jeez,' he said. 'It looks like a bomb's gone off. Holy smoke,' and they both giggled.

'How awful,' said Elisabeth.

'Wish I'd seen it burn.'

They walked to the tea house by the lake.

'You think there'll be a war?' said Toby.

'No, of course not. Why would there be?'

'Boys at school say the fighting in Spain will spread. Peecock's brother's gone to drive an ambulance. I'd go if I could. To fight.'

'I'm glad you can't.'

A waitress came with a tray of tea and they were silent for a while.

'I wondered if perhaps you'd like to come to Kent,' Elisabeth said. 'You haven't seen George for an age.' She often asked but Toby never came.

'Sure.'

'Do you still like to ride?'

'So, so. I ride sometimes back home. Bruno got a horse for Bonnie May but she's scared to death of it.'

'Your sisters must be grown-up young ladies now.'

'That's what they'd like to think.'

Elisabeth swallowed, put down her cup, dabbed at her lips. 'George and I are considering adopting a little girl.' She could hear herself squeaking slightly with the effort of sounding casual. This was the first time she had spoken about Karen's daughter to anyone but George, and it was strange to hear the words sound straightforward and adoption so ordinary a thing to contemplate.

Toby flicked a look at her. 'Hey,' he said.

'You don't think it's a bad idea?'

'Nope. Why would I? It's great.'

Another silence.

'How is your Aunt Francesca?' she asked, as she always did.

'Don't know,' said Toby. 'I haven't seen Frankie much lately. She's been in Italy and Greece, and somewhere else, Corsica, I think. They came back last week.'

'How wonderful. She's been travelling with a friend?'

'She got married. She married Michael Ross. You know him. He used to live in Kent near you and George. Well, now he lives in Bloomsbury with Frankie.'

• • •

It was a surprise to get a telegraphic booking from Frau Landau so soon after the last time: three nights, a child's bed in the room, a sea view, and also a booking for Mrs Mander: adjoining suite, two nights.

Stubbard entered the details in the ledger. It was typical of the Frau to assume there would be vacancies to suit however late she left it. As it happened there were, but Stubbard had half a mind to put her at the rear without a view just to make a point. He didn't, though; the fuss wouldn't be worth the satisfaction.

As it turned out, he was glad they had nice rooms. Frau Landau's child was a fairy of a thing, tiny as a wisp and so pretty your heart would break just to look at her. They all made a fuss. Pearce bowed and shook her teddy's paw, and she took a shine to Awkward Sidney, who seemed to understand her even though she hardly spoke and neither did he – maybe that was why.

The Frau was a surprise – as loving and tender a mother as ever there was, and so quietly proud, Stubbard could see it, to have so much attention for her daughter. It caused a stir having the little one on the premises and everyone was in a tizzy wanting a slice of Antje Landau. Mrs Cubsy took her down to meet the girls, Chef made her a plate of

273

toffee, and Elsie and the other maids went broody so you couldn't get any sense out of them, or any proper work.

But it was pleasant, Stubbard thought, to have all the staff drawn together, and Frau Landau was a different woman this time, gentle and polite to people, hardly able to tear her eyes away from Antje as if she'd disappear, as if Frau Landau was hungry for every precious second of her daughter.

'They grow up so fast,' said Mrs Cubsy wistfully. 'They're gone before you know it without so much as a backward glance. I understand how Mrs Landau feels.'

Mrs Mander arrived and for the following two days they were off out the three of them in their summer frocks, coming back windswept and full of sun. Every day, little Antje had too many treats to carry, paper windmills, a kite, a bucket or balloon, or some other seaside toy her mum had spoiled her with. The women seemed easier together with their attention on the child, and who wouldn't be content in the company of so sweet a thing. It almost made Stubbard have regrets.

The last evening, after dinner, Frau Landau came to the desk alone. She paid the bills for herself and Mrs Mander, and booked a taxi for four o'clock next morning. Four o'clock! No breakfast, and she said she would put her luggage outside the door so the porter was not to knock. An envelope was to be given to Mrs Mander in the morning.

Stubbard did not see Frau Landau again. She left before his shift.

Mrs Mander came down at nine and the little girl was hanging on her skirt or pattering behind, looking all around with those big smoky eyes and not mithering or asking for attention but quiet like she always was.

Pearce did his turn, bowing to her teddy, and Awkward Sidney mumbled and blushed, which made Antje nearly smile, then Mrs Mander took her hand and they stood outside on the step together looking at the sea, silhouetted, just like the first time when Mrs Mander came two months ago.

They waited there a minute, the two of them, until a big old yellow Daimler drew up at the kerb.

• • •

When Elisabeth had woken up, Antje was beside her. Karen must have brought her in and put her in the bed. Elisabeth leaned on her elbow and watched Antje sleeping in the blue half-light. Michael's daughter, deep inside soft untroubled dreams. Soon the first day would begin, and as the mornings came and went this little German girl would disappear. To be so small and lose everyone, everything, was so hard a thing to bear.

The sun was lighting up the curtains. Michael would be waking beside Francesca Brion.

Elisabeth got up and dressed. As she clipped on her earrings, she saw Antje in the mirror standing behind her watching, barefoot in her nightdress. 'Mutti,' she said. Elisabeth picked her up, wrapped her in a cardigan and stood at the window pointing to the waves, then to a woman with a dog, a fishing boat, a pigeon. 'Sea. Lady. Boat. Bird.' Antje stared into Elisabeth's face, watching the sounds coming from her lips. See. Laydee. Boht. Berd.

When they left, the staff all came to say goodbye. Mr Stubbard at the desk handed Elisabeth a manila envelope which contained some documents and a letter.

*Elisabeth, here are the papers you will need. They have been prepared carefully and there should be no difficulty. You and George must sign where I have marked. The witnesses have already signed.*

*She belongs to you now. If she ever asks, you must say you know nothing about me. She must never know who I am. Promise me. You think you understand how it is in Germany, but you do not.*

*Please don't write any more, and if you must for any reason, I ask you from my heart to make sure you never mention her. No one must know. I beg you.*

*Please don't think badly of me.*
*Karen*

The adoption papers said the child's mother died two years ago. The father was unknown.

• • •

'Darling, would you like some milk? Milk?' said Elisabeth, pointing to the milk jug.

Antje stared from the dusty corner by the press where the brooms were kept. She had dressed herself, put on her coat over a party dress

275

with pink silk rosebuds round the hem, and knitted trousers. Her colouring book and crayons and her nightdress were in a heap at her feet. Elisabeth knelt down and Antje pressed herself against the wall.

'She can't talk,' said Christina. 'She only knows words I tell her.'

'What shall I say, Christina? What will she understand?'

'Crayon,' said Christina. 'Paintbox. Teddy.'

Elisabeth held out a cup of milk but Antje turned her face away, pushing her chin into the velvet collar of her coat. 'Sweetheart, have a drink, please, my darling. You've had nothing at all this morning.' Antje winced as if Elisabeth's voice hurt her.

'She doesn't like milk,' said Christina.

'Talk to her, Christina. Will you? Be kind to her.'

Christina put her arms around Antje's neck, kissing her hard on the cheek. Antje gasped. 'Not too much, Christina, gently,' said Elisabeth.

Christina looked into Antje's face, their noses almost touching. 'Antje.'

'Let's call her Alice,' said Elisabeth.

'But she's Antje.'

'She says it differently, that's all. Her name is Alice and that's what we must teach her.' Elisabeth gave Christina a cup of water and she put it to Antje's mouth. Antje drank and water dripped down her coat. 'Take Alice into the sitting room to play,' said Elisabeth. 'It's warm by the fire and I'll bring you some biscuits.'

'On dolly plates,' said Christina, 'with cups of real tea.'

'Yes, real tea. Leave Alice's things, I'll look after them.'

The two little girls went off hand in hand. Elisabeth picked up the nightdress. Wrapped up inside it were some beach pebbles and one of Karen's scarves.

Alice wandered through the house opening doors, running her hands along the furniture, climbing up and down the stairs, as if the movement stopped the tears from catching up with her. Elisabeth would find herself throwing down her duster, or dripping soap suds from her hands, leaving saucepans boiling over on the stove and running through the house to look for her.

Alice drew pictures with her crayons: a mountain and a house with rows of windows, a man, a woman and a boy all with yellow hair and blue, blue eyes.

Elisabeth felt as if Alice was dismantling her, so she couldn't fit herself together any more. She couldn't make decisions on the simplest things and sometimes she couldn't breathe for the weight of loneliness that seeped from Alice into her. They were too much alike, she and Alice, incomplete and always waiting for something that would never come.

Once, at a tea party for Christina's dolls and Alice's teddy on the hearthrug in the sitting room, Alice shouted, '*Mutti, Mutti, schau mir mal an!*'

Christina pushed the teddy bear into Alice's hands. 'He's so sad.'

'Does teddy have a name, Alice?' Elisabeth asked. 'Teddy?' She pointed.

Alice turned the teddy over in her hands. 'Stefan,' she said.

She had the dazed unearthly calmness Elisabeth had seen in Christina's eyes as a new-born, before infant incomprehension overtook her. It was a kind of wisdom, an acceptance of the terror of the situation, and a trust that somebody would come.

Elisabeth had never felt this for Christina, this binding of her soul so tight it never eased – or she had forgotten. Perhaps time had settled the feelings for her own daughter to an easy equilibrium.

The love for Alice seemed older, simpler, as if it had always been there, waiting.

# 30

It feels like a reprieve when Elisabeth goes shopping in Hythe and doesn't bump into Rachel. Eddie plays cribbage with George sometimes of an evening, but Rachel never comes any more to do her knitting or her mending with Elisabeth.

If Elisabeth had to explain, she'd call it a misunderstanding. Rachel thought one thing and she thought another. But that wasn't true and the shame of knowing she won't confess to Rachel makes an apology impossible.

Elisabeth is haunted by the conversation in which she delivered the lies so flatly that Rachel was left dumb and unable to challenge her. It was months ago, but the memory still keeps Elisabeth awake almost every night.

Rachel had arrived one morning carrying a shopping bag. She was shaking with some anxiety or upset, and Elisabeth was frightened at the sight of her. 'What's happened, Rachel? Is Eddie all right? Is it Vera?'

'It's you. Tell me I'm wrong. Tell me you wouldn't do this to me.'

Rachel has been helping Vera clear out some cupboards at the bungalow, and they come across an old chocolate box of Nanna Lydia's in which she kept drawings Granddad Lemy did years ago. There are also photographs, dozens of them.

Rachel empties the shopping bag on Elisabeth's kitchen table, scattering the contents: manila envelopes and sheets of cartridge paper. She searches through, extracting a pencil drawing of a toddler and also a watercolour of a little girl wearing a too-big gingham dress and sitting in an armchair. Then she pushes through the heap, selects an envelope, tips out the photographs and finds a picture of the same little girl on boy-Michael's shoulders holding on to his ears, and another of her puffing out the candles on a birthday cake. Rachel lays out the pictures on the table.

Elisabeth almost smiles with the sudden pleasure of seeing Alice's face.

'Look,' Rachel demands. 'Look.' Her eyes are furious and terrified. She points to each one as if Elisabeth might not understand.

Elisabeth looks and says nothing.

'They're of me, but if you didn't know you'd think it's Alice,' Rachel says. 'I know she's Michael's daughter. I don't know why, but Karen gave her to you. Don't lie to me, Elisabeth, just tell me.'

'Alice's mother is dead.'

Rachel stares at her.

'Alice is an orphan, Rachel, and we know nothing much about her.' Elisabeth doesn't look at the pictures any more. There is Michael. He can't be more than ten and he has a clear untroubled smile she has never seen before.

'I've got a right to know,' Rachel shouts. 'Why should you have her, any more than me? You've got Christina. I should have Alice.'

Elisabeth hates the splinter of a laugh she gives. It is nerves but the sound is superior and spiteful. 'Heavens, Rachel. Children aren't things to be shared out fairly.' How could she say it? 'I'll show you the adoption papers, though I don't know why I should. You can look at Alice's birth certificate. No one knew her father.'

Rachel is so still it seems as if she isn't breathing, as if her heart has stopped. 'I know him,' she says. She turns, walks out, and Elisabeth hears her footsteps on the path. Alice and Christina are in the garden and Elisabeth runs outside. The two little girls are playing and Rachel has already gone.

- • •

Hidden well, a secret is difficult to examine, even by its keeper. As Elisabeth remembers it, the secret she must guard for Karen is clear of outline, honest, loyal. Concealing Alice's past is a burden, Elisabeth tells herself, and a painful complication in their lives, but it must be done for Karen.

But there are whispers at the edges of Elisabeth's mind: *Perhaps it's good that Alice can't be shared with Rachel. Would anyone be happier? Rachel would want too much of Alice, and I deserve to have a part of Michael for myself...*

As buried things do – unless they're made of gold – the secret has tarnished and distorted over time. It belonged to Karen but it serves Elisabeth now.

1938: a year since Alice came to England and six months since Rachel guessed the truth. People know that pretty Alice Mander is adopted, but the kindness of the Manders and why they took the orphan girl has ceased to be a talking point. The secret is settled, buried.

Then, suddenly, one November night, it shows itself again. It has grown fat and monstrous in the dark. Elisabeth's guilt is swallowed in its jaws and Rachel's hurt is crushed beneath its bloody iron hoofs. Karen and little Alice are nothing to it; it always had its yellow eye on greater things. Now it has a name: Kristallnacht.

A German boy who lives in Paris has heard that Jews are being deported from the Reich, crowding at the borders without food or shelter and shot if they defy the orders of the Führer. The boy's family have been evicted from their home in Hanover because they are Jews of Polish origin, but they're also German so Poland doesn't want them either. At the border, destitute and starving, they wait with hundreds like them for someone to relent. The boy's parents write to him and ask for help.

He is seventeen. He doesn't understand it is already too late. He buys a revolver and a box of bullets, then goes to the German embassy in Paris. He shoots an embassy official. In his pocket he carries a post-card to his parents: *May God forgive me. I must protest so the whole world hears . . .*

The world hears but hesitates. Jews in Germany are beaten and assaulted in revenge for the assassination. Some ordinary Germans, mistaken for Jews, are beaten too. Synagogues are burned or ran-sacked, Jewish graves are desecrated, and windows of Jewish businesses all over Germany are smashed. Kristallnacht. Night of broken glass.

*1941*

# 31

A pregnancy at forty-six had caused some consternation at the hospital and when Michael came to visit, Frankie's letter said, he'd probably cause even more. *Watch out for She who guards the prison gates. She'll think you're my little brother, so when you tell her you're the proud pappa, run for cover.*

Michael saw the Matron appraise his uniform, his stubble and his sling. He hoped she'd assume he'd been shot. When he introduced himself, she recovered her composure swiftly. 'Your wife is sleeping, Mr Ross. You may take a peep at Baby if you wish, but I suggest you come back at five.' She stood between him and the closed ward doors, and through the porthole glass he could see a line of iron bedsteads. 'I'm sure you'll persuade Mother to take Baby to the country. We all have a responsibility to keep the little ones from danger.'

He knew Frankie would not leave London. 'Francesca told me she couldn't be in better hands,' he said. The Matron's downy chins pinked with pleasure.

'You have a boy, Mr Ross. Well done.' She twinkled at him. 'A little miracle, if I may say so – and handsome, just like Father.' She looked at the watch lying horizontal on her bosom. 'We had a tiring labour but we'll be pleased to see you later, I'm sure.' She folded her hands across her bulk and shifted to obscure the porthole with the wings of her cap. 'I suggest you arrive at fifteen minutes to five if you'd like Mother to see you lead the visitors on to the ward.' She leaned in. 'It's so encouraging if Father shows an *interest*.'

He backed away. 'Quarter to five. Thank you.'

'Congratulations, Mr Ross, a fine healthy first-born,' she called after him as he walked away along the corridor.

The morning outside was foggy and he stood on the hospital steps wondering what to do. He had forgotten to ask to see his son. It was a fluke that he was here at all; he had been sent home with a broken collarbone, not an injury of war but of rugby. One afternoon in the square of a devastated village they had improvised a ball with a lump of rock-hard dough they'd found in the rubble of a boulangerie.

He had wanted to stay in France. His injury wasn't serious and he was an artist for the Commission. He could still paint if he couldn't fight, or cook if he couldn't paint, but they said he must be signed off for a month.

As a war artist, he had special privileges, and as a Jew, special sympathy. People assumed he would take the war personally, but there must be thousands like him in Europe who were suffering for something they were mostly indifferent to. They were marked for cruelty as he was marked for kindness. He did not feel Jewish but had given up denying it. Acknowledging what he was had come to feel like loyalty, long-owed, to Lemuel Jacob Roth, who had given him his art.

When Michael landed back in England, a message was waiting and he went to the hospital straight away, grateful that attention was diverted from his unheroic homecoming, but he was too late – the baby was born. Frankie would say it didn't matter and all he could have done was pace the corridor and smoke cigarettes.

The news of Frankie's pregnancy had astonished him and Frankie's joy made him joyful too, although he couldn't imagine how they would be parents together. His work had been halted by the war but he'd had four successful exhibitions and there were plenty of commissions waiting. Frankie liked to travel, to hold her soirées, stay in bed till noon and entertain until dawn. The shape of their life together had set.

Their marriage had been a leap of faith, both trusting that the past would be enough to build a future. Or perhaps neither he nor Frankie had anything to lose.

When she turned up at his studio one summer evening, they held each other tenderly, mistaking gratitude for love. How many times had he written letters to Elisabeth asking her to come to him then thrown them in the fire? She had a husband, a good man who cared for her, and if Michael loved her, he must not see her again. He had fought with himself to stay away.

He thought Francesca would save him from the endless wrenching of his heart, and for this he would cherish her and not look back.

At the wedding, Michael felt a kind of desolate relief that there were no more choices to be made. For a while, hope and fondness for the past eclipsed the strangeness of their situation, but gradually they realized that they barely knew each other. Francesca still mourned McCarthy Brion. He grieved for Elisabeth.

Frankie worked hard at happiness and he admired her courage and her determination to ignore the disappointments of her life. She knew he still loved Elisabeth but she trusted him to keep it hidden.

He knew he ought to be content and he sometimes was. Francesca was beautiful and clever, they had money and freedom, and now they had a son.

The day stretched out. Michael could not face the empty house in Bloomsbury and thought of going to the restaurant where he and Frankie often used to eat, knock on the door and ask Marco for some breakfast.

Fatherhood seemed postponed until the evening visit, and Michael wondered if he would feel the transformation inside himself that friends described the first time he held his son. At the moment, he felt nothing much at all.

It was late April but as bleak as winter. The fog was so thick the boarded-up statues and heaps of sandbags for makeshift shelters were invisible. London could have been the same. Grey shapes of people in overcoats passed him on the pavements. Car headlamps and cheerily lit buses loomed up and disappeared again into the yellow gloom. He looked for a café but the district was unfamiliar and he had no idea which way to go. People had their heads down, hurrying to work.

He felt a flutter of jubilation. He must look different. Something about him must have changed. He tried to catch glimpses of the faces passing, but people were wrapped in scarves. He wondered if the men he saw were fathers, if they would recognize him as one of them. Then all at once, between one pace and the next, he remembered. He stopped, someone trod on his heel and a bus passed close with faces staring from behind the streaming glass.

This was the beginning of another lie, added to the lie that had grown up between him and Frankie. This child was not his first. He'd never told Frankie he had a daughter, because a moment never came when he could be sure it wouldn't hurt her. If he ever thought of little Antje, it was only a brief, vague contemplation, as if she was a half-remembered dream.

In the doorway of a tobacconist, he stood staring at snuff boxes and pipes and bowls of tobacco. Brown paper was pasted on the window against the blasts – a picture of Tower Bridge. It looked like something a child would do at school. The shop bell rang and an old gentleman came out to ask if he could help. He handed Michael a cigar. People were generous to injured soldiers.

The light turned lemon as the sun came out above the fog, illuminating precipices of broken buildings, caves of rubble, a rug hanging over a joist as if it was ready for a maid to beat out the dust, a dissected bedroom with floral wallpaper and a dressing gown still hanging on the door thirty feet above the ground. Beside him, beyond a rope barrier, was a flooded crater with an upended car nose down in water. On the other side of the chasm was a Lyons Corner House.

Michael sat with a cup of tea, hardly aware of the din of crockery and hissing urns. A door was being prised open inside him. 'Is everything all right, sir?' a waitress asked him.

He paid at the counter and left, and he took a taxi to London Bridge. The next train had been cancelled but a blackboard said the one after would run on time. He had seven hours: the first child would be seen before the second. It was ridiculous and made no difference to the lie, or to Frankie, but he had to. Some part of his mind was jeering at the belatedness of this journey and how ludicrous it was to think that visiting his forgotten daughter would absolve him.

On the train the memories flooded in and he sweated at his disloyalty; on the day Frankie had given birth to their son he was thinking of another life he might have had, and the daughter who was his revenge on Artur Landau.

Antje would be seven – or eight. He had no idea when her birthday was. He had never thought of it before and to his surprise it hurt him that he didn't know. Today he would walk to the Manders' house, knock on the door and ask to see his daughter. He wouldn't give anything away and would never go again. He'd have a cup of tea like any other visitor, then leave.

In Kent it was a day of towering clouds and a striding wind. Michael turned up the collar of his greatcoat and started walking. The horizon of hills was the same but the station was ringed around with red-brick semis and suburban gardens. A rash of bricks was everywhere in England. He passed some half-built houses with mock-Tudor façades and leaded windows. Ragwort and nettles were growing amongst the piles of sand and the abandoned wheelbarrows. So many things were interrupted by the war.

Away from Hythe, the landscape hadn't changed. The scent of pastures floated with the stink of farmyards, and the orchards were coming into bloom. The rhythm of walking seemed to wear away the urgency that had brought him here, and at the bend in the lane where the chimneys of the Manders' house came into view he stopped.

He stood, unable to go on. The feeling for Elisabeth was the same. This was the disloyalty to Frankie: not the child he'd had with Karen but the truth of what he wanted. It seemed that nothing, no span of time, could wear it away. He had never felt this for his wife and he never would. It might be an illusion, nothing more, an unfulfilled desire, an idea of love, but the belief that it was real made it so – and that was all any love could be.

Elisabeth. He wondered why they had never kissed in all the times they were alone in the black hut on Dungeness – he had wanted to and he had seen in her eyes she felt the same.

If it was an illusion or a fine enduring love, it made no difference now. She was married and so was he. Today was the start of a new life, and coming here had entangled it with the old. He turned back from the house. How many times in this life would he walk away from her.

The rain was coming in and he went inland, hoping to settle his mind while walking the miles of flat deserted lanes. His daughter had brought him here and even though he would not see her he should keep his thoughts on Antje.

Four years ago, on an afternoon as blustery as this, he first heard that she existed. He was beside the Thames with Karen, but the memory of a swan was clearer in his mind than Karen's face. If he'd had money then, he wondered, would he have said he would look after Antje?

Soon after, he married Francesca and had more wealth than anyone could need but then it seemed impossible to ask his new wife to be a mother to his secret daughter. He thought Frankie wanted to erase his life before their marriage. He thought she didn't want a child.

He had turned out to be wrong on both counts; she had always wanted to be a mother, she told him, and she was not unnerved by secrets or jealous of the past. *We've lived a long time, Michael, you and I. Neither of us can pretend we're starting here.*

It was almost three o'clock and he should get the train back to London or he would be late to meet his new-born son. He cursed his stupidity in coming here on a sentimental impulse, prodding into life what should be left alone. He took a short cut towards the station, along a track across Eddie and Rachel's land – he hadn't seen Rachel for years – and saw a little girl standing on a gate ahead of him. She was so still he didn't notice her at first. She looked over her shoulder, tossing back a curl of hair as vivid as a flame, and watched him walk towards her.

• • •

Alice wasn't well and had been kept away from school. When Christina came home, they did puzzles and colouring, and played battleships, but Elisabeth said Christina must go outside for a while to get some fresh air.

The sky was clear after rain and there was a faraway moon. Cold came up through her boots and socks, and Christina looked forward to the warm sitting room and the burn of her nose when she sat by the fire for tea. Her fingers and toes would ache.

It was not interesting being outside on her own. She walked along the lane, then ran as far as the post box, then back the other way to the half-built house where the trees were cut down. The earth was churned up but grown over now with weeds. It was sad to see the places that would never have wild flowers again. The badgers would move somewhere else. Perhaps they had already gone.

A dappled mass which must be cows was moving across a field, but it was hard to see because Christina had forgotten to wear her spectacles. The cows belonged to Mr and Mrs Saunders, Eddie and Rachel, her mother called them. Eddie Saunders came to the house sometimes to play cards, but they only saw Mrs Saunders when she waited at the bus stop in a hat with a shopping basket on her arm. She had slim ankles and heeled shoes although she was a farmer's wife. Mr and Mrs Saunders had no children to be friends with.

Christina stood on the gate and waited for the herd to come. The cows mashed the mud around the gate, and when their hoofs landed on a stone there was a grinding scrape, and with each suck out of the mud, a hoof-shaped hole was left for a second, then the mud caved in, watery as soup, and the hole was gone. Hoofs, dozens of them, smack, suck, splatter, the holes appeared and vanished almost too quickly to see.

The cows jostled, lifting their wide slick noses to breathe the smell of bruised grass into Christina's face. She breathed back at them, wondering if she smelled of sherbet lemons.

A soldier was coming towards her along the track. Christina saw him give a start, and the cows skittered, barging into each other. She had been still and quiet so as not to frighten them but she'd frightened him instead.

The soldier had his arm in a sling. He had a nice face, Christina thought, although there was something wrong on one side. He stopped and his eyes were level with hers because she was standing on the gate. Up close, she saw he had a scar. He looked into her eyes, at her hair, as if he was searching for something or she was particularly unusual.

In towns, people didn't introduce themselves if they passed on the street, but here on the Marsh they did – it was politeness – so she said, 'Hello. I'm Christina Mander.'

'I know,' he said.

He couldn't know, but what adults said they knew often seemed impossible. Christina got down off the gate. He was tall now that she was standing on the ground. 'Have you crashed your plane or did someone shoot you?' she asked. 'Is that why you've got a sling?'

'No, actually I fell over.'

'Oh.' Christina wondered what more she could say to make conversation. The soldier did not resume his walk. Some people liked to talk if they were troubled and it was kind to spare a little time. Perhaps his arm was painful or his friend was dead. Christina was just about to enquire when he said: 'Is Antje . . . Is Antje well?'

The name ruffled something in her mind. 'I don't know. She isn't in my class. I'll ask my sister. I didn't catch your name. Are you local?' Christina had heard her mother say these things.

'You have a sister,' he said.

'Oh, yes. I've got two. A baby one, Maud, and Alice is the same age as me. We're eight. Well, goodbye,' said Christina. 'I'm going home now. I expect I'll see you another time. Good luck, mate.' People called this to the soldiers marching to the boats, but he might be an officer underneath the greatcoat so she added, 'Good luck, sir.'

'Thank you.' He smiled and looked away over her head. 'I wonder if I could give something to you, Christina.' His breath streamed out of his mouth like a ghost.

She knew she ought to say no but the soldier reached into his pocket, took Christina's mittened hand and held it up, palm open, higher than her face. He folded her fingers over something too big for them to cover and held her hand in his. He touched his forehead to his hand, with her hand and the thing inside.

Christina stayed very still. It must be very precious. Then he let go and stood back. 'I've been carrying it with me much too long and I'm glad I've given it to you. Thank you.'

She had never been thanked by someone who'd given her a present; it seemed back to front. He was walking away and very soon his earth-coloured coat was just a blur between the hedges.

Christina opened her hand and in it was a locket, brownish-black like a pebble from the beach, a nasty battered thing. She could see it had once been the shape of a heart but now it was dented as if he'd trodden on it. No wonder he didn't want it any more. It was puzzling that the soldier who looked so nice had given her this ugly broken present. She dropped it in the mud and poked it with her toe.

'What are you doing?' Alice had walked up the lane without Christina noticing. She had a scarf wound round and a bobble hat pulled down. Her arms stuck out and her stomach bulged with all the pullovers she must be wearing underneath her coat. Her legs were twigs in red wool stockings. Alice bent down and prodded the locket with her finger. 'What is it?' She looked up and her eyes were like peaty puddles in the rain.

Christina waved her arm. 'I found it over there. You can have it if you like.'

'Thanks.' Alice put it in her pocket.

'Do you know a girl called Antje?'

Alice blinked.

'Well, do you?' said Christina impatiently. '*Antje*, I said.'

'Antje who?'

'Antje no one.'

Alice swivelled her eyes up to the sky like someone pretending to think. 'Nope. Not ever. What shall we do next?'

'Quick, he mustn't see us!' Christina shouted.

'Where?' shrieked Alice. 'What?' There was nobody, but Christina ran, screaming, and Alice ran screaming behind her.

After tea, Alice wanted to play *Peggity* and Christina forgot about the locket and the soldier because meeting him had not been interesting, so there was nothing to remember.

*1944*

# 32

On weekday mornings, Rachel would put down the bucket for the hens and run across the fields to the trees near the lane. She waited in the shadows for Alice to go past on her way to school with the other little girl, Christina.

Nanna Lydia used to say Rachel had a lioness's heart and it may have been true long ago, but she was different now. Since finding the photographs, she'd never had the courage to question Michael. What would be the point? Choosing not to tell her was another way to turn his back and another betrayal. He might not even know if Alice was his daughter – it would be just like Elisabeth and Karen to have lied to him as well.

Michael never came to Kent and Rachel never visited him in London. He had fallen into a different world when the pretentious American widow snared him, or perhaps he had snared her money and connections.

He had left a hole in Rachel to add to the other holes of Albert and Vera and Nanna Lydia. There was the bitter loss of Karen and Elisabeth too, and the ghost children pleading to be born. There were so many holes but what was there of interest to explain to anyone? There is nothing to be said of absence other than that it is.

The women at the shops in Hythe all seemed to be martyrs to abundance and of that there was always plenty to discuss. Little gatherings of wives with prams would dam up the pavement outside the butcher's or the grocer's. 'Good morning, Mrs Saunders. Come and have a peek at Mrs Wilson's new arrival. Go on, dear, he's fast asleep. Up all night and now look at him, butter wouldn't melt. Aren't they all the same? I was just saying to Mrs Paine and Mrs Turner here . . .' Rachel had to listen.

Oh, the trials of being needed, the women confided in each other, the relentlessness of babies, and the children, the children, the children clambering all over you and dragging on your hands. The organization of crayons and Plasticine just sucks the life right out of you, and oh the utter weariness of washing little clothes and reading bedtime stories. How hard it is to be a mother but how funny and unique it is when baby Susan yawns. And Keith, he's such a little gentleman and only six, and Marilyn lost a tooth the other day, her first, and asked if Father Christmas would bring a new one!

Rachel saw the women's eyes glaze over while they waited for their turn to speak, although there must always be a smile with aahhs and ooohs from the audience however dull the story, because that was the etiquette.

She seemed to be the only one who listened. A heart that's being cut apart always pays attention.

She stood quietly, singular and tidy with her smallish shopping basket on her arm: just a few things for her husband's dinner. They must think she was used to it.

*It's a shame no babies came along for Mrs Saunders, but it's not the joy she thinks. She just doesn't understand. Well, you can't, not until you've had kiddies of your own. She's got no one to consider but herself, no worries about accidents or upsets like you always have with offspring, and look at her, in her thirties and the figure of a girl, that's got to be a plus. No veins or drooping derrière, or little problems down below. Don't we wish we had the luxury!*

If Elisabeth had told the truth about Alice, it would have been different. It would have gone like this: Rachel would glaze over too, then take her turn, raising her voice a notch to drown out the competition, 'My Alice? Oh, heavens, yes, she's eleven now, started at the grammar and doing very well. She's got two left feet thanks to me, but she's talented, artistic, she gets that from her daddy.' Hushed, leaning in: 'Michael? He never comes to see her, poor little scrap. I blame the wife. It's a funny situation but you know how it is. Families! You do what you can and make the best of it. My brother's always been a dark horse.' A sigh, a wistful smile: 'And Alice, she can be a little madam – well, they are at that age, aren't they, but she's a good girl, she really is. She's my Eddie's angel, he adores her. We couldn't ask for more.'

This other Rachel Saunders lived behind the curtain of Elisabeth's deceit, and Alice, the real Alice, was oblivious. She probably never thought about the odd reclusive neighbour who fed her hens, had no children and might as well be living on the moon.

Since Alice and Christina had been going to the grammar school in Folkestone, they walked in the opposite direction and Rachel never saw them. On clear days, she shaded her eyes and thought she could make out two specks in the distance in blue dresses, swinging their satchels or swinging their school hats. They dawdled, heads together, discussing nothing as girls do, then sudden bursts of skittishness would start them running and their shoes would be clacking on the lane. Rachel imagined it; she couldn't really see them, they were too far away.

She had never spoken to Alice and Christina except for the time she came upon them in Eddie's hay field on a hot breezy afternoon in the fourth summer of the war. There was a tangle of woolly tracers high up in the blue – the dog fights were over and this was just the Hawkinge boys practising their loops. Rachel was collecting wild plums and cherries from the trees that grew along the ditches, and the girls must have been lying on their backs looking at the sky because they suddenly sat up out of the grass, both with pairs of cherries dangling on their ears. Their ribbons had disappeared and their little manes were stuck with bits of straw and grass as if they'd been playing in the hay. They scrambled up and stood side by side in their shorts and cotton blouses, holding hands.

Ten years old, fine and long like foals, flat chests and still with that delicate bluish tinge beneath the skin that little children have. Christina was the bigger of the two, with Elisabeth's molten copper brightness in her hair.

And Alice: the smoky eyes of Michael although her colouring was fairer. She had the same long unruly curls as Rachel but pale brown with glints of fawnish gold like rumpled beach sand in the wet.

Alice looked at the ground, twisting her hand in Christina's and fidgeting as if she was about to run.

How strange this must seem to them, Rachel thought, a grown woman out here in a field in the middle of the day with her hair as wild as theirs, bare legs and an old print skirt bunched in her hand to carry the fruit she's gathering. They must think she was a gypsy.

Christina said, 'We hope you don't mind us being in your field.'

'No,' Rachel said. 'You know who I am?'

'We often see you,' said Christina, surprised. 'We only live just over there. Didn't you know?'

Rachel couldn't think of a reply that wouldn't open a door which must stay shut.

'We like your old pony and we stroke him sometimes,' Christina went on politely with the effort of a smile. 'He used to belong to Toby. We know Toby Schroëder too. He's in America and you're Eddie's wife, you're Mrs Saunders. We've always known about you, haven't we, Alice?'

Alice flapped at a fly and the cherries on her ears jiggled. 'Your name is Rachel,' she said. 'Eddie told us.' Her eyes flickered up for a moment, and the look in them was embarrassment and boredom and anxiety all at once.

Rachel could say nothing more and after a long moment, the little girls edged away and ran.

*1946*

# 33

The Saunders' cottage was a mile away behind a line of poplars Eddie planted eight years ago. When Elisabeth stood at the sink she could see the silvery tops of Rachel's trees way off in the distance and she sometimes wondered if Rachel was washing dishes too, both of them up to their elbows in suds, looking across the level fields lying beneath transparent or hazy air, or the mists, or the rainstorms that seemed to bring the taste of salt into the house.

They shared the changing Marsh weather and sounds that carried, like cuckoos calling on still days and the occasional motorcar. If a goose honked overhead, Elisabeth knew Rachel would hear it in her sky a moment later.

When the Blitz was on and Elisabeth was woken by the night bombers heading towards London, she would think of the house in Catford and the other houses she used to know – in Neate Street and Richmond – which might all be rubble by the morning, and listening to the enemy going north across the Kentish Downs she knew Rachel would be awake and thinking of Michael too – Michael and Francesca Brion in London, Karen somewhere in Germany, and Vera and Nanna Lydia both gone now and spared another war.

Elisabeth wondered if Rachel ever thought of her. They hadn't seen each other for all the time the poplars had been growing. It was only a mile of sheep pasture and reedy ditches, but it was a distance impossible to cross.

Eddie still came to play cribbage with George, and Elisabeth asked after Rachel because it seemed strange and awkward not to.

'She's well,' Eddie answered in that neutral kindly voice of his that said, *I have no part in whatever trouble is between you. I shan't be drawn either way.*

'Give her my love, would you, Eddie. I expect she's awfully busy.'

'She's busy enough,' Eddie said. 'She doesn't leave the farm much these days.'

'Oh, I know. There's always too much to do what with meals all the time, it never stops. I'd love to go out more, to Folkestone or even Rye, but I just can't get away.' She knew she was prattling. 'I know what Rachel means. I feel just the same.'

'Not the same, Elisabeth,' Eddie said, the gentlest of admonishments. 'She says there are too many children. She stays at home because it's better not to see them.'

In the strange months following the end of the war when anything could happen, Elisabeth turned her back on the breakfast things waiting by the sink and walked with Karen to Eddie and Rachel's farm.

It had been easy to do ordinary things that morning because she wasn't really there. She was flying over the ruin of Germany, searching. The letter must be a mistake.

'I'll stay at home today,' George had said. The light was playing on his spectacles, which were besmirched with little smears here and there, and she couldn't see him clearly.

'No, George. I'm fine. I really am.'

He smoothed her cheek, which was perfectly dry, and kissed her. He took Maud to school on his way to work and Christina and Alice sauntered off in the sunshine in their blazers and velour hats to catch the Romney train to Folkestone.

When the door shut behind them, the kitchen settled. Elisabeth was tired already. The activity and all the little knots and tangles in a family's mood were difficult to follow with her mind elsewhere.

She heard Christina and Alice talking to each other as they walked past the kitchen window. Alice was saying softly, 'It's sad about Auntie Karen.' Their footsteps on the gravel turned the corner of the house, then stopped. 'I wish we'd met her.'

'I know,' Christina said. 'We haven't even seen a photo.'

'They weren't like you and me,' said Alice. The footsteps started up again, with Christina's voice very faint: 'Perhaps they didn't love each other much. Some sisters don't. Perhaps they didn't even like each other.'

A noise had been gathering all morning, deep inside her head, and Elisabeth leaned over the sink to let it out. The blast of it would split her open, the sky would shatter like a cup, the fields would curl up in a ball. The roar would be infinite, immaculate. But what emerged was a withered little cry, hideous, like a rabbit in a trap. Then the feeling vanished.

She wiped her mouth and sat down at the kitchen table in a patch of sunshine. The clock snipped off the seconds, each neat-edged bit of time dropping on the one before. Surely the matter of a square of paper was not enough to make a death.

She swept the floor and changed the water in the flower vases, hung some washing on the airer and made the beds, considering the oddness of a woman who had been whimpering and dribbling at the sink and was now folding perfect hospital corners and plumping pillows.

The woman's sister was dead. And with the thought, she was running downstairs and scrabbling through the paperwork on George's desk to find the letter which might be different this time.

*Cause of death: unknown. Gestapo prison, Kaufering.*

Some happenings are like a spill of bleach on the mind, burning off the pattern of mundane thoughts and eager little human wants. The selfish colour is taken out entirely and what is left is raw and unadorned, the plain material of a soul.

Time begins here. The human heart does not evolve, each one starts from scratch. There's no knowledge on the subject and no one who can tell her; Elisabeth must discover for herself what it is to be the sister left behind.

She feels her mind turn white and then the understanding comes, pristine and astonishing as if it has never opened its wings before. The truth is this: everything is in her keeping now, two lives belong to her but one will be invisible. She must not forget that Karen's hands are always warm and she likes blackcurrants more than strawberries. Karen sings too loudly and doesn't care, and she will share or give away anything she has.

Elisabeth must look after every scrap of Karen or she will be lost. There is no one else to do it – no Ma who became Mrs Mole, dead in the arms of Mr Mole, buried in their Anderson shelter. No Nanna Lydia and Vera. No Michael.

There is Rachel.

Another moment and Elisabeth is standing in the kitchen. She notices the crockery ready to be washed, also some cutlery and a milk pan. But how to begin? What was it she had been meaning to do the moment before this?

She has a letter in her hand and she needs Rachel.

Elisabeth steps outside into the birdsong and the fragile air. She walks along the lane, across the sheep pastures and plank bridges, over the reedy ditches, to Eddie and Rachel's farm with Karen beside her in the aqueous morning light.

'Hello,' Rachel says. The passing of eight years is subtle and it's hard to see exactly what has changed, but Rachel's skin is sallower and her eyes have shadows round them. She is drying her hands on her apron. 'I wondered if you'd come.'

Rachel's dress is green and blue, and her apron has a merry print of frying pans cascading down the front. Elisabeth didn't expect her to be colourful. There are white threads in Rachel's hair, which is long again and loose. Perhaps she leaves it down because she won't be going out and usually no one comes.

'Eddie met George and your little Maud on the Brookland road. He came back home to tell me.' Rachel has finished drying her hands and she regards Elisabeth. 'I'm sorry. Poor Karen.'

Elisabeth feels obliged to respond in some way but the weight of all there is between them makes speaking impossible. The time for saying sorry is so far in the past, an apology is useless now.

'I've got to feed the chooks,' says Rachel. 'Come with me.' Her voice is ordinary. She pulls the door behind her and picks up a bucket by the step, then they walk across the yard together as if they do this often and there's nothing unusual about today.

One of Bruno Schroëder's black mares is still in Eddie's paddock. The mare's spine dips with age and the shine has gone from her coat. Eddie doesn't ride her any more, Rachel says, because the other mare died two years ago and this one grieves so much she can't be parted from the pony – it's only Toby Schroëder's old spotted pony can console her.

And there is the pony, Little Bear, asleep with his legs folded underneath him and his nose almost resting on the grass. Elisabeth walks across to him, he's snoring, his ears flick and his head jerks up with a grunt but he doesn't seem to see her. When she reaches out her hand to stroke him, her fingers understand the minute texture of each single oily hair coarsened with the wind and sun. She had always thought the pony was a cheerful vacant thing, but now she feels how wild and secretive he is. A muscle beneath his skin shivers to dislodge a fly. She has forgotten why the morning sun is terrible. She can't lift her hand away.

'Let's leave him now,' says Rachel softly.

The hens come running when they hear Rachel's voice, dozens of russet Orpingtons with a froth of chicks in tow. Rachel makes little clucking sounds as she scatters the feed. The chicks squeak around her boots.

Elisabeth dips her hand into the bucket too and some hens sprint off towards the glittering shower of corn she makes; others stay loyal to Rachel. The chicks mill about and concentrate on cheeping. A few starlings arrive and then a crow, but the hens square up to him and he lazily flaps away.

So this is what happens every morning below the line of poplars.

Afterwards Rachel sits on the side of the cattle trough and Elisabeth sits beside her. The sunlight flexes and the light solidifies.

Rachel says nothing when she unfolds the letter and reads it, but she holds Elisabeth's hand, and all of Elisabeth seems to rush into that hand, all the fear and disbelief and gratitude swarm to the place where Rachel touches. Something is eased and weakened, breaks apart and the mewing cries which have no words begin again.

*1947*

# 34

The freeze started in December 1946, when fuel supplies were already running low, and as the temperature plummeted coal stocks dwindled to almost nothing. There was still a healthy talent in the country for resourcefulness and making do, and the prospect of empty scuttles with no hope of filling them inspired a fashion for electric fires. Consequently, the Electric became endangered too.

In February, the Kew Observatory recorded no sun for twenty days, there was pack ice in the Channel and ice floes in The Wash. German prisoners were put to work shovelling the ten-foot drifts to get coal along the railways but defeated soldiers don't feel much urgency nor do they take an interest in helping those who've beaten them. Little was accomplished.

Mr Shinwell, His Majesty's Minister for Fuel and Power – or lack of – solved the problem of supply by cutting down demand. Electricity was rationed along with jam and soap and margarine. Factories across the country were forced to close, television was off the air, broadcasts on the radio were reduced, also the size and thickness of the newspapers. Not much coal was saved and people were miserable for nothing. The war was over but life was still a battle with rations even meaner than before.

Vegetables had to be dug out with pneumatic drills. Sheep and cattle froze to death. Starvation was a possibility. But if people thought this was the worst to happen, they hadn't tasted Snoek.

The Ministry of Food imported a million tins of it to ease the crisis. *Snoek, South African cousin to the British mackerel*, the posters said, was nutritious and wonderfully versatile; *Snoek Piquante* would impress at any dinner party, or mashed with an onion it was equally delicious plain for everyday. The average British palette even numb with cold found Snoek repulsive and most of the consignment was served to British cats.

On 5 March, the worst blizzard of the century, and on the 10th, a thaw. The ground was frozen solid and the snowmelt couldn't penetrate, so water pooled and turned into streams, which poured into rivers, which flooded into lakes as big as parishes, which joined up into seas as big as counties. Farmers fought to save their livestock from another peril.

Eddie Saunders found himself wading through his pastures again with the swimming collie and the half-barrel for rescued lambs. This time, Rachel worked beside him.

She was glad she hadn't seen Elisabeth again. It might have been the weather, or grief, or guilt that had kept her away – Rachel didn't know and didn't care. There were too many troubles in the present and too much owed to Eddie to waste time mending ruptures in a past she was sorry she had shared with Elisabeth and Karen Oliver.

Another spring turned up at last and so did Elisabeth for a second time. It was almost a year since she had arrived on Rachel's doorstep, dumb with shock at the news of Karen's death.

This Sunday morning Eddie was cleaning the shoes on the step and the collie was basking in the milky sun. Rachel was reading in a deck-chair in her sunglasses and Eddie's coat. She heard Eddie speak and when she looked up, Elisabeth was there.

'I hope you don't mind my disturbing you,' Elisabeth said. Her face still had the stony look of grief. Rachel did not close her book. Whatever had brought Elisabeth here again would be for her own purposes and Rachel was not inclined to make it easy.

'I wonder if I could talk to you and Eddie.'

'Well, here we are,' said Rachel, not getting up.

Elisabeth stood looking at her feet and at the reflection of herself in Rachel's sunglasses until Eddie intervened. 'Let's go into the house and sit comfortably.' He lined up the polished shoes, putting the brushes in their box. 'I expect Elisabeth would like a cup of coffee with us.'

Elisabeth sat at the kitchen table with her handbag on her lap and Rachel wondered why she was so smart when she had only walked along the lanes. The war had made George Mander wealthy so perhaps a fur coat was nothing special to Elisabeth. There was a time when Rachel would have dressed fashionably on Sunday too, and would have tried to fill a silence, but not now.

'I've come to tell you something,' Elisabeth began, looking at the coffee cup which Eddie put before her. 'This is difficult. It really is.' She looked around the kitchen wildly as if she was having second thoughts, then she said, 'It's about . . . it's about Karen's son. His father is dead, he died somewhere in Poland, we think, and Stefan is alone. He's coming to live with us.'

'Oh? Is that a fact,' Rachel said. 'That's nice. Another one.'

Eddie had come to stand near to her and he put a hand on her shoulder. 'Shall we listen, Rachel? I think Elisabeth has more to say.'

Elisabeth stared at the clasp on her handbag. 'George believes . . . George says we must explain to Alice that she's . . . that she's . . . You were right, Rachel. About Alice. She is Karen's daughter and . . . and Michael's. I wanted to tell you, Rachel, I really did, but I promised Karen I never would. Everything is different now.'

Rachel felt Eddie's hand holding her still. The anger with Elisabeth was worn out and stayed meekly quiet. *Everything is different now*, Elisabeth had said, but it wasn't because this house, this life with Eddie, the women in Hythe who tormented her kindly, couldn't change. All the years when Alice should have known her were gone, and all the ordinary things aunts and little nieces do together would never be.

Rachel leaned her elbows on the table and her head was a boulder teetering on the matchstick of her neck. Alice's family was Elisabeth and George, Christina and Maud. It could never be Rachel because Elisabeth had lied. It was too late.

Eddie's hand was very warm, which was good because it was the only thing that ever soothed her.

Elisabeth continued, picking up speed now the confession was over. 'George and I will take Stefan away for a few days when he arrives in England. He'll start at George's old school in Yorkshire and he won't come home for a month, so it'll give us all some time to get adjusted. It will be hard but George and I will explain everything to Alice.' There was a pause. 'Rachel?'

'She's listening, Elisabeth,' Eddie said.

'So I wanted to ask you, Rachel . . . I wanted to ask if you would like to look after the girls while George and I are away with Stefan. You can get to know them. Will that be nice? Alice won't have been told by then of course, and I'd ask you to respect that, but very soon everything will be out in the open. Everything. I promise you.'

Eddie's voice was somewhere close. 'I think Rachel must have some time to think this over.'

Rachel didn't need more time. She said from the dark behind her hands, 'Will you really tell her?'

'Of course.' Elisabeth sounded surprised. 'Of course. George and I have agreed we will.'

'Then, yes. I'll look after her. Only Alice.'

'Christina and Maud won't be any trouble.'

The old anger sparked and Rachel could lift her head to look Elisabeth in the face. 'It would be convenient, wouldn't it, Elisabeth, if I do as I'm told. But I'm telling you, this is what I want and you owe it to me. I'll have Alice, that's all – the other two are nothing to me.'

Elisabeth was silenced for a moment, then she said carefully, 'But we can't leave Alice on her own, surely you can see that, Rachel.'

'She'll be with me.'

'She doesn't know you. What will we tell her?'

Rachel was too tired to take much notice of another hurt inflicted so easily, and the answer had been waiting all the years, the days and hours and minutes since Nanna Lydia's photographs showed the truth.

'You'll think of something, Elisabeth. You're good at telling lies.'

# 35

Stefan is uneasy about leaving the school in Yorkshire for the holiday. He has grown accustomed to isolation and he likes it. Although he has been surrounded day and night by boys, he can tune them out.

A claustrophobic home with conversation and attention on him is an unappealing prospect, but when he comes to the house in Kent, he finds his new English family undemanding. For most of the day, he can avoid them. The house is large, he stays in his room, and he walks alone on the Marsh. They don't require him to be sociable and for this he is grateful.

It is Maud's seventh birthday a week after he arrives and for the first time he is expected to participate. She wants to play Crazy Golf, so George drives them in the yellow Daimler to the little port of Rye, which has a silty tidal river, some tea shops and a park with a bowling green, swings and Crazy Golf. A woman in a hut tucks her knitting under her arm to receive George's money and to hand over a club and a golf ball for each of them.

Crazy Golf is the maddest thing Stefan has ever seen. The game is to hit the ball across the drawbridge of a model castle, then up the trunk of a wooden elephant, over a humpbacked bridge the shape of a shoe, and along a slalom course between little metal flags. They take their turns and the girls shriek all the time, especially Maud, who knows this outing is for her. But soon there's confusion about whose go is next and which ball belongs to whom. Stefan is befuddled by the pointlessness. Other adults are playing, bent double with mirth and whacking golf balls everywhere. He wonders how these people ever won a war.

Across the park, the town rises up on its bluff. Rye is knapped flint and timbered houses, and he can pick out fire-blackened windows and gaps in the skyline where bombs fell. There are sea defences in the harbour. These things make sense, Crazy Golf does not.

He lays his club on the grass. The more delicately primed the anger, the more careful any movement needs to be in order not to detonate it. He strolls across the road and up the hill into the town. They let him go. No one calls him back and no one follows him. He feels a liking for them he hasn't felt before.

When he first came here, they tried to distract him as if he was a child or an idiot. A heap of ash in the fire might start him shivering, or the wireless howling off the wavelength, or Maud chanting as she skipped on the path. When the shaking started, it couldn't be reasoned with and resided in a place inside him which was inaccessible.

He wasn't troubled by anything at school in Yorkshire, perhaps because the place seemed familiar and not so different from the Reich School – except that English boys were not united by love of their country as his friends at Mittenwald had been, but by a cheerful contempt for everything, including each other. The headmaster instructed Stefan not to speak German or talk about his past, but the boys in his dormitory went on and on baiting him, thinking he had a shameful secret. Patriotism might be different in England; bullying was the same. Eventually, he told them he had a girl, a blonde with techniques they couldn't imagine, and his father had been an SS officer who put a bullet through his head rather than be taken prisoner. The information spread, the little ones scuttled out of his way, and the thugs wanted more detail about the blonde and to take him on.

Stefan was tall for his age, and strong. After a while, they left him alone; Stephen Lander, the mongrel English boy.

His father used to say he was a mongrel German and sooner or later the weakness of an English mother would show itself. Now it had. He was living in the country she longed for and he was homesick for the place she hated.

After he deserts Maud's Crazy Golf, he walks to the top of the town. The afternoon is tawny gold and seagulls clamour round the fishing boats down in the harbour. There is distant bleating on a briny breeze, and Stefan sits on a bench looking out across a flat expanse of fields. A notice says that two hundred years ago this salt marsh was the sea. A gun on a plinth also has a notice, which says it was fired at Spanish galleons.

Stefan ponders on the uselessness of a sea port without a sea and cannon aimed at sheep. He laughs out loud and knows he must seem crazy, though the madness brought on by Crazy Golf has gone and he is sorry he has spoiled Maud's treat. She seems fond of him and likes holding his hand, although it makes his muscles ache and something alter in his mind like a creature stirring in the dark. Unaccountably he wants to cry. Elisabeth notices his discomfort and coaxes Maud away. 'Leave Stefan, Maudie darling. He needs some peace.'

It's often as hard to tolerate Christina and Alice, whose presence can be unbearable. He loathes their calculated coyness, despises Christina's doltish Slavic face and furnace-coloured hair no less than Alice's cunning gypsy eyes and contrary mouth. At other times he likes them and enjoys their two kinds of prettiness, even though their conversation bores him and he'd prefer it if they didn't talk to him.

They are fourteen, the same as Gerda, and they remind him of her – not because they're like her but because she was so different. For all her ugliness and stringy pallor, he longs to be with Gerda Seffert.

His thoughts turn to her, over and over. He closes his eyes to find the room in Müllerstrasse where they lived together and sometimes he has a fleeting remembrance of its chilly twilight smell of mould. The house was dying with a hole in its heart because half a blazing plane fell through the roof and was embedded in the basement.

Rain floats in the chasm, down past the truncated landings and dissected rooms. The wallpaper runs with black and peels like skin. The stink of leaked fuel and charring intensifies with the wet and there must be a corpse somewhere – perhaps it is the British pilot – because the smell of rotten meat permeates everything. Stefan tastes it in his mouth and smells it on Gerda's breath.

At night she lights candles in the dry part of their room, and they feed the fire in the marble fireplace with the smashed furniture which is always to hand. Although the house is filthy with soot and debris, plenty of things survived the scorching passage of the plane; they have a nice hearthrug, a chiming pendulum clock in a glass dome and some ornaments of shepherdesses on the mantelpiece which Gerda dusts and rearranges when she does her housework. They aren't starving any more because she gets food from the Americans, who are far from home, Gerda says, and lonely for their wives.

She gets vodka and schnapps, and cigarettes as well if she can. When she comes home, Stefan pours them both a drink and she tells him about her day, or night. They roll around on the floor, splitting their sides and shouting with laughter at what the Americans ask Gerda to do. They especially like my BDM uniform, says Gerda, and she hoots with mirth. Stefan grabs her and pins her down to kiss her, and she whispers what a soldier taught her this time – then she does those things to him. He is astonished at the exquisite brutal happiness she can magic in him. He can't imagine loving anyone but Gerda for as long as he lives.

They lie on their mattress and smoke Lucky Strikes while they contemplate America, where a baby deer called Bambi makes grown men cry and there's nothing on God's earth can beat blue jeans on a girl.

They drink vodka from Venetian glass and imagine the rich people who lived here once upon a time and the dead man in the plane downstairs, idly wondering if his limbs and head are still attached and if he has turned into a see-through ghost with a lovely shine like vodka.

Rain falls past the hole where a wall once was and it catches the light of the fire, twinkling streams of stars, then turning black again on its way down to the rusting half-plane in the basement and its decomposing pilot.


There are times when Gerda will punch him if he touches her and bare her teeth. In this mood, Stefan can't follow where her mind goes or why it bounces off certain subjects and dives into the depths of others. She used to giggle on and on, but now he has to put up with monologues he mustn't interrupt or she will set about him with her fists. The things she says are vicious, mysterious, and he wonders how Gerda's fragile throat can give voice to so many vile things. While the mood is on her he reminds himself it won't last long and he has plenty of practice at switching off his ears.

This night he cannot stop his ears, or stop Gerda, or stop the thing that happens.

Gerda hasn't spoken since she came home. He lit the candles for her, but she doesn't thank him and he knows something is brewing when she lies down on the mattress beside him and sniggers at the ceiling. After a while, he thinks that's all she'll do, but then she begins to mutter, too softly to hear at first, then, as the quiet settles, he picks up words: '. . . *What a pretty . . . all soapy wet she turns around . . . hold up the towel and out she steps . . .*'

Stefan has stopped breathing because he wants to listen now. This is not Gerda's voice but it often happens that a different Gerda possesses her. '. . . *White lacy panties, nice as pie stepping in, the flimsy kind the Jew can work a finger into . . . then madam says that's all, off you go . . .*'

His heart jumps at the name. Their housekeeper at home called his mother 'madam'. Stefan feels dread, a dread that swallows him. 'Gerda, please stop. Please don't.' He leans over to kiss her, but she punches him so hard he sees sparks inside his eyelids and his nose starts to bleed.

'. . . *The Jew was punished, nicely bashed first time around, but oh, yes, madam wanted more – a second helping – whorish cunt, my Artur said . . .*'

'Gerda, stop. I swear I'll stop you if you don't shut your mouth.' Stefan jumps up from the mattress and grabs some clothing – it might be his or Gerda's – to staunch his nose. His heart is rushing and he leaps across the room and stands braced in case she fights him. The voice in Gerda ceases for a breath, then starts up again. '. . . *The Jew, the English goat. Michael Ross, she liked the taste. Ha! Baby Antje, out she popped, Jew-brown eyes and pretty as a strudel . . .*'

Stefan is transfixed by his sister's name amongst the gibberish. Sweet little Antje can't be part of Gerda's nightmare. And he hears the English name, remembering another story Gerda told him long ago about his mother's death. He hauls Gerda up. 'Who is Michael Ross?' and he shakes her hard. He is ready to fend off the punches but she flops against him. '. . . *Our baby girl is gone and madam, she's gone mad, the bitch is sorry for herself . . .*'

Stefan wants to hit Gerda hard enough to shock her to her senses, but all he can bring himself to do is push her away. She staggers back against the wall, then feels her way along it with her palms as if she's blind. '. . . *Madam's not the only one to grieve, my heart is broken too . . .*'

Gerda stops. The wall has gone and there's empty air down to the basement. She sways, her eyes are shut. '. . . *Oh, yes, she asked for it, we know, oh, yes, Frau Landau thinks we're daft, the skinny little tart . . .*'

He knew his mother's name would come. Suddenly Gerda flaps her hands and the voice is higher, sweeter. '. . . *What's the matter, Gerda? Tell me, darling, what is it?*' Then Gerda's own voice shrieks so loudly that Stefan cowers. 'RUN! *Run quick, run please, now* NOW! *Quick now . . .*'

Gerda is dragging at her hair, yelping and whooping. She stamps the splintered floorboards at the edge and Stefan has to back away. There are many voices now coming out of Gerda's mouth and they are hoarse and bellowing. '. . . *Got her, here she is, hold on tight, she'll have to learn, yes, she will, punch the slut . . .*'

'Shut up! Shut up!' His own voice is nothing against the might of Gerda's and she doesn't even pause.

'*. . . Let's see the goods, yes, ha ha, hold her legs, a fighter this one, ha! Wants a smack, yes! This is what she likes – watch out . . .*'

Then suddenly it stops. Gerda sighs. The voice is soothing. '. . . *Hush . . . it's no one, Gerda Liebling . . . go home . . . look away . . . it's nothing . . . nothing . . .*'

Gerda hangs her head and the fetid draught rising from the basement lifts her hair. The room shudders like a bell. Stefan reaches out to draw her back and his fingers touch her lightly between her shoulder blades – the place where wings might grow. She tips forward, her arms fly up hopefully, even though they're thin and featherless, and the little cry she gives is Gerda's own voice come back to her.

Then something happens which Stefan's memory can't explain. Wings unfold from Gerda's back. They are huge and muscular, brighter than the moon. Blue light fills the room, and the gust from the first slow wingbeat pushes Stefan back against the wall and snuffs out the candles. Gerda is lifted up an inch or two, then she flies into the darkness.

The Kentish breeze is on his face and he wonders at the faulty memory of Gerda flying. Wherever she is, he knows she's waiting because while he thinks of her he feels flesh and blood again and she lights up every particle of him.

He can't remember why he left the house in Müllerstrasse. The flashes of tumbling down the ruptured staircase must be faulty too because he recalls the wreckage of the plane glistening in the dark, and searching with oily bloody hands – for what he doesn't know.

Then there is the oddest memory, or perhaps another dream to which his mind keeps on returning: beside the plane he finds a little deer lying in the wet with blood running from its mouth. Its hoofs are human hands reaching out to clutch his shirt and the fingers have bitten nails. Its back is broken and it cries, *Mutti, Mutti*, which makes him weep because he feels broken too. He wipes the filth from its face and rocks it in his arms until it's quiet, then he carries it to the garden and covers it with rubble.

There is white noise in his head until a doctor with metal eyes talks to him. He doesn't answer, not because the man is French but because Stefan has forgotten how to speak.

Now he's sitting on a bench in Kent looking at a salt marsh and it is difficult to work out how these things join one to another to bring him here. What is clear is that this is just a pause in the real business of his life, and he must go back to the house in Müllerstrasse so he and Gerda can put their heads together and work out how to mend the roof and get the plane out of the basement.

Gerda had said a name, Michael Ross, and Stefan had heard this name before, years ago on a summer evening when Antje was playing with the blossom in the garden. Hede and his mother were arguing, and for a long while they didn't see him standing by the door. They need not have worried; he couldn't follow anything they said. All he remembered was the name.

None of it really matters now. Whatever it might mean is buried in the wreckage of the past, and he is weary of searching and finding only broken, sullied things. What he knows for sure is Gerda.

He hears Rye's church bell chiming five. Swallows are squealing in the dusk, diving up under the eaves of the houses. He left the others playing Crazy Golf almost two hours ago and he should go back.

The sky is still light, but the cobbles under his feet are in shadow and as he descends the hill he stumbles, cursing loud enough in German for people to hear.

• • •

The next day, Christina sought him out with a proposition. 'You said in Yorkshire you would teach me to shoot, remember? What about today?' She laced her fingers and twisted her hands in a knot, looking quickly up at him, then at her socks.

His preference for her over Alice had grown. There was something about the placid lustre of Christina that took his mind to Gerda – not the real Gerda, but a biddable unblemished Gerda with a soft stomach and milky skin who came to him in the quiet moments when everyone left him alone.

Today he liked Christina's glossy pony tail and the little reddish curls by her ears and on her neck. She was so clean. She was wearing blue jeans sent from America by someone called Toby Schroëder and

Stefan had never seen jeans before except in Western films. It was true what Gerda's Americans said about blue jeans on a girl.

Christina's jumper had a pattern of snowflakes round the yoke, like the jerkins children wore for skiing in Bavaria, and he couldn't help being distracted by the way the knitting stretched across her chest and the snowflakes distorted. He could tell she wasn't used to her brassière because she squirmed against its tightness, even in front of him. She had no idea about the things Gerda used to do with the Americans and he wondered when some boy would teach her.

Christina said, 'Would you, Stefan? I've thought of a place where we can go.'

He laughed at the collision of his thoughts with hers, and she smiled, assuming they were friends. She waited expectantly for his answer, but it was an effort to summon up the will to speak as happened more and more these days, even though his throat had healed and didn't hurt him any more. Most things he started to say seemed too trivial to persevere with.

'Would you?' Christina said again. 'Alice and Maud are going to ballet this afternoon. I said I have a headache.'

'Ja,' he said. No more was necessary. He was already tired of this conversation and he stood watching her until she gave up and went away.

He waited on the drive, ready to direct Elisabeth when she backed the car out of the garage. He would have offered to do it for her, if he could have been bothered to explain that he'd been handling bigger vehicles than this since he was twelve. All *Hitlerjugend* boys learned to drive.

As Maud and Alice were chivvied into the car with their ballet cases, Stefan could see Elisabeth's mind running over the problem: *Should I leave Christina alone with him? We can't always be watching . . . but can I trust him?*

If she had asked, Stefan would have told Elisabeth not to worry, even though he sometimes sat on the stairs outside Christina's room in his vest and trousers and smoked a cigarette in the middle of the night. Her door was always open and she sounded like someone on the wireless acting an impression of sleeping. He imagined that in years to come, Christina's wholesome lungs would calm a wholesome husband when he woke up in the night worrying about something or other. Stefan didn't envy the man, although it would be good to have a girl like Christina, who did not rant or punch him, good to unfold her from drowsiness and discover a sweeter body than Gerda's. He and Gerda were as good as married and he would never be unfaithful, but he liked being near Christina when he couldn't sleep, that's all, just near her; anything more would be crossing the threshold to another life. It was comforting to see its possibilities laid out in front of him like the view along a pleasant road, knowing he wouldn't ever choose to go that way.

He would not want to be alone with Alice. She stirred up his thoughts, which were unruly enough as it was; they ran amok like a pack of dogs hunting out things to pounce on, or flee from. Alice's face troubled him so much he couldn't take more than a glance at her before he had to look away. She was a wire in his brain that set off a gruesome little reflex, like an electrode in a frog. It ought not to cause him pain because there wasn't any thought or reasoning behind it, but it felt like a spasm of terrible yearning for something he had forgotten, or forgotten how to feel. Perhaps a dead frog yearned to hop again.

Little Maud he loved so much it had already begun to hurt, and this was good because it proved to him the numbness of his heart was only temporary.

•  •  •

The Daimler had driven off ten minutes ago and they were alone. Going shooting with Stefan Landau would be the first time Christina had been anywhere alone with a boy, and as she rummaged in the cupboard for her shoes, she wondered how something could feel so entirely new when she was fourteen and had experienced quite a lot of life already. Her head was upside down, tying her laces, fingers like sausages and the blood rushing to her face, when she heard Stefan coming downstairs and opening the front door. She licked her finger and smoothed her eyebrows like the girls in the Milk Bar in Folkestone, picked up her spectacles, put them down and ran, buttoning her corduroy jacket that had got too short in the sleeves this year.

He was standing by the porch, wearing George's coat, with a rifle on his shoulder and smoking a cigarette which he let fall and ground with his heel. Then he gave her a longish look.

He was sixteen and too old to be a boy, she realized, nor was he the bony ghost she met in Yorkshire. She felt her face heating up again.

Sometimes it did really seem as if her head was on fire and not just her hair, which appeared that way.

Stefan looked out at the hazy nothingness of the sky and his eyes were the colour of the air which had too many blues to count, millions of glassy motes of new-made sunlight. He turned up his collar.

'You are sure you would like to do this?' he asked – a long sentence for someone who rarely spoke and had never asked her a question before, and suddenly, unaccountably, she knew he was untrustworthy and also that she could trust him. He was asking if she would lie to Elisabeth and George this evening at the dinner table, whatever might happen, because those were the terms.

What would she say if there was an accident, Christina thought, if one of them fell in a ditch and couldn't get out, if they got lost somehow or forgot the time, if a bull gored them? What would she say, and would it be worth it?

'Yes,' she said.

He began walking and she fell into step beside him, noticing the intricate decoration on the rifle that she would put against her shoulder this afternoon and aim as he directed. It didn't look like a gun a Nazi would own and it wasn't like the rifles chained in the cabinet at home, which were plain cumbersome things she could barely lift.

They followed the track towards the Saunders' farm, which was well used as far as the heifers' field and then became overgrown. Stefan went in front to stamp a way through, holding the nettles and brambles aside to stop them whipping back in her face. The hedges closed in above them, dripping and glittering so Christina could hardly see for all the tangle of watery pulpy greens, and after a while she found she was walking in a dreamy, fascinated way because the patterns of the shadows and the rhythm of turning her shoulders one way, then the other, to push through the foxy-smelling leafage filled up her mind.

How long they had been walking she didn't know, when suddenly the track came to a dead end. It should have opened out to pasture, followed by a path that led all the way to an empty pebble beach where they could fire the rifle and no one would hear. But a tree must have fallen last winter, bringing down other shrubs and saplings with it, and now the whole heap had started growing. There was no way through.

They stood facing the wall of foliage and listened to the quiet after all their thrashing and stamping. 'We'll have to go back,' Christina said, finding she was whispering as if they were intruders, but Stefan ducked underneath a bough and dived into the mass of leaves. He was gone.

For a second she was alone, then Christina dived too, putting up her arms to protect her face. She felt his hands on her sleeves guiding her through.

They were in a lush little clearing. The track had disappeared completely and greenery encircled a lawn of fine bright grass and a shallow pool. Birds were calling amongst the leaves and water trickled somewhere under the vegetation. They stood awed by the silence of the place.

Stefan hunkered down, laying the rifle at his side and resting his arms on his thighs, and Christina stood looking down into the water at the bits of bright reflected sky, a leaf floating on nothing and, below it, peaty dark debris. They seemed to have agreed without speaking that they wanted to stay for a time.

Christina said, 'Do you like it here?' She meant something more along the lines of *Do you like being in this pretty secluded place with me in it too?* But it had taken quite an amount of rehearsing in her mind, and nerve, to say anything at all.

Stefan didn't start at the sound of her voice, as a person who is sometimes jumpy might; he plucked a blade of grass and threw it into the pool. She thought he wasn't going to answer.

'I should not be here, Christina,' he said at last, and to her astonishment his eyes were full of tears, brimming but not running down, as if they were stuck there, shimmering dangerously on his eyelashes with nowhere to go.

'Oh!' The cry came out of her quite softly, her eyes filling up too, although she knew her injury was just a bruise and his might be a mortal wound. She realized the enormity of their misunderstanding – how she had meant one thing and he understood another. She had asked a lumpen selfish question and he had heard an infinitely more sorrowful and lonely one, a far older question than she knew how to ask.

She couldn't hold his hand to comfort him as she would Alice, or take him on her lap like Maud, without an even more mysterious confusion arising. She must try to imagine how a girl of much more than fourteen would gather up this mistake and be sorry but not ashamed, understanding that she had simply opened a door without meaning to.

If she spoke again, she must not compose the words in her head but discover with her heart what he needed her to say, and this would be a different way of talking, a way she had never tried before.

'Where should you be?' she asked.

He looked up at her immediately, as if she had surprised him. 'With Gerda,' he said. He started picking at the grass and she wondered how things looked to him distorted through a lens of tears. He said, 'I don't know where she is. I do not know why I left her. I can't remember.'

'Perhaps it doesn't matter now,' Christina said. 'She's your girl, isn't she, and you love her so you must find her. She won't care what happened if you're sorry and you tell her so.'

The old Christina would never have said all this – or should it be the young Christina, who would have been hurt by the mention of another girl and wouldn't have known how to talk to a man in love and in need of advice.

'Yes,' he said. 'I must go back.' He stood up and rubbed his face as if he was cleaning something away. He took a step towards her, close enough for her to see the down on his jaw and the white healed stitches in his throat. He put up his hands, so for a second she thought he was going to touch her face, but he moved back her hair, which had half come undone in all the struggles through the bushes.

'This is very beautiful. Your boy gave it to you?' He was looking at the silver locket she wore all the time.

'Oh, no. It's from Alice. Well, yes. Actually a man did give it to me first.'

'I hope he is a good man.'

'I don't know. I only met him once, years ago, by accident, in the lane. I'm not sure why he gave it to me, he didn't say. You see? It has an E. It was meant for someone else. He wasn't in love with me or anything. I'm only fourteen, Stefan, I'm just a girl.'

Saying this felt more grown-up than pretending and she liked talking to him in this private easy way as if she was quite used to it.

'He was bewitched by you.'

'No, I don't think so,' Christina said. 'Actually, he was wounded. He had a sling so I expect he was mixed up by the pain.'

Stefan smiled – so slight a smile it was almost nothing. 'If you were my sister, I would make sure of this man. I would take care of you.'

'You have Gerda to take care of.'

'Yes,' he said. 'I wish . . . I wish you would come with me.' It was the truth, she could tell. 'But I do not want to spoil it with this man who loves you, beautiful Christina.'

Now he was joking but not entirely; also he was sad and more happy than she had ever seen him, and the contradiction between these different Stefans existing all together almost defeated her. Perhaps another aspect of being older was that she needn't mind if people made no sense.

'Thank you very much, I'm sure,' she said to match his teasing.

Something moved way off in the undergrowth, and they both started and turned towards it – a badger, probably, or a deer – then it was still again.

Stefan said, 'Christina, have you heard of someone called Michael Ross? He knew your mother, and mine too.'

'No,' she said. 'No, I never have.'

They listened to the trickling water and a singing bird, then the rustling started up again, coming nearer. The thing was cracking branches and crashing through whatever was in its way, like King Kong beating back the jungle. The bushes were moving and soon it would burst through. There were no dangerous beasts on Romney Marsh, but Stefan picked up the rifle and Christina moved behind him.

The greenery parted and the spotted pony stumbled out.

'It's Toby Schroëder's pony – I mean the Saunders' old pony. It's Little Bear!' exclaimed Christina, hearing straight away how confusing she was being.

It was a ruin of a pony. Little Bear's dusty coat was rumpled and his mane and tail were threadbare. He dipped his nose to drink, standing motionless in the water, joined by each leg to his reflection. He blinked his pale blue eyes, breathed a sigh and fell asleep, camouflaged by the dappled light and greenish shadows – a sagging equine shrub growing in the water.

Another rustling, the bushes parted again, and Mrs Saunders was standing on the far side of the pool, as startled at seeing them as they were at seeing her. She was wearing galoshes and farmer's overalls. Her hair was under a woollen cap, so she looked almost like a man. 'I thought so,' she said. 'You wouldn't think he'd go wandering off at his age. He gets through the hedge and always comes here to have a drink, I don't know why.'

'Hello, Mrs Saunders – Rachel,' Christina said, doing her best not to be flustered at being discovered though she wasn't, strictly speaking, doing anything wrong. It seemed polite and correct to introduce everyone. 'Stefan, this is our neighbour, Mrs Saunders – Rachel, I mean.' Recently her mother had become friendly with Mrs Saunders and they had been asked to call her Rachel. 'Rachel, this is my cousin Stefan from Germany.'

'I know who he is,' Rachel said, which seemed an abrupt reply.

Stefan didn't speak – he often didn't when there was nothing in particular he wanted to say – and Christina had no idea what anyone was meant to do next.

The pony groaned gently in his sleep.

'Rachel, do you need something to lead Little Bear?' Christina asked, deciding it was best to just change tack. 'You can borrow my belt if you like.'

Rachel might not have heard. She appeared to be weighing something up, standing very still but agitated in her mind with a problem Christina supposed was connected with the pony, though what could be difficult about leading him back to his field was hard to guess.

But when Rachel spoke, it was something else entirely. She looked at Stefan and said, 'Has Elisabeth told you yet? I don't suppose she has. Elisabeth's promises never amount to much.'

Stefan didn't answer and Christina wondered if he was ever going to help with this awkward situation. On his behalf, she said, 'We don't know what you mean, Rachel. We don't understand.'

Then Rachel said another thing that made no sense. 'He'll remember his little sister, I expect.'

'Antje,' Stefan said – one solitary word and nothing more. Something jarred in Christina's mind, as if she'd heard the name before. She put her hand on Stefan's sleeve and thought he was shaking her away, but he wasn't, he had started shivering. 'Let's say goodbye, shall we?' she suggested quietly. 'Let's go.'

'So her name was Antje,' Rachel said loudly, as if it was a challenge. 'You must have noticed Alice has your mother's mouth. As a little one, she was like me.'

This conversation was baffling and lacking in courtesy, in Christina's opinion. She had no idea why they were discussing Alice and they didn't have the manners to explain, so she decided to interrupt, seeing as they wouldn't notice her unless she did. She spoke up loudly. 'Actually, Stefan and I were just talking about a Mr Ross.' She coughed to keep everyone's attention. 'Stefan's mother knew him and we think my mother did as well, so I was thinking, Rachel, you might know him too.'

It was quite a speech but it vanished immediately into the leafy shadows, and the three of them were silent again. There didn't seem much chance of Rachel Saunders having heard of Mr Ross – why would she? So it was a jolt when she said to Stefan, 'Michael lives in London. He can tell you everything.'

This was another mystery, one Christina had no time to ponder because Stefan had gone crashing through the branches back the way they had come.

As she fought through the whippy brambles and nettles, Christina realized she hadn't said goodbye to Rachel Saunders before she turned and followed Stefan. He must have been moving fast because she couldn't see him up ahead, and when she walked the last few yards of the track, there he was, leaning his hands on the house wall with his shoulders heaving.

She leaned beside him, gasping, and she scraped her hair off her face with her throbbing, nettle-stung hands. 'You mustn't mind Mrs Saunders, Stefan. She can be peculiar.'

'Perhaps she is not,' Stefan said.

'Who is Mr Ross?' Christina asked. 'And you have a little sister! Where is she?'

'She is dead.' He said it plainly; a thing too terrible for words.

Although the shock gripped her heart, Christina stood quietly so Stefan would understand that she wouldn't shy away, even in her mind, from what he'd told her. If Alice or Maud were dead, she couldn't go on living, and it was so cruel of Rachel Saunders to mention Stefan's sister – unless she hadn't known the little girl had died.

Rachel mentioned Alice too – what for? If Alice looked like Stefan's mother, how would Rachel know? And in any case, Alice couldn't look like anyone because she was adopted – they had got her from the Orphans' Home in Folkestone. Christina had scraps of memory of when Alice had first arrived: her made-up words and her teddy bear called Steven. What did it mean? Something? Nothing? Too many questions filled Christina's mind, but now was not the time to answer them.

She put her hand on Stefan's arm. 'Antje will always be your sister no matter what, and Alice is mine,' she said softly. These were facts in every way that mattered and all the rest was impossible to grasp.

Stefan might have felt comforted because he put his hand over hers. It was warm and large. A boy's hand. 'I have to leave, Christina,' he said. His face was different and she could see he had already almost gone.

'To find Gerda?'

'Yes. And Michael Ross.'

'When?'

'I'm going now.'

'You won't say goodbye to anyone? Not even Maud?'

'No. Only you.'

Christina felt as if part of her was tearing. She had never had this feeling in her life before, but she could see that Stefan already knew about goodbyes.

'I need money, Christina.'

'I haven't got any. Maud's birthday used up what I had. My Post Office book won't work if I'm not there.'

'Is there anything? Any money at all?'

'Wait a minute.' She ran into the house to the little sitting room. In Elisabeth's bureau there was a purse for the housekeeping and Christina took it and ran back outside. 'Take it. Quick. Before they come.'

They stood facing each other. 'Have my locket,' Christina said. 'I know you like it. Please don't say no. For Gerda. For when you find her.' She turned her back, holding up her hair so Stefan could untie the ribbon. She felt the warmth of his fingers almost touching her, and when the locket was gone her neck felt cold without it.

There was not much more to say and this was almost the end, but he seemed to hesitate – there was something else and when he asked, it seemed so odd and funny she almost laughed.

'I would like to have your blue jeans. For Gerda. Please.'

Christina pulled off her shoes, then he turned his back. It was the last time she saw his face. She took off her jeans, standing in her socks and pants and jacket, knowing it was something she never could have done on any other day but this. He put his hand behind him and she gave him the blue jeans.

'Promise me you won't turn around until I'm gone,' she said. One last look: his golden hair, quite long now over his upturned collar, the rifle on his shoulder, her jeans in one hand and the silver locket hanging from its ribbon in the other.

She picked up her shoes and reached out her hand to touch his back very lightly to tell him goodbye.

# 36

Stefan jogged across the fields to the station, and on the train he put the window all the way down so the air beat on his face and filled up his mouth. He huddled in a corner seat, swallowing the cold and concentrating his mind on the thud of the train, which was like a heartbeat in his chest with no heart of its own any more. He was leaving another place and each leaving became lighter.

He saw his face reflected in the glass against the streaming dark of a tunnel and could not decipher the expression in the black eyes staring back at him. The face seemed closed, unknowable.

The thing the woman, Rachel Saunders, said could not be fathomed: how she knew that his mother and Alice looked alike. It was true, he saw it now, and perhaps that was why Alice's face had always troubled him. Elisabeth must have told Rachel Saunders this, but what was the 'everything' that Michael Ross could explain?

How difficult would it be to find this man in London with nowhere to start except that he was an artist and a Jew? He would find Michael Ross and talk to him, though about what wasn't clear. Then he would go home to Gerda.

He stared out at the land he would be leaving soon, the piebald cows and thatched barns, the sudden gleam of a river and the pink brick cottages. The English could play Crazy Golf because the war had never happened here. One day he would bring Gerda to this peaceful untarnished land to help her to forget.

He stowed the rifle under the seat and felt in his coat for Christina's locket. It was warm to the touch. There would come a time when Gerda would hold up her hair as Christina had done and he would tie the ribbons, kiss Gerda's neck and be happy to give her so beautiful a present when she had almost nothing. He knotted the ribbons round his own neck to keep the locket warm all the way to Germany.

Although Christina had asked him not to, when they said goodbye he had watched her running to the house in her socks, carrying her shoes: a glimpse of white knickers below the ribbing of her jersey and the too-short corduroy jacket, long bare legs, the tendons flexing at the knees. Her limbs were smooth like the china figurines Gerda used to have on the mantelpiece in Müllerstrasse. Christina knew almost nothing, which must be why her skin was perfect. Gerda knew more than she could bear and she was always bruised.

Someone touched his shoulder and Stefan opened his eyes to see a man in uniform holding out his hand – 'Tikitpleesa' – and for a moment Stefan did not understand, as if his English had disappeared in his sleep. The man clipped the ticket and went away.

The sky had darkened to pinkish mauve, the hills cast long blue shadows and the wind through the wide-open window had been buffeting his face while he was asleep. He was cold. He put up the window and stretched his legs to ease the stiffness, took out a cigarette, grateful to George for leaving the packet in this borrowed – stolen – coat. There were no matches. He could go along the train asking for a light, but he was a thief, a fugitive, a filthy Jerry bastard, people would say. He stuck the cigarette between his lips anyway. Even an unlit cigarette slightly appeases hunger and gives some comfort.

The purse Christina stole for him was in the coat too. When he had bought his ticket to London, he put the remainder of the money in his trouser pocket: three ten-shilling notes, some silver and bronze coins, which were called two shillings, sixpence, one penny and one farthing. How much it came to in Deutschmarks, which were worthless now anyway, he didn't know, or if this money would get him back across the Channel when he left London.

The purse smelled sour and the silk lining was so frail with age it was disintegrating. A name was written on the silk: *Elisabeth Mary Oliver*. There were some shopping lists and unpaid bills for meat, coal and groceries. In an old envelope were two faded bus tickets and a yellowing photograph with *Folkestone 1932* written on the back.

In the picture, three young women are standing on a promenade with their arms round each other's waists. One is his mother and Stefan sees that she is not much older than he is now. She wears a dark full skirt and summer blouse and he knows that her hair will be a dozen shades of gold in the seaside light. She looks happy and there is no caution in her smile. She has twelve more years.

Beside his mother is Elisabeth, and the third young woman he recognizes too. Rachel Saunders does not look like a farmer as she did today, she wears a tight pale suit and heels. He sees the subtle proportions of her face that all good Germans of the Reich have been taught to recognize. It was clearer in her youth than it is now. She is a Jew. But no one who saw this picture of the three together could think they should not be friends.

Stefan leaned back in his seat and angled the picture to the light. It was 1932 when he came to England with his parents. He wondered where he was that day, and where his father was. Did his mother, or Elisabeth, or Rachel Saunders, already know Michael Ross? What were they doing at the seaside?

He examined the faces, but there wasn't any more to discover, and he put the photograph in his shirt pocket.

In another compartment of the purse he found an old visiting card stained the colour of flesh, although the deckled edge and the name were still gold:

*Mrs Francesca Blanche McCarthy Brion*

The address was a place in London called Regent's Park, and written on the back in pencil:

American lady who knows M. very well.
Given to me in Fitzroy Street outside M's
studio. Lunch hour
March '29. Invitation to call.
E.

He put the visiting card in his shirt with the photo.

The light had almost gone. Far away at the house on Romney Marsh, the fire in the sitting room would be lit and George would be home from work. He and Elisabeth would have gin and tonic before supper, while Maud demonstrated what she had learned at ballet, and Alice and Christina would sit on the arms of the sofa and scoff or applaud depending on their mood.

Stefan wondered what Christina had told them and if they thought he was still out walking on his own. When the time came, he hoped she would deny knowing anything about the stolen money.

He put down the carriage window and threw the purse out into the dusk.

Lights began to cluster and string along the roads. The fields and cottages became suburban gabled houses with long gardens, then row on row of chimneys and black brick terraces so close together there could be only alleyways between them. He began to pick out empty spaces, the shapes of battered half-demolished structures, and sometimes there were neighbourhoods of ghost streets with pavements and kerbs, but where the houses had been completely cleared away. Weeds had grown through the remnants of foundations and there were solitary trees which must have been in gardens once.

The damage to London seemed slight compared to German cities. The bravery of the Luftwaffe didn't amount to much, but perhaps it was good they never knew at home how little was achieved. Stefan wondered if the pictures of the Blitzkrieg had been faked.

The city gathered itself together, holed in places but closing in around the train. The upper storeys of houses and tenements were level with the railway, which ran along a viaduct. Through the lighted windows, Stefan glimpsed the English people in their sitting rooms and kitchens: a man in a vest shaving at a scrap of mirror with his braces dangling, some children jumping on a sofa, a girl lying on her stomach on a hearthrug, a woman in a floral apron reaching up to pull the curtains. Then the train crossed a bridge. The Thames was busy with tugs and barges. Yellow lamps along the banks cast reflections in the water.

At the station, Charing Cross, Stefan walked through the ticket barrier and out to a street. The sky was royal blue and the air was warmer than in Kent. The city sounded like a forest, with the din of birds twittering in the dusk above the lights of cars and buses and shop windows. Damaged buildings were scaffolded in readiness for repair. Everything seemed orderly and hopeful.

He walked past a rack of bicycles, a horse and cart, a boy selling newspapers, and joined the flow of people on the pavement, not knowing in which direction he should go. There was a large square with fountains, stone lions and a statue on a column. The scene was familiar, like walking through a picture he had seen a hundred times.

He asked the way to Regent's Park, struggling to find the English words. For the first time in months his thoughts were in German. A man gave him directions, then pointed to the rifle, saying something that may have been a warning. Stefan had not forgotten how to make his body still and ready. The man backed off and walked away.

Stefan asked for directions twice more before he found the address of Mrs Brion. It was a villa with a grand porch set back in an almost empty garden. On the scrubby grass stood a strange melancholy shape which could have been a rock worn into holes by the sea. It looked lost, the same as him, and people had chalked their names on it. Some-one had drawn a cartoon of a buxom naked girl, and it seemed wrong that this lonely thing had been defaced and made to look ridiculous. Stefan walked across to rub away the drawing with his sleeve. He smeared the chalk across the stone but a ghost of the girl remained.

Half a dozen dustbins, a few bicycles and prams were by the porch steps. Toys lay about on the bald gravel drive. Several windows were broken and boarded on the inside, but there were lights on all over the house and he saw a row of new bell buttons beside the front door; Flats 1 to 8, with names. None of them was Mrs Brion's.

*P. Fairhaven & O. Layne* was painted on the wall by the original brass bell and he pressed it, hearing a jingle far off inside, then after some minutes the door scraped open and woman's narrow face angled up at him with rodent curiosity. She put on a pair of spectacles. 'Yes, young man?'

Stefan retrieved some English words and said carefully, 'I am look-ing for Mrs Brion.' He held out the card and the woman took it.

'Oh, my, you're way out of date. She's in Wyoming. She hasn't lived here for years.' The woman was an American. 'And you are, if I may ask?' Her wiry ginger hair was receding slightly and her forehead gleamed in the hideous light from a naked bulb.

'My name is Stephen Lander.'

Another woman's voice shouted from the open door Stefan could see across the cavernous hall. 'Who is it, Pixie sweet?'

'It's a nice young man after Frankie Brion,' Pixie shrieked over her shoulder.

'Frankie's in America!' the voice yelled back.

'I know, Ollie. I told him. Stop hollering at me. I'll bring him in.' She said to Stefan, 'I have an address somewhere, though it's years since I've made use of it. Francesca's never one to keep in touch, and I'm just hopeless when it comes to pens and paper and the like.' She giggled and two yellow teeth hooked her lower lip.

Stefan followed her into a room so packed with furniture he couldn't see a route across to the man with a turquoise cigarette in his mouth who had swivelled round to look at them.

'Here he is, Ollie dear, a visitor for us,' said Pixie gaily, setting off. Stefan followed her along a winding path between occasional tables and footstools, whatnots of china animals, standard lamps and magazine racks, to the modern tweed armchairs – his and hers – on either side of an electric fire. The room was brightly lit and sweltering. It smelled of old beef dinners.

The man stood up and said cheerily, 'Heavens, Pixie, the boy has got a gun!'

It was the voice that had shouted to the hall – a woman's voice.

'Ollie' was wearing flannel trousers with her shirtsleeves rolled up to her elbows, and her clothes were rather flattering to her large bosom and narrow hips. She had abundant, cropped, two-toned hair. She rested one elbow in her other palm, holding the cigarette between her long stained fingers. 'What a splendid thing – your gun, I mean. Put it over there by the wireless. We don't want it going off and killing old man River upstairs in his bed.' She shook his hand. 'I'm Olivia Layne.' Her face was lined and heavy in the jaw, but she had a fine complexion and clear hazel eyes. 'What a treat. A gorgeous boy – and wearing silver.' She was referring to the locket. 'Let me get you something, darling. Whisky? Gin?'

The pink-faced Pixie patted a chair and Stefan sat, then she went to a bureau and started searching through papers. 'How is it you know Francesca Brion?'

'She was my mother's friend,' Stefan said. The lies came easily but English didn't any more. 'They lose . . . they lost . . . connection in the war. But now I . . . remember it, she told me Mrs Brion is in America, but I forget . . . forgot. I would like to smoke, please. Do you have a light?' He took out George's cigarettes.

'Oh goody, Players. Olivia only ever has Russians,' Pixie said, when he offered a cigarette to her. She gave him a box of matches and he lit her cigarette, then his own. The smoke in his lungs was a relief.

'There is someone in London my mother likes me also to find. A friend, she says, perhaps of Mrs Brion, so I come – came here to this house to enquire. Michael Ross.'

'Hah!' Olivia slapped her thigh. 'What a hoot! Does your Mama know that Frankie nabbed the Hebrew? You remember, Pixie sweet – Michael Ross, the Hebrew. He was divine. Didn't we *all* just lust after him. But Francesca was the one who got him up the aisle.'

'They are married?' Stefan asked.

'It didn't last, poor Frankie. I don't think he ever really loved her. There was a girl, Frankie told me once. His heart belonged elsewhere and always had.' Olivia handed Stefan a drink. 'I say – it wasn't your mother, was it?'

'Ollie! Hush! What a thing to ask.' Pixie had pushed the papers back inside the bureau and forced it shut. 'Then you don't need the American address,' she said to Stefan. 'You'd better try our old house in Bloomsbury. It belonged to Mama, you see, and Frankie used to live here in Regent's Park. That must be why you have this address. Lordy, *such* a muddle when Daddy lost his money in '29. We were in Amalfi and the pool had only just been filled. I thought I'd die. All our lovely houses had to go. Frankie bought our Bloomsbury place and said I could live in this one. So here we are, aren't we, Ollie dear? We've survived.'

'Indeed we have,' said Olivia. 'What times they were – until another blasted war and rations bored us half to death.'

'Oh, *yes*,' said Pixie dreamily. 'I so miss steak.'

'Remember, Pixie, Frankie Brion's soirées – in this very room?' Olivia mused. 'Frankie brought in fascinating poor people for us to talk to. We all *so* adored genuine *naïveté*. She found the Hebrew in a park, if I recall. And how we travelled! Your mother's bijou castles and the like across half the bloody globe. Happy times, Pixie darling, weren't they just.'

'After the Crash, Mama took to living on the river steamer Daddy bought to ease her lung, and my brother, Huttlestone, turned tragically to ballet . . . but you don't want to know all that,' said Pixie forlornly.

'So I will find Michael Ross?' Stefan said, standing up. The room was suffocating and he wondered why the women didn't need air. 'You know the house?'

'No rush, darling,' Olivia said. 'Enjoy your drink, chin chin. I'm afraid Michael isn't there.'

Pixie said, 'Is he in Wyoming too?'

'No, dear, he came home in '41 or thereabouts to witness the hatching of the first-born, then off he went again, to Africa or some such illiterate warring place. Poor Frankie was exhausted with all the dashing underground to dodge the bombs and the water off every other minute. You can't bathe a baby in a sink of bloody vodka even if you are Francesca Brion. She took the child to America in '42, to her sister, Ingrid. The house in Bloomsbury was mothballed.'

'I didn't know all this,' said Pixie peevishly. 'No one tells me anything. So where *is* the Hebrew, Ollie? The boy needs to find him. Doesn't anybody know?'

'He never went to join Francesca, I do know that much. He could be anywhere. He had a studio near the Tottenham Court Road. Francesca used to say he practically lived in it before the war. Perhaps that's where he is.'

'I shall go now,' Stefan said. 'I trouble you too long. You can tell me where I will find Tottenham Court Road?'

'I'll sketch you a nice little map,' Olivia said, downing her drink. 'Are you sure you won't have another?' She perched her cigarette on the mantelpiece amongst an arrangement of china kittens and opened the bureau, setting off another slide of correspondence.

'While Ollie draws your map, I'll show you Michael Ross's work,' Pixie said, ushering him along a different pathway through the furniture. 'When I was just a girl, he *begged* Mama to let me sit for him. He told me that of all the beauties he had ever painted, I had the *most* exquisite skin.'

On the far wall, amongst framed tapestries of cats with balls of wool, was a painting of a girl. 'There,' Pixie said. 'Mama says it's so *me*.'

In the picture, the young Pixie's back was turned and she looked over her smooth bare shoulder. Her copper hair curled down her back and over the dark blue satin of her dress. An open fire or candles were somewhere near, edging her lips and cheek and shoulder with light.

It seemed to Stefan impossible that it was a portrait of the florid little woman standing beside him, with her horse teeth biting on her lip. 'You were like this?' Stefan said, realizing too late how rude it sounded, but Pixie seemed accustomed to people noting the discrepancy between the youthful portrait and her middle-aged self because she didn't look offended.

'Oh, yes,' she said, taking off her spectacles as if that would do the trick. 'Michael was entranced by me. Bewitched. I was his muse, you see.' She peered foggily at the picture. 'He painted flame-haired girls for years and years. I was his Janey Morris. His Lizzie Siddal.'

'He was an artist with unusual vision,' Olivia said crisply. She handed Stefan a piece of paper. 'That'll get you somewhere near the studio, then you'll have to ask. I don't suppose you'll find him. Do come back if you need a bed for the night. We have a put-u-up behind the piano.'

Pixie blinked her chalky lashes. 'It's surely been a pleasure.' She led him across the room via the electric fire, then back along the route towards the door.

'Good luck!' called Olivia. 'If you find him, tell the Hebrew we're still alive and single.'


Stefan was glad to be outside after the stifling meaty air of Pixie and Olivia's flat. He had Olivia's map to follow but as he walked out to the street, the thought came into his head that he should go to Müller-strasse. Weariness was overlapping different times and places, and he knew he must keep reminding himself that he was in London looking for the Jew. What he would do if he found Michael Ross, he did not know. The hatred and the reason for it seemed vague, like something he used to understand but wasn't sure of any more.

He walked along a street Olivia had drawn for him: Portland Place. The moon was hidden in yellow clouds and misty rain had people hurrying with their heads down. No one took any notice of a young man walking alone.

The map directed him into an adjoining street, so he left the pavement and cut across an empty expanse of concrete gleaming with puddles. Thickets of weeds grew up here and there. A halved building was on one side with a mountainous pile of rubble against it.

Stefan stood for a moment with the clean English rain on his face. It was peaceful away from the street lights. The scent of nettles reminded him of the walk with Christina on Romney Marsh a few hours ago. It seemed like another life. The ruin gave off a subtle smell of rotting wood and old burning which was repulsive but comforting, because it reminded him of the place where he and Gerda had lived.

He climbed the pile of broken bricks and sat on an upstairs window-sill to have a cigarette. Below his hanging feet were charred joists and, below them, a void with water at the bottom where ripples glimmered – rats swimming, he supposed.

He lit a cigarette with the matches Pixie told him he could keep and wished he had talked to her about America. He hadn't thought it out before, but perhaps he and Gerda should forget Müllerstrasse, just pack up and go to New York or California. Why not? Gerda had her blue jeans.

Then with a shock he realized he didn't have them any more. They were not with him at Pixie and Olivia's flat so he must have left them on the train or dropped them somewhere in the street. The jeans were for Gerda – what she most wanted in the world, and he had forgotten all about them.

His stupidity and carelessness made him wince, his mouth flooded and the walls of his throat squeezed tight with the fear he could never keep at bay for long. He had lost so many things, there would come a time when he had nothing left. The shaking started.

He touched the locket around his neck to calm himself, fixing his attention on the vaporous drizzle lit up by the street lamps. The floating rain was specks of gold dust, spinning when he exhaled, then drifting down again. He followed the minute drops of moisture, barely falling, alight, then extinguished by the shadow.

He remembered rain like this, lit up, then disappearing down into a void, and Gerda standing by a space where a wall should be. A draught lifts her hair. She has been raging but now she's quiet, and he puts out his hand to ask if she is all right. But instead of turning when he touches her, Gerda's arms fly up. She tips forward into empty air, her body rolls over, and she's gone.

Time draws back, reluctant to go on. It cannot be: there's an empty space where Gerda was. What has happened is impossible.

He crashes down the broken staircase, hearing Gerda in the dark amongst the wreckage of the plane. When he finds her, she clutches at him while he tries to wipe away the blood and filth from her face. He lifts her up and a ragged shriek comes from her mouth, so he sits in the water holding her while she cries softly for her mother, *Mutti, Mutti*.

After a time she lets go of his shirt but she is too heavy to hold and she slips down. Black ripples bump against her cheek. A rat tiptoes along a nearby joist and Stefan scrambles away, sending an oily wave over Gerda. The water folds her into itself and she disappears.

This happened. Stefan knows now. The memory was snarled up in the clutter of his brain but now it's broken free: wings did not unfold from Gerda's back and there was no wounded deer calling for its mother. It was Gerda and she died at the house in Müllerstrasse.

The sound of footsteps on the pavements ceased. The city turned dark at Stefan's back and Moon amongst her constellations laid silver on the roofs and spires. The nettles grew a fur of frost and the shadow of a fox, Fox himself invisible, paused to taste a human scent somewhere high up, still and barely breathing.

Stefan leaned his cheek against the air and the quiet held him softly to itself. There was no need to search for Gerda.

The stars took note and drew their graceful diagram for the coming day. The moon accomplished her arc and the stars withdrew. The sky turned violet. Birds began to sing.

# 37

The disappointment was greater for Francesca, Michael knows now. When they married, she had trusted in the infinite possibilities of love and it was painful for her to discover she was wrong, and also wrong about herself. She found she didn't love him after all. Michael wanted to tell her it didn't matter, but that would hurt her more.

For two years they lived uneasily together. Their need for sleep and food and sex did not coincide, and, their natures being equally selfish and equally peaceable, life became a succession of apologies and counter-apologies which it still makes Michael weary to remember.

He started sleeping at the studio and her fantasy of their life together, 'not at all respectable', as Frankie put it, remained intact. Michael could go walking at dawn and she could sleep past noon without either feeling guilty. Their incompatibility was proof to her that the marriage was unconventional and therefore a success.

'You're not like anyone in the whole world, Michael,' Francesca once said to him. 'You're someone I can't even imagine.'

The war and Francesca's pregnancy forced a helpless contentment on them both. What they wanted for themselves was suddenly irrelevant. When Michael came home on leave and Francesca returned from the hospital, they lived together for a month and almost fell in love.

Michael would walk back and forth across the bedroom with his new-born son in his arms and Frankie would sit by the fire in a bright silk kimono, hugging her knees and smoking. Those were the best times, when they were simply content in one another's company as they used to be.

He loved Frankie's dark eyes and the silver in her hair, and when she was naked he wanted to paint the fineness of her bones under the cool white skin. He rarely wanted to touch her.

They talked about how life would be different and marvellous when the war was over and they could be a family together. Their dreams bore no relation to who they were.

He was sent to Tobruk and Francesca struggled alone in London, writing brave letters that touched him and sometimes made him laugh. Life was difficult and dangerous, but fleeing to the country was impossible for her. 'I'd go mad, Michael. I know your English villages, all mud and scones. The quiet would swallow me whole.' After a year, she took the baby home to her sister in Wyoming.

When the war was over, he went back to London, took what he needed from the house in Bloomsbury and moved into the studio.

He wondered at this half-marriage he and Frankie had. Their letters never acknowledged that it was finished, and Frankie sometimes talked about returning to London when life was easier again. She did not ask him to join her in America and he understood it would be wrong for her if he did; she needed to keep the illusion of him perfect.

So he was alone and glad to be so, but freedom, he had come to realize, was as difficult as living with Francesca. There was always money in his bank account, earned from paintings or deposited from time to time by Frankie. He could have lovers if he wanted, and do anything at any hour of any day. He was nearly forty, and time sprawled like a flood with no landmarks and no tide to take him anywhere.

London was subdued after Germany surrendered. People seemed baffled by the victory and the mood was sullen. Grief and hardship had exhausted people and the aftermath sometimes seemed as terrible as war.

One weekday afternoon, Michael went into a news theatre to shelter from the rain. He sat in the flickering dark and watched a newsreel of stone-eyed creatures with bone claws hooked on wire fences. Without flesh the people did not seem naked although they were. But, for all their suffering, he felt them pitying his ignorance. He was a creature who did not know its own kind.

These were the concentration camps in Germany and Poland. What could not exist except in nightmares did exist.

Cartoons came on and then the reel of news again. Michael watched twice more because his mind could not comprehend what his eyes were seeing: the human body nullified.

That final summer of the war, a city was destroyed in a single burning breath, and then another. Horror was perfected. Lucifer had woken and now it seemed he worked for good as well as evil. The human mind could accomplish feats of devastation beyond its own imagining.

The dead were a multitude too vast to mourn, so the living turned back to the small things they were masters of. A kind of life resumed.

He sometimes went to Dean Street of an evening, to an artists' club above a trattoria where Muriel presided – a chalk-faced woman Frankie would have hated. Muriel would clamp her black-red lips around her cigarette and tell him, 'Your work is sentimental, Michael. Beauty is old hat. You think your gods are grateful?' She stroked his greying hair and laughed. 'Poor darling. A fine old angel when there's no call for angels any more.'

Occasionally, he walked to Hampstead Heath to visit an ageing sculptor and his wife, who was a painter. They still believed art could repair a damaged soul although their faith was wearing thin.

Most days Michael worked until noon, had lunch in a café and slept for a while, then worked into the night and slept again. He would go out before dawn to walk and see the light take on a colour.

This morning there is a frost. The days are warm but the dawns are still cold. Michael is swaddled in a heavy sweater, scarf and gloves, and the cashmere overcoat Francesca bought him one Christmas. He is amused that he's dressed like an old man, but his arthritic hands and damaged leg will suffer if he does not keep warm.

When he leaves the studio, a woman is still asleep in his bed and she will have gone by the time he returns because this is always the understanding.

Fitzroy Street is empty. The cold seems to fall from the buildings, which sparkle with rime in the grainy neutral light. There is a gap in the terrace where a bomb fell. Vast oak struts support the houses on either side, and a cat sits neatly on a first-floor mantelpiece looking down into the weeds.

He is aware of people sleeping behind the upstairs curtains and he tries to walk quietly. Occasionally a basement light is on where a maid or a housekeeper is already up, but not so many people have servants these days and most of the houses have been turned into flats.

He has never met his neighbours or the people living above or underneath the studio, and he wonders if they know he exists because he never hears them. The studio is hidden in its labyrinth of staircases and passages. As Frankie once said to him, no one would ever find him.

He walks until the dawn turns violet and then stops for breakfast at a café in Covent Garden, where business started hours ago. He buys some dark blue delphiniums which remind him of Elisabeth although he has forgotten why.

Coming back along Bloomsbury, through Bedford Square, he is not far from the house where he and Francesca used to live, but he has no need or inclination to go there, then along Bayley Street towards the Tottenham Court Road.

He reaches the corner, turns right and what he sees stops him dead in the middle of the pavement. A sudden wonder grips him and too many sensations come at once.

There is a boy walking towards him with a rifle on his shoulder and at the open neck of his shirt is Madame Baumanière's silver locket. The boy's blue eyes are bloodshot and his hair is a dozen shades of gold. He has almost walked past. His lips are mauve and he stares ahead. On the stock of the rifle he carries, there is a design of flowers and curling ribbons.

Michael touches the boy's sleeve, which causes him to flinch away so violently a man passing on a bicycle turns to stare. The anguish in the boy's eyes is terrible and Michael almost flinches too. He says, 'So you've found me.' What other reason would bring this ghost except to find him? 'I live just round the corner. I'll make us some coffee.' The words sound oddly banal.

The boy doesn't seem to understand but when Michael starts walking, he follows. He has the loping gait of a youth but the height and stature of a man. He might be sixteen, seventeen, not much more.

In the studio, it is still dark although the muslin at the windows is lit up by the early light. It is not quite seven o'clock. The firelight casts a pinkish glow across the floorboards and the boy stands in his heavy country coat staring at the embers.

When Michael comes out of the little kitchen with a pot of coffee the boy is lying on his back by the hearth. He looks as if he's fallen down. The rifle is across his chest and he is asleep. His face looks younger coloured by the fire, his skin is very fine though down is beginning to show above his lip, and his nose and mouth have outgrown their childish neatness. The jaw is clumsy and the cheekbones are too prominent. The planes of his face might settle in the right proportions as he gets older or they might not.

His eyelids are like waxy petals and Michael finds it strange to be so moved by a child he doesn't know – because, for all his size, the boy seems not much older than a child. There is an untidy scar on his throat from a wound that was probably infected once – it occurs to Michael that perhaps the boy hasn't spoken because he can't – and lying near the scar is the silver locket, which has been repaired and polished since it was given to Elisabeth's daughter in a muddy Kentish lane six years ago. It was tarnished then, and dented from having been in Michael's pocket during the Munich beating.

The rifle looks the same. After nearly twenty years he still knows every curl of the inlaid ribbons and he can recall the feeling when he lifted it from the iron rest above the fireplace at the house in Mazamet.

Jean Baumanière's rifle and Emmanuelle Baumanière's silver locket have been reunited. Michael would ponder what it means if he thought there was some purpose or design in the conjunction, or if there was a message to be deciphered in these objects from the past. Fate can be spiteful or generous, that's all. Chance can look symmetrical, but it means nothing.

What Michael believes is that a kind of random magic has occurred and something will be altered by this boy. A succession of small convergences and ruptures, decisions and accidents, has brought him here with the rifle and the silver locket.

The boy doesn't stir while the morning begins to come into the room with the sound of motorcars and footsteps and, occasionally, horses' hoofs. Michael puts the delphiniums in water, then starts to paint, and he feels an odd companionship with the sleeping figure by the fire. Usually he can't work with anyone but a model in the room. He makes more coffee, wondering if he should take off the boy's boots and put a pillow under his head, but he is gripping the rifle even in his sleep and Michael leaves him alone.

By ten o'clock, the sun shines straight in, making prisms bounce from the bevelled mirrors. The muslin across the windows diffuses the glare but the ricocheting light is tiring at this time of the day. When Michael moves, dozens of subtly distorted reflections do the same. At one time he thought of covering the mirrors, but he has become accustomed to the multiplication of light and movement and he hardly notices it now.

It is almost eleven o'clock. The work absorbs him but for the first time in years he notices the smell of the paint, the linseed oil and fumy turpentine, and he wonders if the boy's dreaming mind notices it too. The thought makes Michael look across and the boy's eyes are open. He hasn't moved but he gazes at the ceiling, then he turns his head when he feels Michael watching. His expression is peaceful and curious, as if he doesn't know where he is but he doesn't mind. The sleep has done him good because whatever frightened him has receded.

'There's still coffee if you'd like some,' Michael says. A mass of questions crowd in and one of them will start the unravelling of the story, but it's too soon. 'I don't know your name,' he says.

The boy's lips part and he licks them.

'*Qui êtes-vous?*' Michael asks. '*Wie ist Ihr Name?*'

'Stefan,' says the boy huskily. His coat creaks as he shifts, puts the rifle on the floor and sits up, rubbing his scalp so his hair fans silkily through his fingers. The proportions of cheeks and jaw are better now he's upright. He yawns and swallows hard.

'*Ich hole Sie Wasser.*' I'll get you some water, Michael says but he can't bring himself to move. The sound of German has momentarily invoked the past and he catches a glimpse of Artur Landau. The likeness vanishes and the boy is just himself again.

There is a pause when nothing happens. Michael stands by the easel and Stefan sits on the floor and blinks sleepily, then his expression changes as if a switch is thrown. His eyes redden and flood and the myriad of thoughts and reflexes that give a face complexity are wiped away because there is only one single thought: he has remembered something which was forgotten in his sleep.

Michael has seen it many times in war and in its aftermath – the sudden recollection of a fear that brings back the fear itself. Stefan begins to shiver. He doesn't weep and hang his head or hunch into himself. Whatever it is must be too terrible to cry for. Michael can sense only its outline but for the first time he feels frightened too – not of the boy, who could almost be Artur Landau's son, but of the horror that is present in the room.

'*Was ist los?*' Michael asks softly. There's a plea in Stefan's eyes. He wants the thing undone, or unremembered as it was in the seconds after waking. Michael knows this longing too because how many times has he tried to make a memory disappear. He never could. Unknowing is impossible.

If he had succeeded in erasing certain things, he would have chosen

346

badly, he realizes now, because in these last few years he has been grateful to have the memories of Elisabeth, and glad to remember his father, even at the end. And if the beating in Munich had been forgotten, the kindness of the Jewish doctor and his wife would have been lost too. A life can't be partitioned and perhaps there's nothing it's better to forget.

As always, when he thinks he's found a truth he is proved wrong, because he sees that Stefan is recalling something intolerable and the horror of it will never change. The boy will not become a better man because of it, or a kinder one. Whatever this memory is, it will distort him and will always torture him.

Stefan shivers inside the coat. Nothing can be done. The air feels solid, as if the two of them are fixed in glass.

Ordinariness is needed to break the spell – a cup of tea or food – so Michael moves. What happens next is hidden in the light.

Perhaps when multiple figures seem to move on every side, Stefan reaches for the rifle and scrambles to his feet. Michael backs away to show he is no threat and his reflections do the same. Stefan sees grey-haired men retreat, but blond young men swing their rifles wildly around. There is a shot.

A rectangle of air seems to crumple, then drop slowly like a waterfall sending a tide of shards out across the floor. The young men still have their rifles raised and whichever way Stefan turns they always aim at him. There's another detonation, another mirror falls, another tide of glass.

There is silence. Michael straightens up and something has altered. After a while he says, 'What a mess.' The floor is strewn with bits of aquamarine and silvered glass and it is everywhere, even in the fireplace amongst the ash. 'What a mess,' he says again, although it looks rather beautiful.

The rifle is on the floor. He didn't notice when the boy put it down. At the first shot, or perhaps it was the second, he felt a dull clenching and unclenching of his nerves as if he had touched a raw electric wire. It is difficult to gather his thoughts together but he notices blood pooling at his feet. It has filled his shoe and his trouser leg is soaked. There is so much blood running down it looks like skeins of paint but he's not in pain and he wonders where it's all coming from. His chest feels bruised somehow, nothing worse than that. He pats his chest and sees his hand – his little finger with the ring that used to belong to Nanna Lydia, his thumb with charcoal under the nail, and between them is a mess of flesh and bone. Three fingers have disappeared. Blood goes down inside his cuff and starts filling his sleeve, but the arm is too heavy to hold up for long so he lets it drop again.

The boy rushes to the sofa where the models pose and he hauls off the cover, wrestling with it crazily to find a hem to rip, then he is hobbled by the trailing cloth, falls over and flails his arms like someone beating off a dog.

Laughter rises in Michael's throat. He wonders where his missing fingers are. 'Get someone,' he says. His hand throbs softly in time with his heartbeat, and Stefan staggers up with the cloth bunched against him but he doesn't seem to know what to do. He shifts and the glass grinds under his feet.

'It was just an accident. I can walk.' The voice is coming from somewhere else.

Then he's lying on the sofa and his hand is swaddled in the cloth, which also covers his chest. When he looks around the room is empty but footprints of his blood track across the floor. There is so much of it. He remembers hearing thunder over Romney Marsh, but perhaps it was the boy running along the metal corridor.

He isn't anxious any more. His mind is clear and he is content to lie in the sunshine with the room glittering around him like the sea, and it comes to him that the rippling green mirrors turned out to be water after all and two have burst and flooded the floor.

He moves his head and knows this is not a dream because his neck clicks and he hears himself swallow. He must have passed out, the boy carried him to the sofa and wrapped up his hand. Soon someone will come. A brief fear grips him because the door is shut and he knows he can't get up to open it – but they will knock it down, that's all. It doesn't matter.

He remembers Nanna Lydia, whose dog came back to see her with the hens from Neate Street while he and Elisabeth sat by the bed holding Nanna's hands. He looks around but the room is empty and he is still alone.

The scene jumps. The sun has moved. The wad of cloth is soaked through and he notices its weight. The sofa behind his back feels sodden too but there's no pain.

In the street below the window someone is sweeping and he has never heard so quiet a sound outside before. Perhaps he never listened. Close by is the mothy flutter of muslin moving in a draught, and his ticking watch.

All his life he has tried to paint the light and now he sees it's made of restless beads of salty blue. The perspective of the chair is wiser than he thought and he never noticed that shadows have quiet voices.

He remembers his missing fingers. He will have to learn to paint with his left hand, relearn for a second time, and by then he will have forgotten all this. With the thought he does forget. The air vanishes and the shadows are silent. His chest aches with sadness and he can barely draw in a breath; he'd rather die than never see again what he has just seen – and then suddenly the marvel returns.

Every piece of broken glass strewn across the floor carries its last reflection, and if he were to pick up any one, it would show a fragment of the room as it was this morning. This seems to him miraculous because it means his hand can be made whole again using the reflections on the pieces. He must remember to tell the people who come to help not to sweep up. The thought flickers like a reel running out of film.

It is pitch black and he feels the boy's arms around him heaving him up so he half walks, half staggers in the darkness. The boy is strong and doesn't let him fall. On the sofa, the cloth is wound around Michael's injured hand, and although there is no light, he sees the boy pull the silver locket from his neck, break the ribbon and put it inside the wad of cloth. It hurts the boy to let the locket go. His grief has caused the blackness in the room. Then he leaves, shutting the door behind him.

Michael opens his eyes and knows he has been dreaming. From the way the shadows slant across the floor, it must be late afternoon. The boy left a long time ago.

In the dream, the boy put Elisabeth's locket inside the cloth but Michael knows that moving his good hand to search for it is too great an effort and he wonders if he can see the locket anyway with the new sight he has acquired. He can. It is there deep inside his chest, a silver heart beating strongly. He is glad he is still all right.

The room stretches away, beautifully sunny but very cold, and Dungeness lighthouse stands on the splintered glass. The thud of the sea comes through the floorboards and into Michael's body.

When the door opens, he expects it to be the boy returning, but it is Elisabeth. There must be a sea mist because her face is wet. She puts the basket on the table and lights the stove, moving quietly because she thinks he is asleep. From time to time she looks across and she doesn't seem to know he sees her.

# 38

Alice said, 'I don't think this fits me well at all.'

Elisabeth had pins in her mouth or she would have said something about the ingratitude of daughters. She remembered Karen at Alice's age, when life moved forward with such force that things were said or done before they could be considered, and she wanted to smile at the memory of Karen in spite of the pins and Alice's rudeness, and the agony of accidentally kneeling on the handle of the scissors.

The evening was hot. The doors to the garden were wide open and the August moon was shining across the lawn. Alice stood on the piano stool while Elisabeth shuffled on her knees, trying to get the yards of skirt evenly hemmed. The dress had been cut from a voluminous silk coat given to her by Ingrid Schroëder many years ago. It was a handblock print, expensive and exclusive, as Ingrid Schroëder's cast-offs always were, and there had been plenty of yardage to remake it as a dress in the New Look style Rachel had shown Alice in a magazine. Elisabeth fought with herself not to resent Alice's head being filled with nonsense about fashion.

'Alice, your middle is baggy,' said Maud. 'And your top.'

'Well, it's your fault,' said Alice. 'I never should have given you my coupons.' Maud's class at school were collecting clothing coupons to send to the Princess Elizabeth Alexandra for her wedding dress. Christina had given hers without regret but for Alice it had been a sacrifice. The dress was her consolation.

Alice had altered in these last few months. She was elated that her neighbour, Rachel Saunders, was her aunt. The story told to her was a sketchy version of the truth: some papers at the orphanage had been discovered and the connection with Mrs Saunders had come to light. Alice accepted the vagueness of the details and the coincidence. She wasn't interested in what was over and done with, only in the present; this was her nature, like Karen's. If her father lived in America, Alice said, she would look for him one day but not just yet.

Elisabeth felt a new and different tenderness for Alice and Christina. The separation was beginning – from her and from each other.

Christina looked up from her book, taking off her spectacles and rubbing the bridge of her nose. 'I think the dress is nice,' she said.

She had been quieter since Stefan left, turning in on herself as a young girl does when her heart has encountered something she has no name for.

The night Stefan disappeared George was telephoning the police when she told them Stefan had gone home to Germany. 'His girl is called Gerda,' Christina wept. 'He wants to be with her. Please don't bring him back.' In spite of her tears she said nothing bad had happened to make him leave, he just realized he should, that's all, and they must be happy for him because he loved Gerda and that was that.

The port authorities at Dover had no record of a boy alone having been a passenger, but George had gone to Germany to search for him. Finding Stefan seemed impossible unless he wanted to be found. The Landaus' last address could not be traced, no paperwork had survived for Artur, nor was there a record of his death in Poland. The Gestapo prison at Kaufering where Karen died had been burned down.

George said he would go back to Germany again. 'He's our family, Elisabeth. We must know he's all right even if he doesn't need us any more.'

To Elisabeth, there were two Stefans – the orphan, Karen's boy, who shivered with the memory of horrors that could not be imagined, and the almost-man, Artur's son, calculating, watchful, and far older than his years. She wished him safe, but she did not wish him back.

She hoped that explanations and confessions to Alice might never be necessary now. 'Why should we tell her unless we find him?' she had said to George. 'It will only hurt her.'

'For the same reason all the other things we've hidden should be told – because Alice's past belongs to her,' he had answered, baffled as he often was at Elisabeth's reasoning. 'Surely you want her to know who you are?'

'She does know,' Elisabeth said. 'I'm her mother in every way that matters.' If this was right or wrong, she had no idea. Her motives and loyalties, the decisions they all had made over the years, were too tangled to understand.

'Turn,' Elisabeth said, patting Alice's tanned legs, and Alice revolved on the piano stool. Elisabeth sat back on her heels and the heat prickled on her skin. There was no breeze coming in and moths flickered round the light. 'Would you shut the doors, please, Maudie darling? We'll suffocate but we can't have insects in the house.'

'Then Maudie better go outside,' Christina said.

'Put her in a jam jar!' said Alice. 'Ouch, a pin. I'm stabbed.'

Elisabeth got up off her aching knees, pushing back her hair. 'Let's stop now, Alice. It's too hot. I'll finish the hem tomorrow.'

Alice had already jumped down off the piano stool and was jiving across the carpet in her pinned dress.

'Alice, help me squash the insect!' Christina yelled, and her book fell on the floor. Maud shrieked and Christina tickled her.

'*Toot, ta toot, ta toot-tootle-ee-oot toot toot . . .*' Alice was singing.

Elisabeth put the heavy scissors and the pins in the sewing basket. She went to close the doors, but stepped outside, shutting them behind her, and walked across the terrace to find the breeze that might be coming from the sea. Through the study window she saw George at his desk under the yellow electric light, running a hand through his hair and rasping his stubble. The wireless was on and Elisabeth could hear voices and then applause.

She leaned on the garden wall and listened to the frogs croaking in the ditches and sheep bleating out across the Marsh. The night air moved and the damp on her skin cooled.

She remembered the painting Stefan had given her, unrolling it and seeing herself and Michael. A shapeless hope or the memory of a hope had pulled at her as if a thread from the past was tightening. She had thought something would happen. Nothing had. Stefan had left them and gone home to Germany.

The more she examined it, the more absurd the feeling seemed. There was no reason to think the painting was a sign, or the girl was her. The face was in shadow and long auburn hair was not so unusual. It must be someone Michael had met in France.

And the memory of the studio in Fitzroy Street was nothing too. She had simply walked with him on a winter afternoon to a dusky rose-lit room where he made some tea. There was a painting on an easel and she imagined or dreamed something. That was all.

She knows this isn't true. She had glimpsed beneath the opaque shifting of her life to something luminous and certain. Perhaps this is what she longs for: a single moment which seemed to hold more life in it than all the years that followed. If it could be found again, she would know it this time and she would understand.

Two days after Stefan disappeared, thoughts of Michael and the need to go to Dungeness had got hold of her once more. Suddenly, on an ordinary afternoon which should be like any other, time seemed folded back, as if fifteen years had disappeared and Michael was there waiting for her in the hut out on the Point. The girls were at school and George was at work, she picked up a scarf and the car keys and locked the door behind her.

As she turned on to the shingle track, her heart lifted as if Michael would be there. She stopped the car and got out. The pearly air, the stones rolling under the waves and the lighthouse against the sky seemed the same. Sea spray was carried on the wind. She walked along the shingle bank and back again to find the place where the hut had been.

Here would be the door, the table, and on the other side, above the wooden bed, the window which looked out to sea. She closed her eyes to feel the current of the past and Michael, somewhere, knowing she had come. *When I open my eyes, I'll see him.*

Slowly, the feeling fell away. There was driftwood and seaweed on the shingle, nothing else. Even the stove had disappeared.

• • •

There was a theory that the atom bomb which finally beat the Nips also put the earth out of kilter; the blast had jogged it nearer to the sun and this explained the scorching summer. Other people reasoned that the recent atrocious winter proved all the seasons had been disrupted by the war and this was punishment for the evil men had done, and for the devastation.

Eddie was not one to think that anything the human race could do would trouble Mother Nature or provoke her to revenge. Working on the land soon teaches a man how small and insignificant he is.

On the Romney Marsh, the summer dawns were crystalline pink, poised on the edge of blue, and Eddie and Rachel rose at four to work until the night breeze from the Channel dropped and the heat thickened with the day. There had been no rain to speak of for weeks and the ground was like rock, so Rachel put down a heap of straw in the paddock for the old pony to rest on.

The sheep blundered after any shade or scent of moisture. Eddie had to keep hauling them out of the ditches so he called in the shearers to give the animals some relief.

The men sweated through the night, working by touch and moonlight. They sat round the lamps to drink the beer and tea Rachel brought out to them and agreed there had never been a hotter summer. The trees against the stars and the soft clicking of moths on the lamp glass made the world seem innocent and trusting, so the men talked about brutal unsettling things to keep the magic of the night from overwhelming them: a spaceship had landed in America at a place called Roswell and the Russians were edgy and belligerent for no reason anyone could understand. Another war was on the cards and if it wasn't the Ruskies, it would be the Martians.

By July the pastures were yellow. Rachel's new niece, Alice Mander, often walked across to see them, and she and Rachel sat in the cool of the kitchen talking about fashion and suchlike – things Eddie didn't understand. In their summer dresses with their arms and faces beautifully brown, they looked comfortable in the heat, like creatures born to it.

The summer had divided the population, Eddie noticed, into those who burned in the sun and sweated like him, and those who thrived. Elisabeth and Christina belonged with Eddie in the scorched tormented tribe, Rachel and young Alice, with glints of sunshine in their eyes and hair, were in the other.

The other likenesses between Rachel and her niece were subtle. They discovered that their ears were similar and also the shape of their ankles and their knees. Eddie was touched by their fascination with the evidence of their shared blood, but he didn't let himself dwell on it too long. It was an ordinary joy he would never have in this life.

Rachel had gone up to London to see her brother Michael for the first time in years in the hope that a family of sorts could be salvaged and he would want to see his daughter, but the house in Bloomsbury where he used to live was closed up. The neighbour said Mrs Brion had returned to Wyoming and no one had lived there for years. They used to see her husband occasionally but not for months now, and everyone assumed he'd joined Mrs Brion in America. There was no forwarding address.

'I can't do any more,' Rachel said to Eddie. 'Michael's always been the same. He'll turn up one day, he always does.'

So Rachel's brother had disappeared, but she had found a niece, and Eddie was glad that fate had been kind to Rachel at last. He was thankful for her happiness. Although the years of painful disappointment could not be wiped away entirely, Alice was a gift that had not come too late.

It was odd about the German boy. He had been at the Manders' house for only ten days or so when Eddie met him out in the fields late one evening as the dew was falling.

The boy was taken by surprise by the unexpected encounter, and he looked tensed to run, like a wild thing with good reason to be afraid. Eddie said, 'Quiet, lad. Steady. I'll leave you now,' and went on his way.

Two days later the boy had gone. George Mander went to Germany to look for him, but Elisabeth seemed to put the whole affair away as if the brief visit in their lives was of no account.

Eddie would keep the memory of the meeting in a misty Kentish pasture. It was only a passing moment of the boy's lost life, of no significance or interest to anyone, but it was right that somebody should remember him.

# Acknowledgements

Thanks to the following for their advice and wisdom, and all their help in getting this story into shape: Richard Francis, Mark Vidler, Val Bridge and Christine Purkis; to Peter Garner for his memories of Paris and Germany; to Beverly Stark and Jonathan Carr for our seaside conversations, and also to Jules Stanbridge. To Heather Malcolm for the sustenance she has given me in all ways; and to Ruby Wastvedt for her golden optimism.

To Mavis Cheek and Paul Sussman for their faith and encouragement when it was most needed; to my agent, Judith Murray, and to Venetia Butterfield at Penguin.

To my father, and to my mother, whose letters from Gerda were the beginnings of this story.

C